The Black Harvest

A Novel of the American Civil War

Daren Dean

Livingston Press
The University of West Alabama
Livingston, Alabama, USA

Printed on acid-free paper
Printed in the United States of America by
Publishers Graphics
Hardcover binding by: HF Group
Typesetting and page layout: Joe Taylor
Proofreading: James Moran, Matthew Mason
Cover layout: Joe Taylor
Cover image: George Maddox,
Wikipedia Commons

—For Chris

first edition
6 5 4 3 2 1

The Black Harvest

A Novel of the American Civil War

"I wish that strife would vanish away from among gods and mortals, and gall, which makes a man grow angry for all his great mind, that gall of anger that swarms like smoke inside of a man's heart and becomes a thing sweeter to him by far than the dripping of honey."

Homer, The Iliad

CHAPTER 1
A Fire in Zion

Yellow-visaged she stood in my dreams, and would forever stand in my memory, at the door dressed in homespun with a warning to join Quantrill in the Sni Hills. Even after all these years, she makes an appearance in the penumbra of my slumber, but now she is mute, and her face has begun to disappear like a daguerreotype treated roughly. The sky is a sickening green. Looking out over the tobacco crop, a hand to block the sun, waving to a boy in the field like some hateful ocean in the roiling breeze. Next, she stands on the porch in a snowstorm of pollen, waving near, and then the scene is played out again on a ridge; a hemp field overlooking the Missouri from a limestone bluff covered in honeysuckle and vines; the rail of a sidewinder; she gazed up from a watery grave wearing a linen gown, shimmering maroon and serpentine, gripping a brace of pistols across her dun breasts; the Lady of the Lake in the time of the Border Wars.

My elder brother, Gideon, was out fighting in Kansas and western Missouri with the boys he rode with, mostly terrorizing old men, spinster women, and children who sympathized with the Federals—and even an unlucky few who didn't. Looking back on it now, I wish I could have avoided the misery sweeping across the land during those years just like that dream boy out in the field behind the mules, but now I understand neither one of us could.

In dreams I see myself as a youth, flying in spirit overhead, simultaneously watching *the boy* doing chores around the farmstead our father called a plantation. But it wasn't really a plantation as much as a farm with ambitions at the height of Father's Christian pride. On the Sabbath, I smoke a cigar, and in my reverie I dog the boy's steps like a wraith as memories of the Civil War appear like magic lantern slides.

I sat there at my kitchen table in *La Fayette* County, as it was commonly pronounced then, with that son-of-a-bitch journalist John N. Edwards. Edwards was a Major who had fought as an adjutant to General Jo Shelby's cavalry, the western front's J. E. B. Stuart, apparently still trying to resurrect the Southern cause. He had already made Frank and Jesse James living legends with his chicken scratches, not to mention all those editorials in the *Kansas City Times* newspaper. He sat there without so much as a pencil to write down what I had to say, his eyes hungry for a truth, *his* truth, that I didn't feel inclined to give him. I suppose he hoped to do the same with Colonel Quantrill's reputation or Captain Bill's, and that's what my statement is meant to redress for posterity.

Edwards was irksome at best, but what I resented about his literary style was his penchant for hyperbole. He was destined to smear what should have been the real person for a symbol, inventing a counterfeit persona in order to further his own dubious literary reputation. He had asked me to come deliver my statement to him in his Kansas City office as if he were judge and jury, but I told him in a letter that I would come to him but he would be required to provide a significant gift of some kind. If he wanted my story, he'd have to pay for it. I didn't much give a damn about his designs on fighting the war over again. I put in my time. I'd surely earned my rest. I'd stood my ground and turned to fight them all in a circle at one time or another, if you get my meaning.

Edwards thought he looked rough, but to me he was ridiculous, despite serving under Shelby. One of the undefeated, indeed! He look more crazed than fierce, with his hat cocked at an angle that suggested someone might have just woke him from a thunderous snooze after a prejudicial bout of drinking. He tried to hide the tremor in his hands by placing them flat on the round oak table or holding on to his overcoat as though it might sprout wings and fly out of the room with him in it. He wore a Van Dyke that had grown a mind of its own and threw out roots like a cypress draped in salt-and-pepper Spanish moss. The facial hair, a ruse, failed to hide his bulbous nose and gin-blossom complexion.

Understand that most of us were not fighting for a cause of any kind, whether one believed in the peculiar institution or was an ardent abolitionist. No, the way things were then in western Missouri (what would later be referred to as the Burnt District), everyone from a boy of fourteen to men on the threshold of old age had to make a choice for the Federal government or the Confederacy. Why? Because you were likely to get scalped, shot, or burnt out no matter if you took the oath of loyalty and refused to swallow the dog. Loyalty tests were rigged worse than a witch trial by the Missouri Militia. There wasn't a right answer as far as they were concerned. Many of us fools in the Little Dixie tried to remain neutral during the war for a while and fine folks paid a hefty price for it. Many a proud man lost his life and that of his family if he was too eager to declare himself.

It was 1888 when I handed over the ambrotype I had made to the former journalist (originally not more than a couple of months after I joined up with Bill Anderson's outfit) as a gift for my mother. Edwards had arrived by carriage from Jefferson City in a desperate attempt to revive his own fame attached though it was to the memory of Jesse James and the late war as his chronicler. By then it was plain to see that Edwards had the red-faced complexion of an alcoholic whose liver had long ago raised the white flag, but he still had some ambition that had helped the Democratic Party destroy the Radical Party and Lincoln's Republican Party.

I had rushed off with countless other young men (lying about my age, of course) who had joined General Sterling Price down south at Wilson's Creek, when a Union ball scored a direct hit to one of our cannons. It had flown through the air like brimstone straight from hell, killing the boy standing between Gideon and me without leaving a single mark on either of us save blood and brains from the boy, who, if I recall correctly, was from Joplin. That's when the notion of serving under an officer left a foul taste in Gideon's mouth, which was transferred to me as my own opinion. I vowed to return home and fight no more. I was so naive. All of fifteen years old and a veteran after one battle.

It was then that my father decided I should take up the cross of our Savior and become an officer in the Army of the Lord. I do not wish to sound disrespectful toward Father, because he was a man I loved above all other men. As much as I loved him, however, I did not want to be him. Even now, after all these years, his grave face comes unbidden like a specter dislocated from his body. I see this anomalous image even without closing my eyes. This visage has always been indomitable, as if he were haunting me.

"You were—" the sound of Edward's dragging on his cigar, "—a handsome young man, Mr. Marchbank. Now, however . . ." but sensing that it might be inappropriate to discuss my physical frailty and jaundiced skin, he allowed his statement to hang in the air. He passed back the daring ghost (my younger self bristling with Navy Colts in the daguerreotype) with as much fear as courage showing plainly in the set of his features.

"I was drunk when the image was made." I coughed, hocking blood into his kerchief. I had just turned forty-four and I was dying of the consumption if a man could believe what his country doctor told him. Although I did not need to explain this to Edwards. I could have gone off to a sanitarium I had heard about in Denver, but who wants to face their mortality head-on? And besides that, I loathed most of the sawbones I had known.

Edwards took back the framed picture and sat it nearby on the table face down.

"That photograph was made right here in Lafayette County."

Edwards exhaled a mist of blue smoke intermingling heavily with the memories of the dead. Even the journalist could not help entertaining the notion that the spirits might be invoked in the smoke when their names were called. "What we agreed upon then." Edwards slipped a few coins across the table, I quietly slid the money back. You see, I did not want to be bought. "How old are you, then?" Edwards stared down at the paper in front of him.

"In years forty-four," I said, "but a hundred and fifty in experience."

The journalist glanced quickly up at me and smiled thinly, nodded as if to himself. He poured two fingers of whiskey into each of our glasses. I threw back my drink in a single motion to steady myself. I was nervous because I wanted to get it right, if nothing else. Occasionally the sound of Edward's nub scratching paper made its way into my consciousness like the ostentatious proceedings of a spiritualist before he conjures the departed for his gullible old women. I needed to get it right. I owed it to all those dead boys and their families—the ones I had grown up with in what was later referred to as the Burnt District.

"Anytime you want to tell it. You just go right ahead. I'm here. We want the truth about the war out this time. Frank and Jesse—now didn't you tell me you fought with them?" He pursed his lips with skepticism and palpable disgust. His hands were blackened with his cheap newspaper ink. He gave the impression of a man who inhabited his own world, as I suppose some of the literary bent cannot help themselves from doing. There was such a self-righteous zeal about him—he reminded me of one of Falstaff's men—that I couldn't help but dislike him intensely despite his politics. He didn't know I had seen Edwards once before look delicate when I rode into Boonville with Captain Bill Anderson. Captain Bill had made a gift of dueling pistols to Price before it all unraveled. No doubt if Edwards had been on his own, he would have given our party the cut sublime and turned his admiring gaze upon the clear blue sky until we had passed. Price and his men about fainted when they saw all our scalps and ear garlands. *What a pussy,* Captain Bill said later on. He was the very picture of a gentleman, or at least, what passed for a gentleman to us brush boys.

It amused me to taunt Edwards so I pushed my whiskey glass toward him with my fingertips. "I fought with them crazy sons-of-bitches. They are not the heroes you make them out to be, or the devils others think, either."

"Funny," Edwards said in a tone of thinly veiled contempt. "Jesse never mentioned you."

"Well, he mentioned you. He told how you turned your back on him when he needed your help!"

I spat on the floor like I might get up and dispatch the journalist with my bare hands. Edwards flinched backward for a moment as I leaned forward, my saliva flecks lightly spraying his face. I suppose the journalist reminded himself of the reports of how I had cut off ears, fingers, scalps, and even a Federal head with an Arkansas toothpick in stony-faced detachment. This is not an idle brag or something I am proud to admit but just a regrettable fact of the times. I believe he observed the former bushwhacker who appeared to just scarcely have himself under control, hands closing into fists, opening; the cords on his neck standing out, no doubt. It was the old feeling, the burning blood, I used to get before the killing had to start as we flanked the militia on their nags.

Edwards dabbed at his blanched face with his kerchief. He was what we called a real Admiral of the Rear!

"Now, now . . ." Edwards half stood up out of his chair with his hands held out in front of him. "You actually sound like him when you talk."

"Who's that?" I asked, ready to reach out and tag him on the nose.

"Frank," he said, very soberly. "You share the same sense of humor."

Another memory overtook me during the journalist's interview: Ephron calling me in to supper. Ephron brought her own brand of despair with her to the Marchbank family when Father, the Reverend William Drury Marchbank, bought her in Liberty speaking some foreign Houdou language. She revealed to me once that she had served in a brothel, when little more than a child, in the New Orleans French Quarter. He had been so taken with her that he brought her back to our place in Howard County, not too far from the Missouri River and the town of Glasgow. Her first name was recorded by the enumerator in 1850, with a dash following and then "mulatto." In the Bible she couldn't read, her only possession Mother allowed her, flowers were pressed and dried like hope. Deep down, that hope was the only religion she had allowed herself, even though it was fated. It was like a bullet wound that had been cauterized but still constantly ached. She had been with our family for three years and it was that time and the memory of her that I would never recover from, although I did not know this at the time. She had cooked all our meals. I remember watching her in the summer months as she cooked in the kitchen out back away from the house. Her skin always smelled of bread and cinnamon. And now they were all gone. How tenuous our human relations. When we are children, we believe things will always remain as they are.

"Are you all right?" Edwards nudged my forearm.

"Did I say I was drunk when that photograph was made? Because it wasn't the first time, I can guarantee you that."

"Just do your best, Mr. Marchbank." Edwards relit his cigar with a Lucifer match. His rhetoric turned evangelical: "For the annals of Missouri history, for our common Southern cause."

It didn't sound convincing, even coming from him. Though perhaps at one time he had been rabidly for the Cause, but at this point it sounded hollow and shattered.

CHAPTER 2
The Marchbank's Farm
(Near Glasgow, Missouri)

When I was sixteen, my brother Gideon came riding up to the house with his devilish friend John Thrailkill. John's mount was decorated with the foul-smelling scalps of some unfortunate bastards. Some said Indian scouts taught them scalping and cutting off ears for war trophies or that they had started the practice in retaliation for what the Red Legs were already doing along the western border before the war. Jayhawkers and bushwhackers (as they called us) alike were known to go so far as to cut off the genitalia of their victims. There were a few partisans on both sides who had started these indecent practices years before the war had officially begun. It came to us in Missouri much earlier than it did to the rest of the country. Others said it was those wily veterans of Doniphan's expedition into the Indian territories were the ones handy with the knife and taught the younger ones. But most of the boys I knew were just that—boys—at least, in the beginning. The men over thirty were busy with crops, wives, and children. You take a nineteen-year-old and train him to fight and you will never find a more cruel soldier under the right circumstances.

"Hey, Dingus!" Gideon grinned at me, standing up on his stirrups.

I gave him a half-wave. "Hey, Gid."

Normally I would have been insulted at the nickname he had

bestowed on me when we were boys, but the day was fraught with excitement and as his little brother I heard it commonly enough. He also presented me with a fine slouch hat he'd bought for me in a shop in Kansas City. He had placed the bloodred feather of a summer tanager into the hatband himself, which made it look right smart. Still, it made the hair stand up on the back of my neck because I was something of a hothead, but the gift took some of the sting out. Besides, he was always japing me about having my head in the clouds, reading the Bible our father had given me for my sixteenth birthday, or simply for being left-handed. There were good folks in the congregation who said left-handedness was the Devil's hand, but Mother would not have it. When Gid or my father became too wound up about it, she was the one who stepped in and told them it would be fine in the end. The good Lord Himself had seen fit to make me the way I was.

My knees weakened when I saw a scalp with some blood and gore still attached to the hair. I stole a glance at my brother, but he pretended not to notice. For our mother's sake no war trophies decorated Gideon's roan, but there was a rawhide necklace, almost like a rosary, around his neck with three knots tied in it. Our mother, not one given to expressing strong emotion, came bustling out onto the porch to embrace her son. She was proud to have a son fighting against the Yankees.

As I mentioned earlier Gideon and I had already fought at Wilson's Creek and because of that we had to sign our names as officially disloyal and had to pay $10 commutation tax to avoid service when the Enrolled Missouri Militia was established by Major General John M. Schofield. They gave us our paroles and a passport showing we were under the protection of the Federal

Government, but they weren't worth the paper they were printed on. A Yankee sergeant with a thick chevron mustache handed us our walking papers and said he hoped he saw us again, so he could personally cut our balls off.

This new militia was loyal to the Union, radically abolitionist, and the Marchbank family was having nothing to do with it. Especially not our matriarch, Isadora Augusta Marchbank, who, to hear her tell it, had ridden out and participated in her own midnight raids. Of course, I am spinning a yarn here, but she could be a fierce one when her ire was raised. Only my father could keep me from going into the bush sooner, with his eloquent talks about serving the Lord and establishing our Savior's Kingdom when they threatened the life of my beautiful cousin Lizzie if I didn't enlist in the state militia. Father flatly rejected the proposal because he told them I was too young, but they said I was old enough. He conveniently left out that I had already been in the regular Confederate Army down in southwest Missouri fighting under Price. No matter what they said, I refused to become a Paw Paw. The Paw Paws were those boys who had been conscripted to serve in the state militia ostensibly for the Union, but actually they were southern boys, or Copperheads, miserably going through the motions.

Fifteen or so rebels taking refuge around the farm and in the wooded acreage behind the house were like golden idols come to life as I watched them caring for their impeccable mounts: piebalds, bays, roans, grays, and black horses nervously carving the air with their hooves while their hides flickered against *gallinippers* so large they could have shouldered a musket. A walleyed horse tied to a cedar tree bucked wretchedly against the deerflies landing on his back. A set of dun horses stood head to withers swatting away the green flies with their tails. Carbines and revolvers clanked at the sides of the men. I noted with wide eyes that many were not much older than myself. Horse blankets were thrown over shrubs, some used as tents to rest their eyes from the especially odd glare of the sun that day.

There was a magnetism about those boys, despite the fact that I was attending William Jewell College, where I labored over the Word of God. The Great Commission was strong on my conscience, but then so was the War. Everyone had said since I was a child that I had the Call. God had put his mark on me. I was even more compelled to follow my father's wishes since Gideon had managed to kick against the pricks of my father and our Christian family and become a bona fide rebel. There were times when I was not entirely sure of my calling. I had up to that point visited the mourner's bench to confess my sins and claim salvation a half dozen times at least, which would stick with me for a while, but after enough time went by, I'd begin to lose the feeling and my taste for the entire enterprise. The wild side of me wanted to raise up and fight any man who stood against us.

I could not help but get caught up in the excitement of the moment, with the thundering hooves of the horses and the smells of the impromptu camp. I could hear the sound of the blood coursing through my veins like heathen voices in that motley company. The pistols were the most intriguing; even the poorest member had three or four and another couple holstered in their saddles with lengths of rope or twine tying them to the saddle horn. And when I say poor, I'm saying as poor as Job's turkey! Thrailkill carried a special Buffalo gun. He was the marksman of the bunch. Not many of them carried rifles even then. The Sharps were only good for one shot and took too long to reload for the kind of Indian tactics they employed with their revolvers.

A one-armed man with a ragged beard was acting as a barber for another who took his turn sitting on a stump out in the yard with the chickens waddling around. Mother told Sarah and Ephron to prepare a meal for the regulators. Ephron was just two years older than me, or so she said, but I loved her no matter her age. I didn't know how she felt for sure. She had already lost a husband from the Benton farm who was sold out of state by his owner. I did my best to comfort her up in the loft. Her beautiful honey-brown skin was magnificent in the moonshine, but I knew I should put her out of my mind. My better judgment told me to leave Ephron alone, but she had been with us as long as I could remember. There was about her a tragic sadness that made her all the more intoxicating than the young virgins of my father's church.

I prayed for forgiveness but still wanted her, which made confessing my sin yet one piled atop another. My greatest fear was of grieving the Holy Ghost, since there was no pardon for such an act. Had I gone too far already? Now, those hazel, Creole eyes of hers, with a nimbus of gold, cut through my innermost being and held me for a moment until one of the men started hollering and raising such a fuss one of the dogs ran beneath the porch with a yelp prompting an eruption of laughter.

Ephron went inside and I couldn't help noticing the whistles and rough remarks about her beauty. I was hot with anger. I balled my fists with bitter, angry tears filling my eyes. I saw her for a moment looking out the window at the boys under the pin oaks behind the house. Only Gideon, and perhaps Sarah, knew my genuine feelings for Ephron. Gideon did not approve. We'd had a childish fistfight over her one day in the shade of the apple grove. He loosened my front teeth and I gave him a shiner over one eye. I loved her and would only learn years later that one cannot altogether help who one loves and who one does not, or the relative appropriateness of those feelings. Now Gideon gave the boys some hard looks and they put their heads down like wayward children with mischievous smiles still on their lips.

I felt conflicted about everything: the war, slaves, Jehovah, and what part I was to play in it all. But I exulted in my spirit because there I was, right in the middle of them with their .36 caliber revolvers. I reloaded Colts, Eliotts, and LeMats and all varieties of smaller pistols for the boys, since no one wanted me to be in the middle of the fighting, out of respect to my father's wishes that I became a man of God. They even employed me in an adjunct way to drip hot candle wax over each of the caps to seal them from rain. But hell, we were all taking our lives in our own hands simply trying to live there. Loading the weapons was a dangerous job, but one I took great delight in, focusing my concentration on the task at hand, filling cylinders with powder and lead balls, ramming it home sealed with grease. The loading took long enough that each rebel carried as many as a half-dozen Colts at once. There was a real art to it. Just the right amount of powder made the shot more accurate and deadly.

Five rebels sat down to play cards on a "table" made of a blanket over a wheelbarrow flipped on its side. A boy everyone called Cy kidded me about being afraid to lay a bet, but I had to get out to the fields with a hoe, even though my heart wasn't with the tobacco and mangling cutworms. Amaziah, the slave who had been with our family the longest, accompanied me out to the field with an amused expression playing across his features. Until suddenly he began to wave his arms as he turned and ran toward the house not too far distant. I half-turned to see Yankee riders sitting their horses along the tree line. Their leader gave the signal and their horses tore down the tobacco plants as they came at us. Before I knew it, two hairy free-soilers had caught me, one by each arm, and wrestled me down to the ground like a calf. Aye God, it was none other than the infamous Jayhawker Charles "Doc" Jennison and his Seventh Kansas Cavalry. Father had read about his exploits in the newspaper out loud to us, and the accounts had upset our mother so she had left the room huffing under her breath. I kept trying to twist around to Jennison but his men had me pinned to the ground on my stomach.

Amaziah stepped forward and a man in frayed clothing rode his mount into the slave, knocking him a few yards distant into the plowed earth. The Jayhawkers unceremoniously shot the mules. An important looking man, Doc Jennison, wearing his bizarre, tall bear hat, sat on a pale horse. The Yankee grunted as he leaned over his paunch and pricked my cheek with a saber, a mocking sneer on his lips. The scar that would indelibly brand my soul with hate toward him and all Yankees. A broad-shouldered blond boy with a drooping moustache leapt off his paint horse and kicked me viciously in the ribs.

"How you like that? Fucken secesh!"

I expected a fight to erupt between our boys and Jennison, but all the bushwhackers had skinned out like ghostly rumors from around the house, as if they had never been there at all, though their smoking breakfast fires, saddlebags, and bedrolls left in haste proved differently. It was reprehensible that a man or a soldier would harm children, women, and especially a preacher, but Jennison's conscience was in league with Satan and John Brown. They lobbed the bight of the rope around my waist and drug me back to the farmstead, tearing up the delicate tobacco plants as we went.

When I came to, I was on the ground in front of the house. Mother stood indomitably on the porch, all six feet of her, with her arms crossed in front. Her iron gray hair pulled up and away from her face into a high bob of hair atop her head like the crown of a particularly savage queen. Ephron and her children, Auggie and June, huddled in terror into the shade of the listing porch. Sarah looked on from the window behind a sash of curtain. I wanted to throw myself down between the Jayhawkers and my family, but I was beginning to wonder if the Jayhawkers weren't about to execute Father just like all the stories Gideon and John had told him about the families up and down the border of western Missouri.

The Bradford family who lived just west of Lexington were burnt out and the men executed by Jim Lane and his crew. I saw the place and the bodies, with my own eyes when we came back from a trip to Kansas City with my father. The men were shot, burnt, and dragged, before their ears and noses were taken for trophies. The barn, smokehouse, and other outbuildings were set afire and went up like a house of cards. The only thing left intact from it was the scorched weathercock.

Finally, the Kansans came pulling my beloved father with a noose around his neck and handed the end of the rope over to the bellwether officer as if he were a dog commanded to heel.

"We know you been providing hospitality to the bushwhackers," Jennison said. "Even if half their belongings were not already strewn over all creation, we'd know what was going on here. Now, where have they gone to hide?"

The obvious answer was they'd probably gone back to their

hideout in amid the gorges and thickets of the Sni-A-Bar, but the Jayhawkers didn't have the stomach to follow them there.

"Mister," my mother, said. "I don't know a damn thing about what you all are talking about." She spat off the porch like a man with her hands on her hips. She was a formidable woman, even in her petticoat and apron still tied about her waist.

My father visibly cringed where he stood. Jennison's pale face went splotchy that a lady would speak to him thusly. A guttural, commanding voice issued from his chest, giving orders to the mounted men who held Dr. Marchbank between them. I could tell they had beaten my father and that he had remained silent no matter what he was asked. He stared off impassively. A cut above his left eye oozed blood.

"Hike that man up over yon sycamore branch," Jennison bawled to his men as he tore off his tall fur cap to reveal a head of fiery red hair. His hair stood up like an angry porcupine's. "Give him a swing, and see if his memory returns."

"He's a man of the cloth." Mother shook her cane at Jennison. "How can you do this?"

"What kind of preacher imprisons his fellow man?" Jennison said. Then he squalled, "Hoist him up! Haw! Haw!"

The pair told their horses "git up," and they pulled Father off his feet as if he were disappearing into the eastern sky to be with his savior. The rope made a hissing sound against the tree limb, he was yanked up so quickly. I had always thought that tree to be good for climbing when I was a boy and my father warned that one day I would fall out of it and break my neck if I didn't take care. The Reverend's pale violet eyes bulged, as heat lightning flashed in the west. The air was so charged with electricity and violence that I prayed it would roll back on itself and destroy these heathens. It had never occurred to me that one day I would witness the death of my father from the branches of that tree. Or, that there were men capable of subduing him. My father's neck tipped to one side, the rope tight on it and eyes swollen. Father's legs thrashed in the air against the rope.

"That's right! Do the dead man's dance!" A Jayhawker called in a voice too cynical. He was scarcely more than a boy. "Watch him dance, Mr. Doc!"

A shot roared out from the side of the porch. The horseman, grinning like a demon at the fruits of his wicked labor, flew backward off his horse like a pullrope had been attached to his waist. Sarah stood there with a Sharp's rifle in her hands. Her eyes were wet with tears. An angry militiaman raised a quaking pistol at her.

Dr. Marchbank's body fell to the earth like an owl I had once seen fall, stone dead from its perch, as the rope unloosed. Father gasped and his legs flopped as he turned a circle on his shoulder, his hands still tied behind his back. Then the legs quit twisting and the choking red face went pale.

"Damn it, man!" Jennison said. "Disarm her, Ford! All of you, out of the house, and off the porch!"

Mother called to me, "Ashby!"

The man called Ford, a stocky man with one milkdead eye, yanked the rifle out of Sarah's hands as he shoved her off the steps. She landed on her back with scarcely a sound. I lunged at the soldier but caught a rifle butt in the face for my efforts, causing my nose to erupt in my hands; it was now my turn to writhe on the ground at the feet of the Jayhawkers.

"Tie them both," Jennison ordered before taking out his Navy Colt and whipping the bearded, hawk-like face of Ford in the jaw with a backhanded blow. Through my pain, I saw the man subtly genuflect as he obediently absorbed the blow and stood up again quickly after an appropriate amount of time.

I watched as everyone I held dear in the world was lined up. Jennison paced up and down in front of Mother, Sarah, Ephron, and Ephron's children. In my heart I prayed that Gideon and the others would come riding out of the treeline with their pistols blazing at these damned fanatics. Instead I heard the sawing of the cicadas, a cloud of witnesses, in the long grass and in the burr oaks as the afternoon stretched out into eternity. Jennison unsheathed a heavy broadsword from his saddle with a wicked gleam in his eye. He was the sort of man whose soul feasted on violence and mayhem. He went to the immobile body of my father, the Reverend Thomas Marchbank, and in one fell stroke decapitated him. My family was visibly devastated by this heinous act. I could not bear to look and reflexively tore my gaze away, not wanting to believe it.

Jennison next ordered a man to start with Ephron and then the slave children in the summer kitchen. Ephron's children were crying as she hustled them out back. The men were laughing and pulling at Ephron's shirt, but she turned to face one of her tormentors. In one swift movement the man leading her away raised his Bowie knife and cut her across the neck. Her hand went to her neck as if she could stop the wound, but she fell, throat cut, writhing on the ground. June still held her hand as her mother's body fell to the earth, along with my impossible world. Ephron lay unceremoniously on her face, lifeblood pumping into the grass, a most terrible offering to violent gods.

The whole thing was otherworldly. I wanted to die then— even if it were a mortal sin to think it. Where was Jehovah in this hour? What would He say if some hard-faced cracker asked Him if He was sound on the goose? I wanted to scream, but no sound would come out. The children, I was given to understand, would be set free in Kansas. I suspect they didn't know what that meant anymore than I did. More likely, Jennison would sell them to a slaveholder in the next county over if it suited him. He might have been an opportunist, but one thing I was certain of—he was no abolitionist. This time of violence was simply justification to ride roughshod over anyone he could.

The Jayhawk leader's lips moved unconsciously as he fixed his eyes on Mother, but she would not give an inch. She defiantly stamped the floorboards of the porch with her hickory cane. She was tall for a woman and as flinty-eyed as any man, a Tennessean by birth and raising. You couldn't have told by looking at her what had just happened to her husband. Her face remained impassive. Jennison ordered his men to fire the house, but then he had a better idea. He had one of his men put the torch in Mother's hand and forced her to set her own house aflame. She looked at the man defiantly with an expression of pure hate even as the place caught fire with smoke and flame. Next, Jennison cut Sarah's pretty alabaster face across one cheek with a twine-handled knife from his boot. She held her bleeding face with her hand, crying out in a muted sob, her bonnet off her head of disheveled auburn hair. It was not a pretty sight to behold. Some of Jennison's men took her to the barn kicking and screaming to have their way with her.

Jennison came to me last, his lips moved and spittle landed on his face, but try as I might to listen the Jayhawker's words were not clear. His lips mouthed the words: *No paroles. No second chances. Kill this baby Secesh!*

Then his man, Ford, shot me in the chest with his Colt. The billowing clouds, like smoke in their aspect, plunged down at me like Elijah's chariot come to take me to glory and up to the right hand of Jehovah. Mother knelt over me weeping for a time, until the blood-orange sun faded to a pinpoint of light. The last thing I heard was the sound of her voice singing a hymn we had oft sung on the Sabbath. Rough hands picked me up like a sack and threw me in the back of a wagon with other dead men. This life wasn't for me. I was meant for the Resurrection.

CHAPTER 3
Bad Company

I awoke in a copse of woods down the side of a ravine with the bodies of two men I did not recognize, hoping not to be struck by the serpent tongues of purple and yellow lightning illuminating the parched earth. It was night. The minié ball in my chest pained me terribly just below my left clavicle, a reminder that I was alive. The ache pierced me with every movement. I had hoped it had gone clean through but knew I was likely not going to die. I had never felt anything like it, but I didn't know how much longer I could remain conscious. Dried blood clung to my shirt and was encrusted on my face from the inverted angle. I was weighted down by two Navy revolvers in my belt that I had wrested from the two doomed men lying on top of me, though I remembered no such action. Hunkering down beneath my stolen Federal coverlet, which I'd wrapped around me like a cowl, I studied the naval background engraved on the cylinder of the Colt like I had studied Gid's a hundred times. Beggar's lice clung to my pants. There were cracks in the earth from the late drought.

A feral dog came chattering up through the sticker bushes at an odd slantwise gait. *Get!* I hollered but the dog kept coming with its ears flattened down on its skull. The dog's eyes were empty, its bared teeth were yellow, patches of fur missing on his body, and a froth was on its face. I shot him less than twenty-five feet away, near a hawthorn, without ever taking off the blanket. The dog yelped and lay still.

"Death to dogs," I growled between clenched teeth.

An old man yelling blood and murder at his mules came along, pulling the wagon up the deep rutted road. He looked unkempt, smelled bad, and his salt and pepper hair stood on end as if he had recently lost his hat. He stopped and asked me if I was "sound on the goose," to which I allowed I might could be. He grinned scornfully, spat on the ground, and nodded. The blue coat I wore didn't appear to fool him one whit. He just looked me up and down and gave a derisive snort, despite the hand holding the Colt against my thigh. I crawled up in the back and winced with each plunge and sway as the driver headed toward the evening sun.

"Looks like you died yesterday," the driver called back to me.

"Could be I did," I agreed and fell into a fitful sleep.

Two days later, I was informed by a Doctor Ridge wearing nankeen trousers and a white shirt without a collar that, in point of fact, several days had passed. I was informed that I was in the bustling city of Boonville. I could hear the shouts of the stevedores down along the Missouri River. It was early morning by the light from the window. His breath smelled foul from liquor. I was in bed and completely naked save for an itchy nightshirt. My wound was cleaned and dressed. Someone had covered my wound generously with a salve. Dr. Ridge had given me very damn little laudanum for the pain.

The sound of a fist hammering on the door below caused me to sit up in bed, tearing open my wound—I passed out again. A blue-eyed slave girl took the chamber pot from under the bed to throw it out. She stared at me wordlessly in the doorway with her mouth slightly agape revealing two buckteeth. The days passed alarmingly in their speed. I lost consciousness and slept so hard I had no dreams.

When I awoke again, a man's voice echoed in the hallway, a softer woman's voice attended, and I heard "lucky boy" and "passed through" and "missed his vitals." No doubt the breath behind those voices smelled of cloves. On the bedside table was a bottle of Dr. Sappington's anti-fever pills and a bitter-tasting liquid I knew from experience was quinine water. I hauled myself carefully off the high bed, put a foot down on a step-stool, and stumbled to the window for a look. The Missouri was visible from the second story. A fancy home was being built up on the bluff, which I could just make out. *How did I get here?*

Scuffling shoes in the hall sent me scurrying around the room to find my possibles. I didn't want to have to fight in a nightshirt. My clothes were freshly laundered and folded on a bench at the foot of the four-poster bed. The revolvers were nowhere to be found. Disquieting laughter filled the room as if punctuating my distress. The scullery maid knocked briefly. This was the girl I had seen before. I knew they called her Kate from eavesdropping. She came mincing into the room with an amused smile, although she kept her dark eyes respectfully on the floorboards as she gave me a bowl of broth. I was amazed at the whiteness of her teeth compared to her coffee-colored skin. At least I knew I was in a home of folks who supported the Secesh.

After recovering there for a mere four weeks, I awoke to find the blue-eyed maiden placing a wooden pineapple onto the end of the bed, raising her eyebrows with a telling glance. The pineapple was my southern message from the host it was time to take my leave. I knew enough to realize the owner of this home, Moran, was a businessman with a reputation to keep who dealt in cotton, corn, hemp, and tobacco on the river. The girl rolled out a carpet that appeared to look right nice in that room. My weapons—Navy Colts and a bowie knife—lay on it. I wanted to get a shotgun and another knife, just to feel like I could protect myself properly. I still hadn't had the nerve to use them since Wilson's Creek. Even so, I doubt any man fell by my hand. Creeping down the back stairs, I noticed the creamy plaster walls with occasional rosettes and even one mosaic of cherubs with a span of pink ribbon stretched between them.

One of my Colts needed reloading—I had been shooting jays and squirrels for target practice—so I carefully tore the cartridges with my teeth behind the carriage house. I needed to keep my skills sharp. I worried about the dizziness and double-vision I'd been having. It was like looking at your warpy reflection in a store glass window. I had been looking for the boy inside ever since what should have been my fatal wound stopped me cold. I'd found Gideon's bushwhackers, or they had found me. What had happened to me, my bullet wound, had started the boys talking about Fate and the supernatural.

The Irishman got them all started on calling me the Preacher, as if it were divine providence instead of dumb luck. I would soon find that this Irish was known to pull the longbow, as the saying goes. Gideon continued to call me Dingus, every other name in the book besides, and said the only thing I was fit for was to lead blind monkeys to evacuate their bowels. He had been shot in the leg and lost his mount on a simple foray to steal a wagon from a man between Fayette and Boonville. He berated himself between clenched teeth for turning his back on the old jackleg. He had been shot twice now and still alive to tell it.

I wanted to get back home to Mother and Sarah, still on the farm. Gideon, had he been there, would have told me to steal a horse from a German, but I couldn't bring myself to hurt someone who had done me no harm. Damn the Dutch! So I walked on, every nerve bristling, as I intended to jump off the road to hide behind the girth of an oak or under a weeping willow whenever I saw too many men on horseback riding together. I was scared to death, but ultimately conscience didn't stop me from stealing a horse tethered behind a stately summer kitchen in Fayette—I looked both ways and called out to boot, a trick I had learned from the Stanford brothers who had been little more than horse thieves in Kansas. I was traveling in an ever-widening circle, attempting to stay within the bounds of the known universe of central Missouri to find Gideon.

I slumped over my stolen bay, tears streaking my dirty face. I remembered my dream, Ephron telling me to find Quantrill and join up. I had not met him and couldn't imagine how to approach him by horseback alone without getting shot. How did one explain a dream or a vision? The militia would not only kill their prisoners but cut off ears, and they hanged the rebel bodies for the crows. No mercy. In Kansas and Missouri, neither man nor boy could count on dutifully mouthing the words to the Oath and expect it to be the end of the matter. It was illegal to cut the bodies down, even if they were friends or loved ones.

Ephron's voice in my dreams kept me going until I found the Sni-A-Bar hideout. A young Missourian from Johnson County named Archie Clements gave me an appraising look and then said,

Looks like you seen the bad side of hell. No answer was required. I would later learn that the short, slight young man who stood maybe five feet tall was referred to as "Chief Devil" to Bill Anderson.

Clements introduced me to a tough-looking bunch of dangerous young men: one man referred to himself as Henry Starr; and there were the Anderson brothers, Larkin Skaggs, a stuttering boy who gave his name as "Pony," and a wide-shouldered boy with a shock of red hair who announced in a rough brogue, "Mulvaney," he said, "though I'm known far and wide as the Wild Irishman!" He jumped to his feet and did a dance in the dirt, all the while making rolls and trebles with his mouth like a fiddle, his Colts waggling toward the heavens as if to prove his point, while the others laughed at his antics.

Ephron had told me to join up and now I'd gone and done it. Now here I was with the wildest bunch of rebs: Fletch Taylor, George Todd, Dick Yeager, and Bill Anderson were all there in camp playing at cards. As soon as I saw Bill, I admired him right away, though he terrified me. He didn't seem so much older than me, but he had a way of looking at you that said we would get away with whatever we wanted—and it would be easy! He wore a porkpie hat with a gold star sewn into the brim and what's now called a red "guerrilla" shirt. I came to find out later he had several of these shirts of slightly altered styles and hues his proud sisters made for him. His hair was long and down past his shirt collar, he wore a full beard. His face had fine, chiseled features, but it was his penetrating light blue eyes that really cut through you. Jim Anderson, Bill's brother, was standing at his elbow as he made his way joking and giving instructions to one group or another. The Anderson boys cut handsome figures in their fine clothes and even after spending time patrolling the country looked more like

Southern gentlemen than the horse thieves and cutthroats they were rumored to be.

Not too far away I saw some of the men I knew who rode with Bill standing around trading stories and drinking chicory coffee: blond-haired Little Archie Clement, Buster Parr, Hi Guess, and Butch Berry. Ed Koger and his brother John were singing a song called "Alley's Ball" that I'd already heard a couple of times. Koger played his banjo with gusto and John sawed his fiddle with a bow:

> *Ole Rile Alley gave a ball,*
> *The Feds came down and took us all*
> *Over the ice and over the snow—*
> *Sing-Song Kitty, won't you kiss-me-o!*

> *Ole Rile Alley gave a ball,*
> *Planned to catch Quantrill and bushwhack all,*
> *But Quant was smart and didn't go—*
> *Sing-Song Kitty, won't you kiss-me-o!*

Sitting a little off from everyone else was John McCorkle scribbling a letter with a nub of a pencil. I gave a wave as he looked up from his writing and he surprised me by breaking out in a big grin of recognition. He even gave me an abbreviated salute—the ultimate compliment, to my way of thinking. Gid had brought him to the house once, where they ate a hasty breakfast of fried sausage and black coffee. McCorkle drank a glass of fresh milk like it was the best he had ever had. I remember Gid telling me he was from Jackson County.

"Mulvaney," George Todd said, appearing from behind a cedar. "You're the sorriest issue of your daddy's jism I ever seen. Shut your goddamn mouth, lad." He had a strong Scottish brogue that might have been considered musical if he weren't always threatening friend and foe with violence. Little Archie told me he had killed a man in Scotland and escaped to Canada before ending up fighting in Missouri.

"Ye are a brave one, Todd!" Mulvaney taunted. "Begorra and ye need to be!"

Todd reared back with his entire being and laughed a big belly laugh and made obscene gestures as if he were pleasuring himself in front of us.

Clement told me he didn't care so much for Quantrill and rode with Bill Anderson's bunch. "Don't let anyone fool you. Some of those Yankees have sand, but they have shitty horses and sorry Enfields."

"Where do you think he is now?" I said.

"Quantrill? Probably hell." Clement pushed up his hat with a jokey grin. "Or maybe Kentucky. He might be relieving himself in yon bush."

"I would sure like to meet him."

"You are an eager one." Clement looked at me with suspicious eyes. "Be careful how you talk around here. I know you don't mean nothing by it. Besides, they made Quantrill a colonel and he was talking about fighting in the regular army. George tried to talk him out of it, but his head's got too big for his hat to fit. Say, what line of work were you in before the war?"

"Farmer . . . I was about to follow my father's footsteps and become a man of God—until some Jayhawkers killed him."

"You're pure d shitting me!" Little Archie put down a week-old copy of the *Missouri Statesman* he had been fitfully trying to read since dusk fell. "You was fixing on saving everyone's souls and now you want to send them all to hell! I have to respect that, boy. Otherwise, what's the point of hell? Some people need to be sent there before they'll see the error of their ways and even then they still might not believe it."

Laughter abounded around the fire at this comment.

"My daddy was a preacher too." A serious young man, with a large nose and ears to match named Frank James introduced himself to me with a nod. "Seems fitting to me." There was something I liked about him, he seemed trustworthy compared to some of the others, which may sound queer, but it was one of those things you feel in your bones about a person. I mean, the big bad bank robber—trustworthy? But he was.

I held my tongue and Clement repeated what he had said to the other boys. They all laughed, but they looked at me askance now.

Much later that same evening, the campfire they had gathered around was silent as the temperature dropped. Not more than two or three hours went by. It was the Irishman's turn to stand watch and after he chunked a piece of wood into the fire, he fell to his knees and shook me awake like he was in the grips of an evil spirit.

"I heard ye are a man of God. Bless my pistols, Fader," he said in his thick brogue. "Despite our desperate calling here, I believe in the hope of a better world."

"I am not really qualified—" I felt apprehensive that anyone would look to me for guidance or blessing of any kind, especially a boy who was at least a couple of years older than me. "I'm not Catholic or a real preacher. I never even—"

"Please, Fader." The boy's eyes were wet with tears. It was

clear that it didn't matter and that a refusal might have been unhealthy to one worked up into such an emotional state. He collapsed on me and made my chest hurt as he clutched at my arm and whispered breathlessly, "Don't tell anyone, but I'm afraid to die. What if my immortal soul ends up in purgatory? It would put me mind at ease." He whipped out two ancient-looking pistols of heavy iron.

I put my hands on the pistols and nodded to him, hoping to calm his nerves. He smiled and nodded with what looked like relief. But then he disappeared into the underscrub with a mist across the pasture laid out almost like a table top, a common feature I'd observed about the land. It was as if the darkness had enveloped the Irish like the Howard County fog. I thought, we are scarcely more than boys. Even the leaders were more like brutal older brothers than leaders. The moon came out and split the thunderclouds wide for the stars and the valley ducked below as it was bathed in a hoary light. The river fog was rising and I remembered a story Ephron had told me about the souls of the drowned inhabiting the mist. It was an ethereal night. I forced myself to chuckle aloud to relieve the tension, but it was the quality of night that made it hard not to believe those superstitions.

Little Archie was staring at me from beneath his blanket as if he were measuring me before he gave me a steely nod and said, *You are in damned bad company now,* and then turned his back to the fire.

CHAPTER 4
Argive Dreams

"Death to the Federals!" a hot-blooded group of men exulted. All I could do was sway wearily in response to them that required it. The weather had grown colder and the men would be returning home to blend in with the general population until spring released their fury again. This was what I had overheard one of George Todd's sleepy-eyed regulators say to his pard. The seeds of retribution kept growing in my heart every time I thought of my father or Ephron as I stood over a pile of turgid bodies. This band of feral pups, their expectation of apocalypse and an eternity in the hell Father had always warned about. The beating of archangel wings of reckoning accompanied my every heartbeat thumping into the cottonwoods. I just wanted to get on with it.

Little Archie brought me a small but likely-looking skewbald plug and handed the reins to me with a sardonic grin. She looked barely green broke to me, but Arch said, "Hell, no, she's spirited is all!" She spun around with me a few times just as I put my foot in the stirrup, causing general laughter to break out. He said she was a good Missouri mare and if I took right good care of her I might just stay alive.

"Don't say I never gave you nothing, Preacher. She's fleet, she is."

"William T.," Arch said. "This here is Preacher. Preacher, this is Bill Anderson."

"Who give him that horse, Arch? We can't have a coward like him traipsing around the countryside with us. Best set him on yonder mule and send him back to the parsonage."

I turned the horse so she was facing Anderson head-on.

"Climb down," William T. motioned with a dagger in his hand he had been using to pare down his fingernails. I hesitated only for a moment before those icy, hooded eyes. I did what he said, but I was pissed and scared to death all at once. I handed the reins back to Arch with a shrug of feigned indifference.

A drummer boy led a mule by a halter to me. I understood Bill had been a dyed-in-the-blue Union boy but now considered himself a Confederate. He had that bloodthirsty look in his eye that I had noticed among more than a few men who had seen too much. He offered to help me up, but I stood stock still instead. The men thought this was great entertainment, so much so that the boy led the mule around me a couple of times. Its rabbit-like ears flicked comically to and fro.

Bill Anderson was taller than me and swaggered when he walked. On his head was a purloined hat, rakishly turned up, with a golden star sewn on its brim. He stared down in my face until I wasn't sure if he meant to kill me right there. Arch had retreated with the spirited pony and was standing under a lightning-struck tree laughing at my plight.

"Your name's not Preacher," Bill Anderson said. "Who are you?"

"Zechariah Ashby Marchbank," I said. "They call me Ashby . . . sir."

"Marchbank." Anderson pointed a finger into my chest. "How come I never heard of you until now? Are you a spy? Come out here to try to report on Bill Anderson to the home guard?"

"No. Besides, ain't you really Quantrill's men?"

"Listen at the mouth on him," Arch said. "Don't let him talk to you like that, Billy Boy!"

"I think you are a coward and a spy." Anderson circled around me once before he stood in front of me again. His men gathered around now to watch the entertainment.

"What do you say to that, ole son?"

"Let me prove myself to you, Mr. Anderson," I said. It terrified me to think that not only would I no longer be allowed to ride with these boys, but I might be taken for a spy. I couldn't abide for them to believe me a traitor, so I tried to think what I could say to put his mind at rest.

"You won't regret taking me on. I can shoot and ride with the best of them. Heck, you know my brother Gid, don't ya now?"

"Listen to him." Anderson looked around at the men. "Talks nervous like a spy too."

The men had fallen into a silent expectancy like prairie wolves waiting for their leader to bring down the prey so they could all jump in and tear the rabbit apart. Anderson took another step closer to me and I could smell the chicory on his breath. His hair fell in ringlets to his shoulders; it smelled like the decay of leaves in the woodland. The smoke on his clothes from the campfire was strong. On his person was the jacket of a U.S. Army officer he had no doubt slain. Those eyes were cold and pierced mine as if he were trying to discern my very nature, his features a cross between an eagle's and a snake's. He half-turned away; then suddenly he jerked around and spat directly in my face.

Now, no one had ever done that to me before. Out of reflex, I wiped away the saliva. I didn't have time to consider my actions before I had struck him above the right eye with a roundhouse punch in a fit of insanity so unexpected it caused him to stagger back and steady himself on the arm of one of the boys. Gid had taught me to fistfight and I put them up and shook them to let him know I was ready come what may. My face must have blanched in fear then but instead of going for his revolver, as I'd thought he would, he smiled shrewdly.

"Bang." Arch shook his head as if to clear the stars and pointed his finger at me with a cruel glint in his eye.

The wolves in their appropriated blue hooted coldly.

I didn't bother to reach for my own pistol. They would have been only too happy to gun me down right there. I guess being Gid's younger brother didn't testify to my character. The blood ran out of my face until I could feel my own paleness. Anderson's men were loyal. Some of them were from Clay County or very nearby.

Anderson's face was grim. He worked his jaw back and forth like he was deciding just how to end my life. After just a bold step or two he was back in my face again, breathing hard, but his own nervousness was gone now, replaced by a coolness of a decision reached.

"You're one of us now, kid." He grabbed my right hand in a crushing grip and shook it vigorously. "We'll call you Preacher. You're the *fightenness* preacher I ever saw. Any young man who would dare strike me with all my men around me has cojones and deserves to be one of us."

"I never seen a preacher punch like that!" Arch said.

"I do attest he kicks like a Missouri mule," Anderson rubbed his jaw.

A general chorus of "Preacher! Preacher! Preacher!" went up to welcome me.

"Arch, swear him in."

"Will do." Arch took me by the arm and led me to where a blanket was stretched out over a bush, functioning as a tent. He handed me a tin cup of black chicory and busthead whiskey.

I thought maybe he was taking me over a few feet away just to put a ball in my forehead, but he said, "You'll take the black oath now." Little Archie's malevolent stare unnerved me.

"What's the black oath?" I asked, unable to control the tremor in my voice. General laughter erupted in the wake of my question.

"I'm glad you asked," Little Archie said. "You have to agree to it first."

I nodded. "Yes, I agree."

Mulvaney was skulking within earshot, pretending to talk to a tree stump.

"The Irishman too."

"Aye!" The Irish bounded over to stand at my shoulder. "Don't mind if I join up."

Arch turned his eyes upward as if he might have a fit of his own coming on. I wondered if he might start slobbering at the mouth, but then I knew he was attempting to remember something he had memorized. He recited the following to me, line by line, in a scathing oratory approaching the evangelical fervor of a Methodist circuit-rider and bade me and the Irishman repeat him after each line:

"In the name of God and Devil, one to punish, the other to reward, and by the powers of light and darkness, good and evil, here under the black arch of heaven's avenging symbol, I pledge and consecrate my heart, my brain, my body, and my limbs, and I swear by all the powers of hell and heaven to devote my life to obedience to my superiors; that no danger or peril shall deter me from executing their orders; that I will exert every possible means in my power for the extermination of Federals, Jayhawkers and their abettors; that in fighting those whose serpent trail has winnowed the fair fields and possessions of our allies and sympathizers, I will show no mercy, but strike with an avenging arm, so long as breath remains!"

A cheer went up, followed by rough hands pounding our backs and grim laughter. I wasn't sure if this were said tongue-in-cheek or if the whole lot of them were in earnest, or more likely it was a bit of both.

"We're riding out in a couple of hours. You're both coming with us. Your souls belong to Quantrill now."

"Turn the other cheek, hell!" The words came from a large raider in his early twenties who wore an irregular uniform handstitched in Confederate gray without chevrons to indicate rank. He wore the long coat of a cavalry officer and shining buttons with fine gold embroidery. When he heard I'd had the audacity to swing at Anderson, he clapped me on the back, "Now that's my kind of preacher!"

And that was how my life as a bushwhacker began in serious and deadly earnest. Not that I hadn't been doing my best until then. I had fallen in with one of the bloodiest devils in all Missouri and that was fine by me. The setting sun at twilight revealed the hint of darkest blue infinity in the heavens with the moon setting low and bloodied on the horizon. The evening was just revealing her early stars. I'd vowed to protect Missouri or die.

CHAPTER 5
The Enigma of Henry Starr

I was turning my back on polite society of farming hemp or tobacco. Let me make it clear: at the time, we Southerners in Missouri would have been surprised to find that we were in the minority, until Price failed to take St. Louis in '64. Hell, Price never made it to Missouri. He was too busy collecting laurels from loyal citizens as if he were a savior. We knew then he was through engaging the enemy mob before he had even begun. Ole Pap was the most backward moving general in history. Men like Price wanted an "honorable" war, where both sides stood up, beat on their chests for a protracted length of time, and then shot at one another like duelists. We bushwhackers, though, weren't going to be pawns to get shot for an officer who might throw away our lives just to further the military's own often pointless objectives.

There were critics who said we didn't fight with honor, but we were fighting for our state, our country, Missouri. We had been called "the *Secesh*" in the newspapers so much it began to sound like a new political party, until a boy named Wyatt (I had made the acquaintance of before his head was summarily blown off) wrote cleverly to his mother about how much he loved *Secessia* and would never leave *her*. He read the letter aloud to me and I found it shrewd. It sounded right nice to the ear. As time went on the government declared us outlaws.

The boys were already well past advanced in their tactics by the time I started fighting with them. Frank told me he had a brother about my age, but he didn't think he was old enough to join with us yet. Jesse had other thoughts on the subject and was bound to meet up with us directly. I thought it was a curious thing to say, since there were a few boys younger than me, but I didn't have the inclination to ask at the time. I assumed he meant his brother was too immature or small in stature, but I began to hear from the others stories that indicated he was not only steady for one so young but fearless to the point of injudiciousness. Frank handed me my own Yankee jacket to wear, although the sight of it was repugnant to me. It made some of the boys around me smile to see the look on my face, but Frank said it was how we did business. I slipped it on. It was tight in the shoulder but long in the sleeve. It didn't seem like an honorable way to fight, and I said as much.

"We're outnumbered and surrounded." Frank clapped a hand on my shoulder as he led me away from the others. "It's the only way we've found to make this offensive work."

For the next few days it was difficult to tell if anyone was in charge. We rode along seemingly without a point; or, if there was a point, it was not explained. I struggled to stay on my mount since she was green broke and had a habit of jumping three feet into the air at any noise in the brush—that would often as not turn out to be a squirrel skittering in the leaves. We came up to a boundary line of osage and elm, where we sat our horses until a horseman rode forward to investigate a hamlet just ahead called Franklin.

When the horseman returned, he spoke to Captain Taylor at length, who, after smoothing down his moustache with his thumb and forefinger, waved to us all, and off we went. There was nearly a hundred of us to do God only knows what. There wasn't much to the place. An old woman dressed in rags carried a bucket of slops.

A dirty boy of about twelve ran behind us poking at the horses with a stick until the Irishman aimed a kick that left the boy flat on his ass. Fletch pointed at Yeager, Bill, and Arch. Arch waved me on with them. We tied our horses to the hitching post in front of the store. The street was scarred with deep gouges baked hard into place by the recent drought.

"We need a few supplies," Yeager said. He cocked his revolver as he led the way into the mercantile.

"How can I help you fine Southern gentleman?" the grocer eyed the blue jackets of our disguise but did not appear to be taken in.

"By giving us some whiskey and food to eat!" Yeager shoved his pistol in the grocer's florid face.

"You are selling any embalmed beef and salt horse for the trail?" Arch demanded in an ironic tone that sounded like it should have been a question. His face contorted like a demon let loose in a church. "You're going to let it go for cheap?"

"Why, sure," the grocer said, standing with his hands settling on his paunch like a pregnant woman. "Young man, I've the best prices you will find in these parts."

"Don't give me that 'young man' business," Arch said. "Aren't you a good Southern man?"

"Of course." The grocer moved toward his counter in an unnatural movement, which warranted some suspicion.

"Call me, Sir," Arch said.

"Yes, sir," the grocer said, but he made a face when he said it and Arch balled up his little fist and hit the man on the end of his nose. He fell to his knees, holding his ruined nose in his hands in disbelief. Blood flowed down his shirt and apron. He looked up at Arch but not in fear. I saw a defiant look come over his features.

It became clear to me that this grocer had likely served in the military in his younger days.

"Don't you want to contribute to the cause?" Bill Anderson shouted down at him.

Arch gave me a hand sign, setting me into action. I crossed the store and before I knew what I was doing had backhanded the grocer where he lay in a heap, now with a bloody mouth to match his nose. He did not look so crafty-eyed as before. I went around the counter, where I found an old-fashioned musket and a fat wooden club. I held it up for everyone to see. Dick Yeager shook his head in disgust as if to wonder if the grocer were really fool enough to try to confront us with a one-shot musket and a club. He stepped on the man's hand and stood there while the old man attempted to pull it out from under his boot. Fletch gave orders for more men to come in and plunder the store. They used the man's own horse and rig to clear out his supplies and filled the buckboard wagon with powder, bacon, whiskey, and sundries.

The sound of a fight outside revealed two of my brethren in an argument over a fancy box. Upon closer inspection the box was of the type that held dueling pistols and these two young rebels were fighting for them sight unseen. They were wrenching at the box like children in a tug-of-war until the lid fell open. A pair of ancient though obviously finely crafted pistols clattered into the dirt.

"Damn you, Starr!" The larger man with a trimmed Vandyke bellowed. "I was only showing you, not making them a goddamn Christmas gift." I should have realized that they were in fact charged to be our lookouts on either end of the dirty street, but I was studying my own thoughts of father, Ephron, the War, and God. My head was full of lofty sentiments when I was a young man instead of the "practical matters of life," as my folks might have referred to them.

The grocer was brought out of his store by Anderson with his hands bound behind his back and a noose around his neck. They had worked him over in short order. Now I feared what would happen next. I was personally acquainted with the fear the man must be feeling and wanted to reach out to him in some way, though I had just smacked him in the face. Arch came out the door with his Colt drawn. The grocer kept pleading with Bill in a strong Eastern accent not to kill him, but it was plain that this man would not see another sunrise.

"Don't try to tell me you love the Confederacy," Bill said. "If you did, then you would be out fighting the blue bellies instead of coming here to profit off other folk's misfortunes."

A memory of the Jayhawker who shot me flooded my mind. The sudden movement of his gun hand haunted the moment. The explosion penetrating my chest. I gasp out loud still at the memory as if it had just happened. Jennison's giant bearskin hat almost laughable were it not for the ferocity of the man and this notion that I had long held that I had actually died at that moment. However, in my case the deformity was not visible but one of the heart and soul. I felt as if I were floating along the rooftops for a moment. Anger enveloped my entire being. Still, I was loath to do anything to mortally harm the man, even if he were a staunch Unionist.

Bill shot the grocer in the forehead unceremoniously, and yet he was still alive. Arch threw him on the ground and scalped him and rushed to adorn the reins of his horse standing a few feet away with the gory trophy. He wiped his hands and Bowie knife on the man's apron with a sweet smile of a choirboy that chilled me so that my whole body shuddered, just as he turned away. The little fiend took my Colt out of my own holster and shot the man in the stomach three times. The smell of his bloody insides made me immediately feel like retching. Arch then ordered me to place a hemp rope around the grocer's neck and pull it tight.

"Get over here, Preacher." Bill held out the rope. "Can you write?"

"Of course." I was relieved to be asked a civil question.

"Write a note to raise a few eyebrows," Bill said. "Write a note that says, 'I sell supplies to the devil.'"

I dutifully wrote the note and Bill pinned it to the grocer's shirt. He laughed like hell about it. It was a chilling sound and caused the gooseflesh to break out on my arms. I felt the hair of my scalp standing on end like a feral dog when cornered. The smile disappeared and he handed me the end of the rope and motioned that I should help him heft the man's body under his sign. After doing so I tied it off at the post. I couldn't swear to it, but the paunchy man still looked to be alive. Maybe I was too religious back then—it had been beat into me after all—but the hanging man made me think of my father and then of Christ's crucifixion as the amber light of the sun shone from around his body. It must make no sense to anyone who hears it. The words sound strange to my own ears and embarrass me just to hear them said aloud, but it reflects the state of mind I was in. I was torn between wanting to live peacefully or fighting like a wild beast against the Federals.

All of a sudden, the boy who had been fighting over the dueling pistols with Starr fell to the ground clutching his abdomen. Tinny gunshots rang out. A troop of Federals were charging down the lane at us on plug horses. An officer led the way, whooping, with his saber drawn. The sight made my blood run cold. Bill threw a laugh at Arch.

Later, I discovered how much it amused him when these Yankees chased them with only old rifles and sabers. They were outmatched for the rapid-firing Colt revolvers that we had. We would find a dry creek or ravine to lay in wait and come out like howling banshees as we were given the high sign. The whole business reminded me of the fiasco at Wilson's Creek.

Arch shot the officer's horse out from under him and I could see it pleased him greatly. This appeared to distract them and they pulled up their horses, uncertain as what to do until their captain was pulled up on a horse. Arch attacked the ancestry of the Yankees while they milled around uncertainly and our outfit set fire to what supplies on the wagon couldn't be easily carried. Dick Yeager set fire to the store for good measure.

"We'll hold them off, Bill." Arch raised a rebel yell as he fired with both hands at the horsemen.

"Don't have all the fun." Fletch Taylor leapt onto his horse with the wounded boy and roared out of town. Dick Yeager and his men soon followed suit.

Henry Starr stayed back with us and fired at the Yankees without aiming. He couldn't hit the broadside of a barn. Later, to embarrass him, Arch would probably tell tales about what a great shot Starr was at the taverns. It was tough to decide if Starr was the bravest man I had ever met or just the most foolish. The Federals were all over him and yet none had shot him—or even aimed their rifle in his direction. It struck me as downright memorable.

I unloaded one of my pistols into the knot of uncertain Federals. Before their officer could issue new orders, we reined our horses around and went off in a westerly direction instead of following directly after Bill. Like a rabid pack of dogs, the Federals gave chase for a couple of rods, but we were too well mounted and the weather was grim. The clouds were an angry purple. A purplish-black anvil swept toward us low across the sky. Black tendrils reached toward the earth from the center of the cloud's righteous indignation with man. Lightning flashes of judgment licked the earth. We were riding in a marshy field of wild milk-weed as the wind stirred it around like a painting. It was so beautiful in color and I couldn't help but wonder that all things, the creation and man himself, were fearfully and wonderfully made, even given the present dire situation.

"Something wrong with your horse, Starr?" Arch hollered over his shoulder as the first drops of rain began to pelt us in the face.

"She needs a rest," Starr said.

"You better ride her or join up with the blue bellies." Arch pulled up short and stared hard at Starr.

The wind hit suddenly. We were getting pelted with chert, leaves, tree limbs, and other debris. I lowered myself down low on my horse's neck. With my left hand I gripped the saddle pommel just trying to stay mounted. Arch was well ahead. Hail was falling out of the sky like locusts. It looked like the storm was moving so fast it might pass us by, if we were lucky. The black anvil hovered over us like an angry god searching the earth for a human sacrifice. Arch was under a swaying Indian bean tree, still on his horse, waiting for us. An abrupt lightning flash revealed lightning-rendered trees in stark black and white. Arch's eyes were an electric blue in the volt.

"Where's Starr gone now, General?" Arch called over the wind. It was violently shaking the trees as he passed me by. Little Archie and the other boys liked to call us all "Colonel" and

"General," especially the ones who hadn't been around long, but I aimed to give a good account of myself.

"Hell if I know," I said and pulled my hat down to protect myself from the hail. We rode into the weather knowing that they'd give up the chase. The sluicing rain watered us down; my horse's skin crawled at the first splattering drops.

The storm abated. The winds died. The dark clouds rumbled east. Wispy tendrils of clouds like ghostly fingers passed overhead that looked like the leavings of a twister. The hail covered the ground like a diamond field. Most of the regular army was in the Eastern Theater fighting the Confederacy proper, leaving unmotivated farmers on nags. Even the ones who were serious about ridding the state of bushwhackers weren't armed well enough to get the job done. But there appeared to be no end to the sheer numbers of state militia. If they came along, a man or boy loafing on the farm, the Missouri Militia might compel him to do his duty as the home guard. Some of these farmers were Dutchies and couldn't have cared less about duty, country, North, or South.

We came upon the boys near a bridge, gathered together looking like they were on a Sunday lark. Arch stood up in his stirrups and waved at them so they wouldn't think we were Yankee scouts riding up. Yeager waved back and Starr appeared behind us from between a stand of pines.

"Howdy boys!" Starr said.

"Howdy," Arch touched his hat in a two-fingered salute.

I thought it was strange the way Starr couldn't keep up with us, when it was clear he was a good horseman. His horse was tired like ours, but to the eye she didn't appear to be lame. The boys were beginning to look askance in his direction.

We had a laugh at the expense of the Federals and rode across the bridge over the Blue River. There was a narrow lane much used by carriages and wagons where it led under a white archway. We followed it to a house, covered in creeper vines and surrounded by musky cedars and walnut trees. It belonged to an elderly farmer named Cummins and he allowed us to rest in his back yard even though he warned that the militia was wandering around. The farmer immediately had his bowlegged wife cook beans, cornbread, and strong chicory coffee. Yeager himself called her "Mother" out of respect and thanks.

CHAPTER 6
The Spy

I was eating beans with a tin plate over my lap and noticing how fine the plate was. It dawned on me it was most likely the Cummins' rarely used wedding dishes. The boys were in high spirits in the main despite the sun playing peekaboo behind the clouds and a bit of drizzle a quarter-hour earlier. I felt a little more comfortable, but I have oft been accused of being a worrier. The farmer's dogs were lolling around looking for handouts among the boys. Henry Starr was patting a little fice on the head while holding his plate with the other. Starr had made what I thought was a grandiose show of checking on his mare's condition earlier to make up for his lollygagging. He readjusted his short Spencer carbine in its makeshift scabbard slung low on the right side of the horse. He had promised in front of the boys to give me the Spencer if anything ever happened to him.

Little Archie was conferring with George Todd. Todd did not think it was a good idea for him and Yeager to have their men together except for extraordinary raids that required a good deal of manpower. I noticed Todd always kept his pistol strapped on his hip as if it were an appendage. No doubt he needed it for friend and foe alike. Arch favored his knives and there was one wicked little dagger he fingered out of habit.

"You've a face like a *skelpit erse*!" Todd bellowed at Little Archie over some remark, real or imagined, he disagreed with.

Daren Dean

At best, Todd was down in the mouth most days. His conversation was all about his sour grapes over this or that involving Quantrill. At one time Todd had been Quantrill's right-hand man but as of late he had been bucking for a promotion even if it came from himself. He gave me deadpan looks, too, whenever we crossed paths. When he was particularly angry, his eyes narrowed and his voice grew whispery. One night Arch had revealed that Todd was an illiterate bridge mason from Canada via the Scottish highlands. He didn't talk much about himself, so there were only rumors to go on.

"What kept you, Starr?" I said.

"What?" Starr asked. "Oh, well, I circled around just to see if they were going to keep following us right after the storm hit."

I noticed he had recently changed clothes since I had last set eyes on him. Now he wore what could best be described as farm clothes consisting of a pair of canvas britches and a wool shirt. I wasn't the only one to notice. As Starr slid off his horse, Arch gave a nod to Todd as if to say 'Have a look at that' and we were all looking. The young man's freshly scrubbed cheeks burned red like a boy's will when he's feeling embarrassed at some turn of events.

"And," I said, "were they?"

"Oh, now," Starr took up my plate of food off a rock and shoved a great helping of beans in his mouth by my personal spoon, "this here's a good dog. I used to have me one like this when I was a lad."

There was the sound of a pistol being cocked and then a shot ringing in my ear made me jump and knock my plate all over the ground. Blood and brains splattered on my shirt and face. I looked over just in time to see Henry Starr slumped forward. His dog yelped pitifully and ran off around the house. Some of the men were on their feet with their revolvers out, looking around to fend off an attack. I snatched out my Colt and rolled onto my side and came up balanced on one knee aiming the barrel right at Captain Todd's chest. He paid me no mind and spit out a wad of *bacca* juice on Starr's body.

"You're a damned spy!" George Todd was crazed, kicking dirt over Starr's body, and cursing incomprehensibly besides in his thick burr. He shot Starr a couple of more times to make sure he was dead. "Don't come in here spying on us. Now, you're dead! Tell the Devil I sent ye!"

Henry Starr was lying at an unnatural angle, his body weight supported by his head. His neck would never have bent like that in life. His eyes were already going dead, though I could still see tiny puffs of air coming out of his mouth. The body quaked and quivered with shock.

It had not occurred to me that Starr was a spy. He had been acting strange for true, but I had taken him for a daydreamer or a shirker. Yeager stormed over and stood up to Todd so they were standing nose to nose. The men liked Yeager, but they feared Todd, so everyone was waiting to see who would kill who. Would Yeager and Todd's men start fighting it out too? I was still new and not altogether certain who to a man belonged with each outfit. It was a tense moment. It was hard to hear, for the ringing in my eardrum. Todd's revolver must have been right next to my ear when he pulled the trigger.

"Lower that damn Colt, lad!" It was one of Todd's main men, an older man who looked to be in his thirties named Ed Speight wearing a singular porkpie hat I'd never seen him without. Gid had told me all about him before I ever laid eyes on him. He was a particularly rare breed and he brooked no arguments and did not suffer fools lightly. His deep set black eyes, sunken mouth, leathery skin, and skeletal face caused me to imagine the Angel of Death riding around central and western Missouri under the black flag. He did not say much, but when he did, men listened. I felt like the child I was then in his presence, but there was nothing in any wise comforting about it. I did as he said and looked around wide-eyed for an explanation, but I kept my hand over my pistol in case circumstances changed.

"What the hell did you kill Henry for?" Yeager demanded. He had his hands on the shoulders of Todd's blue-belly coat and pushed him backward. I noticed he didn't push the Scot back too far before he pushed forward again and the men stood inches from each other.

"He was a spy!" Todd shouted. "Just ask Arch about it if you can't take my word for it, Dick."

"There was something not right with Starr, Captain Yeager," Arch said. "He wasn't keeping up with me and Preacher. He was dogging it bad. Ain't you never had doubts about him before?"

"Who is Preacher?" Yeager's head jerked around to look at me. "Maybe *he's* the damn spy for that matter?"

"Preacher ain't no spy." Arch walked over to Yeager perfectly calm. Arch was a cold one under pressure and I was relieved he stood up for me. "He's a good boy. I personally vouch for him. His pa was Reverend Marchbanks. Jennison and his boys hung him. Cut his head clean off the way I heard it told. That's why he's with us. He's got blood on the line. He ain't new business to us like Starr there was."

"Henry wasn't a spy," I said. "I . . . don't reckon he was."

"What the hell do you know?" Arch yelled harshly in my

ear, but his voice sounded like we were standing in a tunnel to me. "You're just an ignorant boy! Wet behind the ears! About as useless as a damn Dutchie in this war."

I dropped my pistol and held my hands up over my face. It was terrifying to see Henry dead before me and kicking in the dirt and thinking the devil might call my number up next. Later I figured Arch had done me a good turn by dressing me down. I might have been killed just as nonchalantly as Henry Starr had been if he hadn't.

"I guess this is yours now," Ed Speight thrust the Spencer into my arms without even looking at me. "Don't forget to pick up that Colt, boy."

"Shit, Todd." Yeager wiped saliva from his mouth with the back of his sleeve. "Next time say something and I will do it myself. I can't abide no traitorous spy in our midst."

"I'm sorry we had to do it," Todd said. "You are right. We should have parlayed with you in the first place."

"Exactly George!" Yeager said. "Do talk with me first since we have damn few men enough as it is. We have to be sure about these things. I could have questioned that boy and seen in his eyes if he was lying or not."

It could be that way sometimes. You were eating or drinking with a man, the next thing you knew he was dead. Henry was a damn abolitionist anyway, I told myself though I didn't altogether believe it or really hold it against him. Why shouldn't the black man be free if he could? Of course, it wasn't the time to go flying off at the mouth surrounded by killers. I wasn't fighting for or against slaves as much as I was fighting to avenge my father and to keep the man next to me alive. We were like cousins warring with each other one minute and wolves fighting a bear the next.

Yeager cared more about another captain usurping his authority than he did about Starr. I doubt he knew the man very well. I don't know how Todd knew without uncertainty that Starr wasn't a decent man, but considering the times, it worked to one's advantage to be a little nervous.

Arch sent a young boy, Frank's brother it turned out, named Jesse, to help me bury the body. The boy's face already looked like a man's who had seen too much. I noticed his spade-work and how he used the devil's hand just the same as me. We made quick work of it and the chore seemed to set our friendship. I was only a year older, but the age difference seemed much greater at the time. His horsemanship was impressive but common amongst most Missourians. His eyes were pale blue and penetrating. The well-worn clothes he wore looked to be his brother's. Even burying the spy, Jesse wore three revolvers and one of his brother's bushwhacker shirt with its pockets full of lead balls and percussion caps. I had heard Frank mention his brother, but had never met him until recently.

"Preacher, would you mind saying a word over him?" Jesse's eyes welled up. He looked intense and angry rather than mournful.

"Did you know him, Jesse?" I asked kindly.

"No, not well," Jesse said. "I just know that's where most of us are headed. Except for those who are called to do something more. You ever feel you were called on to do something important? Maybe even called by God? You being the Preacher and all, you must have heard the call?"

"Not the way you mean," I said. "But no, I don't think that way. My pa did."

It fell quiet between the two of us for a few minutes. The sound of a cold northeastern wind blew through the conifers and cedars listing on the hills. A redheaded woodpecker hammered on a tree not far away with an industry unnatural to the mood between us.

"I do." Jesse cut his eyes to me through narrow slits. "So why don't it make me happy?"

There wasn't anything to say to what turned out to be a prophetic statement. He had a habit of speaking of himself in these terms, causing men to laugh at him behind his back. Todd sauntered over and constructed a little cross with Starr's epitaph scratched on it and planted it into the ground like he would shove the point down to Hades:

We kill Yankee spies like the one buried here!

When we got back to the Cummins' yard, we could see camp was breaking up. The captains had decided to break apart again, if the truth be told, because they couldn't stand each other half the time. Captain Todd and his men had already ridden northeast in the direction of Fayette in Howard County. I felt like I was protecting the people of my own country in Howard, but I feared Todd would turn funny at any moment. The man was quick to get blackassed over the mildest comment. I had felt safer in a larger company, just one of the boys, but now we were back down to fifteen again. Todd said we'd draw too much attention with such a big company and he was right.

The urge to see my mother and sister again was growing strong around then. Being a bushwhacker was still new and I couldn't get the image of the storekeeper out of my head. Arch mentioned the boys would go their own way as soon as the leaves fell from the trees: it was too hard to hide from the state militia boys without the leaves on the trees. The bad weather would follow and the countryside would be almost impassable for lightning-quick strikes and hasty getaways.

The memory of what Jennison had done was always occupying my thoughts when we were on a raid in Kansas or riding from Feds along the Marais de Cygnes. Arch was recounting the way he had scalped the grocer for everyone. Even though I hated the Yankees, his story made me feel a bit *all-overish* to think about it. I certainly couldn't imagine doing it. A man killed when he had to, but scalping struck me as devilish.

It was at that exact moment when the Lord in His wisdom decided to commune with me. It had happened before maybe a half-dozen times. I knew when it was going to happen. I had a feeling that cannot be described. I wanted to go off somewhere, but there was nowhere to go, so I just sat down in front of Arch on the ground. The sky turned a greenish aspect. His mocking face contorted as the world loomed. The imp's evil laughter was in my ears. My eyes rolled up into my head and I imagine I flopped on the floor in front of him like a catfish fresh-ripped from the hook and tossed up on the muddy bank.

When I came to he looked at me like I had horns on my head. It was a hurt-eyed expression not easy to fathom. I told him I would be all right. His earlier attitude had calmed, replaced by something like fear. Maybe he worried that what I had was catching. Arch even put his Bowie knife away in his belt and turned away from me on the log he was sitting on.

"I seen a man do that once't in St. Louis." Arch shook his head. "He bit the tip of his tongue clean off."

"Did you try to help him?"

Arch turned his head toward me, "No sir, I did not."

There was a part of me that admired him. I wanted to be like these men—boys really—and most of them my age. I wished I had the courage or was hardened enough to go cut the 'nads off the enemy, but it wasn't in me then. Another part of me was terrified too. If they knew how insubstantial I felt to meet the demands of what we had to do, someone might have popped my head off with a twist right there like a frying hen.

Long ago, Father had decided it was the Lord talking to me instead of admitting it was the epilepsy. I think he was ashamed of me for it though it wasn't anything I could control. Once he even intimated to his parishioners that I was *slain* in the Spirit and embraced by the Holy Ghost. I think most of them knew better. It frightened Mother the first time it happened in her presence. It had even happened once during an Easter morning service just four years earlier. Old Man Williamson told my father he believed me to be in league with Lucifer. Doc Barker said he had seen it before and called it "epilepsy" —I kept telling folks about it and calling it a "Caesar" instead, until Sarah pointed out to me what I was saying.

I felt that familiar feeling again. I felt confused. My body twitched spasmodically. I fell to the ground and the world faded to black.

When I returned from the vapor this time, Arch wasn't the only one looking. I was lying on my back with a half dozen faces staring down at me. At first I thought the Yankees had caught me. Maybe they were about to torture me or cut off my ears. After such fits, I often had a lapse of memory.

A hand descended on my arm, I swatted it away. I tried to bite the hand with my teeth. I wasn't in my right mind.

A grievous voice said, "He just growled at me. You don't

want a man to bite you. It'd be better to be bit by a hog."

"It's okay, boys," another familiar voice said. "Give him some room. Are you all right, Preacher?"

"Fine," I said. "Arch? Where's Archie?"

"Uh huh," Arch said. "What was that all about?"

"I was communing with the Lord," I said. The men were thankful to be able to laugh under the circumstances. "Praise His holy name!" I spoke in the loud, cadenced tones Father often used when he gave his best Sunday sermons.

"It's lucky you came back to earth when you did," Mulvaney said. "They were about to leave you here, but your true friend, the Irishman, would never leave ye! Amen and Amen! Aye Father!"

They were all laughing and hee-hawing because it made them feel better about themselves. This crew was always hunting for a man's weakness but not all of them were convinced that I *wasn't* talking with the Lord either. A couple of the younger boys, one tall and one short, had their hats off and eyes downcast in fear and awe. They seemed to look upon me now as a Celtic wizard or a prophet, seer, a revelator. One rugged country boy, a giant really, named Bass helped me up off the ground in a kindly gesture.

I sat up, rubbing my face with both hands. My head was groggy and my muscles were aching from the convulsions. I needed to rest. I was never quite myself after such spirituals. But the men hoisted me up on my horse by the shins and my body remembered what to do as I clambered aboard the mare, seeming a bit calmer than usual, as if she might recognize my smell or my weight upon her backside. She was as gentle at that moment as some horses when you put a babe upon their backs. I had some difficulty holding the pommel and allowed my legs to dangle with my feet outside the stirrups until one of the young boys from earlier came and slipped my boot into one stirrup and then ran the front of the horse to repeat the act on the other. He gave me a respectful nod, adjusted his pistol in his belt, and ran back to his friend the giant. I noticed he had a small feather from a bluebird in his hatband.

Nobody said much as we mounted our horses. We rode down the back pasture toward a shallow ford of a fast-running stream. I watched the tiny rapids, a nacreous white, as they flowed over a logjam and fed the deeper pool beyond. The leaves were still green and thick, but the way the boys were talking, you could almost see them in your mind's eye turning maple orange, yellow, and rust. The veterans were speaking of returning to Arkansas or Texas for the winter, but Jim Anderson said it was months away and the boys just wanted a rest. We were thundering through the trees, low-hung branches hacking and ripping at us in a blur as we rode away from the main roads and cut across seldom traveled cow trails.

I did not know it, but I had joined up at the time of the most critical and bloody of our war. We didn't give much of a damn for what they were doing back East, just so long as Lee and Jeb Stuart kept whipping them. As bad as it may sound I only had the time and proclivity to care for my own people in Missouri.

Daren Dean

CHAPTER 7
The Four Horsemen on the Western Plain

Just as the sun was breaking out from the clouds, my gaze was distracted by men on horseback on the ridge above us. The sun backlit them so that they appeared to be appalling shadows of death. The Four Horsemen. Not a man among us who thought they had simply run into state militia; we envisioned a more lethal Federal troop—their mounts were easily the best we had seen for some time. But the chimera passed as it became apparent that they were wearing gray uniforms.

Captain Fletcher gave them a secret hand sign, which they returned. It was the kind of practice we had picked up from the regular Confederate army and the militia had resorted to it as of late. Arch gave them a wave with his hand sweeping across his body with his palm parallel to the ground, they waved back. Fletch told Bill and me to reconnoiter the situation, so we rode down the vale toward them. They sent a sergeant and a captain to meet us, the captain wearing a clean uniform as if he were merely out on parade.

"Is that fucken Charlie Harrison?" Bill relit a cigarillo with a Lucifer match he had been chewing on most of the afternoon.

"Colonel, fuck-ing, Charlie Harrison," the officer corrected. "And this fine lad is Sergeant Connelly. I am Captain Park Mc-Lure."

"What's he want?" Bill said.

"He's been given a commission," Arch said.

"Might I have your name?"

"General Archie Clement, at your service," Arch snickered. "But I don't stand on formalities myself. It's always the lowborn that seems like they have to puff themselves up with titles and such." He was laying his country boy act on extra thick.

"Who gives a shit?" Bill added.

"He's been given a commission," the sergeant struggled to keep his daft horse from turning in a circle.

"By the Secretary of War," Captain McLure said, "James Seddon, to find and select loyal men of the South and of courage to persuade our brethren in Colorado and New Mexico to fight for the Cause. Of course, a man needs the courage to go riding through the Osage Indian reserve."

"That's what I call a dangerous assignment," Bill said. "Why would we cross over into abolitionist Kansas, travel into the uncharted wilds of the red heathens, and risk our precious necks when we can continue to guard the women and children in our fair state of Missouri?"

"You," said Captain McLure, "of all the partisan rangers, should have no need to fear Kansas, Bill Anderson. Yes, I've heard of you. There's money in it for up to eighteen well-armed men of your choosing. Besides, this area is about to be lousy with roaming packs of Union men. Give yourself a break. Get some men together."

"Does Seddon offer an incentive?" Bill took his smoke out of his mouth and exhaled.

There had always been talk of Bill's madness in battle, greatly exaggerated I assure you—a madness of which he was the chief author and progenitor. When he was bored, he would tell any of the boys who would listen how he foamed at the mouth during a fight, but most of the time he was smart and kept a cool head. He knew how to terrify the enemy. Nobody was as lucky as Bill Anderson was said to be. He could be a cold-blooded bastard when the situation, like this one, called for it.

"He said to tell you," the sergeant interrupted with a sardonic expression, "that the part of Kansas we're going through—there's a pretty girl behind every tree."

Not being widely traveled at that age, I didn't get his meaning until the two of them started laughing at my confusion.

"Say Preacher," Bill took and untied his reins from around the pommel. "The only problem with that proposition is there ain't too many trees in Kansas. Nary even a hill you can use as a windbreak."

"I'm in charge of this outfit, Bill," Dick Yeager said. "I'll thank you to move to the rear."

"Is that right?" Jim Anderson bumped Yeager's horse broadside.

"Don't tempt me, Dick," Bill said. "Don't even start." He cocked his Navy Colt and held it down by his side, watching Yeager closely, ready if he drew down on him.

"I guess I can't have all the fun," Yeager said. "As long as Quantrill's not around, that always leaves one of us in charge."

"I'll say you're in charge if you let me have all the loot then." Bill laughed, but there was no humor in his eyes. There was a coldness of expression that caused Yeager to ride off nonchalantly, but ride off he did.

Captain McLure presented Bill with two dragoon pistols and Federal cash money, which had become scarce and almost worthless. Bill laughed at the money, but took it anyway. Bill looked around at us and said he liked ole Park and wondered if he had ever fought with Quantrill or any other rangers. McLure nodded as if it were a sad thing indeed that he could not claim the honor of having served in such august company. The scout nodded over his left shoulder and two boys led horses with supplies: whiskey, carbines, ammunition, new boots, and other sundries. Bill looked up to the bluff and gave a smart-ass salute to Colonel Harrison. Harrison did not offer any sign in the way of valediction but turned his mount and his men retreated behind him.

"That son-of-a-bitch used to ride with Quantrill." Bill took my horse's reins as I dismounted to gather the lead lines for the supplies, made up of broken mules and sway-backed plow horses. It was a wonder the animals had made it this far into the bush. I said as much to Bill, who was pointing at two of the retreating figures. "Cherokee scouts was how they found us. They would have rode in circles back around Liberty without them. Them Cherokees are surely more Southern than you are, Preacher. They love the Southern way of life—they even have slaves. Some of them try to live like white men."

"I never heard of anything like that," I said.

"You just keep your eyes peeled for the wonders you will see out in the heathen lands. That is, if you can keep your scalp from getting snatched by the Indians. Besides, it's a good way to get out from under Captain Fletcher. He's beginning to chafe me. Hell, it might even be a distraction."

We galloped our horses back to Captain Fletcher and Bill relayed the plan. He eyed the ponies with a green eye, but he said he didn't have any intention of trying to twist arms out West. If they wanted to be in it, they would be here already fighting with us was the gist of Captain Fletcher's position. Bill had about fifteen to twenty boys that followed him more or less regularly at any given moment. A couple of the older rangers bowed out, since they had families in the surrounding counties they could see anytime they took a notion. Fletch rode off out of temper with four of our men trailing behind.

"We better skin out of here quick," I said, "if we're going to catch Colonel Harrison." I was in an agitated mood. It was bad enough to ride around in circles in a country I knew, but now to go out West where there was nowhere to seek help frightened me. It was the kind of thing I thought a brave man wouldn't admit to when I was that age.

"Don't fret yourself," Arch said.

"It's only Charlie Harrison," Bill added more to Arch than to me. "It won't take long to catch his bunch, Colonel or no."

Arch was tightening the girth strap while the horse made little perturbed noises and then he remounted and said, "I never knew Charlie Harrison to do anything in a hurry."

We rode off in single line up the stony ravine, our horses' hooves clattering over stones resembling a crumbling ruin of a staircase. I was in the rear, leading our newly acquired supply train. The mule was particularly obstinate so that in my consternation I tied the lead line to the saddle horn, dragging him for a quarter of a mile before he deigned to accompany us.

A hawk spun off in the distance, hallucinatory and constant, as if he were leading us to where our fates were calling. Our men were discussing whether the presence of the bird of prey was a good or bad omen. It was still wheeling in the sky as, according to Bill's calculations, we crossed into eastern Kansas. Colonel Harrison rode methodically, as Bill had said he would, never once turning to acknowledge Bill or his men because Harrison considered

Bill's men as Quantrill's. It grated on Bill's nerves and I noticed him uneasily fingering a knot on the rawhide charm he wore.

On the second day of our journey, we were on an overlook to the west, taking a cold lunch of salt pork Colonel Harrison had supplied for us. This seemed a delicacy compared to the hardtack and salted meat we would have to make do with on the way back to Missouri. For the last few hours, the land had been flattening out, just as the trees had begun to vanish, and the vista offered some relief to the boredom. I began to feel a constriction in my chest at a landscape so devoid of cover should we be attacked.

A slope-shouldered young man named Robert Huff rode up next to me and proceeded to scorch my ears with his worries about the expedition, to which he did not require that I respond. His hair was down to his shoulders and he wore a top hat, not quite a stovepipe that he must have taken off some dead landowner, as his clothes were ragged and dirty farm clothes. The boy told us he had been riding with Captain Fletcher, but he didn't like the treatment he had lately come to receive. Evidently his share of the plunder was being siphoned away by the captain, and the rest of the boys were jealous of his good looks. He took up with us, he said, to fight with good old boys. It was all said with dry humor, so we didn't worry about him too much. We were rangers anyway, so we didn't worry about undying loyalty to a captain. Men were appointing themselves captain thus-and-so on a regular basis. Huff wasn't exactly handsome like he claimed, but he wasn't terribly disfigured either, other than a left eye that appeared to droop like an invisible finger tore at the skin around it. The eye itself was milky, but I allowed he just might see a little with it. His lips were full and an unseemly red but his teeth were yellowed and rotten in his head. He said the disfigured eye kept him humble, but I doubted that. His face was ebullient with the confidence of youth.

"Got this in Osceola working for the smith last year," the boy scratched at the few blond whiskers growing on his chin. "It was midnight and I was watching out of the loft of the barn where I was sleeping. Lane and his men were coming to town. I saw their guns glistening in the moonlight. I wished I'd had a rifle then. I could have blown off that damn Jayhawker's head for the rest of his life!"

The boy's bravado was a diversion at first, but mile after mile he wouldn't shut up. Once, Arch rode back and did not say anything but rode silently with his ear cocked to the boy's soprano repertoire of anecdotes with a bemused grin on his face. Arch stole a glance at me and grinned before he whistled loudly with his fingers in his mouth into the boy's ear and rode back along our column to where Bill led the way for us, although still at some distance from Colonel Harrison.

"He's within striking distance," Bill nodded grimly toward Harrison and his men.

Robert Huff did not seem to notice Arch at all and told me all about how his family had moved to a farm outside of Sibley from Tennessee. By his own account he had even worked at a ropewalk, served as an apprentice in a carriage workshop in St. Louis, before finally joining up with the partisan rangers. It was difficult to separate truth from lie the way Huff told it. He did not look old enough to do all the things he said he had done by a quarter. And yet he was so entertaining and high spirited about it all that I couldn't bring myself to call him out as a bare-faced liar. If nothing else, his oratory probably had been rewarded with shots of busthead whiskey, but at the time, he was so young that I decided his manner of speaking was foremost a habit of personality rather than merely artifice toward manipulation—It was both though. By this time in our acquaintance, I allowed my ears were bleeding and his lower jaw was soon to fall off its hinge.

Bill hailed Colonel Harrison to comment on an analogy he had already tried on me, comparing Harrison to Moses leading the Israelites in the desert for forty years. It wasn't the length of time he meant, but just as in scripture, there wasn't a soul to be found out on the plains. Harrison for his part was not amused and ordered Bill to the rear. For someone who was said to be a demon in battle, Bill proved he had a fair sense of humor. He came back to ride with Arch and me and he would laugh to himself that he had tormented the colonel for the better part of an hour. Bill recalled that Quantrill had ordered Harrison to go home, not because he wasn't an able-bodied soldier but he had to be told what to do every second. Even needed to be told when to conduct his business in the bushes.

Suddenly the plains weren't so empty: a body of men were riding to meet us at a full gallop. Harrison raised a hand to stop his men and it was a sight that caused your insides to freeze up as if your veins were full of storebought molasses. The Colonel stood in his stirrups and peered across the plain through a pair of brass binoculars. Bill guessed there were one hundred and fifty Indian warriors coming at us on their mounts like trick riders in a tent show. Even with Harrison's men and ours combined we were badly outnumbered. Harrison nodded that his calculations were correct. Most of us had well-oiled pistols, the standard for the kind of up-close fighting we did but on the prairie we could have used some Springfield rifles. Colonel Harrison's men had rifles, not many of us had thought about an eventuality like this. Even Bill was silently cursing himself. He snatched the short Spencer carbine I'd inherited after Captain Todd had killed Henry Starr.

Bill glared at me like a madman now, "This should be in the hands of someone capable. I hope you do agree, Preacher!"

I only nodded mildly in return. My legs were beginning to shake numbly at the sight of all those Indians galloping toward us and making their war cries at us.

The massive body of red demons froze in a tableau when their leader held up his hand. He regarded us with great dignity and we could hear his commanding voice speaking in an unknown tongue. It wasn't long before the horde gave out another bloodletting cry and their ponies thundered across the rocky field before us. It turned out he could have spoken to us in English but it amused him not to.

John Thrailkill unsheathed his buffalo gun like Excalibur, and in the most impressive example of marksmanship I have been personally witness to, he managed to pick four of the warriors off their horses like the hand of Jehovah. The troop stopped after the fourth hit to circle their ponies for a parley on the subject and a couple of men let out a cheer, but the savages were not going to be deterred. They knew they had us and would eventually catch us. Colonel Harrison himself led the way for the retreat and Bill and Arch took it upon themselves to form us up as a rear guard, after forcing Harrison's men to give up a few rifles. If it had not been for Bill and Arch, I would have ridden as hard as I could back to Missouri. The Indian ponies were sorry but Bill warned us with a word of dubious encouragement that if they caught us they would do far worse than kill you.

Bill Anderson hollered against the wind as if he were telling the best joke he had ever head, "They will cut off your Peeder and stuff it in your mouth, son. Be certain to save a pistol shot and shoot yourself in the head before they catch you."

"And other terrible things besides," Thrailkill said as he mounted his black. "Take heart, though. You'll be dead when they dishonor your mortal remains anyway."

We tried walking off our horses in a southerly route not to signify retreat but that we were merely going this way over here. Their horses were painted with barbaric suns and white symbols indicating their heathen belief in animals instead of our Christian God. Their faces were painted too and some of them wore the hats of Jayhawkers and Missourians alike. They were no respecter of persons.

I rested my horse for a moment on a rocky hill near an overlook above a creek and, looking down on the savages, met the gaze of one with long hair and eyes with all the compassion of a bird of prey. His horse's head looked to be painted red and yellow like something out of a nightmare. His look said he fully intended on sending me to the next world as he notched an arrow to his bowstring, so I spun my pony around and dug my heels in to charge hard after my brothers down the trail. The larger body of Indians gave chase to Colonel Harrison as his men raised up a plume of dust to the northwest. A smaller band was hard on our ass. We were still outmanned but we were more confident that now we could give a pretty fair accounting of ourselves.

When they charged us, screaming, sounding at this distance like a flock of geese, curiously enough, Bill gave us the signal and we leapt onto our horses and rode for all we were worth. A boy from Clay County was shot off his horse and we all knew his fate, but just then we began to ride up an earthen mound. and Bill, never one to admit defeat, said we were going to give them a taste of righteous indignation. So, as mad as it sounds, we turned to charge the savages and were shooting with both hands. Our mostly pur-loined pistols were made for this kind of close fighting.

I killed my first Indian with a lucky shot to his throat. He let go of his reins to grab at it as if he were swatting biting insects. There was no time to admire my work or contemplate man's dark-er intent toward his fellows just then. My horse was shot out from underneath me and then I was hit in the shoulder by an arrow. It did not hurt at first, but I figured I was as good as dead. My hand went to the arrow of its own accord and snapped it off short. I had not yet pissed myself when that crazy Huff boy hollered at me. He jumped down and pulled out the arrow, but I barely noticed in the excitement.

"Your prayers have been answered." Huff wrenched at my clothing to find purchase. "I got you now, Preacher." The boy whipped me onto the back of his horse before hopping on behind me. I did not relish the time when I would hear his retelling of how he had saved my hair from being lifted, but right then I didn't entirely believe we wouldn't be killed yet.

What trees there were went by us in a blur. My vision was wobbly from my wound. The grassy plains roiled with the winds and purple-black clouds sped overhead like a nightmare. The blood on my shirt and hands was, conversely, vividly red. It seems my unlucky body attracted bullets and arrows. I remembered that Biblical line, *No weapon formed against you shall prosper.* Clear-ly, I had not been living right.

They chased us for several rods. Potshots rang out. Every so often a bullet found its mark in a man or a horse, but there was no way to call a truce with savages. Some of us were riding dou-ble now. We were riding for our lives. Arch and Bill agreed later on that they were probably Delaware Indians. We rode the horses hard and we intended to ride them until they fell over dead.

Huff's horse was not going to continue on much longer carrying double. It was lathered in a milky-white sweat. The horses were foaming white at the mouth and standing on shaky legs when we pulled up at a little stream with some cover around it. I had lost a bucket of blood, but I could still fight. Having my feet back on solid ground made the sick feeling in my guts go away. The Indians gathered around us, and all hell broke loose. They fired on us for minutes that stretched out like hours.

"Make straight the way for the Lord!" I hollered, standing up to shoot an Indian with a head as big as a pumpkin right off his pale horse. I hadn't even aimed carefully but later found that was the best way in a fight. "Let the Spirit quicken your mortal bodies, boys!" I was clearly out of my head at the time, but this spiritual exhortation seemed to help.

A warrior raised up off the grass and shook a fresh scalp from one of our fallen pards, which clearly ticked Anderson off, but they were out of the range of our pistols. Thrailkill calmly leaned the buffalo gun over a rock, sighted down its length and squeezed the trigger ever so calmly and the Indian fell to the earth. John was a genuinely gifted rifleman. The regular Confederate Army back East should be so lucky as to have a marksman like him, but some men considered it immoral to shoot a man from such a distance. It was, some reasoned, more honorable to engage a man from a more suitable distance to test your moral fiber.

I was not of that ilk.

"You *Thrailkilled* him," Little Archie shouted. It was true, but the Indians were still giving better than they got.

"I'd wager the chief of this bunch is that Indian Quantrill was always talking about," Arch said to Bill.

"Joel Mayes." Bill pointed at an Indian sitting a gray horse on a little rise giving orders. We didn't have time to do much more than spot him at the moment.

"That's one hell of a white-man name for an Indian." I squeezed Huff's tiny waist with everything I had.

"You don't know what you're talking about, kid," George Maddox said, riding alongside us. He rode by me and Huff brandishing a Remington army revolver, looking as pretty as if he were going to visit a sweetheart instead of fighting the savages. He was vain, charming in his way, and liked to fight. The man always seemed to be impeccably dressed, even out in the wilderness.

I didn't know then what the boys were talking about, but it was told to me how Quantrill had rode with Mayes and the First Cherokee Regiment under General Ben McCulloch when he fought the Union at Wilson's Creek. Mayes was more Southern than some Southerners in his devotion to the Southern way of life and believed strongly in the institution of slavery. He was in that regard a mannered patrician from Virginia.

Frank Roberts was shot through the head and fell from his horse. I stopped to see how badly he was wounded, but it was no use. I had the presence of mind to slide over and acquire his fine charger that I remembered was named Dante's Infernal (and not inferno which you might reasonably expect), plain "Infernal" for short. Captain Park McLure, with a dozen men, came thundering over the rise; all were screaming and firing from horseback. I can tell you we all got a warm feeling in our hearts for McLure to come back for us like that. Colonel Harrison was a stout man and even from this distance I could see him bringing up the rear on his sorrel horse. The Indians clearly thought there were many more white men on the way, but a force equal to our own still came at us like banshees, screaming and hollering like whorish, painted-up nightmares.

Captain Park McLure's saddle came loose from his horse as he was turning it and signaling a retreat. McLure fell backward as he ascended a modest tor. He fell right into the bloody hands of the Indians, but there was nothing we could do for him. He was screaming as several of them leaped down from their horses with knives and began stabbing and cutting on his body. Even his horse had arrows protruding from its flank. They would probably eat the beast later. They gave McLure this treatment because they hoped it might unman the rest of us. Even Harrison was shot in the face and captured. I remember entertaining the notion that had he been caught by the Yankees in a similar situation they might have paroled him since he was a regular Confederate officer. We later learned Harrison's body and those of his men were found nude, scalped—their peeders crammed in their mouths for good measure, just like Bill had said.

Ever increasing numbers of Indians were riding up now until we were nearly surrounded. We pulled our horses together in a bunch. Bill rode around us, telling us we had to break through the cordon immediately. A strange smell came into my nostrils, almost like that of blood and burning flesh, but I could not detect the source. I'd smelled the odor once before when the Jayhawkers killed Father. Most of our horses were stamping their feet, but Infernal stood his ground like a warrior. I knew not to give him his head, though, because he had bitten more people than anyone could count, including even his former owner, Frank Roberts. I allowed myself to think one more time of all those dear to me but now as insubstantial as ghosts or figures from a book I had once read. I gave a quick silent prayer to be reunited with what little family I was still blessed to have. It made a man weak to think that way, so I put it aside and thought about killing red men instead.

Bill waved his pistol in the air and gave a rebel yell. Aiming his black stallion at the savages, he drove right through them and we followed with our hearts in our throats. They had killed about six of us by then. We rode hard for a couple of miles until we were near the Verdigris River, where they almost caught Huff, who was trying too hard to be a hero, shooting with both hands, and had slipped off his horse. Bill and I went back and returned fire to our pursuers to give Huff a chance to get back up. Huff smiled a remarkable smile at us at just that moment, causing Bill to swear in admiration of the boy's spirit. Huff swung back up onto his horse in a slick piece of horsemanship that would have made us whistle under any other conditions.

"This way, boys!" Huff shouted as he spurred his horse on.

We lost ourselves in the cover of the bank and followed the course of the stream. Mayes must have known where we were but had finally given up. After darkness fell, Bill forced us to dismount and walk our horses for another several miles despite the grumblings. Everyone was exhausted, but we didn't want to wake up dead either.

We wanted to cross the river, but we had to wait because dogs were barking on just the other side of the river and we were none too sure if this was a heathen village or an abolitionist town. Either way, we had to keep moving on. When we did finally make camp, Arch wouldn't let anyone make a fire. We went hungry that night and slept with our hands on our weapons closer than any lover. I left the saddle on Infernal in case we had to hit the trail in a hurry. To make matters and our moods worse, one of those notorious Kansas storms hit us head-on with first sleet and then hail.

No sign of cover or so much as a dip in the landscape to hunker down for the night. We were pelted by hail for a quarter of an hour.

We remounted and hunched over in the saddle, hoping the hail didn't grow any larger. I started humming "Just Before the Battle, Mama" to keep myself awake and make sure I didn't fall asleep, fall off my horse, freeze to death, and get scalped.

"I don't care if you are a preacher." Huff rode up next to me.

"I'm not."

"Wouldn't you like to find a warm whore on a night such as this?"

"What would a kid like you know about whores?" I turned in my saddle and pretended to busy myself with my blanket roll behind the cantle.

"Just what everyone knows about them." Huff's tone changed from jokey to morose in a second. You could see he was torn up with desire over the subject of whores. Whenever someone told the boy an off-color joke around the fire, he blushed so hard I thought he might faint. "A warm cunny would fix us up right nice."

The Irishman rode up, not being able to resist our conversations. "Maybe he's worked as a whore and he's propositioning you?"

"Better be careful, Mulvaney," Huff said. "I might just have to start my own necklace of peeders instead of ears." It hadn't occurred to me until Huff made the remark, but the potato eater's ears were as big as saucers.

"I suppose you fancy yourself the original cocksman?" the Irishman hollered over the howl of the wind. He made a wave with his hand as if to signal that such mirth was not worth it in this storm.

"That wild Irishman," Jim Vaughn came up alongside me and

shook his head. I marveled at the way large men like him maintained such an even temper. It must be unusual for big men like Vaughn to have to prove themselves physically when a simple threat would have done the trick before the war. A smaller man has to be prepared to fight hard and dirty unless he wants to end up licking boots his whole life. Little Archie was the perfect example of a small man who would cut a man's throat in an instant over an offhand remark.

I vaulted into the saddle and Infernal pranced around uneasily for a moment. Huff rode off alone ahead of us like his name. The Irishman grinned at me, not knowing whether to jape with me like a pard or treat me like a man of the cloth. His complexion and especially his ears were aflame with what I took for mortification at Huff's comment. It seemed that no matter what I said, I couldn't convince him, particularly him, or anyone else that I was a man just like them, bent on avenging myself against the current government. For some reason, no one wanted to believe it. Maybe they felt like God was fighting on their side if one of Christ's own was in the middle of it. I could talk rough, kill and torture Jayhawkers and do my bloodiest at all times to destroy the aura of godliness that clung to me, but try as I might, their gall in calling me Preacher only increased with time. Eventually I decided it was part of my luck for the duration of the war; I would let it ride with me as long as it might.

Now, one would think what we had just been through would be enough to contemplate, but perhaps I felt that way because of my wound. Our force had been cut in half by the dirt-worshippers, and that's not an exaggeration. It was not enough for Bill Anderson, though. His eyes had an edge to them.

Even if Bill was not the outspoken type like Arch Clement,

who was as wily as they come, Bill was muttering about the heathen Joel Mayes, who he held responsible for the Indian attack. He didn't care what kind of Indians they were, but Mayes was a Cherokee Indian who as I might have mentioned before loved the Southern way of life as an ideal. Which is to say he thought it was proper to turn your enemies into slaves, not being burdened with the Christian conscience of a Northern abolitionist. Now Mayes was nowhere in sight. Probably back in Kansas on the reservation, so Bill had to make do with what was at hand.

We rode upon a farmstead just outside of Wellington that looked to have been burnt out. An old man with the pallor of death hobbled off his porch in a way that suggested his feet were lighter than air. It was a comic gait, but the flesh of his face was turned down with sorrows no one could ever make right. The barn and a couple of other outbuildings were burning. A couple of shoats were out in the mud in front of the cabin.

"Hello! Hello!" the man stumbled off the last step in excitement.

"You love the Union?" Bill Anderson asked.

"Well," the man eyed our blue jackets cagily through his tears. "They were just here and burnt down the barn over there, but I put the cabin out before it went up. They ran off with my daughters." At this he started sobbing. It was clear he didn't care what happened to him anymore.

"Sounds like you got some Dutch in your accent," Arch said. "What's your name, mister?"

"Meiers," said the old man. "Henry."

Arch said, "You must have pissed them off, Dutchie."

"I gave them everything they wanted and more," Meiers suddenly dropped to the ground in a heap in front of us. Frank and

Jesse pulled their pistols out as if the old man were drawing on them, though it was clear this old man had never carried a weapon other than maybe a fillet knife. He threw his hands in the air and let them drop in his lap. "They took my daughters. That's the only thing in this world I care for. *Diese Männer waren Teufel.*"

"Hey, Dutchie," Arch said. "We were going to rob you. Your kind lining up behind the wrong side and all."

"I am not any side," Meiers cried into his hand like he might bite it off at the wrist. "I just want my family together. I don't care about all of this." He motioned to his farm, but truth to be told there wasn't much left besides the corn and a little garden out back.

"It's time to decide if you're sound on the goose!" Bill said.

"We'll just take your pigs," Arch tested the German, but the old man seemed not to care. He shook his hand at us to take whatever we wanted, attacked by demons of grief as he was. "I guess you'll pick a side now!"

"Come on," I said. "Let's leave this poor bugger in peace. Is there some place you'd like to go?"

The man waved us away with one hand. *"Neine. Bitte geh weg."*

Bill did something extraordinary then. He dismounted his horse and came out of his saddle bag with a pouch containing five hundred dollars. He reached down and pulled the man up by his shoulders and looped the pouch strings around his wrist. There was no way to save his daughters. Who knew why or where the Feds would take them. They had probably raped and killed them by now. The man nodded wearily and put the bag in his pocket with no more concern than had it been a scrap of meat leftover from dinner. We still took the hogs, and we rode off down the road and left the old man on the steps weeping miserably into his hands.

My shoulder was killing me, so they found an old Mormon woman outside of Independence who cleansed my wound and wrapped it in clean linen. The woman, Ruth, lit a lantern and set it on a table. She made a point of looking deep into my eyes once and said, "Yes." It was disturbing the way she looked at me, as if she held some secret knowledge just between her and the Lord. The more I looked at her, the more pointed her face became, the more gray and wild her hair grew. Not that I ever believed in such things, but it came to mind that she was probably a witch. I never disallowed things as witches and ghosts. Most folks I knew made reference to them, so I figured it was reasonable they could be around, despite Father's belief to the contrary. The night was filled with thunderstorms and lightning was in the air. I felt rejuvenated by the lightning in the atmosphere.

At the first smear of dawn we rode until we hit the Sni-a-bar Hills, a warren of thickly wooded ravines, thickets of prickly thorn, and cottonwoods bursting into green. Anderson told us to rest up until he could plan some new devilment. He was looking contemplative and sour, but it could have just been the same exhaustion that we were all feeling. Men always expect their leaders to show a better example than they would give themselves. Bill Anderson wasn't even as old as a few of the boys, but any of us would have done anything he told us or died doing it. He was that charismatic. Even Todd and Quantrill recognized it in him. It was like Quantrill's magnetism, but focused and icy, with vengeance in it. Todd's men followed him out of a respect born of fear. I didn't like George Todd or respect him either one, but he was a right handsome devil. We were all relieved to make it back

Daren Dean

to Missouri. Three ravens sat idly grousing in an oak tree, spirits roaming the country.

Chapter 8
The Wedding

"He's just trying to get the farm," I told Mama when I had gone back home for a visit after the weather had become too cold, the ground too mush, and the cover the leaves provided were gone until spring when the boys would meet up again.

"That's what I am counting on," Mama said.

"What?" I was inspecting Infernal's hooves for sand cracks and anything that might have become lodged therein. I crouched, holding his foreleg between my legs and trimmed it at the point of the frog with a knife as she talked.

"I'm counting on greed to help me seal the deal," Mama whispered although we were alone in the house. "I know he ain't interested in me . . . that is, he has no strong feeling . . . "

"Mama—"

"I am not completely without decorum." Mama folded her tea towel across the back of a rope-bottom chair as she spoke. "You wanted an explanation. Be enough of a man to accept it when it's given."

Mama went to the window, where the wind was bending the trees as cherry, gold, and russet leaves flew dead and dying through the air. The mornings of late had been turning bitterly cold. I had spent a couple of weeks flat on my back sweating and taking vile emetics according to doctor's orders. The past week I had spent the mornings hefting an axe endeavoring to teach myself to cut wood right-handed without much luck. It was nice being in polite company and living indoors again, with Mama and my sister Sarah. Even Gid looked no worse for the wear. Gid came over and clapped me on the arm and comically felt my biceps and said, "Look at those chicken wings!"

Nothing I could do would compel them to go to church on the Sabbath. It worried me that their continued absences might end up sending the state militia to our door, but Mama would have none of it. To her credit, as miserable as the war had made her of late, she never once spoke of returning to Tennessee to the protection of kin—except for Uncle Silas, who came with them to Missouri before I was born.

Father's plot was out in the meadow east of the house with a newly constructed picket fence surrounding it. A wooden cross marked the head of the grave. For a man who had encompassed so much, it seemed a negligible tribute to his memory. I opened the gate with my right hand, my left arm being in a sling. Off on another hill, near the woods, were the graves of Ephron and her children. I felt so much looking down at his grave that I couldn't feel anything.

It is a terrible thing to say, but I felt my time with the bushwhackers had hardened my heart. At the time, I had seen enough death to put even the deaths of all of them in a place that didn't touch me, as long as I didn't look there with regret. Later I would learn that when a person who has shared your life passes on, they leave a gap that can never be patched, not even with another person.

It was because life can be fleeting that I asked Lizzie to marry me. I felt like we were too young on the one hand, but on the other I loved her, and she was everything to me. Her hair was gold and it caught the sunlight in the way so as to be breathtaking. She was the most beautiful girl, north or south, I'd ever seen, and I couldn't bear to think of anyone other than me sitting next to her on a church pew or the buckboard of a horse-drawn carriage for the rest of our lives.

We told few what we were about. Not even Mama knew, although we had to tell her folks who were getting on in years and they were agreeable to know she would be taken care of. We journeyed down to the Sni in a wagon Bill Gregg had discovered in a man's barn down the road to drive the wedding party. He claimed to be borrowing it, but even Lizzie laughed behind her hand at such a bald-faced lie.

I put on my preacher suit and polished my pistols and spurs. It wouldn't do to go unarmed in the Sni camp. The boys put on their best, and everyone seemed in high spirits. She looked so delicate in her dress and there was something about when she put her tiny hand on my arm that made me realize the enormity that we were being joined together for eternity in the sight of God and man. We exchanged rings and then we didn't care who knew, although I was worried how Mama might take it. I knew she would be angry, but it seemed like the best way. We stayed at a little farm house a local farmer let us borrow, since it stood empty save for a few pieces of furniture including a bed. Some of the boys took up positions out in the woods around the house to guard us so we could honeymoon in peace, but I was still in no shape to perform my new husbandly duties, though I trembled with the wanting to.

When we awoke the next morning, she said, "Good morning, husband." I said, "Good morning to you, wife." The strangeness of it hit us and we laughed together because we were so happy. We came to each other and laughed and I put my hands over hers and stared into her eyes. I could not believe my good fortune to have such a beautiful woman to love for the rest of my life. Bill Gregg drove us back home, and being in high spirits he serenaded us with love songs and hymns he could remember as he handled the reins and called to the team pulling our wagon. The wheels over the road made the sound of his accompaniment.

I spent my free time healing up and reading. I was a big reader and still am. In the mornings, I would drink coffee and read the *Farmer's Almanac*. Mama and Sarah took turns reading newspapers like the *Kansas City Star*, *Sedalia Democrat*, and the *St. Joe Gazette* and other area weeklies. I read Shakespeare, of course, for Father had compelled me to memorize long passages from his work besides the Bible. When I could sit up and read for myself, I read novels that were on his all but forgotten bookshelves, like one author I stumbled upon named Melville. A friend had brought a copy of *Moby Dick* to our father from back East. Pap had loved reading these stories about the sea though he had been nowhere near an ocean at the time. His official stand on novels had been that they were all immoral and he instructed his flock that it was time idly spent, but he wasn't above reading them himself, I'd noticed. I also read *The Iliad* which seemed to me to embody our War on both sides.

Bending to the mound where he was interred, I scooped some of the clay-laden dirt that had not settled and shook it gently out of my hand as through a sieve over him. The sunlight peeked through the early morning fog and I asked God why He could not speak to me directly to straighten out my thoughts. There were men of God whom Father had introduced me to in the surrounding counties who spoke of a level of personal interaction with the spirit of God that was impossible to grasp. Sometimes these men would put a hand on my head as if to consecrate me to the Lord.

While every muscle strained for a sign from above, I could hear the sound of a wagon rattling down the lane to the house. It was Uncle Silas coming to speak to Mama about her plans for the fallow field. I wondered why he was talking to her about it instead of Gid, but Gid had taken off on horseback at sunrise armed to the teeth, without a word to any of us. I left the gate to Father's gravesite standing open in my hurry to speak to Uncle Silas, but later that afternoon the sight of the open gate perturbed my mind until I relatched it.

Uncle Silas had been appointed the administrator of my father's estate in my absence. He was a solitary, forbidding man who had always rubbed folks the wrong way—it was no different with family. The man was a walking contradiction in that he worked as a farmer on his own small place, but when he went to town or came for a visit, he dressed like a banker. Admittedly, a banker who had fallen on bad times, but it was still odd to see him in his brown suit and bowler hat and still wearing shitty work boots when he would occasion to visit us in his freight wagon.

Uncle Silas was my Pap's elder brother, but none of us ever thought he would hold the reins of the family finances. If he hadn't been nearby, it's likely a stranger would have been named as the executor, and that might have been a more fortuitous situation in the long run. Mama told me about the assessors that were sent out to the place. Including Uncle Silas, Mama referred to them as the Apostles of Satan. After examining the fields and the outbuildings, they came to the house and took account of each household item from the grindstone to every cup and book on the bookcase, including the family Bible. The assessors allowed Uncle Silas to keep possession of the farming machinery so as to make a go of it and granted Mama five pigs, a milk cow, one swaybacked horse, assorted household items including a mahogany table, and fifty-seven dollars.

Mama told me about the auctioneer hollering and neighbors and old friends buying our possessions with stony faces. When a woman loses her husband, she loses everything, but Mama still wouldn't return to Tennessee. She said it was because she was a hardhead. Gideon said it was more like an iron-head. One of the neighbors, a widower named Jim Griffin, helped her buy back a half-dozen sheep, a two-horse straddle row cultivator, a table and ladder-back chairs, and an ancient musket. The auction took place just after Christmas, and Mama said she just wanted to sit down on the steps and cry, but times were hard for everyone. She said it made her harder and anyone could take one look at her face and see the truth in it. She had been born tough to begin with. That was when she started wearing Father's old work pants with alterations. She made a strapping overseer to the farm, but there was Uncle Silas to deal with.

"Being Bill's brother," Uncle Silas said. "Not only should I be the prime executor of this estate, but I should give you the protection and comfort of becoming my wife."

"Is that supposed to sound like a proposal, Silas?" Mama replied.

"Hell," Silas said, "it is one."

"Your ass! I'd no more marry you than I'd marry one of them celestials—"

"Now, Isadora," Uncle Silas said. "First off, it's my duty to marry you as a Christian according to the Biblical principal of the Kinsman-Redeemer referred to in the Book of Ruth."

Mama stood up, wearing Pap's ministerial pants and shirt

rolled up to her elbows, in a threatening gesture that had its desired effect on Uncle Silas. Not long after Pap's murder, Mama had lost what remained of her never quite demure womanhood. She glowered down at Uncle Silas.

"Let's get a few things straight," Mama said. "You may be the court-appointed administrator of the farm, but never presume to officiate over my person. It's all right with me if you want to work the farm. That's your place as my brother-in-law, but I had my children. I don't need no more. And, I don't need another man in my bed. I'm in mourning and will be for the rest of my life."

She dressed in a state of mourning for several years and in Pap's cast-off black suits. There were no black gingham dresses—or dresses at all after that, unless it was to go to a wedding or a funeral. She attended church only sporadically throughout the year despite encouraging visits from concerned deacon's wives.

At first Mama made her household purchases on credit, which Uncle Silas paid off as administrator, but now she simply demanded cash against the estate, and as much as it rankled Uncle Silas, he had no legal choice. Sarah told me they had argued once out on the front porch, Uncle Silas smacked her mouth and bloodied her lip. It was the last time, because Mama balled up her right hand into a fist and smote him so hard he went fell off the porch and into the mud on his backside.

Uncle Silas was not a puny man by any means; it was just that Mama was a large woman with farmer's hands and fierce determination. There was something raunchy-looking about the man. It was hard to believe that he and my Pap were brothers. Uncle Silas had a disarming way of speaking without inflection of speech or facial expression. It gave one the disquieting suspicion that violence was not far behind, but Mama was another species of woman entirely and he couldn't call her bluff. They had known each other too long for that.

Uncle Silas might have been afraid of Mama, but there wasn't a man in the county, other than perhaps a bushwhacker or two, that could have intimidated him. Barring a new husband, Uncle Silas was probably the only thing standing between Mama and losing her property at the behest of the judge. Women couldn't own anything outright in that part of the country. Mama knew it, too, but she knew Uncle Silas's weakness—that despite his wickedness he was a greedy coward. Not many men would venture looking into his eyes that far or for the length of time it would have took to see it. Mama had nothing but time and reliable intuition as to whether a man was worth a damn or not.

So Silas rode up now, smoking a pipe. I hadn't called him Uncle since I was a child, but he still looked at me and saw a boy. It hadn't registered in his alcohol-addled brain that I had killed at least two men now. I was a man. Even if I had accomplished it mostly by accident. The first killing is the hardest, but after that it starts to become part of your whole field of vision about the world. You look at somebody, like your Uncle Silas for instance, and begin to size him up. You wonder how difficult, or not, it might be to kill him if you had the need. Or, for instance, you might speculate on if his head was harder than a split piece of firewood.

"Hey there, young Ashby." Silas tied the reins up with a curt nod. "You back from the Crusades for good?"

"Just healing up." I nodded back, as grim as I could manage. It is taxing enough to look properly dangerous when you are young and can hardly support a yellow moustache and tuft of hair on the chin as I did back then. If you couldn't look menacing, you just had to do what a number of other young guns hoping to make a name for themselves did. Namely, start shooting people—otherwise they wouldn't believe anyone with a baby-face meant what he said. Killing will make a believer quicker out of the worst cynic.

"I heard you was out fighting heathens. Seems like there are plenty of decent white people to fight these days without riding into the reservations or wherever to pick a fight with savages. But I'm glad you're here," Silas looked me up and down like you would a mule you had just bought on market day on the square. Smoke billowed out of his mouth and nose. "Your mama said the Indians shot you? That true?" He looked at me through a sheath of unkempt eyebrows.

"It's healing," I nodded and turned to hobble off. I didn't want to explain myself to the man trying to steal our property.

"Don't turn away from me, boy," Uncle Silas said.

The blood drained from my face. It was hard to breathe or think at that moment. Instinctively, I reached for a phantom revolver at my side, but it was hanging in my gun belt on a hook in my bedroom. It was good for both of us that I wasn't wearing it because he would have been dead and I would have been in grave family trouble. When I turned, he was holding a shotgun on me, but in a casual sort of way as if he thought a fat possum or rabbit might happen by. He was smiling at me as if to say he had rightly provoked my anger and anticipated my response. Even though I was his nephew, I knew he would like nothing better than to have a reason to shoot me dead and then crow about how he had killed one of Quantrill's guerillas—that's how he would have told it. It was like I had been trying to make Missouri safe for Southerners and here comes Uncle Silas trying to take me light. If it had been anyone else, they might have been dead, but the memory of what a family member has been to you will sometimes stop you cold.

He was smiling that yellow-toothed smile of his, too, just making it worse on me.

He might not think so much of himself with his insides leaking out, I thought. A vision of him lying in a rusty ditch on top of a pile of dead Federals came to mind with some satisfaction.

"Were you going to say something, Ashby?"

"No sir." I choked on the words. "Nothing at all." I gave him the most brutal stare I could muster. I'd certainly seen Little Archie and the others use it to convince a few bad-intentioned men to straighten up.

"Good boy," Uncle Silas said. The color draining from his face, he licked his lips, and he now began to stumble over his words. "I realize you're practically an invalid and all with your wound, but I need you to unload this firewood. I cut most of it up last summer down by the creek. Knew you all could use some. I figure if I went to all the trouble to cut it, you could at least unload it. Since it's free."

It was anything but free.

So the whole time I was unloading, Uncle Silas was looking over my work criticizing not only my technique for picking up the wood but the form of the woodpile itself. He never hesitated to tell me how I could have done it better, and if that wasn't irksome enough, Mama came out onto the porch to add a few remarks on the subject herself. I was sick of him mean-mouthing me, and if nothing else, I was going to beat on the back of his head with a hunk of firewood. But just as I was moving to put my hands on him, I heard footsteps on the gallery above again.

"Silas." Mama wiped her hands on her apron as she walked toward the balustrade. "Are you holding up the house?"

"Pardon?" Uncle Silas said.

"Are you leaning against the house to keep it from falling over?"

"Of course not." He pulled at his vest.

"Help Ashby, then!" Mama commanded. "He's still not up to snuff and I don't imagine riding the wagon over here wore you out."

"All right," Uncle Silas said. I couldn't help smiling but kept my head down so he wouldn't see. While she stood there, he even threw a couple of perfunctory logs on the woodpile.

"Is that the proper method for stacking wood?" The sound of Mama's footsteps tapped across the porch as she went back in.

"Woman was made to torment man," Silas said. "That's why I stayed a bachelor so long, for one thing."

"I figured it was either your looks or your personality," I said. "It's probably six of one or a half-dozen of the other."

He did a double-take like he couldn't believe I'd said it to him. I recited 2nd Corinthians 13 under my breath loud enough for him to hear, to the rhythm of grabbing up the wood and pitching it on the pile to keep from braining him with the wood.

Uncle Silas was a particularly easy man for women to find distasteful. He never changed his clothes and only bathed for his annual constitutional or a wedding. I try to put him in a comical light now, but at the time he was a danger to our family as much as any militia or Union soldier or elected local official. He would take everything we owned and liquidate it as he saw fit if we didn't think of something to distract his attention. The other alternative was for Mama to get married, but she needed to find just the right person—a man she could control.

After Mama had been inside for about ten minutes, Uncle Silas gave up any pretense of helping me with the wood. Instead he grabbed the front of my shirt in his thick hand and shook me back and forth. I didn't weigh much more than a stuffed feather pillow. I can still see his florid face and smell his sour-mash whiskey breath in my face.

When I didn't say anything or even attempt to defend myself, his conscience got the better of him after he smacked me across the face with an open hand. Now, I took that as a sharp insult, the fact that he had slapped me with the palm of his hand. I would have taken it like a man had he punched me in the bone-box proper with his fists, but this was almost too much to bear. This act was to show me he didn't even respect me as a man.

Still, I held myself back out of respect. He kept staring at me and laughing in my face. If he couldn't bend Mama to his will, he figured he would take it out on the son. My Pap had taught me to be slow to anger, but I'd always had a hot temper. Mama said it came from her side of the family.

"You are nothing but a runty boy," Uncle Silas said. "You didn't fight no Indians. Hell, they would have scalped you on sight. Just look at you. Terrified of me and I'm an old man. You are nothing but a coward."

My blue eyes stared into his brown eye. I looked deep into the colored flecks of brown, yellow, and black, searching for his fear. The sour stench of morning whisky on his breath filled my nostrils. His hands were still on my shirt, all bunched up in a wad of material in his fist. The longer I stared at him, the more it worked to unnerve him. He was not so sure of himself or of me as I bore into his brain with my gaze. I saw the hesitation in his fluttering eyelids. That was the sign I was looking for.

I held tight to the piece of firewood in my hand. Testing its weight in my hands, I took a half step back and swung from the heels as if to embed the wood in the center of his brainpan. There was a solid thunk like an axe embedded in a tree stump. His knees went wobbly and down he went. I put my boot on his neck and shook a piece of gnarled firewood in his face and thought about crushing his skull for a moment, until something in me relented and I told him what was what.

My wife, Lizzie Bledsoe, now Marchbank, was becoming even more beautiful than ever over the time I had been away. Our love had grown since the wedding ceremony even more than I thought possible. She looked down on me with such tenderness, more than I had ever known or had a right to, and I felt sadness at it because even then I suspected that such exquisite happiness would never last. I should have mentioned her before, but once I awoke with a fever and she was there with a damp washcloth to my forehead singing "Lorena":

> The years creep slowly by, Lorena,
> The snow is on the grass again;
> The sun's low down the sky, Lorena,
> The frost gleams where the flowers have been.
> But the heart throbs on as warmly now,
> As when the summer days were nigh;
> Oh! The sun can never dip so low,
> A-down affection's cloudless sky.
> The sun can never slip so low,
> A-down affection's cloudless sky.

Being Mamaed by a genuine beauty can really work on a young man's heart. At Wilson's Creek I had witnessed a horse-faced nurse get propositioned by a dozen men just because they were away from home, wounded, scared. But for the moment, suffice it to say, Lizzie gave me a kiss once when I cried out for Mama. We were young, and by mutual agreement we decided to keep our love a secret, but as a sign of affection she presented me with a tress of her hair and had her tiny picture made, which she presented to me in secret in a silver locket. What I felt for her, as I'm sure anyone would understand, is impossible to put into words. We wore our rings on necklaces around our necks to hide from the world what we had said in our vows that would never end.

She came to me in the middle of the night with her hair let down and a single braid down one side she had clearly done for me. Her hair shone like an angelic nimbus from a tiled mosaic in the faint light of the candle lantern she had placed upon the bedside table. She sat on the edge of the bed with her hands in her lap as if waiting for a sign. The moonglow streamed ethereal in from the window as I sat up and brushed her cheek with my knuckles. She was wearing a thin bit of cotton with a white shawl around her shoulders that I unwrapped slowly. Her eyes shyly downcast and allowed me sweet liberties as I sat up to help her undress. Standing next to the bed, she took my hand and pressed it against her body, where it roamed along her slender frame from her midsection up to her breasts and slowly down. She knew to be careful, since I was not yet healthy, as she climbed on top of me. She offered up her young breasts to me, and I felt of them and kissed them and suckled there.

She took hold of my manhood, and I groaned softly. She put her other finger to my lips. "Shhh." She laughed. I thrust at her and her lips parted to reveal the gleam of her front teeth. "It's okay. Go ahead. Keep doing it."

"I don't want to hurt you," I said.

"Just do it," she whispered.

We were both trembling and this made us laugh. Our love was special as love always is when it is brand new. Her beautiful face was pale like an alabaster goddess under the moonlight. I brushed the back of my hand across her soft cheek and she smiled as though she possessed a secret.

Seeing me laid up had convinced her that death could come for me at any minute. The last I remembered we spooned together in the bed. When I awoke alone early in the chill morning I knew she had left me in the night. I smiled to myself at the memory of the previous night. Her face was branded in my heart forever. At that moment, I vowed not to die in this war for her. She left a little self-portrait sketched on rough paper in charcoal on the bedside table for me that I suppose she had been working on for some time.

It was early June of 1863 when Frank James rode up. I let him in, and Mama served him some good black coffee. As we had just eaten breakfast, Lizzie fixed him an egg with a slab of ham with blueberry preserves on yesterday's biscuits. She also fed him left-over hoe cakes that were just heavenly at the old mahogany table. I was happy to see Frank but I couldn't keep my eyes from wandering to Lizzie. She wore a gray wool skirt with a forest green sweater over her shoulders and a fetching store-bought bonnet. After Frank ate two of the hoe cakes, he told us some alarming news.

The stubby General Blunt had fallen out of favor with the citizens of Kansas on account of us bushwhackers, but what Blunt did to combat his negative press was going to call down the thunder. They said the man had been a physician and didn't know anything about military matters and the only reason he was a general was his association with the Red Leg senator Jim Lane. There were some other rumors about Blunt, too. The most salacious of these said he traveled with servant girls who responded to his every whim even when he traveled East.

The story was that Will Vaughn, one of Quantrill's own men, was hanged at Fort Leavenworth. Frank James told it that Blunt had made it so bad on Blue Springs men that they either left the area or joined up as partisan rangers. A certain Colonel Penick of the Fifth Missouri State Militia Cavalry was the main culprit who operated out of Independence. Frank said a wild bunch was going to join up with none other than William Clarke Quantrill. I had wanted to meet the man for some time and it thrilled me to think I might be riding along with him any day now. The only thing holding me back was the farm situation and Lizzie. If I had my druthers I would have become a farmer again and turned my back on the whole damn war, but it just turned out I didn't have a choice in the matter. There was no way to call a truce in this war. I refused to die fighting in Missouri under the bloody black flag.

CHAPTER 9
The Tragedy of Robert Huff

As I recall, gangly Robert Huff rode up to convince me to head off to the Sni-a-bar woods with him. He told me to call him Bobby from now on. I wasn't too awful sure I wanted to ride with him. He was an odd one. His mouth seemed too big for his face. If I didn't mention it before, the boy didn't seem to have any particular shape. Unless you consider a lump a shape. I introduced him to Lizzie with a wink and she slapped my arm. I wouldn't have believed it, but damned if Bobby didn't full-out blush until I thought he might faint. The way he joked in Kansas and especially his colorful language left me doubtful that he had any inhibitions at all or even sense for how to act like a gentleman in front of a lady. Even Mother took to him right off, so I thought he must be all right.

"I heard Quantrill wasn't hardly doing any fighting these days," I said.

"Oh that ain't the half of it," Bobby said. "He's spending all his time with a certain Kate King, his lady love, in Blue Springs. George Todd has also become enamored of a lady, I've heard. Fletch Taylor was running both their outfits until that bastard Blunt had Jimmy hanged."

"What are we waiting for?" I said.

Bobby gave me his deadpan look of shock. A bewildered smile spread across his face. He nodded to himself as if my response had settled a matter on which he had been arguing. Despite the fact that Bobby had a powerful smell, I invited him into the house. As I was putting on a new red guerrilla shirt Lizzie had sewn for me with extra pockets for shells in my shirt I grabbed her playfully about the wrists and pulled her arms around my waist. Bobby seemed not to know what to do with himself, so he hugged his arms and looked uncomfortably about the room. Later, I attempted to bid a hasty goodbye to Lizzie behind the barn and stole another kiss of the softest lips a woman was ever blessed with, but she wouldn't hear of it. She marched me up to the house and trimmed my hair, goatee, and even took my cavalry boots into her lap to shine them until I could see her reflection in them.

"I love thee, wife," I told her.

"What if the war lasts forever?" Lizzie suddenly asked, turning her face up to me.

"Then I'm glad we're married now," I said. "I'll be thinking of you every day. I miss you already, Mrs. Marchbank."

I could see her smile behind the bonnet she wore, even if she turned her head away to hide it. I leaned down and she stood up on the tips of her little shoes and kissed me goodbye. After the kiss I saw tears well up in her eyes and she sniffed.

I saddled up the dead man's horse, and we were ready to skin out. Besides his horse, I'd also inherited a nice French Lefaucheux pinfire pistol from Frank Roberts too. But it was the horse that the boys objected to. Some of them tried to tell me I was crazy to keep a horse slower than even the nags the Missouri Militia rode but he was a warhorse and he was fast enough to get my ass out of the Nations in one piece. You could fire a pistol or carbine above his head and he'd barely twitch an ear or shift his weight while you aimed.

The grass was a brilliant green. The weather was warmish

with a heavy breeze. It was a good day and yet as we passed a few empty homesteads of good people that was enough for me to remember not to trust such simple pleasures as good weather. General Ewing's Order No. 11 had seen to it that those with Southern sympathies in 4 counties were forced to leave the general area. I had been living soft at home and had to train my eyes to vigilance again, knowing where I was headed. Bobby kept at me to stop at hotels along the way, though. Now that he had caught up to me, he seemed to care little for avenging Will Vaughn.

We were on the edge of Lafayette County when Bobby took off his hat at a stream. Though most of us wore our hair long, I couldn't help noticing that his hair was longer than most. He smiled up at me in a peculiar way and after filling up our canteens, we continued on toward the Sni and a cave where Bobby had heard everyone was gathering.

Later that night, we were lying on our rolls near a dank pool of water with some wood we had gathered around a ring of creek stones and a small fire for warmth, as it was a cool night. We ate a simple meal of pickled beans and hard biscuits. The chill weather had seeped into the marrow of our bones. A thick fog gathered around the thick, dark forest we were in. The sounds of our voices echoed loudly in the night even when we whispered about what we might encounter on the morn. It was no surprise when Bobby was lying terribly close to me for warmth, but I was nodding in and out of the vapors. Suddenly, Bobby threw his arm over me. Now, at first I thought he was asleep and had just rolled over in the middle of a dream. Just as I took hold of his arm to throw it off like you will in that situation, he raises up and kisses me on the mouth. My first reaction was to beat the dogshit out of him, but as his hat was knocked to the side, I noticed his hair was lying across his shoulders in such a nice way—Bobby Huff was a girl!

"Ashby," Bobby whispered low with a pleading expression. "I've been wanting to tell you a long time now."

"I'll be—" I said. "I'm sorry, I mean. I don't know what I mean."

"Surprised?" Bobby said. The cast of her smile, though not beautiful, made it evident she was a woman and I noticed her rounder and more tender parts against me as well. She turned below and reached up a hand across the back of my neck and before I knew it she had kissed me again.

There wasn't any time to discuss this new development before we heard the sound of riders under the quarter moon riding across a dark field below. Their inky silhouettes bobbed single file along with a flashing lantern as though they were searching for someone. The hoof falls of their horses sounded vaguely like shovels turning the earth. Bobby jumped up and kicked dirt on the fire and dumped the dregs of the chicory coffee over it for good measure. We were lucky they hadn't seen us. I could tell by the way they sat their horses it was the state militia, which meant mostly farmers or paw paws who couldn't have caught us if their name depended on it. One of the stragglers was singing with a broken voice *Just as I am* despite another voice wishing to shush him:

> *Just as I am, without one plea*
> *But that Thy blood was shed for me*
> *And that Thou bid'st me come to Thee*
> *O Lamb of God, I come, I come.*

I looked at Huff and I could see that the song had touched her as she wiped a tear away with the back of her hand. Men claimed to love the Lord yet justified the evil violences they visited upon one another with their own brand of failed human logic. It was about that time the fog began to clear. We got together our supplies and saddled the horses as soon as the home guard had passed by.

Infernal was not happy about it and bit me on the thigh, for which I slapped his nose. He also did his customary bloating up his belly with air, so I had to wait a minute and then punch him in the gut. After he exhaled, I pulled the cinch extra tight. Bobby and me rode with our hackles up, reins in one hand and a pistol in the other. Some sound we made must have carried down to the militia as they began to shoot and holler up at us. Bobby fired on the militia below, though they were too far away to hit with a pistol, but she made so much racket they eventually rode away from us, perhaps thinking there were too many of us to attack without a plan.

When we made it into camp the next morning there were already about fifty others. Arch and Bill were there holding court with their men. I recognized most of the men, but there were many a wild-eyed recruit lately off the farm. You could see the fear in their hollow eyes and the hate, too. Some evil had befallen them at the hands of the blue devils. Bill was leaning against a tree in a rope-bottom chair tipped back, while Arch waxed philosophic about political subjects—although Bill managed to be the center of attention even in his reticence.

"Don't give me that bullshit, Pony," Arch said. "They don't know it yet, but Blunt and those Kansas abolitionists are rotten as a dead Dutchman."

Coleman Younger told us how he had been tending the wounded at a makeshift field hospital that he had to move every so often because of patrols. The men he helped were sure grateful, but you could see the strain of it had marked his face. While he talked, Bobby would sneak a smile at me here and there, but since I was still recovering from the shock of what I knew, I just kept it to myself. There was a reason I was the only one who knew. That's what I told myself. Still, the men liked Bobby and some slapped her on the back when they told their crude jokes—Bobby could spit with the best of them for that matter. She sure was good at pretending to be a man. Even made to poke and prod at her pants as if to make manly adjustments. I shook my head in amazement. Bobby even made like to piss on trees or out in the weeds standing with feet spread a shoulder's length apart like a man. I couldn't help noticing Huff's womanly hips now that I knew the truth.

Bill and Arch were crunching on granny apples from a little basket positioned between them under a shady burr oak. Arch tossed one to me underhanded and I caught it on the fly. Bill, on the other hand, looked to be afflicted with the melancholia.

"Did you all bury them Yanks I heard you captured?" I said to Bill and Arch as I bit into the sour apple. "Oh Lord, that is one sour apple."

"She might be sour," Arch opined with a grin, "but she sure is juicy."

"Nope," Bill said. "Quantrill tried to trade four Yankees for Will Vaughn, but Blunt is hardheaded. They hanged Jimmy Vaughn. Quantrill already had them boys killed and it wasn't long before they sprung up in the trees around Blue Springs with nooses around their necks."

"They picked the wrong boys to bluff," Arch said.

Now another thing I haven't nearly talked enough about was the fact that men like Arch and Bloody Bill might like a fella, but you could never be too sure where you sat with them. If you weren't around them day-to-day and been on the trail with them, they tended to look at you askance. Well, that's how they were looking at me now. Not that they didn't know about my wound from the heathens, but it just paid for them to be extra cautious.

"And that ain't the worst of it." Bill withdrew a cigarillo from a fine silver pewter case, leaned forward to light it off a branch from the fire, and replaced the case in the inside pocket of his coat pocket. "Blunt has given an order to round up anyone in western Missouri, be they man, woman, or child, suspected of giving aid to rebels."

Now the few deep thinkers there were in that bunch claimed to be Democrats, but most of the boys didn't have many political opinions with regards to theory anyway. Even Quantrill, if he had thought to articulate it, was more of an anarchist if he was anything. His talk of the Confederacy was lip service or misinformed rhetoric. In other words, he liked the current lawless state of affairs and didn't care who made it into office just as long as he could continue to plunder Missouri and surrounding areas as it pleased him. I didn't know him but there were many legends around his person.

I knew why I was fighting. I'd never felt so bloodthirsty as when I thought about Jennison and how I wanted to kill him. I'd already killed him a thousand times in my dreams in as many creative ways. I tried to push away the memories of watching my Daddy being hanged, but over and over again the memory of the hanging came to bushwhack me in my dreams.

"They wouldn't really harm a woman or child, would they Bill?" Bobby Huff said.

"I think they might would." Bill exhaled a blue mist of smoke that curled around his head as if he were an amalgamation of a dark sinner-saint. "Anything Blunt's connected with is likely to be without honor or precedence."

"William T. here has vowed to send Blunt back to hell if he ever gets the chance." Arch squatted on his heels and poured himself a cup of chicory coffee.

"Quantrill is here?" I asked.

"Yep," Bill said. "Hope you ain't disappointed, but I think you will like him."

He'd hardly spoke when a tall rider with an impressive moustache and blondish hair approached us, sitting a black mare infamous for her bad disposition. Her scarred hide still gleamed like a new gun barrel. The air could be said to possess an otherworldly tingle as the men around the fire sat a little straighter or even stood as he approached. It had to be someone important. My gut told me it was the man I had heard so much about. His horse was shaking its head and pawing at the air a little, as if it were a demon waiting to be allowed to fall upon us all. Dark clouds seemed to descend low upon our heads just then and became humid with an emotion I can only describe as *disquiet*.

"Allow me to take her for ye, Mr. Bill." John McCorkle came forward and took the horse by the reins with a curry comb in hand. "I'll take care of this one." A jag of blue lightning appeared in the skyline behind Colonel Quantrill. Just at that moment his big black horse turned and bit McCorkle on the arm. The boy promptly fell away with a look of shock registering on his features and began to wallow and shout profanities in a fit of pain and rage. This turned the rarefied atmosphere to comic. I almost wished someone would shoot him just to shut him up as unkindly as it may sound.

"Sorry there, young fella," Quantrill said evenly. "I should have warned you about her disposition. She's a fighter." The great man slipped off his horse and examined the bite. "Just a nibble." He pulled out a pint bottle of whisky from his saddle roll and made a peace offering of it to McCorkle.

"Well, now, I hope you won't mind if I shake your hand." It was the Irishman. "I've been wanting to meet the great Captain Quantrill. And to be by your side at the next donnybrook. Here's to the red hand of victory!"

"I hate to be the one to correct you," Quantrill said in an amused tone to the Mulvaney. "None other than Jeff Davis himself has made me Colonel now." He leaned down from his horse and placed a friendly hand on the Irishman's shoulder.

Todd cuffed the Irishman on the back of the head so that his Hardee hat flew forward and into his own hands. His long hair fluffed up at the blow made the cuff look like a roundhouse right. "Pay no attention to this cunt. He's plumb mad! He's a *culchie* without sophistication."

"My apologies, Colonel. I am but a worm in your service," the Irishman said and slunk away as if he had been seared by Quantrill's presence. Oddly, as he retreated he had a smile on his face that didn't lend itself to an easy interpretation.

The Colonel tipped his hat in a gallant gesture. I sidled up next to him and gave the Irish a piece of cornbread I'd been meaning to eat along with my beans, but I did it to distract attention away from him. He had some peculiar ways that if interpreted rashly could be trouble for the potato-eater. "I'll split this with you," I said.

There had an ongoing debate about an attack on Lawrence, Kansas. It had been talked about for awhile now. The Andersons had settled in Kansas first, before they returned to Missouri under mysterious circumstances. I'd heard other men talk about it around the fires of a night. Some said they were nothing but common horse thieves before the war. But now the flames against Lawrence had been fanned by none other than our Colonel himself. It was a dream of his. He had some personal stake in the matter. I didn't know his experience with Kansas Red Legs back when, other than the regular forays across the border, but the idea excited some although there was general disagreement about how to go about it. We knew their outposts were located about thirteen miles apart; it would be no easy task. A large force might be too difficult to keep secret for the forty or fifty-mile ride into Kansas. A dozen or so at a time might work. Some of the acting captains were for it, but a few were vehemently against it. Even brave men said it was suicide to attack Lawrence.

"You all know me." Quantrill sat his horse uneasily as the demon-horse danced around in a circle. "It's time we rose up against Lawrence like the very black hand of God and smite them, smite them down! Lawrence is where people like Jim Lane reside in comfort while dealing out death to God-fearing Missourians loyal to Southern virtues. They've packed away the wealth of Missourians in their town. I urge you all to consider bringing your men to Lawrence, where we will teach them justice and to think twice before coming across the border to maraud on our land!"

He went on to compare our fight to Homer's Trojan War. He proclaimed himself the chieftain Agamemnon fighting Trojan General James Blunt. It was obvious to all that he was an educated man who knew how to tell us the grand story we wanted to hear about ourselves in his glorious future. The promise of riches and taking what we found there for our own personal coffers was a final *estocada*.

We were all moved by Quantrill's words and some were ready to saddle up and head to Lawrence that moment. Many weren't so sure, though, since there was little hope we could make it back across the border without the entire state hot on our heels. It sounded like certain death, but Quantrill didn't seem to care about his own life. A powerful gust of wind blew up to shake the grove of pin oaks where we were gathered. The rustling leaves above us sounded like applause for our leader. The white clouds fled disconcertingly backward across the sky, toward the west, as if to exhort us on to do the Devil's work.

The men were turning back away from Quantrill and to their fires when he sat up straighter in his saddle and with great indignation declared, "Lawrence should be cleansed! The only way to cleanse it is to kill!" He said it coldly, but we knew he meant every word. A cheer rose up as all were listening intently now at the ideas of taking the fight to where the enemy lived.

Some of the men began to shake their long carbines and pistols, firing shots into the air. It looked like a turning point had been reached. We were all young men in the main. No shrinking violets rode these paths. Still, there were many who weren't yet convinced, but it was something now inhabiting all of our minds. What a chance to get some glory for those of us who had risked our lives fighting in our own local war. It didn't help matters that there were more than a few leaders of small bands who had decided the occasion was more of a social nature and were beginning to get wallpapered as it were. The sound of hooting and laughter could be heard. Quantrill's plan didn't appear too likely just then.

I'd fallen in with talking to Frank James, who introduced me to a determined-looking young man named Joe Hart, a capable captain named Fernando Scott, young Billy Linville, and about a dozen other likely men. I wanted to at least say goodbye to Bobby Huff and the Irishman, but there was no time for that in the present moment.

Joe Hart said Captain Quantrill himself had sent for us with a proposition to harass the homeguard so he could more freely operate in the area. I looked around for Bill, but he had disappeared with the others and Frank said I ought to go along with them. Besides, I knew that Rocheport was the town Bill and Arch favored operating out of. I could return there as soon as I was finished with this foray. Later Captain Scott had a grin on his face as he gave us a report on a daring series of raids to combat Yankee death squads operating all over western Missouri: a jaunt that promised to take us north of Kansas City to the Nebraska line, back through the heart of northern Missouri, and ultimately to Richfield. Joe began to whistle "Old Joe Clark." I followed his lead as we headed straight for trouble, which was in every direction.

CHAPTER 10
Richfield

We were riding along the northern side of the Missouri River when we came upon a high vista and ancient Indian mounds atop the rise. We knew from experience they would offer a chance to reconnoiter the area. Hart gripped the saddle horn and said it wouldn't be long before we came to the township of Richfield. He knew a house in town there where we could take dinner and rest on actual furniture instead of sprawling on our bedrolls on the cold hard ground or in a smelly barn. Frank said he favored a drink and he'd be happy to stop.

The man who ran the house was named Marvel. He looked stout, of about fifty years, and appeared quite happy to see us beyond all reckoning. A bit too welcoming for my taste. He said he hated Yankees and spat pugnaciously on the ground as if to prove his hatred, but there was something in his way that told me he was a liar. What could I do? Joe Hart greeted him like a bosom friend, but it wasn't clear to me that they had ever laid eyes on one another. I began to feel uneasy. So much so that I swore I could feel my scrotum tingle, and my stomach went sick, and I could not enjoy the feast that Marvel and his wife laid out before us. I ate lightly of the roasted chicken, greens, and yams. Afterwards I went outside to take in the evening air. I visited Infernal with a nice apple from a grove just beyond the yard. I made sure my pistols were loaded and at the ready.

Daren Dean

I fully expected some bad business to come our way, but Frank and Joe were roaring drunk on the table wine. Billy wasn't in the mood to drink and just sat with his back against the wall watching the scene before him. Marvel was standing away from the party at the table with a sheen of nervousness on his fat face, and that disquieting enigmatic expression told me he knew something we did not. He stood partially in the darkened parlor, his features obscured from the candlelight coming from the table. As I walked back through the doorway, he nodded toward me in such a cloying way as to make me want to shoot him in the very center of his forehead and be done with it. My hand was itching to take him outside and end him, though until then I'd only killed a few when I was forced. But this man was a danger to every one of us. I walked hard on the floorboards to indicate my displeasure with the whole setup.

I tried to catch Frank's eye and give him a warning, but he just laughed at the coarse joke that Hart was in the middle of telling. Frank pointed at me and, laughing, seemed not to notice at all how out of sorts I'd become. Billy was the only one who seemed to have any sense, but he just shook his head as if to indicate he didn't understand it either. I knew the other boys must be getting impatient out in the woods. I half-expected them to stove the door in and come in firing any minute.

It was an amazement when I realized we weren't planning on spending the night or bathing, as they'd said we might. Captain Scott took Marvel aside by the elbow, his face florid with drink and merriment, and told him we were none other than Quantrill's own men. Frank handed a pipe to me with fine tobacco from the Southeast that Marvel had filled and given to us for our enjoyment. I was none too happy with the way they were acting. I'd thought these men were quite serious, or I would never have fallen in among them.

"We must take our leave," Captain Scott said in a humorous, formal manner. "Tell no one what we're up to."

As we saddled up and rode away from the Marvel house, Frank pointed at me and started laughing. The next thing I knew, all the men were amused. So far I was the only who had shown any sense according to my calculations. Billy Linville was even younger than me, so I didn't expect him to say anything one way or the other.

"Look at this one here," Frank said.

"He's about to bust!" Joe said.

"I fail to see what's so funny! That man is going to report us!" I swore at them all, which only made them roar more loudly. Billy fell out of his saddle and on the ground with mirth as he was more than a good bit drunk. I couldn't help myself and chuckled at his antics. Here was no Yankee killer. This was just a Missouri farmer's boy who would be better off behind a couple of mules.

"Better tie that man in the saddle," Frank said. More roars of laughter followed.

"Listen, listen!" Captain Scott interrupted with annoyance. "Preacher, we know he's an informant. Some Yankees will come looking for us. It's okay. Joe is going to sneak back around later and kill that bloated fool. He thinks he's laid out a trap for us. Well, won't they all be surprised when we loose our own net on them."

"Well, thank you very much for including me in your plan." I was still hot.

"If it will make you feel any better," Captain Scott said, "when Joe returns to let that bastard have it, you can accompany him and have first shot at that plump wife of his." Scott smirked broadly.

They all laughed at that because Marvel's wife was a go-by-the-ground woman if ever I saw one, and half as thick as a foundered horse. She looked like a rotund man wearing women's clothing. I must have turned tomato red as everyone laughed hard and slapped their thighs in mirth. A few even came by and pounded me on the back before putting heels to their mounts. I felt a little better because at least I knew they weren't all daft now.

We rounded up the boys and hid amongst a thick grove of crowded elm, cedars, and river birch. Great vines as big around as a man's forearm spilled from the tree branches. Frogs and katydids were calling from deep in the interior where cypress trees flourished in watery bogs. The silver maples were losing their twirly seeds, just like they did around this time. They rode the breeze and fell lazily on the forest floor, sometimes landing on our hat brims or knocking against our shoulders. We had to slap at mosquitos and other bugs, but Captain Scott assured us we wouldn't have to hide there for long. The spring greening yielded perfect cover for our operations. The canopy was filling out nicely and afforded only occasional bald spots.

The sound of hooves beating the new carpet of grass could be heard just below our position. One of our videttes behind, well up in the branches of an oak, gave us a wave; he scurried down like a squirrel and then rode hard back to our position, keeping the thick cover between him and the approaching men as he navigated the open field.

Scott looked through an impressive spyglass he'd no doubt taken off some dead Yankee and said it was two officers, a captain and his lieutenant. and they were followed by three men. He snapped the glass closed and put it away. Then he gave the signal and, with reins in his mouth and pistols in each hand, bore down upon the officers and their men, firing to kill and screaming the blood-curdling rebel yell as we fell on them like ten kinds of judgment and damnation. The rest of the men soon followed When I finally caught up on Infernal, the captain and a private were already down on the ground, dead from multiple wounds to their head. We had no choice because ever since Blunt gave his no-mercy order, we had to do the same in kind, since if we were caught, they would give us the same bad treatment.

Frank was down and rummaging the pockets of the private he had shot and killed. Scott was standing over the dandy looking captain, who, despite his wounds, was still alive. Scott shot him two more times and his body jumped and the spirit was no longer with him.

I had a big private, a Dutchman with a broad face and ham-like hands, to deal with. His face was grim, but his fat hands were shaking, so he missed his shot wide with the rifle. I ducked to one side and ran him down under Infernal's hooves. Infernal was not a fast animal up and down the slope compared to some, but he was imperturbable in a fight. More than that, he liked stomping the life out of Yankees. As I turned him around to make another pass, I could see the desperation in the man's hairy face.

He threw down his weapon and charged me like a bear, and though I shot him once in the chest he grabbed me by the leg and tore me off Infernal and tossed me to the ground like a sack of beans, knocking the wind out of me. He was sitting on me and choking me by the neck and I was worried at first because I'd lost my slouch hat in the fall. His blood was pumping out of him

Daren Dean

like a fount until I thought I would drown in it. His great yellow teeth and sour breath mingled with the dust we'd stirred it up. I knew it was the end of me, too. To be killed by this slobbering idiot I figured was the method by which I'd leave this earth, but then we were both suddenly splattered with his brains. There was an instant when even he knew what had just happened. His mouth moved as if he were getting ready to speak of some profound philosophy he had just acquired and then he fell over with a thud next to me, stone-hammer dead. One of his arms draped across me like we were taking an afternoon nap together, until I heaved him off in disgust. I was covered in his blood. I could taste the iron of it. I skittered away, kicking at his body with my boots in fear and disgust. The world was limned a violet, plum-color and I worried it might blind me.

A verse from one of my father's sermons came to mind: *The blood makes atonement for the soul.*

"Well, Preacher," Billy said, sitting his horse above me, "seems like a little less mercy and a little more smiting is called for in the future, or you're never going to make it to the end of this war."

"Amen, brother." I rubbed at my throat. He stuck his Colt in his waistband, reached down, and pulled me up on my feet. He wiped his hand on his pant leg at the knee. "If you hadn't been there, I would be preparing a house of many mansions." I walked over and scooped up my hat and beating the dust off across my knee replaced it atop my head. It was a gift from Gid, so I treasured it beyond the practicality of a man needs a hat to keep his brains cool under the sun.

For all his bravado, Billy's hand was shaking visibly as he turned to look for more enemy, but there was no one left for killing at the moment.

"We can't have that now." Scott rode back to where the captain lay. "We're going to have to toughen you up. That blue belly was quite a beast, wasn't he?"

My shirt was soaked. I needed to find the nearest stream to clean up in. I tore off my shirt and wiped up the worst of it from my person, but it was already beginning to congeal. I walked a few feet and was sick.

I gathered up my reins, "You weren't much help that time, Infernal. Did I mistreat you so bad lately? You're supposed to stomp these Yanks." Infernal gave a snort as though he understood me. His ears flickered. A tremor went through his body that I felt in my thighs. Green bottle flies and insects were already beginning to plague me. I used most of my canteen water on my face and hands. I must have looked like a demon.

Frank had moved on to the lieutenant. He had a letter that had come from the officer's mother. "Boys, this here was Lieutenant Graf-en-stein and yonder there is likely a certain captain Sessions." Scott rode over and examined the letter for himself and sent another shot through the captain's head for good measure.

"You want to bury these men?" I asked. There were a half-dozen dead lying on the ground around us.

"Why, no," Scott said. "No, I do not. Leave 'em for buzzard bait, Preacher. You can pray for their souls when we go into town."

It was the middle of the afternoon. Captain Scott and Joe Hart seemed pleased with the day's carnage. Frank and myself fell in behind them. I hupped Infernal to keep up. It was my hope we might ride into town and *get a shot in the neck* as a bit of a celebration for getting another day above ground. I was trailing behind the others as we rode down the rise. I turned to look back over my shoulder and saw two of the slain arise and steal away into the brush. I should have said something, but I'd had enough of killing at the moment, even if it was not the prudent decision to make. No doubt Joe and Frank would have ridden those wraiths down and snuffed out their pathetic souls. I didn't doubt we'd be in Richfield and gone before they made it back.

We came across a creek that allowed me time to clean up properly. After I had dried in the sunshine, I put on the one extra shirt I had in my roll. I'd have to do something about my pants in town when I had a chance.

For all the carnage, it had been a real pleasure riding with this bunch. The men all got along, unlike some of the other bands I'd witnessed to this point. The boys were all in fine spirits, relieved from having survived another encounter with the Feds. We found a hotel in town that we ascertained had a supply of busthead whiskey on hand. After we'd put back a few snorts, we overheard a boy who had just busted through the door to say that Captain Sessions and his men had been jumped by the Secesh. Our ears pricked up at that remark. Captain Scott particularly took umbrage, even if it was a just a runt of a kid.

"What was that?" Scott jumped to his feet and strode over to the boy. "Those dirty bushwhackers are nearby? Is that what you're telling us, boy?" He grasped the boy by the shoulders and shook him back and forth until his teeth chattered. The lad was terrified and he screamed like a feral creature.

"Are you bushwhackers?" the boy cried and visibly shrank down to the floor.

"Bushwhackers? Where are they? Point them out! Me and my men here will go deal death to those vermin!" Captain Scott was about as serious as he could be, but his performance was ruined because Frank could not keep from laughing. The Captain hunched down with his pistols out and bounded around on the hardwood floors as he made to look around for the terrible bushwhackers. The boy and the counterman both looked confused, but the boy explained that Private Rapp had been picked up on the road and was being tended at the boarding house down the street.

"Let's go boys!" We finished our drinks and slammed the tin cups down on the table.

We were high-stepping just to keep up with Scott. A boy named Bayard gathered up our horses' reins and followed behind us in case we needed to get away quickly. When we got to the boarding house, Scott didn't bother to knock and simply stove in the door like it belonged on a child's playhouse. A large woman dressed imposingly in an old-fashioned, black dress met us but Scott pushed by her, as we all did, before she could offer up any complaint. Upon a bed in a bedroom there was one of the men we thought we'd killed, with two bullet holes in him already, but he looked pert enough, all things considered. I couldn't tell if he was one of the men I'd seen escape earlier.

Private Rapp raised up off the bed.

"We done killed you once." Captain Scott drew his pistol. "Do us a kindness and stay dead this time." He blasted the young man right square in the middle of the forehead and his blood and brains splattered the blankets and wall behind him in a bright pink mist. There was a ringing in my ears for some time afterward. The woman began to scream the boy's Christian name, but it was impossible to understand her, for she was in such a feverish state. Scott shouldered his way past all of us and the woman with his pistol raised up over his head. He looked like he expected more wounded boys to leap out of their deathbeds like *haints* to confront him.

He stopped at a dainty oak table where a photograph of a beautiful young girl sat in the middle of a triptych. He froze, picked it up, admired it for a while, broke off the end pictures of Private Rapp posing in his Yankee uniform and tucked away the pale beauty in one of the pockets of his guerrilla shirt where it could compete with ammunition for space.

We followed him right out of the house, took our reins from Bayard, and rode out of town. The streets were mostly empty— no doubt they'd heard the shot—and a clerk popped out of his shop only to duck back inside after giving us the eye. Scott turned gravely, wordlessly, on his horse to regard us with one hand on the reins and the other on the saddle. Impulsively, Billy let out a whoop-whoop to break the tension and thundered out of town before us. Frank gave me a grin and hupped his horse to take out after the boy and then we all followed suit. We'd showed them in Richfield and we'd keep on showing them everywhere we went.

Chapter 11
Hanging of Billy Linville

I was near to freezing to death when I awoke the next morning. My teeth chattered until I thought I'd crush them down to nubbins. I thrust my hands toward my crotch and squeezed my thighs tightly in an effort to warm them. The others were still asleep when I awoke, but I couldn't lay there freezing any longer. I couldn't imagine performing any of the arts of the toilet in that foul weather. We hadn't made much of a fire but I stoked it, carefully added some new wood so as not to smother the embers, and ate a leftover biscuit I had in my rucksack. I wished someone would wake up so I could help one of them smoke their pipe or take out a bottle of liquid fire. I kept hearing robins and squirrels scuffling dry leaves and imagining they were Red Legs leaping out of stumps to cut our throats while we slept. A fog surrounded us. I felt uneasy, so I stepped a ways back into the laurels to do my business but it didn't help. I went back to the fire, added a couple of logs, but could not fall back to sleep.

Visions of the skirmishes I'd been in kept intruding on my rest. I had not slept well in weeks. My eyes hurt in their sockets and felt like they were at half-mast the majority of the time. Nightmares of what I thought might be a future event had come for me all night: I saw a familiar dream horse with a milky eye, opaque in the moonlight, screaming and rearing up to paw at flames; a man with a pig's head for a face giving unintelligible swine orders;

Daren Dean

turkey vultures pecking out the eye of a red-tailed hawk; a young man shot off another horse and dragged from his own stirrup down a burnt hillock; a partisan ranger hanged from a noose high up in a burr oak; an Ozark cavern in the dead of winter with green moss growing along a stone wall built around the entrance, where there should been none; a wildwood boy buried naked in a cave-tomb of green ice and then suddenly as if by witchcraft standing on the curving dome of mounded earth above the doorway, a confederate resurrection.

We had been sure to lose ourselves in the trees and keep off the roads. No doubt the alarm had been raised and the home guard was scouting for us half-heartedly. It was the way they did things in general, but they couldn't be blamed because they were made up of paroled young men hardly more than boys, old men with limbs gnarled by arthritis, and damn-the-Dutch foreigners who didn't care about our war one whit. They were so naive they thought they could tell both sides they were neutral and they would be left alone.

One piece of interesting information we'd learned while still in town was that General Blunt had been removed as district commander and would be replaced by General Thomas Ewing. Before we could rejoice, we heard Ewing was every bit as terrible as Blunt, and a brother-in-law to William Tecumseh Sherman besides. So we got drunk and mulled it over. I thought it might be a good idea to reconnoiter with Bill Anderson and Captain Gregg.

It wouldn't be long before we found out just how terrible Ewing was. He wasn't just out to kill our boys, he decided to make war on our families. It was a sad commentary on the regard we were held in as partisan rangers. We weren't even afforded the same courtesy as our Southern brethren back East but treated as criminals and murderers because we wanted to protect our own. The War had been going on in Missouri for as long as I could remember, long before Fort Sumter Kansans and Missourians had been killing each other.

We set forth before the sun rose and watched the pink tendrils of morning stretch across the sky. The horses were feeling spry, the weather crisp and invigorating as we headed north toward Plattsburg. About ten miles outside of the town we *hallooed* a man out laboring in his field with a swaybacked mule. Joe Hart stopped to shake the man's hand and talk to him about the challenges of farming with so many people riding to and fro, from the Missouri Militia to Kansas Red Legs and everyone else. The man tipped his hat back at a rakish angle to reveal a horrible scar on one side of his face and a missing ear. He said his name was Jim Doyle, born in Kentucky, fought at Wilson's Creek, and later went back to farming, after he'd taken the oath and paroled. His daddy had died after an apoplectic attack out in the hayfield, and Doyle had become the head of a family that included a grandmother, mother, wife with two children, and eight siblings—he'd had no choice but to quit fighting the Feds in order to feed the mouths around the table.

Hart said he knew of a couple of Doyles who rode with Captain George. The man only winked with a sad smile and said he'd heard about those same bastards too. Best of all, Doyle provided us with a bit of information that perked us up to the man. The garrison at Plattsburg was all but empty, with their men patrolling the surrounding area to the east, scouting for bushwhackers. We could, Doyle thought, likely slip in behind them easy enough and make them look like fools.

It was now a race to get to town before they returned. They

didn't know it then in Plattsburg, but the wolf was at the door.

We went riding into town and we shot up the square, but mainly we were looking for blue bellies and Union sympathizers so we could send them to hell. Much to our surprise, about a half dozen men came out to defend the town with ancient muskets. One old man with a great moustache and graying long hair and a nose like a brass doorknob had what looked like a sword from the time of King Arthur and took wild swipes at us. I recall Frank and me had dismissed the old fellow as essentially harmless and we were laughing at the spectacle, until Billy Linville put a bullet in the man's neck and laid him low. It struck us as unsporting and we told him so. He said he didn't like someone trying to send him to glory without facing consequences of his own. Frank was especially put out with Billy and made a point of refusing to talk to him thereafter.

A grocer with his apron still tied about his waist came out and shot his roaring musket at us on the street from the knee, as though he had been trained by Napoleon himself. He even managed to reload a couple of times until he and the rest of them ran out of ammunition. Apparently, the garrison had confiscated everything useful for the purpose of protecting the town although they never expected us to bring the fight to their door. The grocer was cursing wildly in exasperation until Captain Scott laid him out with an excellent shot from horseback. A formally dressed young man with the manner of a duelist came out with a dragoon pistol, the likes of which seemed more appropriate to mount on a wall or better left in the case for discussions of the Mexican War. He boldly strode into the middle of the muddy street and proceeded to shoot one of our rangers out of his saddle. This so enraged Joe that he rode up to the man, who stood in his finery smirking, until the very moment he was shot with a .44 ball in his chest and he crumpled to the ground. Joe later said the fancy lad was an Englishman who must have thought he was invincible and had to be shown different.

Frank rode right into the newspaper office and gutted the place. He made it virtually impossible for the editor to print anything for a while, until he replaced his equipment. He and some other boys broke out the windows. Billy and me went to the local carpenter's shop and scooped armloads of sawdust and placed them at the front and back doors of the newspaper building for fuel. Then we set the building on fire and made crude torches of table legs wrapped in bed sheets and dipped in lantern oil, thus igniting several other buildings down the main road to distract the citizens from following us. We'd managed to steal more than fifty thousand dollars, according to Captain Scott, whose countenance was ebullient at our good fortune.

"Why is it you boys are so fearless and so good at this?" Captain Scott laughed as we leapt into the saddle to make our getaway. As I look back on it now, he may have been all of twenty-five at the time, but that was mature in my eyes.

"I don't know," Billy said. "I never been good at nothing before."

"You found your calling, son," the captain turned his horse and rode off down the dirt street at a gallop.

Billy looked after him in gratitude and admiration. No one had ever paid him a compliment before.

As we were leaving, we came upon a tall man in a bowler hat who fled from the town on a mule. It was obviously a case of a Union man trying to save his own hide and his money and it fell to me to shoot him off the beast and rummage through his belongings, where I found a purse containing five hundred dollars, which

I pocketed and added to my growing nest egg. I'd been building it up for some time now. I thought maybe I could buy a piece of land down along the Marais des Cygnes River or perhaps even up in Howard County, where the dirt was rich and black and the plots of land stretched out like shelves for crops to be planted on, sometime after the war, one fine day with my Lizzie. I imagined all the children we would have together. They would all call me Pap and I might preach at a local Baptist Church. They would only know peace in their lives. The war would become a distant memory that only the old could remember and then only vaguely. The mists of the fantasy evaporated and I looked down at the blood of one of the unfortunates covering my breeches.

We caught a family man wearing a blue jacket with his wife and three daughters riding out of town on a wagon he said he had borrowed from the railroad, but we stopped them too. Scott took great pleasure in grabbing the man by his cravat and throwing him to the ground, killing and scalping him with the same buck knife in front of his women. The mother was crying and holding her young daughter to her bosom so she couldn't see the top of her father's head laid bare and bloody for the crows. The child had blonde hair and was mewling like a creature rather than a human child. I felt sick to my stomach and leaned off my horse and vomited in the bushes not far away. I'd seen a good deal of killing and death at that point, but I began imagining this woman was my wife and this girl was my daughter. It ate my conscience because even after all the killing I had done I couldn't work up the courage to confront Scott about it.

We rode on northwest to St. Joe for another conquest. We had been burning up the miles all day and our luck was riding next to us. Frank laughed that our reputations would soon be as notable as Quantrill's himself if we kept on and we doggedly followed our orders.

We rode on the outskirts of town until we came upon some blue militia men. They recognized us immediately with our long hair, fast horses, and bristling with pistols the way we did. It was as much of an amusement as anything as they chased us on their nags, taking potshots at us. Frank made an obscene finger gesture as we pulled away. Even Infernal seemed to be running more swiftly than usual. I rode with my head low just over his rising, muscled neck.

We split our party into two factions when we were out of their eyeshot. While some of us sat horses in the shadows of a coppice with Joe, the other group led by Scott forced the militia to chase them over a rise and right into our grinning faces. Their expressions went from bloodthirsty to mournful in a split second and we swatted our horses and fell down on them like God's own wrath. We laid them out in just a few minutes and lightened their ascent into the afterlife by taking anything of value from them we could find. One of the men wore a woman's locket around his neck with a portrait of a beautiful Unionist lady inside. Billy immediately proclaimed his love for her and prayed one day he'd get the chance to declare himself and woo her from amidst her obvious state of blue purgatory.

I saw a man and his teenaged son running from behind their house down toward a creek. I galloped down to where they were clambering awkwardly over the embankment, where they thought to lose themselves on yon side of the creek and in the hills beyond. I sat my horse watching their snail's pace, thinking I would let them live if they would just hurry up. They were asking for Joe or Captain Scott to ride up and force my hand; if that happened,

I wouldn't be able to spare them. If Joe saw my hesitancy, this weakness, he would likely kill me first. They wanted me to be the heartless servant of a judgmental God and smite these Yanks, and though I'd lost much myself my conscience welled up within me.

The entire war, for want of a better explanation, was incontrovertibly wrong, and yet here I sat, about to end their lives; death might come for me any moment too. Preachers often used the Old Testament to justify their view that God approved of war but what of Christ and his new blood covenant with man? What of Christ's compassion for all men? I more than agree with Paul's assessment to the Corinthians that we see through a glass darkly. This was no time for love. I slammed shut the Good Book in my mind.

I watched while the younger man held out his hand to the man I imagined was his father. He stood on creek stones covered in green lichen, the current flowing quickly over the tops of his boots. The elder hesitantly reached out his hand. The sound of horses galloping toward me. I knew it would be Captain Scott. I raised up my pistol and shot the young man in the chest and he fell into the deeper pool of water just below the footbridge of stone they were attempting to cross. The other man, the father, was still reaching out his hand for connection even as he watched his son fall into the pool. He turned toward me now and instead of terror I saw rage, he fumbled for a pistol in his waistband and without seeming to aim, he pointed the gun at me and pulled the trigger. The bullet grazed me just above my right ear. Though it was bloody as head wounds tend to be, it didn't stop me from riding to the embankment and shooting down into his face in a fit of terror and rage of my own: the sort of righteous indignation that comes from having your life threatened with eternal death. The father's body stayed in the shallows near a stand of cattails as the other body was pushed along by the current. Looking down at them reminded me of Father's murder at the hands of the Red Legs.

Billy Linville slipped off his horse and scalped a couple of the bodies he believed he was responsible for sending to the next life. It wasn't clear to me that he had actually killed anyone, either on purpose or accidentally, other than the old lunatic with the sword, but he made a big show of attaching the gory trophies along his horse's bridle. He made a bloody mess of it, but he was young and impulsive and full of himself. Whenever I talked to the young man, he was convinced, as few are, that he was the most accomplished blue-belly killer in the entire Confederate army. He was so bloodthirsty that his apparent enthusiasm for killing unnerved even the captains, but from what I had observed he hadn't been notably adept at the practice. On the other hand, he could have talked a whole division to death with his mouth. The boy never seemed quite right in the head.

As we rode off whooping and hollering, one of the militia managed to shoot Billy Linville's horse from under him. Billy had been bringing up the rear and no one realized at first that he was missing. By the time we did, we feared it was too late for him. It must have been a sniper that made such a shot from who knew where. We all rode a bit closer to the saddle with our ballsacks receding like babies at the thought of a sniper on the loose. He could be anywhere.

There was a rock fence that Joe thought would make fine cover for a sniper. He told me to walk up and down the length of it when we circled back around. Sure enough, a young man with a long rifle popped his head up and back down again. I pointed him out to Joe, who took a good quarter of an hour to circle behind him and dispatch him with a pistol shot in the back of the head before he knew any different. We applauded the death of the sniper and cheered.

Scott cursed loudly, "Screw the spooky son-of-a-bitch!" when we told him Billy had been captured, but Joe sent young Bayard to sneak back into town unarmed to find out what they were fixing to do with the boy on the outside chance we could ride hard in after him when the time was right.

The sky turned red in the west before twilight. Hours passed. We thought maybe Bayard had been recognized though when he returned he said the talk was pretty rough and laid out the story for us. He said our worry was for nothing. Since no one paid attention to him because of his youth and he was quite short they mistook him for a young boy. His clothes already looked rather ragged and his hair was getting scruffy. His face was dirty but as smooth as a debutante's.

Bayard led us back into town along down a little stream. The townsfolk were about to string Billy up from a big burr oak on the square when the militia showed up. We had a good view as the town sat down in a little valley. They weren't about to wait for an official hangman or the sheriff to take him up on the platform. They were hopping mad when they discovered what we had done and how we'd outsmarted them by our flanking maneuver. The militia wasn't too happy about it, but eventually cooler heads prevailed. They ushered him into the courthouse and in a matter of hours they rendered their judgment upon him. Billy was to be hanged a few rods southeast of the Patee House.

Soon the yard nearby was filling with a rowdy crowd of families and young men anxious to see revenge down against the bushwhackers. It was going to be the day's entertainment. It would be something they talked about for quite some time in the future.

Men, women, and their children gathered out in the yard in great expectation, as if Billy might sing a song for them. The mysterious power of the Lord stirred the air. A violent young man in the prime of his life would have that life snuffed out because he was likely to kill any of them had he been given a chance. Everyone considered him a walking dead man. Bayard said they talked about him like he was already dead, as calmly as if discussing the evening meal. The lad said only his own terror of death kept him from blurting out, "Don't kill, Billy!" He couldn't bear to see the death of someone he'd known so intimately. He was just being superstitious, for fear a lack of respect might book his passage to Elysium next.

A hush fell over the mob as the instructions of the sheriff and the military commanders were heard by all present. Both sets of authorities decided to work together in this exceptional case. They believed Billy was responsible for the deaths of four of their militiamen just north of town and since the sheriff had acquired a bit more experience lately with hangings, it seemed fitting to them to allow him to handle it. The sheriff was a large man and very deliberate. Billy's hands were bound behind him. He looked remarkably clear-eyed. His face looked as if he himself were about to deliver a sermon. The knowledge of his impending death had washed away all doubts he might have owned previously about eternity. Standing next to the antique sheriff, Billy looked like a child yet. Not a hellish, vicious child who had deprived maybe a handful of men of their lives (which might have been more brag than fact) but a child caught betwixt and between the events of the day.

Then Billy came forward and addressed the crowd: "I was

never involved in the events I've been accused of. It's true I fought at Wilson's Creek for the South, where I was captured and paroled. Since that time I've never raised a hand toward any man. I want you to know you are killing an innocent man today. Let that sit on your Yankee conscience. Don't feel pity for me. The men who did these things may come back at any moment and do the same or worse than you're doing to me today. I pray you never have another moment's rest. May Quantrill and his boys find you in your beds and show you no mercy. I'm not afraid to die today. I expect to find rest in the arms of my Savior before evening descends again."

Billy stepped back and then spit contemptuously on the ground with a movement of his head. This caused a titter of disapproval and excitement, particularly amongst the women. I noticed what I took for a pair of sisters by the look of them fanning themselves more rapidly than before. Their cheeks flushed red with excitement.

Billy began to sing in a fine voice: *We'll hang John Brown on a sour apple tree and feed Jeff Davis on peaches and cream!* The men stoically looked on with their heads erect and backs straight. Many of the men with the garrison had their heads on swivels as they took turns scanning the crowd and the streets for any sign of us partisans. Billy's singing touched a raw nerve. The more consternation among the onlookers and the cries that they should hurry up and hang Billy, the wider Billy smiled in a self-satisfied manner. It was as if they thought Quantrill himself might come riding in and slaughter them all.

There was still plenty of activity in preparation for the execution. A prayer was offered up by a local grim-faced minister dressed in black and holding his Bible like it was a sword. The sheriff leaned toward Billy, spoke a few words and nodded him forward. Billy looked to be without fear as he stepped onto the platform.

The sheriff and a couple of doctors slid the noose around his neck and made morose adjustments so it would do its work right the first time. They handed him a glove so that when he felt he was ready to meet his maker in the great beyond, he could drop it as a signal. The young man nodded that he understood. The black cap was put over his face so that the onlookers would not have to look upon his features if he made faces kicking and dangling in the air. The minister and the other grim-faced men on the platform said goodbye to him and he stood erect with his chest out. The mothers quit their murmuring. Even the children grew hushed. There were birds suddenly chirping and peeping to beat the band, which was at odds with the seriousness of the task at hand. It added that much more regret and sadness to it.

A breeze kicked up. The sound of a church bell went off inexplicably near the square. Billy allowed the glove to drop not long before noon. The cord was cut asunder. The platform let Billy Linville's body fall through. The body convulsed and writhed a moment, but it was the force of the body going to the end of its tether that did the real work by breaking his neck in short order. Billy Linville had departed this life.

Bayard said he was sorry he could not return and report promptly before it happened. Captain Scott said that in this instance he wasn't sure there was anything we could have done to prevent it. The boy had his hand gripping the pistol at his side. His finger was not on the trigger, but it was plain to see he was upset. He hadn't been especially close friends with Billy. If anything, he might have hated him, because Billy was always playing tricks on him and picked on him relentlessly.

It may have had something to do with that fact that Billy had been fearless and not much older than Bayard. The fear of Billy had also transformed to a curious respect. He confided to me that if they could kill him so easily, that he would be nothing for them to deal with. His hands trembled and he made as if to shake my hand but then refused to let go. It was his idea of a manly embrace.

"What hope is there for me, Preacher?" Bayard asked. "There wasn't any way for anyone to save him. If they could kill him like that. Billy went out with not even a whimper . . . it just scares me. Maybe I should go back on home."

"Bayard," I said. "The difference between you and Billy is that you still have a conscience. Because of all the terrible things he had seen at too early of an age, well, he lost his innocence. I believe it is conscience that makes us men. Without it, there's no difference between us and the animals. Not to say we make all the right decisions. War seems to contradict the spirit of God. You hold on to yourself and to what you know is right. You do that, Bayard."

"Yes, sir, Preacher," he said. He continued to pump my hand the entire time I spoke to him. I looked him in the eye and nodded the whole time. His dark eyes were filled with tears. He turned away and wiped at his eyes with his shirtsleeves. He was just a boy.

We all felt bad for Billy. He was so bold we knew the kid was either going to live forever or go charging in front of us and get his brains blown out. I never figured hanging, though.

After some debate, Captain Scott and Joe said they'd had enough and wanted to check back with Bill Anderson and see if he had heard of any larger campaigns brewing. We had wreaked what havoc we could. As we rode south, silently from one copse of elm and yellow poplar to another of tightly packed plum, ash, and the strange fruit of Osage orange, each of us had to think about the terrible price we might pay for fighting for our country. Each clearing we came to we regarded with extreme caution, even when the fields were full of daisies, bloodroot, jimsonweed, and yellow shoots of goldenrod. It was the sort of field all of us might have run barefoot through when we were boys, but now it paid to be careful as the land was full of Federal patrols, Red Legs, and the home guard. We weren't afraid to fight them but we didn't want to ride into an ambush either.

We decided to wait it out until nightfall in a dry creek bed in front of a great sandstone shelf. It wasn't long before the boys took to calling the high-pitched creek bank "the mountain" when we had climbed up and down the slope searching rocks and stumps as hand and footholds to take our turns as videttes. There was a fallen cedar with shorn branches balanced across the forked arms of a weather-cut tree that stood four feet high now. The thorny locust was just beyond the tree line to the north of our camp. It was perfect for getting a view of the valley rolling below like shelves of land that went on for miles to the horizon.

The nights belonged to us. We waited until full dark before making a conservative fire. This is how we moved around the country so quickly, because we knew the Feds were afraid they would run into us after twilight laid out the sun for the night. It allowed us to move freely and undetected, though surrounded on three sides by forces greater than our own.

It wasn't but a week later we surprised some militia in Andrew County that Joe knew. He was glad to avenge some personal grievance. He was riding around like a madman, shouting about killing every man in the county with tooth and claw if he had to do it that way.

He looked back at me once while we were walking our horses in a single line down a cow trail and said, "Devils! They're all devils, don't you know, Preacher?" He had a head wound that didn't seem to want to heal, causing him dizzy spells.

A steady rain began to fall, so we looked for a friendly farmer for a home-cooked meal and a warm barn to stay in. I'd received a slight wound in my heel, of all places, from a stray bullet, and it was damn uncomfortable every time I had to apply pressure going down or up a hill.

A day later we were the ones surprised near Spring Hill by more militiamen and one of the lucky dogs managed to hit Joe in the neck. I saw his hand go to his neck to staunch the flow of blood. When he gave orders a good deal of blood came out of his mouth. He spat and coughed. I tried to tell him we needed to make a stand against the hayseeds who were after us, give him a chance to rest, but he waved us off until he fell off his horse in a ditch feral with black-eyed Susans and died seconds later.

I dismounted and kneeled awkwardly beside him and whispered, "Dear Lord." I thought I might pray, but no other words came to my lips. There was nothing to say. He wanted to say something to me, and he propped his head up at the neck, but then he grimaced and eased his head back down to the earth. He had a terrible look on his face. I knew then that I did not want him to die like he was my own brother just then.

He clasped my hand. His eyes seemed to see into the beyond. He whispered, but I couldn't hear just what. I gave him a drink of water, but he began to choke, and most of it went down the side of face. "Don't go, Joe," I said. We had already been through some wild times and it was hard to see him go down. He smiled at that and he gave me a wave with his hand like he did when he said it was time to break camp.

All expression left his face. His soul left his body. That head wound of his hadn't scarred and it had gone gray like the rest of him. Tears stung my eyes, but I knew the rest of us had to get out as best as we could. I hated to do it, but we had to leave him by the pond just as he was. I knew he was in Paradise with the Savior, though for the life of me I couldn't picture anything golden or heavenly, but I could picture him on Golgotha surrounded by innumerable criminals on a multitude of gnarled crosses stretching on toward the horizon.

They had lost us in this thick knot of woods. We were very near the cattails of a small pond. It felt like we were being watched. There was a face staring at me with piercing eyes and before I knew it I had pointed my drawn pistol at the face with the curious eyes. But it was a crane that stood six feet high, tall-stepping its way through the cattails, regarding us with what I took to be an expression of grave sadness. The bird gave a nod and did an about-face back toward the pond in its hunt for frogs and other morsels. Its footsteps sounded loud and reckless in the water. I wanted to tell it to be quiet and get down. The Federals could discover us any second.

I found I was still holding my pistol toward the retreating giant when I sighed and let it drop to my leg. Before retreating, I managed to get a blood-soaked letter out of Joe's pocket that I'd seen him writing earlier that morning. It was fully my intention to see that his mother and father got the letter, but somehow I knew I'd never be able to deliver it and let it go after a while to the hungry flames of our supper fire that night at the uselessness of it all.

It felt as if the angel of death was dogging our steps now.

After Joe's death I was anxious to meet up with a larger force as much for the safety in numbers as anything. Or ride with Quantrill, if I could find him. Frank suggested we go look up Bill Anderson and his men. My hands had started tremoring. There didn't seem to be anything I could do to stop them. Frank gave my hands a nod and seemed to be asking a question about them and I just shrugged in response. He handed me a small flask of shine and I took a quick sip before handing it back. It felt like lightning in my mouth. Frank held up his hand instead of refusing it outright. He knew I needed it just then.

We were going to head for the Sni, but first we went by my Uncle George's house, who lived not too far away now. It was nightfall. There was a lamp burning on a table that we could see through the window and Uncle George had a nice fire going in the hearth.

There was a pretty neighbor girl named Annie who was helping him with the livestock on account of his bad leg from the Mexican war. She was about to blossom into a beautiful young woman. Boys were going to start taking notice before long. She had golden hair and made me think about Lizzie. I determined it was about high time to visit home again. I would slip away at the first chance, since after Joe, we weren't attached to a captain.

Everything seemed so peaceful, it was like looking at a picture. We *halloeed* the house and he invited us in. Something had possessed him and he grabbed ahold of me like he saw a ghost. That's when I found out that family had been sent news of my death a few weeks earlier.

Apparently, I was dead and buried. Tears were coursing down his leather cheeks as he was telling me about it. He blubbered how it was a nice service all told. Well, that tickled me and I fell over at the waist laughing about it, but Annie looked at me like I was heartless and cruel, laughing at another's pain. I couldn't explain why it hit my funny bone that way. It didn't take long for me to sober up at the thought that Lizzie might marry another man if she truly thought I'd gotten my head blown off. The Widow Lizzie did not sound so unlikely and regularly seeing all the different ways a man could be killed didn't help matters in that regard.

Uncle George had the girl bring in a couple of quarts of blackberry cordial for us boys to share as we sat around the table. It sure went down nice and sweet that night, but we were careful not to get besotted. We could not relax even at Uncle George's house. It was a good defensible house made of solid log construction. There was no one in charge for now, but that was okay since we had decided to rendezvous with capable Bill Anderson. We'd heard reports that Quantrill was out of state. We thought maybe he was down in Texas or back in Kentucky. Still another rumor was that Captain Quantrill was trying to round up the largest force of irregulars anyone had ever heard of to ride into Lawrence, Kansas, but so far there had been few takers. My only fear about Bill was he was reckless and brave and always spoiling for a fight, where I wanted to pick my battles carefully.

Suddenly I felt a chill. My hands began to shake. I felt my body rise up, but it was like watching someone else. It was as though my spirit had stepped outside of my body momentarily. The other me walked over to a shelf and picked up a tiny bell and rang it. Uncle George had seen me have one of these moments before, so he wasn't surprised, but to him it seemed I was doing something impertinent on purpose. Yet I could not have stopped the episode though I wanted to. I carried the bell with me and walked about the table once until my legs went weak. It was as if my body wanted to have a rest, so I laid down on the little green rug and began to shake. My spirit had exited my body again. I could see everyone in the room, including myself, from above. The lantern and candles shimmered like overbright stars, creating halos over the heads of everyone at the table. I heard a woman's voice saying my name repeatedly and then the darkness fell.

Chapter 12
Kidnapped

The journalist touched a Lucifer match to the stubbed tip of his cigar. His ridiculous moustache—more like whiskers on a walrus or some other creature—twitched as he coaxed the cigar back to life. Edwards was a rather Falstaffian character in his way under normal circumstances, but I had seen little evidence of it during our interview. He leaned back in the one good chair in the room as he looked at me wearily, probably disappointed in the story he was hearing or speculating on how he could make my words inspirational to the people in our part of the country, for whom the war was beginning to recede from memory in favor of plans for the new world emerging from the dust and rubble of all we had done.

I remember reading something he had written about us partisans, saying that we were all meant for higher things and could have just as easily ended up as mathematicians or scholars. This was just the sort of inaccurate and laughable statement he wrote in the newspapers. How could anyone take us seriously after reading this, unless they were gullible—though there was plenty of that going around. I must have smiled a sardonic smile just then because Edwards gave me a suspicious look as he chewed thoughtfully on the tip of his cigar.

As I recall, it happened before General Ewing had been able to get permission to kick all the fine Confederate families out of western Missouri that he committed his foulest treachery of all.

The problem Ewing had to contend with was that from just south of Kansas City to the Osage River was held by us; only he called it "bushwhacker country." What he did showed the difference between mere men and what we would rate as gentlemanly behavior. No matter how hot the situation, we would consider it an evil deed to harm women or children. Even if done accidentally, it was unacceptable and not pardonable, either. Ewing was ambitious and took it in his head to arrest seventeen or so of our sisters, friends, and sweethearts. They were women who had stood by their men steadfastly, trying to help in any way they could, including riding into Kansas City to spy on Union troops. Ewing issued General Order #10 to forcibly remove anyone known to be sympathetic to the cause, which was mostly old men, women, and children. They talked of creating some Southern rebel district, but truly they didn't care if people lived or died or where they went, just so long as Ewing's goals were accomplished.

There were about two dozen of us, maybe a few more, at Bill's house on Parchman farm just off the Blue River in Jackson County. We were helping him fix up his house and land for his sisters. I recall it was a blistering hot day. Even the birds refused to fly. I was out weeding in the garden, which I did with two holstered Navy Colts. I would have carried more, but it made it too uncomfortable to bend down in the garden. I refused to go about unarmed in such a time where the enemy had declared us outlaws. There would be no exchanges or paroles, just a noose thrown over the nearest cow tree or a shot to the head like a rabid dog that had to be put down. Some of the boys refused to do work like that since they thought of themselves as soldiers with better things to do, but others of us were used to working hard no matter the weather.

It was work that had to be done and I thought maybe I could save the fair-skinned ladies, Josephine and Mary, from having to do it that day at any rate. The ladies were both lovely and the boys had tired of hearing me moon over a picture I carried with me of Lizzie, and she had made the trip down with her older brother, John, as chaperone. John had fought at Wilson's Creek too and had lost his left arm from the elbow and had one eye blinded by a cannon blast.

I was tickled to have Lizzie at the house. Word had leaked out to her family back home that we were now married. Lizzie told me that my mother knew and was mad as a hornet over it. She had smiled shyly at me over supper, the evening past, when I asked her to *please pass down the peas*. We had known each other most of our lives and now that she was here, she seemed to be stricken mute. It had been long enough since our honeymoon night that time had made us both shy.

The girls were nearly finished with colorful new shirts, that made us boys look dashing. They made us baked goods in the outdoor kitchen and other delicious meals so much better than the corn pone, biscuits and beans, and raw baked potatoes that was our normal fare.

The youngest Anderson was a little ten-year-old tomboy named Jennie. As the baby in the family, she was allowed to follow her own pursuits besides a few light chores around the house. Bill was a different man around his sisters. I couldn't put my finger on it until I realized he was happy. It tickled him to death to let Jennie make flowery garlands for his hair. In truth, we were all in better spirits being able to eat, rest, and talk to one another in a more relaxed manner than we were accustomed to, living out in the woods.

Much to my surprise, Bill ambled up on Edgar Allan, with Little Archie, while we were working, to check on me and Cole Maddox. Now, Cole had become my partner out of necessity as of late. Bill forced us to do all the work the other men didn't want to do when we were out in the woods hunting for small roving bands of blue bellies. We'd ride up to them decked out in blue on some pretense or another and as soon as we got close in, we'd blaze away. Sometimes there was just enough time to watch their eyes widen in surprise or for one or more to utter an oath before we were sending them on to their savior. It almost always worked in those days.

In the woods, I cooked and Cole did dishes. This we had to settle with fists first. The pair of us were the same age and he did not want to accept anyone's orders but our captain's. He pulled out his big Bowie knife and shook it at me, saying, "I dare you to make me." To me it was another sign that he was just a boy, but a big boy that I couldn't ignore. I'd already been in my share of scraps and before he could make a move I'd grabbed him by his wrist, flipped him over my hip, and put the blade up to his eyeball. I gave him a couple of rabbit punches to the head for good measure so I felt confident that the lesson had taken hold of his imagination.

I explained to him that had I not been the one to show him the error of his ways, it would have been someone like Little Archie, who would not have been so kind. His eyes went wide and round with comprehension at this. Archie was the smallest man in our company, but he was also the most brutal in a fight. His way was to slice off an ear, pluck out an eye, take a pinky finger for show, or slit the throat of his enemy. It was no hard chore for him, as I'd already seen him smile with the pleasure he took in his work, and sometimes he would laugh with joy while he was emptying his pistol into some ignorant Union boy's head. Cole generously agreed that this time he would do the dishes. He pouted for a while after that but he gave me some respect and then we became thick as thieves.

If someone needed a nursemaid, one of us was usually elected. If a picket was needed for the night, our names were bellowed out first since we were the youngest. Cole was a cousin to Bill Anderson, and the boy's mother had begged him to train the boy to kill Yankees after the state militia had come to their home near Blue Springs and treated them roughly and killed her husband to boot. Cole had such a crush on the Anderson girls his face would turn tomato red and he'd be rendered mute at dinner by proximity to the female company, which caused no end to the mirth and teasing from the boys. He had not yet become numb to the world from fighting, but that was inevitable.

Bill and Little Archie rode up side by side. They both looked rather fierce and fairly bristled with Navy Colts. It was obvious they were on edge. It seemed like the happiness of the last few days had been gradually siphoned away. The day was beautiful. Ewing's men were carrying out his terrible orders all across western Missouri and no plan had yet been formed against it. Quantrill was out of the state; no one had heard much from him. There was not much in the way of official word from Quantrill's captains who were still in state either.

"Just wanted to see you boys was armed." Bill slipped off his horse and looped the reins around the waist of a sapling. Arch followed suit. "If you weren't armed, well, I'd have to have Hi Guess or one of the Parr boys shoot you in the foot just to make my point. We have to be ready for anything."

"Oh, my, yes!" I said laughing on the outside, but I was boiling my innards with rage. It made me uneasy the way all of them joshed about killing the help, when we were so likely to be killed anyway. I patted the Colts with a comforting feeling. One was in its holster and the other was shoved down into the waistband of my trousers around my backside. "I'll give them something to holler about, any Federals show up here."

Cole brandished two revolvers over his head like war trophies. He could tell from my expression I was irked and he elbowed me. "They're joshing. Don't let their tough talk irk you. They're just trying to get a rise out of ya."

"Well, it worked," I mumbled glumly so only Cole could hear.

"Don't take on so, Captain Ashby," Cole laughed. That was a joke between us that we would call each other "Captain" when there weren't any around.

"What was that?" Bill said.

"Nothing," Cole said.

"There's been reports," Little Archie said, "this morning of a column of Federals in the area. We're going back up near the house soon and make some preparations just in case they do show up. We might take the girls to a neighbor's as a precautionary."

"If very many show up here," Bill said, "you best show them your backsides and hightail it like jackrabbits. You got any water to drink up here?"

"In that wooden bucket yonder by the cedar tree," Cole said.

"Come over here and have a drink with us," Arch said, not unkindly. "We'd like to talk to you boys. It will get you out of the sun for a minute, if nothing else."

Bill and Arch went over and sat down next to the bucket, but just as Arch was about to snatch up the dipper, two gunshots came from the house. We all froze in place, listening for a minute. Infernal was grazing on the other side of the garden and only tethered lightly to a tree limb. He jerked his head, gave an equine cry, and lumbered off into the timber. I cursed myself for foolishness.

"Josephine!" Bill said. "I've got to check on my sisters!" Bill exchanged a look with Arch, and they were both on their horses in an instant.

"They wouldn't dare harm a woman," I said.

"Oh, wouldn't they?" Cole said. "Ride on back with me. You can find that crazy horse of yours later."

I slipped up behind Cole on his sorrel mare and off we went. By the time we made it to the house, it was obvious they were no longer there, but they were not too far away either. Little Jennie came out on the porch before we left the yard. We were all relieved to see her, at least.

"They said they was taking them to prison in Kansas City!" Jennie hollered.

"Kansas City! Why didn't they take you with them?" Arch asked.

"They said I was a little fish, they was throwing me back."

If Lizzie were harmed they would have hell to pay for it. Bill uttered an oath. His horse seemed to do a war dance backward across the front yard. He jerked the reins so hard, toward the sound of horses to the west, that the horse reared up and raked the air and then almost went down on top of his rider but righted himself at the last second and came down on panicky hooves to dash away, churning clods of mud high into the air like he was in a race at the county fair.

Cole pointed and told me to get off so he could catch up with

Bill and Arch and a dozen others.

I was confused at first, but I saw what he was pointing at in the little corral in the front yard: a green-broke white pony that kicked at me, but I was up on its back and digging my heels into his ribs before he could complain much. He whinnied in indignation when I put my heels to him and instead of going out the open gate, he surprised me by jumping the fence and knocking a rail off as he did so. I was worried the horse might be injured, and then he surprised me again when he ran off the main trail and into the brush, fighting the bit in his mouth. I had to dodge low-hung tree limbs, but it seemed Providence had chosen a good route for a shortcut if the fleet little horse didn't step into a hole and break a leg while we flew across a meadow of horseweeds and wildflowers. It wasn't a path a sane man would have chosen for his horse. The horse was huffing down a row of the neighbor's young corn.

"Let's go, you little bastard," I whispered into his twitching ear.

I knew we were making ground on them when I spotted the dozen Yankees who were riding double with the girls ahead on the road to Kansas City, making no attempt at concealment. Because of the lunatic route my mount had chosen, only Bill and Arch were ahead of me now. I really put the heels to him to try to catch up, so they wouldn't have to face off the dread party on their own. I hoped to get the chance to blow off one of their Yankee heads. It was in that moment I understood those men who took war trophies like ears and scalps.

They were wise enough to have a rear guard of sorts. It amounted to six mounted Yankees, which the Anderson brothers were in the process of cutting down with their Colts when my feral pony ran headlong down their gullets even while I yanked back hard on the reins. I found myself face-to-face with a giant bushy red-bearded man who looked like the battle-tested veteran of many a tussle. The veteran took careful aim, but just as he was sure to blow my head off my shoulders with his Remington, the pony did another rabbit hop, resulting in a wound to my shoulder instead of the center of my forehead. The pony bore with a full head of steam into the veteran's big black, nearly unseating its rider, which gave me time to point the snout of my pistol at him and shoot the great bearded troll in the eye.

An expression of shock lit across his face. *How did this little shit kill me?* it seemed to ask. The big man fell backward off his horse like a turd in the outhouse.

The Andersons had already dispatched the other men of their rearguard. I finally managed to control the head of the pony and pulled him back around to gaze upon the impressive-looking Yankee I'd killed. I was lucky to be mounted on such an erratic horse and yet he could have gotten me killed just as easily.

I looked down on the redbeard and wished him safe passage in the valley of the shadow, but he might have to go into Glory missing a finger. I slid off the pony but held onto the reins in case he got a notion to run off. Then I pulled out my hip knife and cut off the Yankee's trigger finger and put it in a little drawstring purse. I had it in mind to start a collection.

"Now you won't be killing no more good Missourians in heaven, you blue-belly motherfucker," I said, but he couldn't hear me because he was playing the harp for St. Peter and the heavenly host.

Cole and Frank rode up side-by-side to where we were.

"It's better to be lucky than good," Cole called.

"My God," Frank said. "What happened to your Christian

mercy? Wasn't he already dead, Preacher?"

"Well," I said, examining my new shoulder wound. "He shot me. He's a dead Christian now. I am overtired of these Federals shooting at me. There's a price to be paid from here on out. I have no doubts that our God is a Southerner, whatever anyone else might think."

It was difficult for me to believe that there was once a time when killing seemed impossible to me, but the ferryman had been paid and I had rode under the black arch of heaven. The realm of Hades was likely my destination.

"C'mon, now!" Frank kicked his mount.

Frank rode off. Some of the other boys blazed by me. The white pony was still acting squirrelly, but I managed to get on his back while he was rearing up. He spun around in a circle once while I had only one foot in a stirrup, until I managed to land my ass in the saddle and give chase again. I could see a line of dark purple clouds in the distance and summer lightning leaping out of the cloudbank like thunderbolts of the gods. I could feel the electricity in the air; for reasons I've never been able to explain, I always felt better when these summer thunderstorms set in. I felt refreshed and alive, is the best I can put it, when these storms cropped up and shook the tall trees by their green branches and made the wheat look like a jade sea as the winds raked over the crop in spirals and waves. It may not make sense now, but I felt that we, I, had wings that day and I was ready to take them all on in a way I had never experienced before.

Lizzie. My heart beat her name.

Bill and Arch were hard-charging on the Yankees with our girls. We had their attention now and they had turned their mounts in our direction to face us instead of retreating. There wasn't much separating us from them but a dried-up creek. We were close enough that either side could have opened fire, but instead both sides were reconnoitering the situation. Bill held up his hand so that we wouldn't shoot. He wanted the rest of our regulators to catch up; they were rumbling up in twos and threes now, until it looked like we were about equal to the kidnappers before us.

The riders with the girls sat them in front to keep us from taking potshots at them. Riders rode double with each of the girls. We were all itching to close the ground between us and lop off their heads, but we trusted that Bill knew exactly what he wanted to do in this situation.

"Throw down your weapons and surrender the women, or we will cut you down where you are!" Bill ordered in his most frightening killer voice.

"You make war on virtuous Southern women now?" Jim Anderson chimed in.

"We will kill them," a corporal's voice trembled in answer. "You shoot at us or our horses and we will slit their Secesh-loving throats!"

"Quiet," the sergeant holding Josephine ordered sharply. The sergeant looked to be a flinty character. There was a scar at his neck and another on his forehead, shaped vaguely like a star.

Josephine, Mary, and Lizzie were pleading with us with their eyes to save them.

"We're already dead!" Josephine said. "If you let them take us away, it will be the last time you see us! Kill them now! We'll take our chances!"

"Hush, girl!" the sergeant hissed. To us he said, "We're not going to kill them and of that I can assure you. They are wanted for their crimes against the Union by aiding and abetting the likes of you! We will not harm them, but if you attack, I cannot vouch for their safety. They will be released in good time. I swear it!"

I put my heels to the pony and was about to let the sergeant have it in the mouth without regard to the safety of the girls. I suppose I was blind with rage, but Cole grabbed at my wounded shoulder as I started on past and bade me to hold back. A couple of other riders were nudging up behind me to follow if I'd gone.

We all looked to Bill. He was our leader. The girls were his sisters. I couldn't keep my gaze from the terror in Lizzie's face. I couldn't believe they were taking my girl away. All I wanted was for her to be safe. She did not seem to see any of us at the moment.

Bill was about to answer the sergeant when we could see a Yankee column coming into view around the bend where they had been previously obscured by the woods. I still thought there might be time for one desperate gamble to win the girls back, but I could see the cold calculation on Bill's face. He was never afraid to be on the offensive in a fight, but he would not risk our lives for the moment on such a fool's errand.

"We better skedaddle, Bill!" Hi Guess said. Hi was one of our videttes and an impressive horseman besides.

"Dear God," Cole whispered as he watched the men in blue draw nearer. It was clear he didn't want to abandon the girls to the enemy. Not a one of us did. "We've been outfoxed in our own country."

"Sergeant Star!" Bill said in a commanding voice meant to temper his own sense of helplessness and growing rage.

The big sergeant looked surprised to be addressed disrespectfully. His hand went unconsciously to the scar on his forehead. Then he pursed his lips and spit on the ground at being dishonored.

"If anything at all happens to these girls, I'll remember you and your life will be sacrificed in retribution. It will not be a quick death, nor a merciful one either. I will hunt you down, cut off your manhood, and stuff it in your mouth for all your brethren to see! I will take your ears as trophies to show to my grandchildren. I vow that my wrath will fall on you and all the men riding with you today."

"Mighty tall words!" But the sergeant gave a respectful nod. They all turned as a man to ride for the safety of the oncoming column.

"I love you, Ashby!" Lizzie's voice rang out softly as a church bell sighing from miles away.

"I love you, Liz!" I would come to wonder if she had said it at all many years later. She was tall for a woman dressed in bon ton dress. A porcelain face that should have been painted and hung on a wall in a museum. Usually she was silent and said very little, but her eyes said it all for me. Her beautiful teeth, high cheekbones, and full-lipped smile spoke to me in way mere words could never quite accomplish. She was a joy to look upon, as it seemed to me a wife should be, and funny and kind.

"And I love you," I whispered again, more to myself than so she could hear me.

A dozen fresh riders were pounding hard down the meadow toward us and yelling like savages. We started firing and levering and cursing at them even as our horses began to dance a retreat back toward Parchman and Brushy Creek.

Bill's eyes met mine for an instant and he gave me a nod. His face was flushed with righteous anger. He put his heels to the big black and off he went. The horse could flat-out run. All of our horses could. They put to shame anything the Federals could put in the field, including their officers. The Army was too cheap to buy decent horses, so we knew we'd lose them by and by. My horse was so green I didn't trust him, but he wasn't much different than Infernal in his reliability, so I was about as comfortable either way. This time I forced the pony to go through the brush, since it had been a good shortcut the first time around. I wanted to mourn over Lizzie, but I knew if I didn't keep my head in what was happening at the moment I could be easily killed this day. Escaping from the Federals was the only thing that mattered. Frank was close behind me now. I allowed him to catch up when we stopped briefly at the second Parchman barn to grab a few personals. Then we were back on our horses.

I was planning on leaving the county in a hurry, but under a weeping willow I found Infernal with a couple of other horses and caught him easily and put the cheap saddle I had for the white pony on him. While I was doing it, the pony took a vicious bite out of my back. He had been waiting on a chance to do me harm. I punched him hard in the nose. *Fucken glorious beast!* I took out a Colt to put him down, but he reared up and ran away before I could take a killing shot. *Damn Yankee horse!*

My nice saddle was back in the barn, it was a good one, and some farm boy would very likely take it as a spoil.

We were masters at losing ourselves in the Sni wilderness. The Yankees wouldn't follow us there. That night we made camp as deep as we could in the wilderness of vines and creepers and trees so close together you could barely fit a horse between the trunks. It was a den we had used many times before. During the winter months someone had come and removed some of the trees in the center to create a little clearing, but it was so surrounded by narrow trees, creeks, and what resembled a Southern cypress swamp that no Yankee would have been too keen on slogging through, especially if he was mounted. A company of mounted men would have to come in one by one and we could pick them off easily that way. They knew it, and none wanted to brave the cow path to our hiding place.

Not far away there was a big room in a kind of natural cave in the side of a hill, which we had widened with spades and shovels ourselves to improve on Mother Nature's work. We unsaddled and hobbled the horses out of habit. Infernal was already hungrily ripping the grass down to the nub. The sound of his ripping and chewing was a comforting sound. Once we were finished attending our mounts, we collected kindling, wood, and creek stones and made a fire once full-on dark had come on.

Frank had me strip off my whacker shirt, cleansed my shoulder wound and had a couple of the boys hold me down while he fished his stiletto hard on one side of my wound and then twisted the bullet so it jumped right out into the palm of his hand.

"Almost seems like you done this before." I forced a laugh.

"A time or two." He smiled.

"When is that brother of yours going to join up with us?"

"Jesse will be back with us before too long. He's barely shaving as it is. You probably ain't much older, huh?" I shrugged. He cleaned out the wound. It was damned uncomfortable but he had a steady hand and I had every confidence he knew what he was doing.

"I'm just a year or so older than him—"

"That year or so of experience makes all the difference," Frank nodded. "He's a nervy boy and he ain't scared of nothing. He'll be a good fighter if he don't get killed first."

"I got a good feeling about him," I said.

"You just rest here for a while," Frank said. "You're fine. It didn't get you too clean or deep."

"How did you end up here?"

"What a question," Frank said. "It's a long, sad story. I'll tell you for true since there's many a man tells a whopper just to look big, but I started out in Ben McCulloch's army. I was captured at Wilson's Creek. Granted a parole. Took the oath, too, but it didn't take."

"Aye, the same here."

"See, we're brothers then." He grinned.

It didn't look too bad. He tried to cleanse it with a bit of whiskey now and then doused it with water again before he wrapped it tight. He bade me drink some of the whiskey. Instead of telling me I'd be fine, he said it wouldn't be long before I was in a good amount of pain. "You'll live, though."

Hi Guess came over with his deck of cards and put his hat on a stump next to where he plopped himself down. Frank moved over to help build the fire and confer with Bill. Hi said he was going to teach me cards and gambling even if I was a preacher. I told him that I was no longer in that line of work, but everyone seemed to determined to call me by that name instead of my own. He kind of smiled and nodded all at the same time. He shrugged and started to deal. I was wound so tight I couldn't concentrate, even with Hi feeding me gulps of whiskey, but he tried to calm my fears by telling me about the boys Bill had settled on for pickets.

I nodded in full agreement when it was expected, but I couldn't help worrying. The thought of Lizzie being rode away with those Yankees to a stinking prison like she was a man or a dog and the knowledge that they had no respect for women was working us all up. Bill was particularly beside himself. From my vantage point by the fire in the center of camp, it looked like every few minutes he remembered what had happened, like he was at war with himself to forget. If he remembered, he might have to jump on Edgar Allan and ride us all to Kansas City and fight them all right then and there.

Bill walked by on his way to the fire to pour a cup of chicory. I looked up at him, almost afraid to say anything. For his part, he looked haggard, yet the skin on his face seemed stretched tight with a pale green vein throbbing like a lightning bolt on his forehead. For as fearsome as he was on horseback, he was also a quite handsome fellow. There was not just anger there but the conceit of a youth who knew he was better than any ten men alive. He squatted down on his haunches with his tin and poured himself a cup and took a sip before letting it cool. With his other hand he combed at his beard with his fingers.

His eyes suddenly cut to mine. It was as if he had caught me watching him, but then he said, "Don't worry. We'll get them, ole son! We'll get those Yankees back, especially that Sergeant Star. If God or Devil will but place him in my path again. But it's the girls I'm most afraid for. In the hands of those dirty soldiers . . . best try not to think about it. How's your wound?"

"I'm doing okay now." I smiled heartily. I was beginning to feel the effects of the rotgut. "My nurse popped it right out of me."

"Ha! He calls Frank his nurse! You are drunk!" He laughed, but it was a bitter laugh. "I could use a bit to fancy up my coffee."

"It's for medicinal purposes."

"Sure," he said.

I grabbed at his sleeve and slopped the better part of his coffee on the ground, but I didn't care. He glared now, trying to understand what I was about. The weepiness I felt was about to come out. It tended to happen when I had too much to drink, although it was a relatively new experience at the time. "Are you afraid of dying, William T.?"

He stood up with annoyance. The good will he had expressed before drained from him. He drank the dregs of the cup, what I hadn't spilled, and grimaced at the temperature of it in his mouth and spat it on the ground as if to punctuate his feelings on the subject. "If I cared for my life," he sneered, "I'd have lost it long ago. Wanting to lose it now, I can't throw it away." Something about the way he said it made it sound practiced but no less haunting to my ear. He shook my hand off his sleeve. "Rest now. We'll need every man."

"Be careful." Cole crept up to sit next to me by the fire.

"What do you mean?" I asked.

"He's not in his right mind," Cole said. "Since they took the girls, he's a bit off his feed."

I gave him a wave of my hand. I felt too weak to talk about anything serious.

A fever plagued me through the night. Sleep would come for a few precious moments and then the shadow of a demon would shake me awake. Faces loomed large. Great eyes, mouths, teeth, and claws reached for me. A giant Pinkerton eye was watching me. Men in blue-black capes and hats shot me again and again in my nightmares. Horses ran me over. A train rumbled somewhere in the distance and the sound made its way into my fever dreams in the form of a sleeping dragon. The locomotive sang a forlorn hymn to the night.

Thunder rolled in the distance. A lightning strike nearby caused me to jolt awake. A couple of the men picked me up and carried me like a sack of grain into the earthen hovel, where a number of men were pinched for space. I wondered if this was what hell was like. It smelled strong of the earth, smoke, blood, and unwashed bodies.

"He's awake," Cole said, stroking his peach-fuzz beard.

"Did I call for my ma?" I tried to laugh at myself.

"Aye," Little Arch said. "You did, Preacher, but we all do that even when we're not sweating out a fever."

"Can I have your boots if you die?" Cole said.

"Enough of that talk. He's not going to die, boy," Frank said. "Just his body fighting it off. He needs rest. He'll be fine."

Without announcement, none other than Captain George Todd came striding into the room with two men. One was one of his lieutenants and the other was called Rube, his well-known colored man who specialized in *Confederate haircuts* with an especially lethal looking Bowie knife. He had to duck down unceremoniously to fit through the doorway. Whispers of "It's Todd's pet nigger" followed him around the room.

These new arrivals shook off the rain from their overcoats and the men nearby held their tongues about any offense they might have felt getting water splattered on them. Todd was a good-looking cuss, too. Tall and blond, with piercing blue eyes, but there was a cruelness to his demeanor. A man who looked into those eyes knew better than to expect mercy. He was known as one of the best captains who served under Quantrill. He seemed to take in everything and everyone in the room at a glance. There was a nod for this one and that one in the chamber. A chorus of "Captain Todd" went up in the room from our men. Men seemed to sit up straighter now.

"I see who's running this outfit and I'm not at all surprised." Captain Todd met Bill in the center of the room and pumped his hand vigorously. "Do I call you Captain Bill?"

Somehow we all felt safer and more proud with the two men together.

"Well, if it isn't Captain Todd!" Bill clapped him on the shoulder. "Captain Bill does have a nice ring to it, but you can just call me Bill like always. I'd say what a good surprise, but it wasn't no surprise at all since our pickets saw you coming a mile away."

"You can't expect a bantam rooster like me to goose-step in his own barnyard now!"

"We don't have much to offer you, but we do have some chickens and sweet potatoes. Are you hungry?"

"I could eat a bite," Captain Todd said in his burr.

"You, up!" Bill pointed at Cole to give up his seat. Cole slunk over to the corner and sat on a barrel.

I was beginning to feel a mite better, but my eyes felt heavy, so I listened to the conversations. All the men had hushed, as much to hear Todd's conversation with Bill as out of any formal respect.

"Quantrill wants to meet with all the captains," Todd said. "Has he sent you word yet?"

"No," Bill said. "Let me guess. He wants us to attack Lawrence?"

"That's about right," Todd said. "He's been talking about it for some time now. It's a dream of his to ride into Lawrence with a thousand men and visit hellfire on it!"

"I'm all for that but it seems like the plan only a madman would consider to tell you truthfully." Bill clasped Todd by the shoulder as if to make his point. For his part, Todd seemed to nod in agreement. "We lived in Kansas for a time years ago, when my father was still alive, but I guess we were Missourians at heart. But first I have other business to take care of."

"I heard about this, but I couldn't believe it at first," Todd said. "Rube, have a seat by the door. You're making me nervous."

Rube's rich voice said, "Can I trouble y'all for some chicory?"

Todd nodded as though he were giving his blessing, though it wasn't his coffee to give.

"It's true," Captain Bill said. "They took my sisters to Kansas City. I mean to either trade me some Billy Yanks for them or find some other way to free them. Maybe they will send them south with the others. I just don't know, but I can't see going to Lawrence until then."

CHAPTER 13
Lawrence Massacre

Lawrence should be thoroughly cleansed,
and the only way to cleanse it is to kill! Kill!
—William Clarke Quantrill

I do not remember the exact date when I heard the news about Lizzie and the other girls. It was a terrible day for several reasons, I can tell you that. A few days earlier Jennie had slipped away. She had been pining for her sisters and went to Kansas City on her own while we were out raiding. The silly girl had been so lonely without her sisters she handed herself over as a rebel. It was yet another reason for us, especially Bill, to be beside himself. So instead of sending the child home they obliged her and locked her away in the rickety building they must have chosen for their most foul deed of all: killing defenseless women. It was further proof of their disrespect and lack of humanity that they treated the ladies so unjustly.

Until this day you will never convince me they didn't mean to kill those girls—there were about seventeen in all—and made it look like an accident too. Besides Lizzie and the Anderson sisters, John McCorkle's sister and sister-in-law was there, along with two cousins of Coleman Younger. We later read in the papers that the building was owned by the artist and Union man George Caleb Bingham, but it had been seized by Ewing's troops to use as a prison for the girls without permission to do so. Some time later we read that Bingham hated Ewing; that caused us all to see him in a slightly more kindly light.

It was a bright, clear day, with white clouds on a deep blue sky. I sat facing the fire. It was Cole's turn to do the cooking. There was fish frying in the skillet. Terrible weak coffee cooking over the flame. I can remember seeing a hawk and thinking it was a sign of good luck. In a time of war you needed all the luck you could find. Of course, I think it's natural when your life is at stake every day and at every moment to look for portents from above.

The wind was on my face like a river current. My arms had become powerful wings. A field mouse froze where it was, in my shadow, but I could spy him perfectly. There was a fancy paddle-boat on the river. The sun reflected off the river like the surface was cobbled together with jewels instead of water. A gentleman and a lady stood on the deck of the boat smiling at one another. The woman twirled a yellow parasol. There were rainbow trout in the river just below the surface awaiting me to pluck them from the depths. A company of Federals were waiting impatiently on the ferryman who was on the opposite shore yanking rhythmically on his hemp line. The sun was brighter than I had ever noticed it before. Soaring above the clouds, I thought the world seemed a sphere of blues, greens, and browns in an opaque mist.

I wanted to stay in the vision of the hawk, but I felt a punch to my shoulder, and my arms were no longer wings. I plummeted back to earth again. Cole was grinning at me like he knew my secret.

"You was humming," Cole said.

"Was I?"

There was one practice in particular I have not mentioned. Throughout the war I took the small leathern Bible I carried and opened it randomly to receive a communication from on high. I shared this practice with Cole and he seemed particularly fascinated. He believed it was proof of my closeness to God. That morning, I'd chanced upon a verse from Daniel, "And it waxed great, even to the host of heaven; and it cast down some of the host and of the stars to the ground, and stamped upon them." Now, I was confused by this. Sometimes I'd just shut the pages and open them again, but I didn't that day. Later, as a personal message for my interpretation, I knew it was the girls in the Kansas City prison, who I was to understand were the stars that had been stamped down.

Two crows flew three times around the old oak I was seated under before they lighted on a branch in the uppermost branches. They were fighting with one another and talking in their loud, plaintive voices. Until, out of nowhere, one was cast down stone dead to the ground. The other crow flew off and cawing in what struck me as a victorious rebel yell. It was not just two crows, you understand? It was a message from glory, a portent of betrayal.

"A rider's coming!"

A young boy on a farm horse came in to give us the terrible news. Arch and Bill ushered him into their headquarters. The ladies, the boy explained, had been crushed when the building they were in fell down around them. The top floor of the building was inhabited by prostitutes who serviced the soldiers—if that's not an indication of what they thought of us! Then he told about the crowd of witnesses who said the soldiers had purposely weakened the foundation so that it would cave in. A foul deed!

Josephine was dead. Mary was crippled for life. She had managed to leap from a window to safety. Jennie had two broken legs and she had been so troublesome to the guards that they had shackled her with a twelve-pound ball adding insult to injury so she was crushed in the rubble instead of being able to follow her older sister through the window. My darling Lizzie was killed by the collapse. I just prayed it was quick and that she had not been made to suffer like Josephine. Someone had related a terrible story: when they were trying to dig the girls out of the rubble they could hear her voice begging anyone to take the bricks off her head, until she finally fell silent. A girl witnessing the events from the adjacent doorways began to sob when she could no longer hear her voice.

The crowd, the boy told us, turned into a cursing, outraged mob. Cries of "Murder" went up that day. Ewing sent his own headquarter guard out with fixed bayonets to keep order. Charity McCorkle died and so did one of Cole Younger's cousins.

Bill became deathly silent upon hearing this news. The color drained out of his face. Arch said they should send riders to spread the news to Quantrill and the other leaders, but Bill shook his head. He said they would all know before too long. It would be in all the papers soon enough.

All the tenderness I'd ever felt began to drain out of me that day as I watched the flames dance in our fire. I saw her face burning in the fire. Revenge. I imagined revenge each day afterward and I would have it too. This war had taken away my future. They would try to kill us all like dogs. I vowed to kill as many of them as I could. Many of their commanding officers had already taken on a harsh policy of *no prisoners* and *no exchanges* when it came to Quantrill's rabble. They called us bushwhackers under the black flag, but they expected mercy from us when we captured them. They asked for all-out war. I aimed to give it to them in spades.

Not even two weeks had gone by when we saddled up to ride to Lawrence with Colonel Quantrill. He looked splendid in his new colonel's uniform. The rank had been conferred upon him in Arkansas by none other than the Confederate Secretary of War, James Seddon (or so he informed us), who it was said had the decaying features of a man dead in the grave for the better part of a month. Quantrill spoke of Seddon in respectful terms, but he also described the aspect of a man with sunken eyes in black hollows, a gaunt face of wrinkled skin plastered across cheekbones and long, straggly hair as was found on a corpse. It was a sticking point, this fealty to the regular Confederacy that had cost Quantrill most of his men to the insolent George Todd, although I didn't know this at the time.

We were as loyal as could be to the Cause, but many of us, having seen the regular military life, said there was no way we would fight in a standard military unit. We wanted to be able to act on our own instead of always following orders and to be able to get our own plunder in lieu of a military salary. Well, let's say we were ruined for it now, fighting under the black flag the way we had been doing out of necessity.

At one time it had seemed a fool's errand, a lunatic fancy, to consider riding hundreds of miles into abolitionist territory fortified with outposts all along the trail. But there we were riding down hell's gullet like some kind of terrible sacrifice, to what end none of us knew. The news said they even had little forts set up just thirteen miles apart from each other along the Kansas border. The Kansans liked to brag about how ready they were to fight Quantrill's men if they ever dared attack. But Quantrill and Bill had both spent plenty of time in Kansas. The Andersons had tried to homestead there until Bill and his brother were unjustly accused as horse thieves, though I'd have to tell it plain and say that even dyed-in-the-wool horse thieves rarely owned up to it. There were rumors that he and Jim were horse thieves before the war, and if that was true, they were probably the best there ever was at the game.

"I'd like to kill me some Red Legs!" Arch growled. He smoked a stubby cigar and smiled as he drew his thumb across his neck and made a whistling sound through his teeth.

When we met up with Colonel Quantrill, there were still many who had objections, but it wasn't none of us in Bill Anderson's group. News of the girls and their deaths at the hands of Ewing's guard had reached them all and that had stirred up the lot like hornets. Most all of the captains people would come to hear about later were there: Todd, Gregg, Pool, Holtzclaw, Younger, Yeager. My regret was we had to hastily make plans to have elder family members recover their bodies from Kansas City. The worst of it was, they weren't even allowed to take them back to our own country to bury them. They were forced south like all the rest, but we all talked of secret plans to return and inter them properly when the time was ripe.

Blackened chimneys stood as brooding sentinels all over western Missouri. One newspaper referred to the area as the "burnt district." There were still some defiant Missourians living out of sight in the area, but they were few. There were razed cabins, springhouses, and outbuildings. We found mounds of hastily dug graves as we traveled parallel to the main roads. Some of the recently departed were marked by mere cairns with jaunty crosses speared into the hard-crusted earth with creek rocks stacked as a foundation. Something in my spirit went still when we came upon a country church, a once proud-leaning spire, half-blackened and half-whitewashed and whole as the day it was built. It seemed a good analogy for men's souls just as this terrible war ravaged us all. Some livestock shot dead in the field. At one farmstead we came upon two mules still hitched together, but one was dead, so we set the other loose. The land had become desolate, forlorn.

It was especially bad one day when we came upon four of our boys hung high up in the trees above us. They had been there for a while, as their eyes were gone and their faces had been pecked clean by turkey vultures and who knows what else. The Federals would kill anyone who took down the bodies but we weren't particularly worried about the consequences. We just didn't have time to give these men a good Christian burial. It was a very real and likely consequence of the work we did.

We all went home for a day or so to bid goodbye to the women folk dear to us. Captain Bill said we should meet up again in a couple of days in the hideout in the Sni. So it was with a heavy heart I rode alone toward Glasgow. I was careful to bypass Fayette, since there was a small garrison there with Union soldiers. Most of Missouri was held by Yankees. It was certain that I was no thespian who could pretend to be a Federal or a farmer. They would take one look at my red v-necked shirt embroidered with flowers, long hair, the half-dozen pistols I carried, and they would know without me uttering a word what sort of man they were looking upon. I am sure I knew some of those boys too but I was in no disposition for a reunion.

I went straight to the home of the Bledsoes and Cole rode with me. Mr. and Mrs. Bledsoe asked us to come in. They both embraced me at the same time. This made me flinch, since in my family no one embraced or touched. It may have been seen as a sign of weakness to my parents, though they talked freely of

God's love. But they didn't seem capable of expressing love of their own in that way.

At the time, I appreciated their kindness to me. They knew I had loved Lizzie and it was common knowledge to everyone I had married her and talked of our children and grandchildren living on the land. Lizzie used to spin the most wonderful yarns about what our future would be like, including the children we would have together. She imagined a daughter that would like me with dark curly hair and blue eyes and a son for her with her high cheekbones and almond eyes.

Somehow I had already missed the funeral. Mr. Bledsoe rode me in his buggy to the Methodist church cemetery where she was buried with her people. Obviously, I'd wanted to attend, but Captain Bill had given us all strict orders to stay away, since the Federals would likely set traps for us knowing we would want to pay our respects. He believed that was partly the reason they had plotted to kill the girls but instead of doing it outright they had tried to make it look accidental.

Before we went out there, I told myself to remain calm and feel nothing, so that when we were at her grave I could retain my dignity and not just blow my own brains out on her grave where maybe we could be together again for eternity. I said something to that effect to Mr. Bledsoe, but he patted me on the shoulder and told me I was too young to throw my life away. If I ever need-ed steady work he could provide it on his farm. He was growing hemp and there was much to be done if the war ever ended and things got back to normal. I didn't ask how he had avoided the General Blunt's Orders No. 10 and 11 but he seemed to be gentle and kind and like many men he may have been trying to play the ends against the middle.

It was not an unusual sight. There were many fresh-dug graves. Lizzie's was at the end of a row, under a line of cedar trees with other Bledsoes who had passed. There was a simple headstone with her date of birth and time of passing. It was a comfort to know she would be with her family in such a peaceful place. I held my hat and looked on. The parson's wife came out of their residence not far away and in a very high soprano sang a hymn. Cole put his arm across my shoulders like a brother. I made a generous donation to the church parson. Like a revelation, a skein of geese flew overhead.

It was a forlorn feeling in my soul. I did not feel sad as I'd thought I would because it was something else instead welling up inside me. Instead it was a knot of anger in the pit of my stomach that spread up into my chest, throat, and filled my head with images of shooting, burning, cutting, fist to bone, tooth to claw. The hunger for the death of those responsible ate me up from the inside. There would be no point in returning to the Bledsoes' house. Working on a farm was a hard thought to entertain when such desperate times made widows of good Southern women and able-bodied men like myself were still above ground and willing to do something about it.

I rode on back to the Sni River hideout to await Bill and his orders.

At about the meridian of the next day a boy name of Bowden from southern Missouri said he knew an Ozark goomer woman who could lay a hex on those involved that would surely be the ruin of them all. He said she had a snake tattoo that stretched from her bosom, up her neck, and its head was on her face with its tongue sticking out. I was laughing about it too, though the boy was in deadly earnest, when Arch appeared and dressed him down for talking about the goomer woman and *haints* to a man of the cloth. I tried to wear an appropriately dignified expression during all of this until Arch turned his face away from the boy and gave me a grin. He was having the boy on. Arch liked to talk hard in the face of these recruits to see if they had the stuff. Some of these boys got romantic notions about what we were doing out here but then found out that men died and real blood gushed in and out of their veins under the right circumstances. Not all of them could take it. We had standards. We didn't take just anyone who wanted to join up.

I watched Buster Parr practice tying a hangman's noose with a length of twine as he sat his horse and seemed to be listening after a fashion. He looked up with a wink when he saw me watching him. He held up the noose with a grim smile. A little salute followed it up. I saluted him back with a bloody grin. We were both as ready as we'd ever be. We had to listen to the men who wanted to cry about never making it back to Secessia. At least, some of these men still felt they had a future in Missouri if they could manage to live through the war.

"Maybe we should wait for Old Pap first!"

"I don't reckon Sterling, or Pap as you so affectionately refer to him, would deign to join us on this one," Colonel Quantrill said. "If we do what I think we can in Lawrence, why they'll call you all heroes! They'll be singing songs about you all."

"Will they name their babies after us?" one man joshed.

While the Colonel was delivering one of his old quips I could hear Captain Todd and Bill talking in low tones as they sat their horses under a walnut tree.

"I'm surprised ole Quantrill left the side of his child bride,"

Todd snickered to Bill, so that only those nearby could hear his comments. He and Quantrill had had a contentious relationship for some time. "Have you seen her? She's not much more than a little girl running around her mama's petticoat. Her name is Bush too. If you can believe that."

"I've seen her," Bill said. "She's Quantrill's wife. I would be careful what you said about her."

"Hell, they're not married! Whatever gave you that idea?"

"Listen, George," Bill growled. "I don't know how they do things up there where you're from, but in this country we try to hold our tongues instead of making indecent remarks."

"Are you threatening me, Captain Bill?" Todd sneered.

They stared at one another for a minute. It worried me they might kill each other before we even left for Kansas. It just wouldn't do not to have two of our best with us in Kansas.

"No, George," Bill said. "But Lawrence is a good long ride from here. Let's try to keep it together so we don't end up killing each other in Kansas instead of the Yankees. They are the ones who really want killing."

George tipped his hat to Bill before moving off to settle with his men near a copse of cedar trees. He laughed loudly, sarcastically, as he no doubt wanted to keep up his insulting remarks to those who would hear them. He hocked a great glob of spit to the ground and then looked at us all.

Todd summoned a genuine cut-throat I recognized immediately. It was none other than the living demon called Speight. Todd whispered passionately to him and he stabbed us with snake-eyed glances. Todd had long been poisoning the men against Quantrill. Bill had said before that he thought Quantrill was a better leader but George bucked under anyone telling him what to do. He had already overthrown Quantrill's leadership of the men once, embarrassed him in front of everyone over claims he was cheating at cards and then put a gun in his face. But while Quantrill could be generous and oft times good-natured, George could rarely be. What Quantrill had, Bill once told me, was a gift for leading men by their noses.

"He seems mad," I said.

"Who George? I don't take it personal," Bill said. "I've seen it before. He's just got to get himself worked up so he won't have to be afraid."

"I did not think Captain Todd knew what fear was anymore."

"Oh," Bill said, looking down his nose at me, "he knows."

"Looks like we better keep an eye on that Speight fellow too."

"Looks like," I was quick to agree. "The man unnerves me."

Bill made a grand show of ignoring Todd. I was glad he was my pilot just then. He cut the figure of a gallant man. I don't imagine he was yet twenty-five on that day, but from my perspective, he was an older, mature man. I laugh when I think about it now. Even he was a young man at the time.

Frank came riding up next to me with a bit of newsprint in hand. "If you want a good laugh, read this one, Preacher!" He rode off hollering at someone he knew from Captain Younger's band. It was a piece from the *Lawrence State Journal*, written by a certain Hovey Lowman, from a couple of weeks former which read:

Mr. Quantrill is not invited to do bloody and infamous deeds upon unarmed men in any part of this State; but we venture to say that his chances for escaping punishment after trying on Lawrence just once are indeed slim—perhaps more so than in any other town in

*the State. Lawrence has ready for any emergency over five hun-
dred fighting men; everyone of whom would like to see Quantrill
in their gun sights.*

"We're coming to see you, Mr. Lowman," I said aloud to no
one. "We'll just have ourselves a little visit in your parlor."

It was August, the most miserable month in Missouri, the
heat was oppressive. It was like trying to breathe fresh air through
a damp dish towel. The day we left Blackwater River, where we
were encamped for Lawrence, Quantrill had about 150 men or
thereabouts. Bill Anderson had about forty of us at that time. Captain Andy Blunt showed up with a hundred men.

I could have cried for a refreshing rain. We were kicking up
the dust across western Missouri, where the terrain begins to level
out and a hint of the grasslands begin. It was hard to believe we
wouldn't be spotted long before we ever reached that abolitionist
capital, but if we were, we would fight where we stood. It was
comforting riding with so many men, all committed to the same
cause, and many of them good Missouri boys in spirit. The hillocks were emptying of small bands of our men as they joined up
with us. The sounds of men talking and japing each other in high
spirits mingled with the sounds of hoof falls and clink of metal
from weapons and bit rings. The cicadas were humming loud in
our ears, seeing us off.

I just hoped I ran into Lane so I could pay him back for all the
evil he had brought to Missouri. He resided in Lawrence, after all.
I'm sure he lived in a grand house with everything he had made
raiding into Missouri and stealing from our good people. Since
the night before many of us had been drinking mighty draughts of
busthead whiskey that had been discovered on a raid. Some of the

boys were saddened by this raid because of the much discussed hopelessness of ever making it out of Kansas alive. They had started off in cheery spirits, but soon enough the alcohol had taken hold, and the youngest boys, not used to drinking, were already crying about their untimely deaths by Jayhawkers and abolitionist scum. How some of them wailed about either their mama or their sweetheart. I began to wish I'd been born deaf. As we rode on, it became clear that some of the men might not make it there in their drunken state, so we lashed them with ropes into their saddles to keep them from falling off their mounts in the middle of the night. Those boys couldn't have seen a hole in a ladder! Soon we'd run out of liquid courage and if they made it to it, they might have to fight for the privilege of stomping on Lawrence. I wanted to be sharp, so I only took a shot in the neck here and there as it was offered to me from one rider to the next.

"I'll hack off their scalps and hang them from thy hacka-more," said a voice.

I turned to see the glowing face of a man known to me as Larkin Skaggs. He was a blowhard and a fanatical Baptist preacher. I gave him a nod and he rode up with a glint in his rheumy red eyes. He offered me a pull from his bottle. I pretended to take a drink just to avoid getting him black-assed toward me. Skaggs was as grievous man as any I ever met. As he rode, he rested one hand on an ancient looking sword straight from Arthurian legend.

"You sure you're ready to go poke the hornets nest?" I said.

"With a stick!" Skaggs winked. "I'll kick against the pricks!" I handed back the bottle. He took a drink and offered it to me again with a shove, but I politely refused with a slight wave of my hand. He offered the bottle to Cole, but then he saw that Cole had his own bottle.

"They speak of my drinking, but never my thirst!" Cole grinned wryly.

They roughly clinked their bottles together. Skaggs rode ahead of us singing lyrics from an opera in a voice less than pleasing but not unbearable. What he lacked in musical skill, he made up for in gusto. "This black harvest of souls is what we're here for, boys."

"I wish I was as drunk as him." Cole cradled his own bottle like a beloved infant.

"You're getting there," I said.

"Aye!" Cole agreed.

These are the kinds of remarks we made to one another that day to bolster our spirits. But what we lacked in faith and courage that day, we made up for in sheer determination. We were meant to have our revenge or die trying to give the Devil his due. We would see what the men of Lawrence were made of when the shoe was on the other foot. See how they liked it when death was brought to their doorstep. These are the words I told myself, but in the back of my mind I was picturing a massive army of Kansans surrounding us on the day of wrath, before we ever made it to our destination.

CHAPTER 14
Day of Wrath

Just before dawn there were three hundred of us at the Grand River in Cass County, about four miles from the Kansas border. A cool, refreshing rain began to lightly fall and bring with it some relief from the oppressive air but not so much as to hamper our column. Some of us looked toward the horizon in the west with some trepidation to see what the weather was going to do. There weren't any of the purple-black clouds that signaled harsh weather or a twister. A summer tanager flitting low to the ground from a hazel bush and blending into the red of the sumac like a scout, a bloodred teardrop in the wilderness—the kind of tears most all of us had been forced to shed.

We were ordered to dismount and take the opportunity to feed and water our horses. We would be riding hard to get to Lawrence by dawn.

There were so many of us, and the area was so heavily patrolled, we had to send out scouts in all directions to detect Yankee movements. This was the benefit in having Quantrill in command; whereas, some who thought they could do it better would have just ridden on whooping and hollering like savages the entire way, come what might, and gotten us killed before we had even made it out of the state. We rode hour after hour in columns of four to beat the sunrise.

Quantrill wanted us to wait there until nightfall to move under cover of darkness. I'm not so sure any Yankees would have been in a hurry to confront us, but he wanted to save us any problems until Lawrence. That was the goal we were aiming for. In the afternoon, Confederate Colonel John Holt showed up with one hundred raw Missouri recruits. Quantrill told Holt the orders we were under. I saw him look Quantrill up and down. He cut quite a gentlemanly figure in his dark pants tucked in brand-new cavalry boots. He wore a commanding hat with a braided gold band around it. Many of us looked like wild men by comparison with our long hair and mismatched clothing. Some wore brightly colored guerrilla shirts while others wore the enemy's blue, but one look at Quantrill made it clear who was in charge of this bunch.

"I've heard nothing of this action," Colonel Holt said. "But there's so much disarray back East that nothing astonishes these days."

"I'm under orders from President Jeff Davis himself via the Secretary of War, James Seddon," Quantrill opined as he smoothed his mustache down against his upper lip. "I reported to Seddon down in Arkansas not long ago. It's a tetchy situation since we're trying to turn the tide of recent setbacks back East at Gettysburg and Vicksburg. This may be the very time to catch them sleeping in Lawrence. We put the false rumor out back in July that I was coming for them then. Now the mayor looks like a fool. Even if someone rode into town now and told them we were here, I doubt anyone would give it credence."

"Very good, Colonel Quantrill!" Holt clapped Quantrill on the shoulder. "Let me offer you my congratulations on your promotion. I knew you were a captain . . . " He let that hang in the air between them but Quantrill coolly waited him out with that dreamy-eyed expression he would get before something terrible occurred, a languid smile playing under his moustache, as Holt appeared to measure him. When Quantrill retained his nonchalant dignity and offered no defense—Holt politely filled the void, saying, "We'd be proud to accompany you and do what we can."

"It's a dangerous move. We're outnumbered ten to one. But it's one we are fully committed to undertaking." Quantrill said. "I know we can use you and your men. We may have some thick fighting for them long before we reach the town itself. You can christen your recruits in Kansas."

"Indeed! Christen them we shall!" Holt rode up ahead disturbing the dust of the road before us until his trembling image vanished into a mythical sea on the horizon.

It was August 21, 1863. The Day of Wrath. The town of Lawrence lay before us just as the pink fingers of dawn began to appear. It was already warm and it looked like another day of temperatures close to one hundred degrees. Many of us, myself included, were still tied into our saddles after riding almost nonstop for a day and a half. Most of us had never been there before nor expected to make it so far into Jayhawker country without encountering a stout defense. It was an impressive town to look upon from the heights of Mount Oread. It was much larger than I had thought to begin with and the streets ran north to south and east to west. There were about three thousand inhabitants. It was clear to see where the fine homes of the city were located. We could see the business district and just where the city butted up against the Kansas River. Dave Pool and his men would stay here to keep a sharp lookout for any Federal activity. The Eldridge House was a stunning four-story affair that Captain Bill and Arch pointed out to me.

"A fine place, worth visiting. But I wouldn't want to live

there." Arch cocked a sardonic eyebrow at the irony of his own remark. "It's where the fine people of substance stay. Just ask Lieutenant Fletch Taylor. He stayed there a couple of weeks back and reconnoitered the situation. Lawrence is ripe for the taking."

Not all of us felt so spry. "I have a terrible feeling about this place," Cole said, wallowing in a state of drunken bereavement.

"What is it? An omen?" I asked.

"I don't think I'll make it back alive." He shook his head like a shade in Homer remembering past glories. His face was ashen. I chalked it up to the popskull he'd had the night before.

"We'll be all right, old son," I said, hoping to cheer him up. He tried to give me a brave grin, but it kept sliding off the side of his face. "Maybe those quail eggs you ate for breakfast just disagreed with you."

"Ashby," he said. Tears had welled up in his eyes, but he didn't bother to wipe them away. "I have to tell you something. I decided I'm too young to die. If I ride into that town, I'll never ride back out. I wish you could pull out your bible and give me a reading on my future. Why, I haven't even laid down with a woman proper yet. That ain't right, is it?"

I made no comment. If he hadn't been so shy, I'm sure Bill or Jim Anderson would have lined him up with a sporting woman. Events had crept up on us and there just hadn't been time for these kinds of issues to come to the fore. I hadn't cracked open the Good Book for awhile and now did not seem to be the proper time. Instead I told Cole the story of how Joshua took the walled city of Jericho. It did not have the effect upon him I hoped it would have.

"Some may think so," Cole said, "but this don't seem like no righteous conquest to me."

"They had the Ark of the Covenant," I said. "Any army that

has it is supposed to be impossible to defeat. Invincible."

Cole fell over at the waist and leaned down across the neck of his horse and vomited. Some other boys laughed at him. Cole croaked, "We could use it about now."

"Here is your symbol!" I wore a silver cross about my neck and took it off now. I held it up for him to see. "Put out your hand!' He did as I commanded. "No weapon formed against you shall prosper!" I put the cross in his hand as his horse shied away. Then I put my heels to Infernal and off we went. There wasn't anything else stronger I could say to him.

Even though we'd made it past General Ewing's border outposts unscathed, not all seemed encouraged. I heard many of our inexperienced young men grumbling about how large the town was. Some were saying there was no way we could attack a place so large without serious repercussions. Wasn't there a home guard? someone asked tremulously. Before Quantrill gave the order to attack, I even heard one faithless soul cry out, "We are lost!" The veteran riding next to him cuffed him roughly on the ear. This was not the sort of remark that inspired confidence before a fight.

Colonel Quantrill conferred with several of our captains over a bit of paper he referred to as "the death list." It contained a map of all the known enemies of Missouri and where they lived in Lawrence. Senator and hated Jayhawker Jim Lane was high on the list. The death list also gave us a key to work with so we could find the other prominent townspeople, including newspaper editors like Horace Greeley of the *Herald Tribune,* who had printed many vile and untrue words besmirching our honor and our country over the years. Men of this caliber were ultimately the ones responsible for the abolitionist presence that had beleaguered our people and caused the murder of our women. All I could think about was revenge for Lizzie and stepping on the necks of fat and prosperous Kansans.

Quantrill positioned himself on horseback before us to give a speech beforehand. He knew how to enthrall young men. There was a mood among some of the men that did not bode well for the work we were about to do, and Quantrill knew it. His hat was in his hand and he sat his horse before us for a moment to get our attention before combing at a cowlick with his off hand. He was particularly good at playing the role of benevolent leader in this sort of situation. It was what many of the younger boys loved him for.

"You, one and all, will understand that the undertaking we are about to commence is one of extreme hazard. It might be that the entire command will be overwhelmed, the ranks decimated as they never have been before. So, I say to one and all, if any refuse to go along, they will not be censured."

Cole sat his horse but he looked like his mind wavered on the question. I knew Quantrill's lizard nature well enough now to know that the proverbial man he spoke of might not be *censured* but he sure as hell would be shot. The ropes binding Cole to his mount were still tight and he fingered them absently, deep in thought. I didn't want to see him go because we had become thick as thieves. He struggled with his conscience and his fear and rode off a ways to avoid my eyes. I had never seen him so morose. Not over fighting. Cole Maddox was the kind of boy who loved nothing better than a fight. I was not sure what he would decide to do but like the Colonel said it would be better for men who didn't have the stomach for it to leave now rather than disappearing when action was called for.

Quantrill's myrmidons looked down at the ground or up to the heavens or at the town below and weighed their futures against what fame or plunder they might gain. A half dozen men arose, went to their horses, and rode away, hooves pounding the earth. Quantrill nodded as much to himself as to the rest of the men. It was difficult to believe that in the face of such a generous speech, any of the men could have had a crisis of faith or allowed their names to be associated with cowardice, but after these men rode away, the colonel continued with his vitriolic speech and spoke of the murderous robbers of Kansas and how everything that had been taken from Missouri over the past two years would be found there in Lawrence. We could take it back and more! Of course, there were the mercenaries among us; rough lads who had come all this way in full expectation of plunder and the spoils of war. He might have lost command for some time after the incident with Captain Todd, but today he was firmly in control. This was his command and his actions this day would reverberate across the country.

The men were formed into units and given specific orders. Nothing was going to be left to chance. Cole was nowhere to be found. I stood up in my stirrups to get a better look around but he was gone. I relaxed into the saddle. No doubt I would see him later.

Hi Guess threw his overcoat down in the brush. "I aim to get me a new one down there," he announced. Several other men agreed and soon a heap of coats littered the ground like some new kind of shrubbery.

"Kill every man big enough to carry a gun!" Quantrill commanded.

Someone gave a shrill rebel yell and others joined in! We mounted up and rode into town by way of Massachusetts Street, discharging our guns at any man fool enough to stick his head out a door to investigate the situation. I followed Captain Bill's command. When I tell you that I looked around and had every confidence in men like Frank, Arch, and the bunch I rode with— so much that I felt invincible in their presence—it should not be discounted. We were going to get our revenge for all the terrible things we had endured while forced to fight from the nooks and crannies in the wilderness like gray ghosts. The boys were worked up now, giving the rebel yell, screaming like the Indians out in the territories.

The acrid smell of burning wood and breakfast sausage cooking on a stove came from a nearby house. Suddenly, without warning, Infernal stepped in a hole before I even had made it into the town proper. I was sent sprawling in a painful manner on the ground. I was laid out like that for some time in an undignified position, but eventually I shook my head and rolled over and sat up. I checked my aching shin bone on my right leg and tested my wretched back. I was fine other than what would amount to bruises and wounded pride. One of my eyes burned and I put my hand to my forehead and felt some blood there. Infernal had not gotten too far away. I collected the reins and checked him over to be sure he had not suffered any sort of debilitating injury, but he was fine. The others were long ahead of me now. I touched at the cut on my forehead with the back of my sleeve and more blood came away. I made a bandage out of my spare shirt to stop the flow. I knew from experience that head wounds bled more profusely than just about any other kind.

There was no telling where Captain Bill had gotten to now. I got back up on my horse and hupped at a trot into town. My head was throbbing, but I did not want to miss out, either. I saw one of ours forcing a mature lady with an aristocratic look and two children at her skirts to put the torch to her own home. Instead of feeling satisfied with this kind of retribution, I began to think of Lizzie being crushed in the Kansas City prison and all our friends and family who had been forced from their homes at gunpoint and ordered to leave the country forever.

Gunfire was popping all over town. The smell of smoke filled the air and there were screams of terror and men shouting. Not too far away I heard a woman's voice crying out, "He's not here, he's not here, sweet Jesus, he's not here . . ." It was the sound of a woman trying to protect her husband. It was all too clear she had hid him away in a secret hiding place, perhaps under the floorboards of the house. It didn't matter, though, since they were going to burn the place to the ground. It was heartrending to hear, but he *was* there! Whoever *he* was. He was doomed. Our men would find him and kill him.

I couldn't help wondering if anyone would weep like that for me, if my life were in danger.

"Kill them! Kill them all!"

"Remember Osceola!"

"Remember the girls!"

I figured I should find Captain Bill and the others, so I began to ride a bit more purposely. The sight of my own blood had unnerved me.

I was attempting to remember where Captain Bill had been ordered to when an old man came around the side of a white-washed shed in his nightshirt. He was pointing a blunderbuss at me from his hip with his crazed, maniacal rusty gut's face grinning at me through his wrinkled death mask of a face. He pulled the trigger but his charge must not have been exactly right as it seemed to blow up in his hands. The old geezer's face fell in disappointment then and with both hands he threw the entire weapon at me with wicked intent, not unlike a hatchet thrower, but I calmly pulled out the Lefaucheux and shot him in the forehead. He went down with a surprised expression as though he had been sure of his own immortality and this death were a stage play.

Just ahead I saw a group of us, loosely in fours, and before them was an encampment of white military tents in a clearing. A few Yankees were coming out of their tents just in time for our boys to put them down like curs. As I rode closer, a big though very young lad came out of one of the tents with his hands in the air screaming, "I surrender, I surrender," and he was shot immediately for his efforts. We hadn't come all this way to take prisoners, we had come to kill!

With revolvers on full cock, we fired a few volleys into the tents from a good distance away, and many of the tents were stained bloodred from the inside out. The cowards refused to come out and fight us. A rough voice was demanding that the remainder of the soldiers cowering in the tent city come out to meet their savior in Glory, but they flatly refused and huddled like rabbits instead. I watched four horses abreast ride over the tents and stomp the soldiers into the earth where they trembled. This caused some of the soldiers to come out unarmed and they were also killed by our guns. The ones who didn't were riddled with bullets where they lay.

As I rode up to one of the tents, I saw a smallish man in blue dash out of the tent with something in his hand. I assumed it was a gun and I shot him square in the chest where a red flower bloomed against the field of his blue shirt. As I rode up to him and realized to my horror that the small man I had shot was no more than a boy of thirteen or fourteen with a hand-carved wooden gun in his hand. Two little boys came out of the same tent and were openly weeping with their hands down at their sides, and again I had the terrible realization that none of these tent-city Yankees were real soldiers at all but merely children playing at war. I'm sure that camping out with the other boys had been a great lark for them until we arrived. It wasn't hard to feature them shouting each other down in fun over which one had killed Quantrill.

One of the boys was even crying and rubbing at his eyes in terror as anyone would do when they know eternal death may be near. The young man looked up at me as if he weren't sure what my disposition toward him might be, until I grabbed him up by the collar of his uniform so that he half clung to my saddle and dropped him off in the arms of a matronly woman standing at the door of a small residence. He looked like a neighbor boy, one of the Gaithers, back in Howard County.

"Thank you, thank you!" The woman ushered the boy into her house. "Save Billy, too!"

The bigger boy I had not been able to save was running toward the woman when he was shot in the back. "Don't murder me!" he squealed, reaching over his head in an attempt to claw at the bullet now lodged in his spine.

"No quarter for you Federal sons-of-bitches," a vaguely familiar voice growled. It was Captain Todd's man, Ed Speight, in his porkpie hat. Now he was staring me down like I might be next. Smoke from a burning mercantile partially obscured him: an exceptionally tall man on a large black horse. There was something about his face that could only be described as mercenary. His eyes were set far back in his head as if he had spent half of his life living underground in a cave. I would never forget the man for he was a lunger. The idea of shooting him right then and there flashed briefly in my mind. It might be best to get the jump on him.

"Ha! Come on with me, Preacher! We ain't here to save souls! Captain Todd told me if I saw you in town to keep my eye on you."

"You just killed a child!" I said. Truth be told, I wanted to give him an anointing like he never had in his life.

"What of it? He was big enough to put on the Federal blue and their kind need some thinning out! You can't deny that. C'mon with us!"

"I'm supposed to be with Captain Bill."

"Well, why ain't ya then?"

"My horse stepped in a hole on the charge into town."

"That right?" He turned and fired a shot at a red-haired man brandishing a hoe who appeared to be the type more comfortable in the burning mercantile than fighting 'whackers out in the street.

"Come with me and I'll watch your back." He said it with a lilt to his voice that I did not care for, but I felt compelled to do as he said, whether out of fear since he was Todd's man or it could have been the kind of dread inevitability that leads us to accept our fate. So follow him I did.

Just then I saw that other preacher, my doppleganger if you will, Larkin Skaggs, riding and shooting his revolvers into the air like a madman, the tattered Union flag tied to the tail of his horse. His voice rose and fell like a savage as he rode down the street singing a drunken melody.

"The secesh is here! The secesh is here!" A redhaired woman was screaming until her voice seemed to be cut off in mid cry.

"Where to, now?" I said.

"Come with us," Speight whooped. "We're under orders to kill all their pet nigger soldiers."

I nodded and rode on with him as the darkness that had followed me around since father's death began to grow inside me like a dark forest.

We arrived at another camp, but there were no soldiers present. It was where a colored regiment was supposed to be, according to Speight, but now the little campsite was completely empty. Captain Todd came riding up with two men flanking him on each side. He was fuming that the entire colored regiment had hightailed it out of town at the first sound of shots fired. The air clattered like fireworks around us.

"Wouldn't you know it would be the niggers to escape scotfree! Send some men down near the river where they may be hiding in the underscrub!"

"Captain Todd!" Speight said. "Look who we have here. It's one of Bill's gang. The one they call Preacher."

"Well now," Todd said gruffly. "Did Bill decide to get shed of you?"

"No, sir," I said. "My horse stepped in a hole."

"That's what he told me too." Speight shook his head.

It crossed my mind that one or the other of them might shoot me as a way of getting back at Captain Bill. As I looked at each of their faces, it was clear as day they wanted to kill me but had yet to think of a cunning way to pull it off, even though Captain Bill had no more love for me than for a Yankee pig at that stage. I was just another recruit who might make the cut or who might be killed in some unjust, pathetic way. The duo seemed like the sort who might kill anyone it suited them to kill, no matter which side of the war they fought on. Todd and his men were straight murderers, from what I had observed, and cared more about the plunder. I'd heard one of his own men say he was not even from this country but immigrants were a common thing so it didn't seem particularly damning on its own. If I let my guard down, one of them would kill me dead. I knew that as soon as I saw Todd and Speight with their heads together.

"I hope you weren't thinking on deserting, Preacher," Todd said. "We shoot deserters."

"I'm no deserter," I hissed belligerently. "I'll take it as an offending remark to anyone who would accuse me of cowardice."

"Well, well," Captain Todd said in a snide tone. "That's just what we were hoping to hear. I remember this one, don't you? But the last time, he didn't have that peach fuzz on his face."

"Yes," Speight said. "He's the one who buddies up with spies. I believe he's a nigger lover too. Wasn't he in love with one of his daddy's niggers?"

"You are one grievous man who deserves death from me evil spirit." I kept my eyes on Speight.

Speight laughed heartily at my speech. He clapped his hands condescendingly.

"My," Todd said, "But I hope you don't shoot me. Such a hard man as yourself!"

"Don't patronize me." I cocked my revolver and leveled it at Todd. The look on his face made me want to smile, though my legs were trembling. I knew him to be a bloodthirsty cuss. "I will blow you right out of your saddle."

"I could see you hanged for this," Todd hissed. "Instead, I'll have you put down. William T. can go to hell!"

"I knew you would try something," I said in reply. "I don't aim to stick my head in a noose for dishonorable trash like you two until I've had my revenge on the Red Legs!"

"Speight!" Captain Todd spun his mount around and roared

over his shoulder. "Kill him. Then meet me at the house of that demon Reverend Fisher! He's on the death list! We must send all Union-loving preachers off to the bosom of their Yankee messiah."

Todd rode off hard as though I were already dead.

Speight kicked his stolen appaloosa and came at me. Suddenly the big man was on me. His horse shouldered Infernal. Off I went, into the dirt. A Colt went flying out of my hand but I pulled out a Bowie knife I always kept at my waist, although it was not much protection against a pistol. *This is how I die.* That was the measure of my thinking at the moment. I recall this thought and the emotion of knowing my life was likely done. It was obvious that Speight found me insignificant as an adversary, owing to my youth and diminutive size.

Fighting a man on a horse is generally a losing proposition. Infernal had been getting better in the thick of battle as of late. In truth, I think it was because he was going deaf, so the shots did not appear to alarm him as much as before. He stood his ground. I grabbed his bridle near the bit to keep his body between myself and Speight. Speight tried to shoot me in the head over my horse but he did not have a good angle. The horses were bumping chests and biting and kicking at one another. I saw the barrel of his gun trying to reach around the neck of Infernal, so I grabbed at his wrist and yanked him as hard as I could and pulled him to the ground with the help of his being off balance in the saddle. I always figured the man was strong so I was quick and on his back and intended to draw my blade across his neck. There was a danger we would both be crushed by the horses.

"What!" Speight said in outrage.

"There's many a slip between the cup and lip," I taunted.

I knocked off his porkpie hat and grabbed a handful of hair; then I yanked back hard to expose the neck, but I could feel his strength in the way he resisted, and just as I was making the cut across his neck—I was determined to cut his head off if I could—a sudden strike to my back sent me reeling off Speight. I was dazed, but in my hands was the knife and a hank of Speight's hair.

One of the horses had kicked me in their scuffle. Again fate had snarled at me. I saw Speight limping and staggering down the street among other horses and panicked townfolk running to and fro, holding his neck in one hand and cursing. He disappeared around a building. I willed myself to get up before he brought back Todd or anyone else to help against me. *No weapon formed against me shall prosper.* I quoted the scripture from Isaiah as a comfort. Infernal hadn't migrated too far away. I pulled up into the saddle. I shot Speight's horse in the head. The beast fell dead as a hammer though Speight would simply steal another. It was a hopeless gesture if anything. Perhaps I thought he would get stranded in Lawrence when the boys left. The noise of a waterfall of bloody rage coursed through my ears.

"We showed them blighted sons-of-bitches!" I said to Infernal. His ears twitched and his hide quivered. He let go a rumbling in his chest in answer.

This skirmish had not lasted nearly as long as I'd thought. There was still much to be done. I was all for rounding up our enemies—the ones on the circulating death lists. Others were more wont to pillage the town, although I wasn't sure how some of them thought they would take their treasures all the way back to Missouri when we would likely have every able-bodied man in Kansas on horseback hot to catch us. Give me a purse full of greenbacks, a new hat, and fine boots. I would buy my own treasure when the time was right.

The world I saw was blurry from my fight with Speight. Many of the important buildings were on fire and smoke rolled from their windows. I saw my own reflection in the warped, old-time windows walking like a nightmare preacher through the smoke. I pulled my handkerchief up over my nose and mouth to keep from breathing in the tainted air. A couple of partisans hopped like magpies around a woman who was pleading with them not to kill her husband. The man she was trying to protect wore a stunned expression and was exceedingly pale. She circled around her husband's body making herself a shield with a flurry of petticoats as she appeared to dance around him. Her voice carried down the street as she went back and forth between English and German.

The men all had their pistols drawn as they each sought a good line on the man, who I perceived to be a lowly muleteer, she was shielding. "Step aside you Dutch bitch!" She did her best to keep herself between both parties. One of the boys managed to shoot her man in the shoulder. The woman held up the palm of her hand as if to stop it with flesh and bone.

"He is one tough son-of-a-bitch to kill!" one cried. Another one said, "Let me try." The pestiferous woman's hand was always in contact with her man, and at one point she threw open her arms as though she could stop any bullet with the sheer force of her will and her love. The macabre scene finally played itself out when she stumbled over a rock and tumbled to the ground. Her husband was left fully exposed and the boys let him have it. "Damn the Dutch!" They were laughing at the sport of it. The whole altercation had been entertaining to them.

The woman screamed. She jumped up immediately, just in time to watch her husband crumple to the ground. There was nothing to be done for him now, but she cradled him in her arms and spoke to him as he was not yet dead. Our boys conferred amongst themselves for a moment. A red-haired regulator caught a horse; another soldier dragged the man's wife a few yards away and made it rear up to trample the man, but it only came down on his legs and he cried out in pain. Finally the red-haired man slid off his horse, leaned in close to the man's face to murmur something hateful and cut the German's throat.

Further down the street, two drunk men were ignorantly arguing over a grand piano outside a burning residence as if they could carry it away on their backs all the way to Missouri. A pale woman with yellow hair piled high, wearing a long black dress, watched mutely with her daughter. She looked like a widow already. I felt sorry for her, but not too much, since the piano probably came from a Southern woman's parlor. The men's pockets were overstuffed with greenbacks, and around their necks they wore what I took to be the lady's necklaces.

"Whose home is this?" I asked.

"We're guarding it so nobody puts the fire out!"

Both of their faces were blackened by the fire and smoke. No doubt they had been inside the house even after they had started the fire.

"Whose home is it?"

"He's awfully demanding," one of them said to his companion.

"He don't look as old as my little brother, either that or he's got a baby face," said the other and spat a stream of tobacco juice.

"Them's the kind you got to watch out for." He took a swig of popskull whiskey. "They's the meanest, they is, because they don't value life, having to fight so hard to get by." He burped out of the side of his mouth.

"Ha! You couldn't be serious at your own execution!"

"It's that damn degenerate Jim Lane's house." The comedian was reaching for the whiskey, though his companion didn't look ready to turn loose of it. They appeared to be friends or maybe even brothers, with a beef. Both of the men held revolvers down by their sides. Just from observing them, I thought it appeared one might shoot the other before the flame devoured the better part of the house.

"Did you get him?"

"Who?"

"Lane! Did you kill him?"

I stole a glance at the man's wife, but she stood stoically and pretended not to hear. How could she have married that particular fiend? She looked proudly away from the house and she seemed to be remembering a happier time. Her dress was torn and dirty and she wore it backwards. Her hair was in partial disarray about her shoulders.

I remembered seeing the remains of the Bradford family outside of Lexington after Lane had rode through. He was a famous Freesoiler. None of us had forgotten how he had burned Osceola up. Some of the men were shouting and murmuring "Osceola" when we first rode into town. The senator had done so many evil deeds personally against people from our part of the country that it made every one of us spit just to say his name aloud. Now it was his fine new house going up in smoke. Lane would not be surveying his fine fields from that colonnaded veranda ever again, unless he rebuilt her.

"Naw," he shook his head sadly. "She said he's not here."

Lane's wife was silent. This bears repeating because of the

din and litany many of the other women raised, begging us not to kill their husbands, not to fire their homes or unburden the family of its savings. The lady stood strong in her stillness, which seemed to set her apart. She was not morose with shock as some were. Her demeanor was entirely different, singular. Silently she stood by with her daughter's hand ensnarled in her own gritty claw. No doubt she had learned a great deal about forbearance; most certainly she had, taking blows from a man like Lane. Her magnificent new home was burned down to the flat Kansas dirt. It was clear to me, as it should have been to her, where the finances had come from to raise it. Red ash from her burning home flittered around us almost like thistledown in the wind.

"Lookee here, what we did get! Show him, Payne."

The young man grinned as he unfolded a patch of cloth into a ceremonial battle flag. They held the flag up between them as it grew larger, grinning for me to see. It was Jim Lane's black flag with an inscription sewed in fine yellow script: *Presented to Gen. James H. Lane by the Ladies of Leavenworth.* They always talked about Quantrill's boys riding under the black flag, but this was one of the few I saw with my own two eyes.

"Bet they give him a little cunny besides this here flag." The boy laughed and grinned like a lunatic.

I gave him a resounding smack on the side of his head for the way he spoke in the presence of the lady. Still, she seemed unperturbed by the boy. She was silent and fixed her deadly Medusa stare on the boys who had put the house to the torch. Finally, she did speak briefly to Colonel Quantrill when he rode up on a carriage. You see, he was overseeing the entire raid, but he was not participating in the mayhem.

"Speak of the Devil," Mrs. Lane said. Her lips went prudish

like a woman sucking on a lemon.

"Speak of the Devil," Quantrill answered, "and the Devil appears."

He tipped his hat to Mrs. Lane, and with that disingenuous, half-mast smile of his said how sorry he was to have missed Mr. Lane.

Mrs. Lane replied with controlled venom between grinding teeth, "And Mr. Lane would be glad to meet you too under more favorable circumstances!" Then she went mute again, after Quantrill was driven off to survey his work in another part of town.

"The big fish got away!" I said. "I hate Lane almost as much as I hate Jennison!"

"Damn, but he's a slippery bastard!"

"He's a devil in the raw," I said to the rider, who cast a familiar shadow. It was none other than Gideon's old childhood friend from back home, John Thrailkill. I recognized his manner of speech more than his physical appearance. His hair was longer. Now he wore a moustache and beard that gave him a wolfish appearance. His eyes seemed an even paler shade of blue than I remembered. The brown guerilla shirt he wore had a swath of blood across the chest, which I thought was his own at first, but it was from some poor unfortunate devil he had killed. Even had I not recognized him, I would have recognized that buffalo gun anywhere, sheathed and tied in a long, custom-made scabbard alongside the horse. The gun marked him as a sharpshooter.

"John!" I urged Infernal over and shook hands with him. Just seeing him made me think of being a boy and how I'd worshipped him and Gideon. I remembered his marksmanship with the buffalo gun when the Indians had chased us down south. I could not contain my pleasure and excitement. "It's good to see you! So good to see you!"

He smiled, but it was plain he was not the same man I'd known. Talk about your strange reunions.

"What are you doing here? You riding with Quantrill now? You always did want to take things to extremes," he said.

"Not at all," I said. "I ride with Captain Bill Anderson."

"Well, now," he said, "I've been hearing wild stories about him."

"Who are you serving under these days?"

"First this one," John said, "then that. Anyone who I think might pay best. I'm in it for the money now. They thinned us out pretty good. I'm just trying to get through this war alive."

"Where were you on the ride?"

"I was scouting ahead for Captain Todd," he said.

"Oh, no," I said. He looked at me as if he didn't understand. I related my observations about the strange tension between Todd and Anderson and my run-in with Speight.

"Keep your head about you," John said. "Todd is brutal. Speight will do anything he says. Killing comes as easy to them both as breathing. I don't trust either of them, but they're willing to go where angels fear to tread. I've got more money socked away now in a Kansas City bank than I'll likely ever make honestly for the rest of my life."

"I killed Speight's horse," I said.

"He will definitely be after you now," John said. "He loved that horse. I think he had congress with that horse more than once on our ride to Texas last winter."

"Well," I said, "he pissed me off. Todd ordered him to kill me like I wasn't nothing."

"They'll want to make good on it too, I'm afraid to tell you."

"Is Gid with you?" I almost didn't want to ask him.

"About that," he said. "Come ride with me to the Eldridge Hotel. It's one of the places we have to secure. Armed men could hold all of us off there until help came. The place is built as solid as any fort of stout brick. It might be a trick taking her. Oh, there's a company of Kansans on the other side of the river who are taking potshots at anyone who rides by. Their sharps have hit a few men. Not bad shooting, I'd say, but just thought I'd mention it. Stay well away from the river. There's nothing down there of value anyway, except a couple of houses that have already been ransacked."

He went on, telling me what I was most desperate to hear: "Gid was wounded trying to protect the family from the home guard. They were looking for the both of you but only found him. There was no one to help him, but I understand he gave a good account of himself, as always. Didn't your mother tell you?"

"I haven't talked to any of them for a while," I said. "I figured they got sent away by Ewing like everybody else."

Just at that moment, gunfire erupted on the main street leading to the hotel. I was turned around, never having been to Lawrence before, so I followed John closely. There were dead men littering the sidewalks and out in the street. It was an uncommon scene that did not sit right in mind or soul.

When we reached our destination, there was a big knot of us gathered on horseback in front of the Eldridge. Nobody was shooting now. There was tension in the faces of the men as they considered who could be in the hotel. Some wondered aloud if whoever was in there was military and they speculated amongst themselves if they had the wherewithal to hold her. The men were shouting and cursing. I thought I caught a glimpse of Cole on the other end of the street but he rode on.

A gong from the hotel sounded.

The men went silent and we backed our horses closer to the buildings across the street, expecting the shooting to start at anytime. I was looking at the upper windows for gun barrels to appear or men with rifles on the roof of the building. This might be where they'd make their stand. It would be a smart choice because of the sturdy brick construction of the place.

In one of the upper windows, a white sheet was thrust out and a gruff voice called, "We surrender! We surrender! Don't shoot!" Quantrill rode forward confidently and waved us to dismount and take the hotel.

We had taken it without a shot! A hurrah went up from our men.

"May I ask who I have the pleasure of addressing?" Quantrill asked.

"Captain Alexander Banks," the man said, "Provost Marshall of Kansas. What do you want with Lawrence?"

"Plunder!" Quantrill answered.

Our men cheered. Quantrill's horse reared up and he waved his hat at us triumphantly. It was quite a sight to behold. It was just such a gesture that endeared him to the men over the years.

Captain Banks came out the front door of the hotel holding his pistol backward in his gloved hand. He had dark black hair and wore a neat Van Dyke. His uniform was immaculate as if he had freshly donned it for the pomp and circumstance of the moment.

"We are defenseless and at your mercy," Captain Banks said and handed his sidearm over with a seemingly practiced sangfroid. "The hotel is surrendered, but we demand protection for the residents."

"Agreed! I'll take some men and secure the hotel, but the rest of you . . . kill and you will make no mistake! Lawrence should be thoroughly cleansed and the only way to cleanse it is to kill!"

Quantrill dismounted and stationed guards before entering the hotel.

The rest of us thundered off down the street looking for more trouble. Some of our men had already broken into the saloons. They were drinking from their own bottles. It was yet morning and the business district was an inferno. The fire was roaring, and the once-proud buildings of the town sent smoking pillars into the air, like incense to our vengeful god. There were bodies littering the ground. Some bodies, those too close to the buildings, were already blackened and crisped from the flames.

The rising thunderhead of smoke would draw Federal troops eventually. I was determined not to kill any more than I had to, especially after seeing those little boys playing soldier slaughtered the way they had been. Anyone who pointed a gun at me or came after me was going to have to die, but I had no interest in going on a shooting spree the way some of our men were. This was supposed to be a fight, but there were no men prepared to give us one. Most of the ones we had really wanted had either hightailed it out or were away from home for one reason or another.

Men were riding up and down the streets wearing jewelry they had stolen from stores. Some wore matched and mismatched new clothing from the finer homes they had looted and were drinking beer and smoking fine cigars. John Thrailkill came out of the mercantile with a new pistol and cigar for me. I thanked him, but I would be glad to be heading back to Missouri after the others had their fun. He was taking long draughts of fizzing good whiskey. He offered me a shot in the neck, but I was in no mood for drinking. He commented on the sallow complexion of my face.

I was terribly conflicted with wanting to do right, but at the same time I wanted to take revenge for Lizzie. The notion popped into my head to kill Jim Lane's wife and daughter, as terrible as that sounds. There was a part of me that wanted to rape them both, slit their throats, hear their cries, and then mount their heads on poles. But as soon as I thought it, I grew cold and was afraid. I feared I would do what I was capable of—what any one of us is capable of under the wrong circumstances. As evidence before me, many of our rangers were committing riotous acts.

Bill's words revisited me, from an evening when we had settled down for a few hours in the mouth of a cave near the river town of Rocheport. His face was long and green that night like the moss on the slick cave rocks in the flickering light of the flame and he spoke in his growly whisper.

"Vengeance is in my heart and in my hand."

What stopped me from exacting mine? I'll tell you what stopped me, mister. It was the knowledge that these were not the people directly responsible for my Lizzie's death. Those men had been in Kansas City and served under General Ewing. These people here might have been culpable for other things, but Lizzie's death was not one of them. They might accuse us all of being cold-blooded murderers; I still had a conscience. A good angel still spoke to me, even at my worst. Not that I didn't approve of the action we had taken but I would rather have fought it on a more honorable front. We had fallen to the level of the abolitionists and Jayhawkers we hated. We had repaid evil with evil, and now the cycle would only continue. To speak truth, I could not have said those words then since they were just swirly emotions. And even if I'd formed them, they were words I would never have spoken to the other boys I rode with.

I walked my horse with Thrailkill, the marksman, and we observed the destruction around us. The town was choking on smoke and fire. Women were shrieking. Children were sitting in the streets crying over their dead fathers.

Thrailkill was hardened to it all. More than I could ever be, even if I lived a dozen more lives. He had already stuffed his pockets with greenbacks and jewelry. He offered to share some with me, but I thanked him and said no, I already had my share and wanted no more blood money. He asked if I wanted some of his whiskey.

"No sir," I said. I did not want any of it.

He took a generous chug out of it. John gave me an appraising look. "You think you're better than me, Ashby?" John said. "Because you're the chosen son of Reverend Marchbank? You're looking down your nose at me? I loved your daddy but these Jayhawkers killed him without mercy. They strung him up. Choked the life out of him with their abolition ropes. Where was God then? I suppose you think the old man's up there with Jesus strumming on a harp?"

"Oh, no, John," I said. "I was there! I saw it. No need to preach to me." I didn't know where he got the notion I was disappointed or thought him in the wrong, but I tended to watch and study people longer than I should. It could be I'd lingered too long with a look, and he perceived it as me taking it upon myself to be judge and jury over his life. I hadn't said anything, but I guess he could tell what was on my mind, and he didn't approve because he felt differently.

"I think that's exactly what you're figuring." John glared at me. "This just some wild hair you got to join up with the bushwhackers because Gideon did? You ain't so fine, you know. Your brother was the good one. You'll never stack up to him. Come with me."

He was fuming and rode ahead of me. We went down to Eldridge and Ford's clothing store, and there were two boys about my age busily retrieving fine shirts, vests, coats, and hats for our boys. They were not the aforementioned gentlemen of the store's name, but it amused John to refer to one boy as Mr. Eldridge and to the slightly older and taller boy as Mr. Ford. In truth, they were just boys who worked for the owners and, in exchange, were paid a wage and allowed to sleep in the back room of a night.

"We would both like a new set of gentleman's clothes, Mr. Eldridge," John said. "Money is no object as I don't intend on paying. I hope that is agreeable with you boys?"

"Yes, sir!" one of the boys said, unnaturally eager. Mr. Ford I guess it was. "Yes, sir." The boy ran to the back room and came out in no time with a white shirt, a fine yellow cravat of silk, and a nice brown suit. He helped John undress and dress up again in his new duds.

"Now, this is how to help a customer," John said. "I hope you're catching all this, Colonel Marchbank? Mr. Ford here knows how to treat his clientele."

The boy smiled affably enough at this remark and began to nod so hard I thought his head might tip off at the neck.

"Looks like I'm going to need new boots, eh Mr. Ford?"

I didn't want to be waited on hand and foot, but the boy did give me new boots and a black jacket, which was probably the most expensive piece of clothing I ever owned before or since. Then much to my dismay, John pulled out his pistol and shot the boy dead in the face where he stood, still holding John's old clothes over his arm like a butler. His mouth made a perfect O of surprise before he slipped into the eternal floorboards at our feet.

"Why did you do that?" I asked. "He didn't deserve that."

"Oh, didn't he, Preacher?" John said "Preacher" with great contempt in his voice. He spat on the floor. "Now you kill the other one."

"Don't call me Preacher."

"You kill him," John demanded. "Oh, Mr. Eldridge, I believe your associate has taken ill. Could you step over here a moment and assist General Marchbank in procuring a fine new outfit?"

"Yessir," the other boy said. He had heard the report of the gun from the back room and how ashen his face was now. He began to whimper and cry at the sight of the bloody gore. He stepped over the body of the other as though it were a box of inventory to be maneuvered around. He held out his hands before him in a self-conscious display. "How-how-how-how, m-may I help?"

"Go ahead," John pointed his pistol at me. "Tell him how he can help. Tell him he can help by dying."

"Oh, dear Jesus." the boy went down on his knees in front of us. He clapped his hands together with the earnest of the worst sinner I had ever heard of. "Please don't kill me too, mister. Oh, please! I'm no soldier and I won't tell. Just please, please! I'm just a boy."

"Shut all that up!" John tapped the boy on his forehead with the nose of his pistol. "I want to see you shoot him. Don't worry. He can't hurt you. You walk around with guns like a big man, but I ain't seen you use them yet."

"Well," I said, "I assure you that I have used them every one. I'm not a murderer."

"Bullshit. I want to see you unholster that piece and send this boy to glory. Now."

"I ain't like you, John."

"I said, Now!"

I couldn't help jump when he yelled like that. The Lefaucheux was in my hand. It was tapping against my leg. He reached down and taking the end of it between his thumb and forefinger brought it to rest on the forehead of the boy's upturned face. Tears flowed from his eyes. He started croaking in a forlorn way. The barrel rested still on the boy, but I refused to fire. What right did I have to end his life? A boy like this that had done nothing to me. Instead of shooting him I holstered it.

"You can go, Mr. Eldridge," I said. "Don't show yourself again for the rest of the day."

The boy looked relieved, but before he could rise, John had more to say about it.

"Think of Lizzie!" John snarled. "Think of how terrible her death was and then I'll bet you can do it. Crushed to death in that Federal building. This here boy is just as guilty as the ones who weakened the foundations of the building. They're all abolitionist bastards. They won't let you live, so why do you have a feeling for any of them?"

"Why are you doing this?" I asked without looking at him. I continued to stare at the boy before us. His eyes were mottled brown with yellow swirls in them. "He is just a boy. What good would it do to kill him?"

He turned and quick as a snake he flicked his pistol at the boy and it barked out death.

"Killing people just seems to make me feel better," John said. He started to walk out of the store, but I remained where I was.

"Come with me now if you ain't a coward."

"I ain't."

Just then a middle-aged, hawk-faced man came down the steps. I suspected he might be one of the real owners of the establishment. He glanced at the bodies of his employees and lifted a rifle up to his shoulder, meaning to kill John but his aim was off, and the shot ripped into the wall near the front door instead. Without thinking I pulled the Lefaucheux and shot the man in the arm, although I was trying to kill him. John looked at me and nodded his head like I had finally shown him the beast in me he had wanted to see.

"How did you like that, Mr. Eldridge?" John strode over to the old man and put his boot on the man's wound.

"I'm Ford, you secesh trash!" The old man was trying with one hand to pry one of John's boots off. He screamed in pain. But unlike most of the townspeople, this man was not afraid of either of us. Even though I had shot him, even lying on the floor at our mercy, he fixed an opaque eye on me. He had one good eye and one bad. His face was beet red and it was plain to see he was strangling on rage. He had either been a military man or even more likely was a Jayhawker who regularly killed the good people in Missouri. There was no remorse there I could detect, only a cold, black hatred.

"Mr. Ford, you are very familiar to me." I was playing with him. I remembered him well, but it was easy to see he did not remember me. "You hate fucken secesh trash. Is that right?"

"Yes," he said. "Your kind is an abomination in the eyes of God!"

His albino, demon-eye stared at me, even pinned down such as he was like an insect.

"God?" I asked. "What has He to do with this? You think

when you're out gallivanting across the great Missouri countryside killing old women and children, raping our girls, stringing up our elders from the highest tree, and stealing from us, that God is riding with you? I'm just an ignorant piece of trash trying to get this right. Do you think God approves of the Red Legs' brand of justice?" Gazing into the man's hateful face I could not imagine a world beyond the grave in that moment. The presence of God I had always sensed nearby and in my mind ever since I was a boy, in the form of the Holy Ghost, was gone. He had withdrawn His presence. I could not abide the forlorn emotion that had overtaken me.

"What?" Ford said. "I don't ride with anyone. I am part owner of this store. I can give you money, if that's what you need. Is that what it takes for you to leave me be here?"

"Don't bother denying it." I talked over his pathetic suggestion. "I can read your face like it was the Good Book. You might as well confess it now. You see, I remember you. You rode with Jennison. Y'all hanged my father, a man of God, and then you personally shot me. This is the man that shot me, John. You probably thought you killed me, but here I am now."

"Well, what do you want from me?" Ford asked. "An apology? You won't have it. Just so you can feel justified, I'll let you know right now that if I had to do it all over again, I would. I could spend all day killing you and all your people!"

"You have no fear in you! You've grown too used to killing people who don't fight back. Now you think it's right!"

"It *is* right," Ford said, and John pushed his boot harder against his neck. "You will see that our way is right. The North has all but won the war. Law will follow. We will be justified. And you will be dead."

"How long, Oh Lord, holy and true, dost thou not judge and avenge our blood on them that dwell on the earth?" I quoted the Good Book. Knowing this was one of Jennison's men made me feel like everything we had done hadn't been in vain after all.

"You tell him, Preacher," John smiled. He stood over the Jayhawker and took his wallet. They played a tug of war with it, but he did finally give it up. The audacity of the man was outrageous. I could feel my own anger well up. His life was in our hands and he was set to defy us even with a boot on his throat.

"Well, I don't remember you," Ford added.

"That's too bad," I said. "Because I am the abomination that causes desolation. You won't remember me but for a minute—or maybe it will be for eternity."

I put a bullet in the murderer's throat and watched life desert him in rusted bloody spurts. I'm not proud of it now, but I have to admit I was satisfied. Not happy, but satisfied in that moment. The spirit of the dead man lingered even after it had left his body. Evil men don't die easy. I could feel his dark nature filling the room, but it was no less malevolent than the black atmosphere we had brought to Lawrence.

We looked down at him for a moment. John spit. He clapped me on the shoulder like a comrade to let me know all was forgiven.

I couldn't let it go. I kicked Ford's limp body hard in the side. I found some paper and a pencil and wrote a note: *I rode with Charles Jennison and killed many innocent Southern people. Now, I am shot dead. Preacher killed me. You should give up on this Cause or you will be next.* I pinned the note to his fine shirt.

"Good!" John laughed. "You want me to help you chop his head off and stick it on a pole out front?"

I thought about it before I answered. There is an exultation and a sadness in killing an old enemy. The hate you harbored for so long still breeds and festers inside you long after the reason for it is warranted. It is strange how emotions can change and get the better of you. How one can be so calm and cool-headed in one moment but then be transformed by murderous hatred the next.

There was no need to answer John. He could see where I had left it. The man dead on the floor of his own store was enough for me for now. We walked out of the building. The sounds of yipping men and general chaos filled the air. The din of the fired buildings was incredible. Bushwhacker horses were tied to hitching posts down a side street with a couple of young, wild boys put in charge of them. The wind blew smoke in our faces and made us gag. Lawrence had become Hell and we were its chief fiends.

As the day progressed I saw many an anomalous sight. On one street, a matronly woman put up a homemade sign outside her front door which had the word SOUTHERN scrawled across it for all to see. More than one deputation of raiders galloped by, read the sign, and soon departed. I suppose she was lucky no illiterates were attracted to her door. Another oddity, almost stopping me in my tracks, was the tableau of a family standing in the street. The man I took to be the head of the clan held a large umbrella over himself and his family to protect his wife and children from the glaring sun. The umbrella seemed to make them an audience, a Greek chorus yet to speak, to the horrors visited upon their town instead of participants. Riders flew by them without a glance.

A man running with a bundle in his arms nearly bowled us over. I ordered him to stop. He obeyed but placed his bundle on the ground before turning. John shot him twice. He groaned and fell over. His bundle of clothes or blankets slumped over to reveal a towheaded little girl who sat where she was in the center of mayhem and wailed. Just seeing the child quieted the rage I had so recently felt when confronting Ford. The child's hair was like a holy nimbus above her innocent head.

"There's his spawn," John said.

Just then a woman came out of a shed and swooped up the child and disappeared from view, turning off at the end of the street. John went over to the man and, squatting on his haunches, calmly scalped him. He held up the hank of hair for me to admire, then affixed it to his horse's bridle, where it almost immediately attracted the notice of fat green bottle flies. The war had not changed him, other than to make him more violent, more calloused than he had been from the beginning.

We walked our horses back to the Eldridge and allowed them to drink from the water trough. We gave them some feed for the ride back. We were both ready to flee. For there could be no other word for it.

One of Captain Pool's men rode into town. He had news that a picket had spotted a large plume of dust stirred up on the northern plain. That could only mean the Federal army was about to slam down on us for sure. In fact, it had been an inevitability all along. Entering Kansas had been too easy, but returning, we would not be so nonchalant. It would not be easy, especially for those who were so drunk they had to be tied in the saddle or those who were trying to carry too much loot with them.

It was nigh time to skedaddle back to the land of the emerald hills. We had laid waste Babylon. When I sat my horse and looked back upon Lawrence, smoke rose up in loud burning pillars, flames surged in angry tongues of red licking the buildings, the homes, the very commerce of the great whore! One explosion sounded, followed by smaller ones reverberated, that must have been the garrison's powder and munitions stores. The roar of the fire could be heard as it ate the town. As much as I hated some of Lawrence's men, I could not help but regret the murders of children and execution of husbands before their wives. Infernal became uneasy and reared up, his hooves raking the air, and that's when I knew we had accomplished the impossible that day. Now, if only we could live to tell the tale.

CHAPTER 15
After we crossed the Wakarusa River

After we crossed the Wakarusa River, Quantrill again hurriedly met with his captains and their lieutenants to discuss our return route. It was decided that if we headed back due east, we would have quite a homecoming party set up for us at the border, so we rode more south than east, toward Osawatomie. Once we could hide ourselves in the dense woodland near the banks of the Marais des Cygnes, our pursuers would be loath to follow us into tight spots because of their fear of ambush.

Quantrill ordered us to burn any homes or property we came across so Kansans would get a bitter taste of their own bad medicine. Instead of riding in a tight column, we spread our forces out to cover ground and create destruction for the Federals to see as they pursued us.

"Ashby!" Cole called out to me. I turned to see him put the spurs to his mount to catch up.

I had lost track of him in Lawrence and now he was riding at my side again. It felt like a relief to know he was alive. I was more acutely aware of the threat from Captain Todd and his man Speight, now that we were in flight. They might think this the perfect opportunity to kill me, when everyone was too distracted to notice my predicament. Cole laughed at me more than once because I kept spinning around and looking over my horse to see who was bringing up the rear.

"Don't worry," Cole said. "We'll soon have every Union man in this part of the country shooting at us. Speight's going to be just as busy as you."

"I still wouldn't put anything past him."

"Besides," Cole added, "Todd is in charge of the rear guard. I'm surprised you didn't see him before now."

"Where?"

Cole pointed and I instinctively crouched down.

"Ah, hell," Cole said. "If they're coming for you, they're coming for you. Just prepare yourself to shoot them first. That's your only chance."

"That's easy for you to say."

A rope tornado spun in the distance behind us. The serpentine pillar trailed us and yet never caught up either. Was it mere coincidence or a biblical portent of God's displeasure? Some thought maybe we should pull up and wait for them and give them what they wanted. Others thought it best to keep moving. Occasionally, to lighten the load, a ranger would sigh heavily and toss down a woman's sidesaddle he had taken for his sweetheart or bolts of cloth and tea services he had tied to his saddle horn: treasures acquired with mortal risk, only to be discarded on the plain. There was no time for treasure when the fallen archangels of Kansas were on your ass.

"Who is following us?" I asked.

"You won't believe it."

"Tell me."

"It's none other than Senator Lane hisself." Cole laughed. "And he was wearing short pants!"

"What? Sounds like bullshit! How do you know?"

"I was still in town with the last of the boys, whooping it up, when he appeared with a bunch of crazed farmers. Half of them ain't even got guns. Some of them have hoes and hatchets! I don't know why Quantrill or somebody don't just turn around and give them what they want. Also, I saw a big Indian, a Delaware, shoot that crazy-ass preacher, Skaggs. Scalped him, too. He was drunk as a skunk."

"Didn't you try to help him?" I asked.

"There wasn't no helping him," Cole said. "I heard him scream. He was surrounded by a mob. If I hadn't left when I did, I would have been next."

"I fought them Delawares before," I said. "They ain't no joke." The memory of one savage in particular haunted me. His skin was red and he wore a painted mask of black across his eyes with black chevrons falling down his cheeks like savage tears. I had only escaped him by God's grace.

"You see me laughing? I rode out of there with the others to save my hide. Larkin Skaggs was no great loss to humanity."

I waved my hand in agreement. One of Infernal's ears was pointed back at us as if he were eavesdropping.

"You think we'll make it back home alive?" I said next.

"Some of us might," Cole said. "There's also a small column of men after us led by a real officer. I don't know who he is, but right now we've got them outnumbered."

"Let's go back and help Todd," I said. "He might could use us."

"You must be crazy," he said.

Without another word, I yanked back hard on the reins and went back to the rear to find Captain Todd. It gnawed at my guts that Lane had escaped us, only to now turn around and give such a damned heated pursuit. When they saw me riding up, Speight charged ahead to meet me. He gave me a hard, intimidating stare and I stared right back. He looked over his shoulder at Todd. The captain, almost unrecognizable, wearing such a fine new blue Yankee uniform, gave Speight the nod. Todd dismounted and tore off his uniform. I assume it was because there was no one the ruse would work upon in this situation. It would be a shame to be accidentally shot by your own men.

Todd knew he needed every man they could get, so he didn't particularly mind my presence in his ranks. If nothing else, he and Speight knew I could give just as well as I could get in a fight. I had a full cartridge case too.

This was exactly the kind of fighting I was prepared to do, not like the slaughter back in Lawrence. We might feud like blood relations, but given a threat from outsiders, all bets were off. No words were spoken directly, but it was understood that after all of this was over, we'd still have something to settle. For now, we were fellow riders in a tight fix. Speight even gave me a grudging clap on the shoulder. When Cole rode up and sat his horse to my right, Speight *hallooed* him in a way that, although not friendly, wasn't hostile either. The men in the rearguard were tense and eyes were filled with nightmare expectation.

There were dark clouds in the distance. I wondered how fast they were moving and how long it would be before the storm caught us. It could be a mixed blessing. Our pursuers might give up the chase if it started raining jags, but if they didn't, we would be hard slogging through the fields. Fortunately, I was used to fighting in bad weather. Missouri had almost nothing but bad weather. It was either too hot or too cold or there were high winds and the rain was too slanted and that was not even to mention the twisters threatening to toss you into the next state.

Todd had about sixty men in his command. Most of the men were keyed up, though edging toward fatigue, and others were so hungover they just didn't have the energy to get tight about every little emergency. Now Todd was wearing his normal home fighting clothes after getting shed of the Yankee officer uniform. Still, he looked every bit the captain now. It was grim business ahead of us as he took stock of our beleaguered army. He ordered every one of us to ready ourselves and our revolvers.

"We need to scatter these boys on our heels," Todd said. "Or the whole lot of us will be lost eventually. This is where we shake them off."

There was a rail fence beside a field of corn nearby. Todd ordered us to take the rails down, as the fenceline was on a rise. This was a huge advantage in terms of Kansas terrain. He ordered some of us to hide in the corn rows while the other half went down the rutted road the farmer used for his cart. Captain Todd gave the command to charge and we lit out with a chorus of rebel yells and went after those Yankees, laying heavy into the thick of them. Gun smoke was so thick it was difficult to see through the curling blue-gray fog bank. I was with the boys in the corn. As soon as we saw Todd leading his men, we came streaming out of the corn to help form a two-pronged attack. Then we saw Don Quixote himself, dressed like a fool of some notoriety, with a straw hat too large for his head and short pants like a child might wear just as Cole had said.

It was Jim Lane. His own men had left him out to dry, having ridden toward us too fast, leaving him all alone. We all started taking potshots at him like he was a proud Tom turkey with his hair standing all on end after his hat blew off in his suicidal charge. He ducked and dodged and had to fall back to where his men were quaking in terror just beyond the range of our revolvers. They had decided to wait for Major Plumb to catch up to their position to avoid a sure earth bath.

We gave them a bit of a spanking as we rode toward them, easily scattering them, until we saw Plumb and his men with a serious military look about them. The traveling blue-black image of them trembled and pulsated in the distance under the broiling heat of the plain. Sun and shadow took turns making patterns on the ground before us as the clouds spirited across the vista. The earth had been transformed in Yankee blue behind us, Kansas men seemed to spring whole out of the stones, the trees, and the very soil itself. The sound of distant thunder rumbled ominously, but there appeared to be no imminent threat of rain, just the sound of the gods pounding their shields as they argued from above, in the big open sky, over our fate.

Plumb's cavalry came at us slow but unrelenting. Shortly after we passed Black Jack, one of our scouts observed about eighty new militia on fresh horses joining Plumb's command. The men groaned upon hearing this news. We fell into a pattern. Plumb would dispatch an officer, a certain Lieutenant Leland, with about 160 men under his command, from the main column, and they would come at us hard. We weren't quite sure why Plumb never sent all of his men at once, but we were relieved he did not. I can still see it in my mind when I close my eyes. There he was again. Leland was coming for us.

Todd gave the order and those of us in the rear guard broke off from the rest of Quantrill's men and formed a line where we waited for them in a state of nervous exhaustion. We desperately needed rest, but none was forthcoming unless we wanted to rest in Sheol for all eternity. It wasn't long before they came riding at us, shooting carbines and their antique pistols. Todd's arm came down and we charged at them, cussing and firing at will until we saw them dropping out of their saddles like drunks on a lark but these men fell wounded or stone-cold dead.

Of course, they managed to hit some of us too. This was to be expected. It was too bad, but we had to leave our boys, about a half dozen, where they lay. The odds were still in our favor in these skirmishes. We were killing more of their boys. If we could just deter them from continuing their pursuit and make it back into Missouri. True, some of us had been lightly wounded, but the pain was the kind of thing that tended to awaken the senses. Death was on his pale horse after all, riding for us straight from the abyss, with reins in his teeth and his pistols cracking while he spurred and cursed at us and shot brimstone from his old-fashioned pistol barrels. It was a battle of attrition between them and us, since we were all near exhaustion. Then Leland would call a retreat back to Plumb. Attack and defend. This is how it went, hour after nervy hour.

"They're trying to slow us down," Todd said as he watched Plumb intently through his gold looking glass. "Let's catch up to Bill and the main column again. We will be damn sure to burn any house we pass close by. We've got to make sure everyone in this area remembers this day until they die, if we want them to stop their atrocities against our people in the future. They'll remember Todd, by God!"

A wounded man under Todd named Joab Perry had disappeared.

"Do you think they got him back there, George?" Speight asked.

"Nah," Todd said. "He was shaking and crying ever since we

knew someone was on our ass. He's probably a deserter trying to make it home skulking through the brambly-wildwoods. If you see him again, do us all a favor and kill him."

He meant what he said. There was no underestimating him. This was one reason why Quantrill gave him command of the rear guard, because it was such a critical position. Only someone with experience and tenacity could pull off these maneuvers successfully. Without us, the rear guard, the rest of the company, would have been overrun and scattered already.

Up ahead, Quantrill assumed any house we saw in Kansas was pro-Union, and his orders were to shoot any man big enough to tote a gun and fire his house and outbuildings. We were easy quarry to track because we were setting fires to every farmstead we came upon.

We were riding hard toward the town of Paola. The sun was burning orange in the northwest behind us now. Twilight was what we were praying for, since Plumb's men might only be able to form one more attack before full-on dark. If we could hold them off one more time, we would make it across the border and into God's country.

Leland came at us again at a place called Big Hill. Even Quantrill's confidence had to be on the wane at this new attack. We were shooting them off their horses and they replaced them just as quickly with fresh men and horses like a macabre cavalry.

There were a few others out there intent on doing us dirty, but they had to catch us first. One of our scouts reported that an unnamed captain was spotted trying to flank us and was heading toward the big creek at Paola. We would later learn it was a certain Captain Clark, waiting to ambush us. Instead Quantrill said we could overrun and scatter them, too, but he wanted to avoid any more confrontations. We had to deal with Leland first. His men, now stuporous from exhaustion, came at us again on horses that stepped in postholes like they had snouts full of busthead whiskey. When we were given the command to face about and charge, they dismounted and hid behind what cover they could find. Some even forced their horses to lie down and then hid behind and aimed their carbines over their bellies. I charged like everyone else but watched my line to make sure I didn't get too far ahead or behind the rest, dressing to the right but it was not much of an issue as Infernal was winding down. Never a fast horse, he was slowing so that I was wondering if he was going to make it.

A man jumped up and came lumbering at me with a rifle. He knelt and fired but came nowhere near hitting me. I ran him down so Infernal could trample him into the dust. This kind of fighting was not to our advantage, as we had mostly revolvers to shoot at point-blank range instead of rifles—it suited our gun-and-run style. Combat across long stretches of rolling hillocks did not suit us, though luckily we had numbers on our side, which was something of a rarity. I had come into a nest of blue vipers but after ten minutes of fierce fighting they were overrun again and forced to retreat.

Cole rode up next to me, "The colonel is leading us around Paola."

"They'll think we're heading that way," I said.

"He's a crafty one," Cole said. "But don't it seem like we should just cross the Marais des Cygnes over yonder instead of heading north?"

"He's got his reasons," I said. "They might have laid some devious ambuscade for us there." I was too tired to offer up a good argument or suppose this or suppose that. For even I had resorted to tying myself to the saddle, just to make sure I didn't end up horseless. I was about to fall over from exhaustion.

We finally crossed over into Missouri and set up a camp on the banks of Grand Creek and slid off our horses with groans. I could barely feel my legs anymore, I'd been in the saddle so long. Infernal laid down on his side, something I had never seen him do before.

This would be a brief respite, since our lives were at stake and there was no cavalry waiting to bail us out of a tight situation. Our scouts said our pursuers had camped en masse at Paola. They seemed to be settling in for a stay. Quantrill, Todd, Anderson, Jarrett, and most of the other captains had a powwow about what Plumb and Clark were planning. It was one of the few times I witnessed a civil military exchange between the captains. In this dire situation they were willing, almost to a man, to leave the final decisions to Colonel Quantrill, who was beginning to look more relaxed now.

Here they discussed how to divide up the money and possessions we'd managed to hold on to as equitably as possible. Each private was given the equivalent of twenty dollars, and the officers took their cut, which I'm sure was considerably more. None were in the mood to debate the final tally, which wasn't much, if you considered our lives hung in the balance for so little, but I reminded myself I had done it for Lizzie and the other girls. This was what I told myself but the memory of those Union boys in blue being trampled or shot as they came out of their tents would not leave me.

There was a report from a local farmer of a large force, over a thousand men, of fresh Missouri Militia awaiting us four miles to the east. It was the First Missouri State Militia Cavalry. Lieutenant Colonel Bazel Lazear was in charge of the lot, the only line of defense between us and freedom.

Quantrill ordered us that could to mount up so as to either evade or fight Lazear's militia. The others would hide in the woods in hollow logs or caves or find a local farmer who would risk his neck and hide some of us in a barn or cellar. There was a wagon full of a few wounded men. We attempted to hide them off in the woods and hope they would not be found. Even Bill Gregg's horse had either died or been killed from underneath him for he was now on foot. Cole and me thought Gregg and the other men on foot were walking dead men now, but ironically most of them (Gregg included) later made it back to the Sni without incident. If we could make it by Lazear, we would split up and each of us make our own way in little bands and try to lose ourselves in the brush. Some were not far from home already. No doubt they would track some of us down, but it was the price we had to pay for the wrath we'd visited upon Lawrence.

I observed Quantrill now. He wore that lizard smile of his as he discussed our next move to evade Lazear. He spoke all this as he watched him through his spyglass. He didn't think we were up to a direct assault on a force that appeared to be closer to the same number of men we had now.

It felt as if all these men chasing us had us on a string and getting away from them would be impossible. We were all but spent. Plumb and Clark were no longer on our tails, but now we had the Missouri Militia to deal with. Thinking how close we had come to dying, and kept coming, it made the ground beneath us livid with life and beauty. I noticed the way the horseweed swayed in the twilight wind, the call of a cardinal to its mate, and a couple of blue herons that took flight from a lake. It was one of those days when the dread of a fight causes you to see the shine on the beauty of the world as the last burning rays of the sun were beginning to slip below the welkin.

"Let's see how well this one has been trained," Quantrill said.

Quantrill had a plan. These young militia officers were trained to do things by the book, he said. He told Gregg to order us to form a line as though we were going to attack Lazear head on. Some of us didn't know exactly what Quantrill was up to, but there was a pattern we'd learned in our skirmishes with the locals, so we sat our horses while the coming darkness made it difficult to see. There we were to be seen by the militia and now it was their move. Then Quantrill saw what he had hoped to see. Lazear gave the order for some of his men to dismount and form a skirmish line according to his strict training. Their horses were taken to the rear. Now that only left about half of them mounted.

"Oh ho now!" Todd laughed. "They're going to fight us on foot."

"Let's slaughter them!" A voice full of bloodlust yelled.

"No," Quantrill said. "Now it's time for us to make a graceful retreat."

"I'd give anything to see the look on their puke faces in a few minutes," Todd said.

We peeled off the line in an orderly fashion. The men who weren't on the main line rode off quietly into the bushes. Those of us who rode with Todd had smiles on our lips because we knew what was coming. Cole gave a wave to Arch and Frank with Captain Anderson and his boys. They made eyes at us, indicating their surprise to see that we were fighting under Todd at the moment. I gave them an ironic little salute. Cole elbowed me to let me know he wanted to join them, but I told him we would catch up with them as soon we got this next bit of unpleasantness done.

Todd took us a ways over the next hillock and had us fan out as we awaited what was to come next. Infernal's ears were drooping, his tongue was hanging out like a dog's. He hadn't wanted to get up but he eventually did. A good number of our horses were in the same state. It was just a matter of time before they began to fall over literally dead with exhaustion. As I imagine it now, Quantrill stared down the militia line until they were all but anticipating his order to charge, but then he spun his finger in the air and he disappeared in the wind with all of his horsemen.

Lazear's skirmish line must have been thunderstruck. We didn't do what the cavalry handbook said we were supposed to do, according to Napoleonic rules of engagement. Lazear had no choice but to order his men who were still mounted to give chase. It would take a while for the horses of the skirmish line to be brought back up from the rear. We heard them galloping hard before we saw them. Now we were using the lay of the land to our advantage, awaiting them as we did just beyond the top of the rise.

Quantrill and his sham skirmish line rode by.

"Hold, boys," Todd said. "That's ole Quantrill. I know. I'd love to shoot him too, but just wait. The militia will greet us momentarily."

Quantrill's men whipped by us and kept riding for the next tree line.

"Give them hell, boys!"

"They're right on our ass!"

We waited now. Each of us had revolvers in both hands. I had my saddle rigged up with holsters on either side of the pommel. I had lost two of my pistols during our retreat, but I still had five. They were loaded and ready to kill the homeguard. They were not the fighters the Kansas men were, nor were they as seasoned. My hands shook from a powerful combination of fear and exhaustion.

Then Lieutenant Lazear with his men came flying over the top of the rise at a mighty fine clip compared to Quantrill's worn-out horses. The lieutenant was close enough for us to see the look of horror on his face as he realized he had been outmaneuvered by a bunch of ignorant bushwhackers. Now he was about to find out why we were so feared, although he had no doubt bragged about catching Quantrill's boys in record time.

"Fire," Todd said in an almost bored tone of voice.

We let loose a volley of hellfire on those boys and watched as bloody men and a couple of horses collapsed like the earth had sucked them into a sinkhole. But the rest were undaunted. Their blood was up now. Some of them fired back. Two of my caps failed to fire in quick succession. A few of our boys fell from their mounts. It wasn't long before the air filled with the acrid smell of powder and a familiar gunsmoke blue. Todd called a retreat and off we went, hard on the trail of Quantrill. I heard the sounds of horses' hooves beating the ground and the wheezing breaths coming from their chests in a riding rhythm into the heart of Missouri, where we longed to find sanctuary. Popping sounds came from behind us, where Lazear's men were finishing off those unfortunate brothers of ours who had been knocked from their horses. We had made good our escape. Somehow we had attacked Lawrence, deep into Kansas territory and lived to glory in the legend of Quantrill's Raiders. We had paid them back in full, but that didn't mean there wouldn't be consequences.

CHAPTER 16
The Burnt District

*The border counties of Missouri have almost as desolate
an appearance as before the soil was trod by by the white man.
Not a man, woman or child is to be seen in the country to which
Order No. 11 applies . . . Chimneys mark the spot where once
stood costly farm houses, cattle and hogs are fast destroyin fields
of corn, prairie fires are burning up miles of good fencing every
day or two, and turn which way you will, everything denotes a
state of utter desolation and ruin.*

—*a Kansas Soldier*

Captain Bill took us on a path through the devastated border-
land like the bitter patriarch of a cursed land. Ash and an otherworldly pall fell over the land that had once been home to many
of the boys, although now it had been fairly tattooed with death.
The families known to be loyal to the Southland had been cruelly
shipped out in droves for aiding and abetting us, except for a few
holdouts in obscure hiding places in the bush or those who, either
through bullshit or by trade, had convinced the Federals they were
loyal to the Union. What was an heirloom watch or silver rings
compared to the farmstead settled by your own people? General
Ewing and his skeevy bunch of abolitionist lovers thought that
without our friends and families to support us we would simply
vanish from the country but we were determined to show him we
were made of stronger stuff.

Wildfires burned out of control. We came upon an area of

scorched earth where a tree was still burning with two unrecogniz-able bodies wearing telltale colorful guerrilla shirts and the long hair of our kind hanged high in the upper branches where no one could easily cut them down. Their faces were puckered with rot. Their eyeballs had been eaten away by the birds. Crows looked down upon us with contempt. A sign was nailed to the tree below them in an unsteady script: *We kill bushwhackers like this! Take these bodies down and you're next!*

The Captain looked grim as we walked our horses over dimly burning coals through one devastated farmstead after another. Ash fluttered in the air like we were part of a purgatorial nightmare. We had taken our revenge but things only seemed worse. God was further away than ever. It felt like He had unleashed one of his Egyptian plagues on the wrong people. I half-expected the sky to open up and begin raining frogs just before turning pitch black at noon. A hazy red sun presided over the still smoking, blackened timbers of a barn. The farm house was burned down to the dirt floor, a lone chimney remained standing.

I rode up to the family farm in Howard County in a fine black cabriolet to see my family before leaving for Texas for the win-ter. I had "found" the carriage abandoned just outside of Fayette and intended it as a belated birthday gift for Mother. She had not changed. She had always seemed like she might be the next to die and yet she was as tough as a snapping turtle. Uncle Silas had died of apoplexy out working in the hayfield. It was a relief to hear the news and I had missed the funeral. When I tried to comfort her she shrugged and waved me away with a fluttering hand.

Now Sarah was engaged to be married to a prosperous farmer named John Lawrence, who lived just outside Fayette in the direc-tion of Boonville. Appearances were very important to Lawrence and he looked at Sarah the way some men might look at a fine horse or a prized family heirloom. He would enjoy great comfort in introducing her at social functions and on the Sabbath at church as "My wife, Mrs. John Lawrence, recently of Glasgow." His acres of fields were laid out on what looked like shelves of land set at an angle to others by Mother Nature's hand. I had always taken the lay of the land for granted but I suppose these "shelves of land" had something to do with being so close to the course of the Missouri. Jehovah had smiled on him and given the kind of luck or blessings to be a success. Providence embraced him and kissed him on his brow. Sarah floated around the old house glowing and doing chores without a word of protest. She was about to begin her new life with a prosperous and mature man.

We had received word to meet up again with Quantrill at Captain Perdee's farm near the Blackwater River, but then Quantrill's camp there or in the Sni had been attacked, so we were told to head toward Blue Springs instead. With winter's bad weather coming on, Quantrill was ready to head down to Texas until spring like he did every winter. This year it seemed particularly vital to head south with the increase of Yankee patrols over the Lawrence affair. On top of everything else, once the trees lost their leaves, there would be no cover. Not even the gorges and thickets of the Sni Hills would give enough cover through winter.

All the outfits were there to ride to Texas together. There we would meet up with Confederate General Ben McCulloch, who commanded the District of North Texas not far from Sherman. I thought about staying up in Howard County where the dread Order No. 11 did not apply but my fight was best carried on since it seemed like maybe Quantrill would pick up momentum again. I had more fight in me, the way I had it figured. Fight or die fighting. Not only because of Lawrence but because, as we thought at the time, the Confederacy had made him a colonel and recognized us all as first-rate fighting men. Some Confederate officers loved Quantrill when he fell neatly into their own plans. Other Confederate officers operating just south of Missouri took some satisfaction that Quantrill was drawing attention from their own activities, while still others condemned him for what they considered brutal tactics. But they didn't realize we were badly outnumbered and we had no choice but to use every trick we could to avoid being shot, hanged, and scalped. General Ewing gave no quarter when he caught our boys. The Confederate generals back East might think it nothing to watch thousands of their men fall in one day and then wax philosophical about their valor, but as for myself I had notions about staying above ground. I didn't want to hear angels playing harps in glory until it was hallelujah time.

I was back with Captain Bill Anderson and the men I had learned everything I knew about fighting from. Cole and me had hightailed it out of Todd's camp as quick as we could. Though the split was agreeable enough, Speight made it clear our little tiff was not yet settled. They tried to get Cole to stay with them and for his part he tried not to rile them, but it was a useless enterprise as we rode off to all sorts of unpleasant things they told us they had planned for us and our "whore" mothers. I looked over my shoulder and smiled at them with hate. It was no surprise then to feel their eyes on us back at the rendezvous site with Quantrill at Perdee's. Cole suggested we should just ride up to them and shoot Speight in the head and then maybe it would be settled. But in truth Todd was the worse instigator, and while I thought together we would be a good match for Speight, I knew Todd was not a man we should trifle with. When I looked into his eyes, only hatred and death looked back. He had spent the last couple of years kicking against the pricks and it had hardened him into something not human. I loved him like the Devil likes holy water.

There was a chill in the foggy morning air. A young girl who looked barely old enough to marry and a man came riding into our new camp in a fine carriage at the Stanley farm. Frank told me it was Quantrill's young bride Kate. She was a pretty little thing but her mouth was full of demons when she spoke.

The colonel met her before the wagon had come to a proper stop. He made a gallant show of helping her down. There was an expression of what I'd call the evil queen in her regal, angel face as she seemed to appraise us like chattel. She wanted to see her husband off before he left for Texas. There was something royal about them both for us boys as we looked on. The look on Quantrill's face said it all. He was lovestruck. He had counseled other men not to marry during this time of war, since he knew it would make them cautious fighters. He also knew it might lead to them wanting to settle down before the war was decided and accept the rule of a wife and domesticity over his bloody statutes. Word was, there had already been a confrontation over the subject between himself and Bloody Bill. Captain Bill had set his cap on marrying a girl who some said was a prostitute. I didn't know it yet, but this would turn out to be the argument that made for a major change in the way the war in Missouri was conducted among our kind.

There were a few, not many, boys grumbling that Quantrill had broken his own rule about marriage while the war was still on, but most of us were happy for him. We respected him and wished him well. On the other hand, the lot of us were glad our necks were not in the noose of matrimony. At first, I thought Quantrill planned to take his wife with us and wondered with a bit of mirth if she would be poleaxing our enemies over their heads with her French parasol, but I learned she was going to spend the winter with her father and wait for Quantrill to return in spring. It was too dangerous for her with us. I'd heard that Quantrill and Todd had renewed their friendship and even spent some time together with their respective wives. This disturbed me since it could prove deadly for me should Todd decide to press his suit against me by bending the colonel's ear. I wouldn't have worried, had I realized how insignificant I really was to Todd. His hatred of me was no secret, but he and Quantrill had an acrimonious relationship as well. As far as I could tell, Todd hated most everyone except the boys under his direct command.

"Do you think you will marry again very soon?" Cole asked as we rode side by side.

"I hadn't thought about that yet," I said. "And you?"

"Yes," Cole said. "I already have it all planned out. I am going to find me a yellow-haired lady. We'll have us a whole passel of kids. The more the better. Maybe we'll go for an even dozen. I'll need a lot of help on the farm. We'll plant hemp, tobacco, and have the biggest garden you ever saw. There's a patch of ground I've seen near the cliffs of Rocheport that's for sale."

"That sounds fine," I said. I had a hard time believing it though, knowing how much Cole loved the ladies. "I'm sure I'll head back to Howard County where my family is, if I live that long."

"You think you might ever return to preaching?"

"I'm not sure that's what God has called me to do ever since the war," I said. "It don't seem likely."

We rode off in a southwesterly direction, passing from the corner of southern Missouri and into southeast Kansas near Baxter Springs. The sanctuary of the Indian territories was not far off. We would all breathe that much easier once we hit it. No abolitionist scum or state militias would follow us there. It was possible we might run into some Indians. They would observe us, but we were a large force to trifle with. Quantrill claimed to have friends there too. The colonel was already full of devilments to unleash on the blue bellies come spring. At nightfall he liked to put pen to paper as he made plans for tearing Missouri away from the Union once and for all. There was an ongoing rumor that General Price was biding his time as he planned to raise up an army from the Ozarks and sweep up from Arkansas, across Missouri, and drive out the Yankees. I could see the colonel did not believe that himself, but he kept his own counsel. If it gave men hope to believe Price might be their savior, Colonel Quantrill would let them believe it. Each man needed to have some hope to get him by.

Our boys were in high spirits and about to breathe a relieved sigh when word came by courier that Dave Pool's advance party had come on some teamsters driving a wagon full of lumber for a tiny fort none of us even knew existed in the area. Word was that it was a small fort built into a large embankment and walled on three sides, commanded by a Lieutenant Pond. The fort was inhabited at the moment only by a bunch of mostly unarmed, black freemen as it was still partially under construction.

The colonel sent Bill Gregg's bunch to help Pool in the event they ran into trouble. Our boys surprised them, though most of the freemen made it to the relative safety of the fort. Pool and Gregg's bunch were ready to dig in and give them hell but then Pond fired their only howitzer and Colonel Quantrill ordered them to forget the fort. It was of no tactical importance and a waste of our time for a force of nearly four hundred.

We had grown weary tearing around the countryside. Even the prospect of Texas didn't set our hearts at rest, since it would just mean McCulloch would be ordering us around, but just then we were overlooking Fort Scott Road from a ridge where we saw a line of eight wagons, an assortment of officers, with a cavalry escort that caused Quantrill to order us to form a battle line to match the Yankees'.

Most of our men wore blue to confuse the enemy and they were not sure what to make of us. No alarm had gone up yet. This would be too easy, we thought, as we checked to make sure our weapons were ready. Cole was especially fastidious about this and could often be found cleaning his guns, checking and rechecking every moving part. If he felt one was not up to snuff, he would bide his time and take a new piece off one of the fallen.

"Two stars," Colonel Quantrill mused gazing through his telescope. "Lady Luck has smiled on us today!"

"Looks like they brought a band with them too," Todd snorted derisively. "Now, don't that beat all. They must know how much I love music. Maybe they think we will put down our arms and hand you over to the Yanks, Bill."

"Maybe we should put on a dance?" I suggested.

"It's time to pull down General Blunt's pants," Quantrill said. He pointedly ignored Todd's remark. He had grown more sarcastic and contentious when he spoke to the colonel as time went on. "We'll give him the spanking he has long deserved."

The boys were getting excited by the prospect of giving old Blunt his comeuppance and riding up and down the line. Bill Bledsoe was tearing ass around us on his horse as if he might attack. Quantrill looked amused at Bledsoe's antics and stuffed his hat inside his coat. He then gave a whoop and put the spurs to his mount as he surged forward. *NO PRISONERS!* The rest of us were on his ass.

The colonel's ill-tempered horse was one of the fleetest I ever witnessed. For his part, Blunt responded, but his men weren't so eager, as they allowed their fearless leader to get ahead of himself. The general began to look left and right and about pulled his mount's head off, making a crescent moon in the dust, as our horses kept on coming. We had them badly outnumbered. Fear was on their faces. The wagons were in the process of turning around to retreat. Blunt's horse was a fast one. It soon passed all the men in retreat down on the plain below.

We were just closing in and firing on Blunt's guard at will. A grizzled veteran with unkempt hair was trying to get his ass-shot horse to stand back up. I shot him twice in the chest as I rode by. The air was alive with bullets zipping back and forth like angry hummingbirds. I saw Bledsoe take out after the most finely attired officer in the entire Union army, sending mean intentions out of the snout of his revolver as he gave chase.

Now I began to wonder if that man wasn't, in fact, Blunt. The officer I'd mistaken for Blunt came out of a carriage with a wonderfully dressed young woman in tow and stuck her on what looked to be the fastest charger alive. She surprised us by leaping astride her horse like a man instead of riding sidesaddle, although she was dressed as fine as any lady I'd ever seen. This wasn't the first time I'd heard of Blunt traveling with a female companion to make life on the trail a little more entertaining. John McCorkle flew by me on his charger with all his whooping and bade me and Cole to ride with him flicking his Colt at us like a finger, summoning us to follow.

McCorkle shot a drummer boy making the mistake of getting out of the band wagon. The boys took to slaughtering the unarmed bandsmen just for wearing the wrong color. A wide-eyed guardsman was holding a Sharps rifle on me, so I obliged him by shooting him in the shoulder. The shot was meant for between his eyes, but I had gone wide of the mark with my pistol. I was above him and shot him on top of his head. For good measure, I shot him in the face, where he lay spread-eagle already. I was sick unto death of these sons of bitches. I told Infernal to make him pay, so he stomped the soldier so far down into the earth he wouldn't need a burial.

Blunt's men were in full retreat now. Some were even tossing aside their weapons in their terror. We were killing them good. It didn't take long before I caught up with McCorkle staring in awe across a wide gorge. Blunt and the young woman were disappearing into the tree line on the other side of the gorge.

"Do you believe that?" McCorkle looked back at me, trying to control his horse. The beast was high-stepping so near the edge, I thought rider and horse might fall into it together. "Both of their horses jumped that gulch there!"

"What?" I said. "Well, hell, why didn't you go after them then?"

"You've got to be shitting me," McCorkle said. "I ain't never rode a horse that could make that jump. Those are some damn fine horses there. If it hadn't been for that gulch, I would have caught Blunt and killed his fat ass and then we could have had us some fun with his whore to boot!"

"Damn fine horses." I shrugged.

He fired a couple of shots in the direction of the fleeing pair, but without a rifle it was useless.

"Don't," I said. "You might make a lucky shot and hit the lady and wouldn't that be a terrible thing to have on your conscience?"

"You're right, Preacher." McCorkle jumped off his horse to have a closer look at the width of the gorge, as if he were thinking of trying to take his horse over it after all but it was much too deep to consider unless you were desperate to meet Lucifer down in his own parlor.

"Looks like the passage to Hades," McCorkle said.

At one time McCorkle would have apologized for talking like that in front of me, but now they knew I was as much a killer as any of them. I'm afraid I'd begun to pick up their habits and cursed more than most of them.

Even so, God was still heavy on my mind. I found myself looking for signs from Him of a night or early before the break of day but everything I had seen of late was inscrutable at best. A vision of a pinkish-orange sunrise with streaming rays of light upon the apogee of the Ozark Mountains. Another time I saw a stork, nearly six feet in height, fishing with its spear-like beak in a waterlogged wheatfield and Queen Anne's lace looking like a cranky old quartermaster. Nothing a man could call a clear-cut sign. No burning-bush moments. No prophetic dreams or guiding visions of the future. Only nightmares that I later remembered were real, that I had been a fully conscious witness to.

But I had been more than a witness. I had committed unspeakable atrocities God would never forgive me for. The visions I lived my life by now: The desolation of Order No. 11, the terror of young women crushed under the weight of their prison, the Biblical destruction of Lawrence, my murdered father, and, worst of all, the death of my wife. I didn't even include all the boys I'd known who were killed in battles in the gory fields of Kansas and Missouri. I knew I would have to fight until they let us be. There didn't seem to be enough Yankees to kill to make up for all the horrors dancing on strings behind my eyelids.

Some of Blunt's boys had managed to make it to their horses and we hunted down every one that we could and riddled their bodies with bullets. At first we told some we'd take them prisoner and do an exchange, just so that we could shoot them unarmed. We couldn't use that one long before they didn't believe us over the gunshots we blasted at their brethren. We chased men for as much as three miles until they met a wider portion of the gorge that Blunt and his woman had jumped. It would have taken a winged Pegasus to jump it at this bend, so all they could do was wait for us to catch up with them and put them down.

"Tell ol' God," Cole said as he leveled his pistol at a sergeant, "that Quantrill was the last man you ever saw alive." The man already had his hands in the air, and he shook at Cole's words. Then a dark stain spread across his trousers. His legs quaked beneath him and he attempted to crawl under his horse, but Cole showed him no mercy as he emptied the pistol into the body and whipped out his Colt and shot the man's horse to boot. "We'll eat good tonight!" he exulted.

As we rode back to what was left of the wagons, I tried to comfort McCorkle over his lost opportunity on account of the gulch. Our boys were standing over nearly a hundred of the enemy, going through their pockets in lieu of a salary. We took their bonny blue shirts if they weren't too bloody. They hadn't expected to be fired on. So they wore nicer uniforms than usual with shined gold buttons. We also relieved them of their paper money, revolvers, and anything that looked valuable and portable. Their canteens were full of whiskey; smiles bloomed all around.

Cole appeared at my side with a fancy silver canteen. I drank and the whiskey burned good as it crawled down my throat. It was a victory but the moment only shone in a temporary light. We might have caught Blunt, but he didn't control things in our neck of the woods anymore, so here we were catching up to the shadows of our past. Blunt had learned every terrible trick he knew at the knee of that animal Jim Lane. The payback we were finally able to give him came too late to be of any use since he was no longer in charge of our district.

"I killed him!" Fletch Taylor cried as he galloped up on his horse. "I've got his damn scalp! I killed that lard-ass, General Blunt!" There was a gory, wet scalp attached to Fletch's bridle.

"My God," Quantrill said appreciatively. "I congratulate you. I wished it had been me that done the deed. I owed him so much for so many men."

"I don't think so," McCorkle disagreed with a mournful shake of his head. "We chased Blunt and his little lady, but their horses bested ours. You should have seen them jump that gulch where we lost them. I'm fairly certain it was him."

Quantrill trusted McCorkle, but there was something about McCorkle that some fellows could not keep themselves from japing him. He was too serious all the time and didn't have much of a sense of humor. He was capable in every way for this work of ours but there was something of the little brother that gets picked on about him.

"That reminds me." Quantrill's eyes cut to McCorkle. "I've been meaning to shoot you, boy."

"Only if you can draw faster than I can shoot, Colonel." As quick as anyone I'd ever seen, McCorkle drew his revolver and held it on Quantrill. All the laughter went silent and eyes turned to the pair in stunned expectation.

"Now, now," Quantrill smiled. "I only meant that I was going to give you a shot in the neck." And with that, Quantrill reached into his coat slowly and pulled out his own flask of something fine. He liked to treat himself to the finer things in life when he could put his hands on them. "You know you're too important to this operation as a scout, son."

"Well, hell, Colonel!" McCorkle smiled self-consciously now. He grabbed hold of the flask and took a languorous draught, but he still had his pistol aimed at Quantrill's guts. "I never heard you joke about killing someone before. That's why I pulled on you as soon as you said it. I am a little too keyed up."

"I won't be making that mistake again." Quantrill replaced his flask into his coat. "The next time you draw down on me, you had better do it, son. I should tell you that."

"McCorkle's a good boy," Cole said as we rode off from the group. "But he's a little slow." Cole pointed to his head and shook it in wonder.

"The way he drew down on Quantrill," I whistled, "I'd say he wasn't slow at all. He's a fast hand with that damn pistol now."

"It's a wonder Quantrill let him live." Cole shook his head. "It's like Captain Todd has been saying. As much as I hate to admit it, Quantrill has gone soft."

The boys had things well in hand. Fletch Taylor had stopped one of the wagons full of men trying to escape, but he and the boys had run into problems. The men were Blunt's band that played for special occasions and not exactly your typical combatants. Sure they could play their polished instruments, but could any of them shoot? If ever we were compelled to take prisoners or show some mercy, it would have been to this group. Among them was a very young drummer boy of about twelve. Fletch was off his horse attending one of our fallen men. As we approached, it was clear that Bill Bledsoe had been shot. He would not be making the trip down to Texas with us. It was a shock. He was one of our best fighters and well-liked and respected by everyone. Bledsoe was the kind of man you see mortally wounded and you know it's all a turkey shoot. Any of us could go out the same way. The rout had gone from a violent lark to macabre just like that. It put some of the men in a dark mood I had not seen since Lawrence.

I squatted down on my haunches next to Fletch. They had meant to take the musicians prisoner and let them go after the rest of Blunt's men had been dealt with, but one of the musicians had popped up out of the huddled mass in the wagon and shot Bledsoe.

"What a damn bunch of yahoos!" he gasped out in his last breaths.

Bledsoe was bleeding terribly bad and his body seemed to convulse. Fletch was leaning over to hear what his friend was struggling to tell him. The lifeblood pumped out of him slowly now like a purge. Fletch turned to me and shook his head, and he showed me his bloody hands. When he turned back, Bledsoe had expired. It wasn't lost on me that his last name was the same as my Lizzie's, though they weren't related as far as I knew. Still, it awakened a terrible sadness in me.

"What did he say?" I asked.

"That outfit have shot and killed me. Take my pistols and kill all of them." Fletch's eyes were black and big as saucers. He stared straight through me.

"Are you going to do that?" I asked.

Fletch seemed not to hear my question. His eyes were vacant; his gaze went somewhere beyond me where he seemed to see some fresh horror on the skyline. "He was so surprised by it . . ." Fletch struggled to fight back the tears. "He couldn't believe it . . . I could tell . . . Just like . . . I can't believe it. Bill Bledsoe is dead." Fletch sobbed like a schoolboy.

Now he looked down at Bledsoe's lifeless form, but this time his eyes could believe it. He took in the sight of his dead friend and understood that no matter how young and strong and courageous you were, death could take you in an instant. It wasn't like he had never seen anyone killed before. Fletch had seen this many times and had done the killing even more often than that. But the sight of his friend's bloody corpse convinced him of his own mortality too. It reminded us all of what we lose in the death of just one good man who has been important in our own lives. It is in that exact moment we know those memories are now lost for eternity.

"Are you going to do what he said?" I asked again. I didn't want to imagine it.

"You just watch me," Fletch said. "Pray for me, Preacher. Pray for my soul, but you should know that I'm not sorry. I guess if a man's not sorry, then he can't really be asking for forgiveness. It's too late for *I'm sorry*, when surrounded by all this death. It is kill or be killed until this war is over, I'm here for the duration, by God."

He wiped globs of sticky blood on Bledsoe's pant's leg as best he could. Knowing Bill the way I had, I could say that he was not a man who was practiced at killing for its own sake. Fletch and Bill had been among those who had wisely held themselves back at Lawrence. I'd seen them sitting outside a boarding house drinking coffee and eating breakfast while others were killing indiscriminately and lining their pockets. Not that I'm saying either one of them was more noble than the other boys, but they weren't mesmerized by the murderous whore of war and its degradations.

Now Fletch took Bill's Colts, deliberately reloaded them, and stalked to the wagonload of men in the band. These latter were no doubt murmuring and hissing in fear as their mules trundled slowly away. Maybe some of them thought they might escape. Obviously, at least one of them was still armed too.

Fletch and a couple of other boys rode up beside the wagon and easily overtook them. They leapt from the backs of their horses and onto the wagon and looked down on the lot of men in the wagon. Cole and I were following along, galloping easily behind them in case Fletch needed more help.

"What are you going to do?" A voice cried out from the knot of men.

"You," Fletch said. "Toss that gun out."

A revolver came flying out of the wagon and landed with a thud on the ground.

"Just don't kill us," the man said. "Please mister. It ain't right. It ain't Christian."

Fletch fired Bill's pistol at the man three times.

"Oh, my God!" A man tried to stand up in the wagon, Fletch shot him down.

Some of the bandsmen were cowering in the bottom of the wagon while others had jumped up and were stepping all over them in an attempt to rush out. About that time the left front wheel came off and the wagon tipped over, spilling the men out onto the ground.

I expected Blunt's men to leap up and attack Fletch and the

others, but instead they stood up meekly with their hands in the air, indicating that they would give up without a fight. But it did them no good. Fletch and his men slaughtered Blunt's boys without mercy by emptying their pistols until none were moving or crying out to God. They even let the drummer boy have it, they were so enraged by Bledsoe's death. A man who was badly wounded claimed to be a reporter with *Frank Leslie Weekly*, but Fletch shot him in the face so he wouldn't have to listen to him cry for special favors. The rest of us were quiet and traded sober glances.

Fletch and his men set the wagon aflame. They began tossing the bodies back up onto the wagon like so much kindling. The smell of burning human flesh tinged our nostrils, but no one made to stop them. I sat my horse and watched Infernal's ears flick back and forth as he stomped and snorted his displeasure. A northerly wind gusted up, blowing the stinging smoke of human flesh into our eyes.

Eventually the slaughter was complete. We all understood Fletch's rage. The drummer boy got the worst of it and though it's true I hate to tell this part. The boy was not quite dead, only unconscious, and when his body made contact with the flame he vaulted out of the wagon with tongues of fire upon him. His body was burning like a living torch. We looked on in mute fascination as he crawled on his hands and knees like he could outdistance the flames. A gruesome preview of what it would be like to be tortured with hellfire on the Day of Judgment. But while this boy's pain was over in a couple of minutes I reckoned our souls would be punished in the Lake of Everlasting Fire.

From across the field of carnage, I saw that George Maddox was about to blow off the head of General Blunt's carriage driver, a man blacker than blue midnight, with thick lips and milky red eyes. He looked familiar. The conk of Maddox's pistol was against the man's forehead. The driver snatched off his own hat and held it in front of his chest like a supplicant. He was about to become another footnote to history while the rest of us gave Quantrill a few huzzahs for finally nailing the reprobate general. Quantrill was proud of defeating him, since a few other Confederate officers had taken their unsuccessful shots at that stout hide before.

No one really thought we were going to win this war anymore, not like we had up until Lawrence. We were still determined to put up a good fight. This is perhaps why Colonel Quantrill seemed determined to keep meeting with Davis and his cohorts to come up with a new strategy to win. They were too gentlemanly and West Point-proud to listen to the likes of us. This would be an important point when Sherman would employ the same brutal "total war" tactics against the South that Quantrill had long used. Only Sherman would go down in history as a great man, a heroic figure, who had only done what needed to be done to avoid more bloodshed. A controversial figure, but still he would be respected, where we would be mostly reviled and nearly forgotten by history.

My eye was brought back to Maddox, who had lowered his gun and was now dragging the slave by the elbow. And now I recognized him, it was George Todd's Rube. We had lost track of him. How he had ended up working for Blunt was another mystery.

"He wants to talk to Captain Todd!" Maddox spat with disgust. "I couldn't believe his guts. The mouth on this nigger. There I was about to send him to glory when he started babbling about Todd."

"McGuire!" McCorkle bellowed. "Go fetch Captain Todd."

"Please let me talk to Mr. Todd, sirs" Rube said. "He'll tell you. Please don't shoot me until I have seen him."

"You had better not harm a hair on his head," Cole spoke up. "Todd will skin you for sure."

"Over this one here?" Maddox laughed. "I think not."

"That's Todd's pet nigger there," McCorkle said and left it at that.

Soon George Todd came walking over with Speight at his arm. They looked at me with smirks on their faces. Things were back to normal between us, which was fine with me. I, for one, would rather see the knife coming as opposed to having it plunged into my back.

Todd's whole demeanor changed when he saw Rube. He took Rube by the hand and pumped it a few times with a smile beaming across his face. You would have thought they were brothers to look at them jawing at each other. I thought Todd was going to give him a kiss on the lips next. Even Rube couldn't help breaking into a cautious grin, as much as from relief at not being killed outright as seeing Todd. Rube had tears of gratitude in his eyes. I had seen them together before, so it was no surprise to me, but George Maddox seemed like the wind had been taken out of his sails.

"How do you know this man, Captain Todd?" Maddox asked.

"By God, it's Rube!" Todd exclaimed. "He was the best barber in Kansas City. He saved my life by telling me about a certain Yankee officer's plan to murder me. You were cutting his hair and heard it all, didn't you Rube?"

"Yes sir!" Rube said. "And I skedaddled right over to your boarding house and told you all about it. Didn't I? Hid you in my cellar for almost two weeks. Helped you escape. Didn't I?"

"That's right, you did," Todd was smiling ear-to-ear. "Listen," he said to the group gathering around them, "the first man that hurts him, I will kill."

"You a no-good bushwhacker," Rube grinned.

"That's right, that's right!" Todd laughed. "That's right!" Flinging insults at each other was some kind of old joke between them. He slapped Rube on the back and Rube clapped him on the shoulder like a comrade. Todd even took off his gun belt and reached around Rube's waist so that he would now be armed. We all looked at each other like maybe Todd had lost his wits.

George Maddox shook his head like he couldn't believe what he was seeing.

"You best come to Texas with us," Todd said and slapped him familiarly across his broad shoulders. "We need a good barber and a passable cook besides."

"You know I can cook. Yes sir!" Rube nodded. He looked to be breathing easier now. He mopped at his sopping forehead with a white kerchief. He didn't even acknowledge nor draw attention to the gun on his hip now but something told me he knew how to use it. "I can kill me some Yankees besides."

George Maddox only just then slid his Colt back into its holster with a look of great disappointment. He had been sure he would get to kill Rube, George Todd or no.

Todd stared at Maddox, "Any man touches Rube is a dead man. He might walk around upright on the earth after the deed is done but he might as well be dead."

"I understand," Maddox said. "He's your nigger. I respect that. I respect a man's property."

Todd growled as he held up a gloved finger and pointed it at Maddox, "You don't know your *arse* from a hole in the ground. He's his own man. He's one hell of a Yankee killer besides."

"Yeah," Maddox said.

"Or you could always settle it now and fight him yourself," Todd pulled a knife from its leather sheath at his waist and proffering it hilt first. "What do you say, Maddox?"

The boys fell silent to see what Maddox would do. Rube pulled his own impressive-looking Bowie to indicate he was game and flicked at the blade with his thumb and forefinger with a smile on his broad face.

Maddox sneered and half-turned away, "I'll take you at your word. Just keep it on a leash!"

Todd seemed satisfied that he had made his point for now. He hooked his arm around Rube and led him over to where his own men were gathered. Speight looked over his shoulder and glared at me. George Maddox spit on the ground so Speight would be sure to see his disgust. As for myself, I liked Rube because he was a good man to have standing next to you in a fight. I did wonder what he was doing working for Blunt, but no one thought to put voice to that question.

"It's a good thing Todd was here," Maddox said bitterly. "I would have stove the boy's head in by now."

The men were busying themselves dividing up all the goods of Blunt's party. They had found some fine food that Blunt and his woman were probably going to eat. They thought it great fun to feed each other, making fun of the lovers. We ate tins of fine delicacies. A good many of us were already well on our way to getting drunk. I know I was doing my fair share of drinking. I'd taken a fancy silver flask off the still-warm body of Blunt's personal guard. In it was whiskey and I helped myself by imbibing as much as I could stand with each swallow to help me forget.

Quantrill said no doubt Blunt had brought the woman along for his amusement on the way and most of us knew what he meant except for a few of the boys who were still virgins. A few of those were so young and naïve they claimed they were saving themselves for marriage. They were good Christian souls who had not yet seen enough of the War.

We had also found the usual ammunition and additional weapons. Quantrill claimed for himself Blunt's fine ceremonial saddle and sword. These weren't everyday items but used for official military functions only. Quantrill took a few practice swipes with it and, satisfied, he belted on the scabbard and replaced the sword. He was a vain man, but vain in a way that the boys wanted to emulate. He did have a style about him. I will give him that. For what other reason would a man buckle on a sword he would never use out in the field?

"We have defeated Blunt's boys!" Quantrill said it like a toast.

A cheer went up.

"Let's put out some pickets. We'll bivouac here for a while." Quantrill graciously received a five-pound demijohn of Blunt's own personal stock of exquisite brandy from John McCorkle and gave him a little approving nod before taking a shot in the neck. Our fearless leader even motioned me and Cole over to share a drink. It was a great honor to us boys.

Most of us were no longer mounted at this point. We were drinking and recounting all the recent events. I offered Cole a shot from my flask. He winced after taking a drink but said it was good, although his face said the opposite. We laughed. After we were good and roaring drunk, he got a little weepy. He wasn't so sure that he wanted to winter in Texas. I felt bad for him when he started blubbering about seeing his mother again one last time. We had seen so much death that we expected to be killed outright. It happened when you didn't expect it. That was nothing new. Why had the man beside you been taken and you were allowed to live? Fate was so random in that way. A few preachers I knew attributed it to God's will or His plan. I reflected that quite often God kept himself aloof from men's doings and allowed them to poleax themselves if that's what they were determined to do. I kept this view mostly to myself, though I did share it with Cole. He did not want to hear these cold, philosophical views. He said he'd rather think about the compassion of God and would continue to have faith in his savior before he flashed a sly grin.

"I don't want to end up in your hell, Ashby." He pretended to dab at his eyes with a dirty stogey. "Even if you are a preacher."

"WERE!" I said. "Was. I was studying to be one. It's all in the past now. You know that. After all this killing . . ."

"Still," Cole said. "It looks bad when a preacher loses his faith. Looks like bad luck to me. Besides, I don't want my soul to end up in eternal torment when I die with your flinty-eyed god."

"You're forgetting one very important thing," I said.

"What's that?"

"Who are you going to know up there?" I laughed. "All your friends, all of us, will be in hell drinking and getting our asses roasted! What will we do without you?"

"We got us another one." Will McGuire had come up and was pushing his prisoner toward us. "This will brighten your day."

It was none other than Jack Mann. Mann was infamous to many of us as a slave who had escaped from his plantation in Missouri and then went to Kansas and joined up with the Jayhawkers to serve as a guide to their mayhem. They must have told him he was doing the Lord's own work, but he had one of those faces that looked like it had just smelled something foul. In his case, that smell must have never went away.

It was another mystery as far as how he had come to be in the service of Blunt. There couldn't have been two more different black men in the state than Jack Mann and Rube, and I wondered how well they got on. Jack Mann was very striking with his hazel eyes and high cheekbones, whereas Rube, though a free man, looked the way you might expect a slave to look after years of hard labor, beatings, and bad-mouthing. But despite his looks, Rube had a different spirit entirely. He had a kindness about his eyes, and he could, and would fight for Captain Todd if not for the rest of us. I heard he'd personally killed at least a dozen blue bellies according to eye witnesses under Todd. On the other hand, Jack Mann had dangerous eyes like a snake waiting for a chance to strike. I didn't want him riding behind me.

At the time, we had more pressing matters to concern ourselves with. One thing I knew was that Mann was not long for this earth. Not only had he served the worst of the other side, but some years back, Maddox had settled with his wife in Kansas. Mann led his new masters, the Jayhawkers, to the Maddox house for revenge on anyone they could take it on. Maddox himself wasn't home, as he was away buying cattle in the Kansas City stockyard, so they had some fun at his wife's expense.

Mann even went so far as to disrobe in front of Mrs. Maddox and asked her if she saw anything she liked. He then dressed up in Maddox's nicest Sunday go-to-meeting suit and preened in front of her. Mr. Maddox said his wife had reported that Mann even grabbed her and kissed her and told her how he knew she wanted it. Maddox had talked about Jack Mann many times and it was an entertainment to listen to all the creative ways he planned to torture him if he ever saw him again.

"What should I do with him? This is Jack Mann." McGuire gave him a poke in the ribs with his rifle.

Mann sneered over his shoulder at McGuire as if he felt sorry him, despite the fact his hands were tied behind his back with a strong hemp rope.

"Oh, we all know who *he* is," I said. "It doesn't much matter what you do with him. As soon as George Maddox sees him, he will be a dead man. Get a good look at him now."

Mann spit in my direction with an audacious disregard for the pistols I carried. I would have loved nothing better than to put him underground to be later disinterred by coyotes and wild dogs. But Maddox wanted the privilege all to himself, for good reason. So I let Mann live for the moment out of respect for George's temper. Besides, I would fight Yankees but simply murdering people after the fight is over turned my stomach. It was dishonorable to kill a man on a whim.

McGuire stepped alongside Mann and gave him a smack in the face with the butt end of the rifle. Mann staggered; blood dribbled from his lips, but his eyes still flashed with defiance.

"Well, I'll be keeping a close watch over him until Quantrill tells me what to do about him," McGuire said. He tied the man so well to a post that Mann couldn't help but cry out in pain. Some of the boys laughed at him each time he hollered out like a great actor on the stage. In between his moans, Mann engaged in a spirited conversation about how this was illegal since he was a free man. "I've got papers," he said. McGuire just laughed at him and even went so far as to pretend to peruse his papers, though he couldn't read and then tore them into confetti and sprinkled them to the ground.

Suddenly I saw McGuire's head snap about when Mann started talking about what he would do to McGuire's mother at the first opportunity he was given. This didn't sit right with McGuire, whose mother had died in childbirth when he himsellf was a boy in Tennessee. He pulled out his pistol and shot Jack Mann right between his eyes, ending his tirade in mid-sentence. A couple of men came up and shook McGuire's hand and thanked him. We were all getting sick of listening to his mouth.

A few of the more experienced men were drinking coffee and laughing about how young McGuire couldn't handle the boy chewing on his ear. But after the initial amusement began to die, we began to think how Maddox was going to take it when he heard he'd been deprived of the chance to kill Mann. Everyone sobered up at the thought of it, since it was likely Maddox would release his rage on McGuire.

It didn't take long before George Maddox heard the news and came riding up on his sorrel. He yanked hard on the reins before throwing them in my direction like I was his servant. I might have thrown them in the dust, but for his considerable ire. His gin-blossomed complexion made it appear as if his head was going to pop, even his mouth looked about to scream like a steam engine on a paddleboat.

"Is it true?" George seemed to hover in the air like some kind of Confederate wraith as he flew to the body of Mann. No one had felt sufficiently inspired to bury his body. It moved me to see how cheap life had become at every twist of this war. Mann had been universally hated as much as those who knew Rube seemed to love him. Still, I suppose it fell to me, in the minds of the others, being the preacher and all, to worry after the freedman's soul.

"He was saying some awful things to me, George." McGuire shook his head regretfully. He was visibly pale with terror at the approach of Maddox.

"You killed him? *You* killed him? Say *you* didn't kill him, Will!"

"I only killed him for you," McGuire offered.

Maddox had both hands buried deep in the folds of McGuire's shirt. His entire body was quaking with impotent rage. He had wanted to pay Jack Mann back for being an "abolitionist nigger," for terrorizing his wife, and for daring to stand under his roof like he thought he was as good as any white man. These were unforgivable sins in his mind but he had McGuire almost off his feet. I feared someone with more authority or brutality would have to step forward, since usually we tried to stay out of personal feuds like this one, but Will McGuire was too young to realize he had stepped in shit.

George threw McGuire down in the dirt and went for his Colt. Then the little Crawford boy jumped, along with John McCorkle. They tackled George to the ground to keep from executing McGuire right before our eyes. The dust was flying as they rolled around on the ground like cats in a fight. They had his arms locked down, but he was frothing at the mouth and trying to turn his head to bite Crawford's ear. I jumped on the pile and managed to lock my hand on the Colt.

George thrashed around so violently I thought we might need more help. He squeezed off a round and the boys were jumping for cover. Finally George lost his grip and I threw the Colt away and George almost immediately went limp. He knew it was no use now. Angry tears appeared in his eyes. We were still wary to let him go, until he said he was all right and demanded it. The dust we had stirred up settled back down to the earth.

I jumped up first and stepped back a good five feet like he was a rattlesnake. It was hard to say what he might do yet. Crawford and McCorkle had not unknotted themselves, when I saw McGuire approaching out of my peripheral vision with George's pistol. I cursed under my breath. Was the boy so ignorant that he didn't know George might take it from his hand and shoot him, still? So I scooted over there in a hurry and took it from him. I hustled him off a few yards.

"He'll get over it," I told McGuire. "I'll give him this later."

"I'm sore afraid he'll try to kill me again."

"Naw," I said. "He'll be all right by and by."

"Bring my pistol!" George bellowed.

"No," I hollered back just as meanly over my shoulder.

"What!" George hollered indignantly. "You mean to steal my Colt from me over this?"

I turned and stepped right up to him. "Just now you need to go dunk your head in the creek and calm down. I'll hand your pistol over later on. I'll be damned if I give it to you now."

His face went red again and his expression said he might kill me with his bare hands. He breathed in and out like a locomotive pulling a hill and bent over at the waist. Maddox had always been a bit too proud of his handsome appearance and wore fine clothes. A half dozen widow women from around the state made clothes for him, cooked elaborate dinners when he appeared at their doorstep, and cared for him like the memory of their beloved husbands. He was not accustomed to hearing the word *no*, such were his powers of personality.

Suddenly, he popped back up again. As I said, the man was partial to his fine clothes, so it was rather entertaining to watch him go through his irritations. He walked off a few feet muttering to himself until he did an about-face and stood motionless before me. His body went limp as he raised his hand up and patted my shoulder.

"You're right, Ashby," he murmured. "You're right." He stumbled off with his horse in tow. He patted the dust out of his clothes. I breathed a deep sigh of relief, now that he seemed able to rein in his anger. We were all patting the dust out of our clothes too.

"Just keep that boy out of my sight for now," Maddox called back to me.

It wasn't long before we were all full of too much whiskey from the canteens. Someone was playing a whining harmonica but not particularly well. It made me think of all the dead musicians as a result of this war. The songs that would not be sung caused an ache in my heart. The boys seemed to have put those men out of their minds already but I knew appearances didn't tell the whole story. I felt one of my spirituals coming on. This was no time to lie down in the chert and start slobbering like a lunatic. I knew it was because I was worried and tired, so I took out my canteen from where it was draped over my saddle and splashed some water on my face. Still, I could not help thinking about the seriousness of war. To kill unjustly set heavy on the majority of us, but until such a time as it was over it was best not to dwell overlong on these battles. Who's to say the men we showed mercy to today would not end up being our hangman *overmorrow*?

A bear of a man was singing every bawdy drinking song he had ever heard in a fine baritone voice. The rest of us would join in on the chorus when we could. We were eating the fine food from the tins we had picked off of Blunt's men and we were genuinely having a high time. The drink was doing a job on me. I was talking out of my head about being a pirate or some such nonsense and picked up a Union cavalry sword and started taking vicious swipes in the air. I crept up to the body of one of the dead Yankees, pricking him with the tip of the sword, and swore at him. I even swatted his ass with the broad part of the blade for good measure.

"Get up! You Federal son-of-a-bitch!"

You can bet I was much surprised when the son-of-a-bitch in question jumped up and started screaming hysterically like he had sat on a pin. I thought for a moment I had somehow managed to raise the dead. He was holding the largely superficial wound I had given him in the abdomen and stomping his feet like a child having a temper tantrum. I threw down the sword and shot him in the forehead with my Lefaucheux and plugged him two more times to make sure. The other boys looking on were just as shocked as I had been, they all burst into laughter.

"What in the bloody blue hells was that?" Cole asked.

"He was pretending to be dead all that time!" A voice called out in disbelief.

"He's sure as hell dead now!" I said.

"You should have seen your face!" McGuire said. "You looked like you were going to piss yourself!"

"I think I did." I began to walk around stiff-legged like I had piss and shit in my britches and the boys wailed in drunken mirth.

Later on, when I had time to myself to think, I wondered if what I had done would be considered murder. I'd murdered the actor-soldier and then made fun for a cheap laugh. Why did I always do what I abhorred myself for later?

Early the next morning the troop mounted up and rode off under Colonel Quantrill's command. We left the Choctaw Nation and rode south into Texas until we crossed the Red River, where the earth was a scorched yellow blaze and the clouds hovered low over us like the white mountains I imagined in heaven.

Here we would make our camp at Mineral Springs near the town of Sherman. We terrorized the town as only idle boys can in such a situation. It would seem like a long winter because most of us were eager to get back to Missouri and take back the state from Ewing and the Federals once and for all, but time was running short as the bad reports came back from the East.

I recalled talking to a young man before the war started who was touring through Missouri like it was a holy pilgrimage, an expression of awe and wonderment upon his face, who referred to Missouri in reverential terms as *Zion*. I wanted to hold him in contempt for the way he swallowed the dog of religion, but even though his religion was different from mine, I couldn't help but feel a kinship with him. He bowed his head in awe at every landmark from bridges to lampposts to live oaks and even ornate hitching posts seemed a wonderment to him. I couldn't help thinking he had the right idea. If we could all see the sacredness in men, places, and even inanimate objects, how much better we would be. I was no Latter-Day Saint, but I felt the same for Missouri. After everything I had done and lost fighting for her, it was hard to see how I could feel any other way.

CHAPTER 17
Gone to Texas

Edwards, the journalist, was bent over his official-looking paper scribbling my words with his pencil like a mad prophet, an ever-present sneer on his lips. There were also the accoutrements of the writer's trade: a quilled pen with an inkwell, parchment paper, red wafer wax and a golden seal and what I took to be lampblack. On the table were a couple of ancient-looking signet rings that might have come from a deposed patriarch.

The journalist seemed to challenge everything I told him with a raised eyebrow or grunt. He straightened out his moustache as subtle commentary with his finger and thumb. I tried to tell myself I just didn't give a tinker's damn but who was I fooling? I coughed up another gob of blood into an already stained kerchief. Gulped a draught of ale from a glass at the table. It wasn't good for me though it went down fine.

I continued on with what I'd come to regard as the narrative of my war. Other men could tell it anyway they pleased. Occasionally, Edwards offered a counterpoint of his time served under General Shelby throughout our interview. The afternoon shadows began to lengthen across the room and the peculiar filigree of dust motes danced before the window like spirits eavesdropping on our conversation.

Mineral Springs, I explained as he fidgeted with a generous pour of a glass of scotch, appeared like a welcome mirage after our long ride. A safe haven of yellow grass, cottonwoods, fairly bulging with quail, wild pig and deer. Quantrill declared it a good place to make our winter camp, lick our wounds, and plot our strategies for taking back our state and our country.

We set about building rough cabins to make it through the next few months. We could fish the Red River to our heart's content. Swim in the creek or hunt up such wild game as we could find in and around it. The captains sent out official hunting parties so we would have plenty of deer meat for so many mouths to feed. It didn't take long for a moonshiner to appear out of the brush, selling his overpriced rotgut to the boys only too happy to part with their wits for a while.

Not too far away was the town of Sherman. At first, the townspeople turned out in droves to welcome us, waving hats and scarves and holding up children on their shoulders. They had heard of Quantrill's men. A few of them were families who had fled Secessia in the mass exodus after their homes had been laid waste. This made us heroes to some of them because there were those who wanted to return. Even for those who had decided to stay, knowing that our boys were still fighting for them made them bust with pride.

They stood along either side of the wide, hard-baked street and welcomed us to town. There were girls making eyes at some of the boys and a few young men who thought they might want to join up. Children and dogs capered around our horses. Old men from the Mexican War pumped our hands vigorously and caught us by the elbow at the same time to welcome us and, so they imagined, to pass along the vigor of their own once youthful blood. One of these celebrants, a white-haired gent stepping in postholes, shoved a glass of bitters into my hand and bade me drink. I drank it down, some of the contents rolling down my chin, and the old man reached up and retrieved the glass, as he was already getting winded. We were told they would meet us in the taverns later and buy us only the good whiskey.

"Hell, we would be happy to drink real black coffee for a change!" I told one slightly rotund hero of that other war. Unbeknownst to me, Quantrill had sold Blunt's ambulance and mules to buy literally hundreds of pounds of real coffee for the boys instead of the weak chicory we normally drank.

I had fallen in with Captain Bill and his men again and brought Cole Maddox along with me. Colonel Quantrill seemed to be growing more and more distant from those of us who served under him, as his greatest desire seemed to be declared bonafide by no one less than President Jeff Davis himself.

On another matter, I explained to Cole that because of Cole Younger, they would naturally start calling him "Maddox," if he was lucky or, worse, some regretful nickname too obscene to repeat in polite society. The James and Younger brothers were already making a name for themselves as full of the Devil.

Cole's face grew pale as he shrugged and told me to start calling him Maddox now, so they wouldn't have a chance to josh him about it. I had already rehearsed the proper introductions in my mind: *Cole Younger, this is Cole Maddox, he suggested we give you a nickname so we don't get you two confused!*

The time away from the fighting caused me to reflect back on those I had ridden with up to that point and now were either killed or disappeared from my life like Robert Huff, Henry Star, and my own beloved brother Gideon. I suspected he was dead, as no one had seen or heard from him for some time. He had grown tired of riding with Quantrill and the War itself. The last we'd heard, he had traveled out West to Nevada territory last winter, where he planned to make his fortune working the silver mines. I had long suspected he had been waylaid somewhere along the trail. In a letter he sent back home, he said he had lost all faith in the war's outcome and, worst of all, he had related to our mother in a letter, he had lost his faith in God. Not that I completely disagreed with him, but it showed a lack of disregard to tell our mother such a terrible thing when she had lost so much already. Now she fretted so over his soul's final resting place in her letters to me.

We were giddy riding into town. The town photographer asked us if we would like our pictures made so we pulled out our pistols and tried to look as menacing as possible for our future generations to admire. I wondered in the moment if we would ever actually see the photographs since I suspected the man behind the camera was either a huckster or incompetent in his art. He spoke to us in such insolent tones that once we eventually saw the terrible photographs some days later, we were incited to smash his camera and wreck his shop for his snide remarks.

This was merely the beginning of our misbehavior in general. When Captain Bill heard about it he insisted we comport ourselves as honored guests in Sherman and we complied out of respect for him. However it wasn't long until Quantrill's men became the worst enemy of Sherman, worse than an invading Federal army. Some of the townspeople were beginning to intimate as much. Even General Ben McCulloch was beginning to complain. Quantrill wouldn't listen to him either.

It was a relief not to be pursued by the militia of two states. Not being expected to kill at every turn made us feel almost human again. A young girl materialized from the cheering crowd and before I knew it Maddox leaned over so the girl could leap up and hug him around the neck and give him a quick peck on the cheek. I sent him a look over my shoulder to ask if he somehow knew her and he simply smiled and shrugged.

I'd never seen so many people so happy to see us. It made me feel slightly light-headed. The fighting of the last few weeks melted away. All the hardships appeared to be more noble in memory, the deaths preordained. It was that kind of mood the day we arrived. Even the sun relented and hid behind a bank of celestial locomotives floating high and fine in the empyrean sky.

Quantrill was ahead of the procession, now clearly reveling in the attention. I could see him from an oblique angle. He patted his great moustache down like a favorite dog and then waved to the ladies in the crowd, much to their delight. He cut an elegant figure on Old Charley, with his fine uniform and its golden tassels. Not too far ahead, to my left, I observed Captain Bill riding just ahead of us with furious black eyes. I have to admit then I admired them both for their comportment. At the time, I assumed Captain Bill had grown to despise the colonel. Now looking back through time's prism I wonder if he weren't more than a little jealous of the attention the great Quantrill received from his admirers! All the captains appeared to be living in some dissatisfaction in the shadow of his legend.

"I almost didn't recognize you," said a man on horseback right next to me. "Oh," I said, startled. It was Captain Bill himself. He had maneuvered himself to ride alongside me without my having noticed.

"You are young, Marchbank. You were there the day they took my sisters. They took your wife as well." It was almost a question he asked and difficult to hear over the din of people shouting and singing and playing instruments. I tried to look at his mouth, so I might catch the gist of what he was saying.

"That's right, Captain Bill," I said, finally. "It was a terrible day. I just the same as lost her that day."

I had tried to stay strong about it all this time. The mention of it caused my heart to grow heavy. My chin nearly rested on my chest. Tears welled up in my eyes. I averted my gaze then from his. I had not meant to start blubbering, but when I chanced to glance at him, his face was red, and he clapped me on the shoulder and I could see unshed, furious tears well up in his own eyes. It wasn't clear to me if he was crying in sympathy for me or for himself, but then he smiled that magnificent smile of his that caused young Missourians to join up with him by the droves. He leaned over his horse and clapped me on the arm. He pulled out a cigar, lit it, took a couple of luxurious puffs and let it down to me. I thanked him and savored the smoke from Bill Anderson's cigar. I must have closed my eyes, because when I looked up again he was staring off toward the horizon. Then without another word he *hupped* his horse and rode ahead.

Later some kindly folks took the reins from some of us and led our mounts around to a stable. It was a rooming house conveniently betwixt a saloon and a cathouse and the madam there was overjoyed to get some new blood and fresh coin for the joint.

That night I met an especially beautiful *entertainer* there with the unlikely name of Bush Smith. She had what we called a bawdy sense of humor. I bought her a drink and turned to tell an oft-quoted limerick to Maddox, when the next thing I knew Captain Bill was leading her off by the hand. In the days to come, the two were seen riding together and strolling through Sherman arm-in-arm, dressed seemingly for a high occasion. She did bear a strong resemblance to his sisters. You could say she looked like an

Anderson already, with that black hair and pale skin, but she was about as plainspoken as any woman of her former profession. By Christmas, we were attending their wedding to cheers and revelry. It was a happy occasion compared to the general backbiting that had taken over in the camps over the preceding weeks.

I just happened to be present when Captain Bill introduced his new wife to Quantrill. "I congratulate you on your wedding nuptials," Quantrill said as he sipped from a drink, then handed it to me to hold like I was his servant; he shook Captain Bill's hand vigorously.

"Thank you," Captain Bill said stiffly.

"Allow me to take a moment of your time," Quantrill said. He gave a look to Bush and some of the other ladies present. "If you wouldn't mind, I shall detain your husband for just a moment?"

The women made their obligatory excuses as Quantrill pressed in close to Captain Bill. His hand clenched the other in what could have been a friendly embrace or the beginning of a wrestling match.

"I'll come straight to the point," Quantrill said, "You remember that I forbade most of the men from getting married until this terrible war ran its course. It's different with you. You are a captain. One of the best. Some of the men throw my own dear Kate in my face, but for a leader there are some privileges. At the same time, though, the leaders bear the brunt of responsibility. Besides, I sent Kate back to her family in Blue Springs until I return."

"What are you trying to tell me?" Anderson's eyes narrowed suspiciously.

"I'm trying to offer you some good advice," Quantrill said. "As leaders we have greater responsibility as I was saying."

"Just don't try to tell me what I can and can't do." Captain Bill seemed to grow in height at the possibility that he and Quantrill might come to violence over this. "Don't tell me about responsibility."

"Please don't misunderstand me," Quantrill said. "I only mean that we can't afford to lose your leadership in Missouri. The boys respect you, the Federals fear you. I'm afraid that if you settle down to a life with a wife and children, it will all be cut terribly short. I beg you not to forget what happened to your sisters in Kansas City."

"I will never forget that!" Captain Bill spat out the words. His face was glowing scarlet with rage. "I don't need you or any man to remind me what those bloody cowards did! But Bush is my wife now, and you will just have to get used to it."

"There, there, Bill. I didn't mean to presume. I guess it doesn't matter anymore anyway. The Confederacy has all but lost the war now. It's every man for himself, between the two of us. If not now—it won't be long." Quantrill took back his libation from my hand as I was still holding it for him.

Quantrill knew how to make a point and he knew when to make concessions with the men but I could see Captain Bill was as shocked as I at his admission that he no longer believed we could win this war.

It wasn't long before it would become common knowledge that Quantrill didn't think his own men could win and that he was really only out for his own glory. Standing as proof were his efforts to curry favor with the high-ups in the Confederacy. But the more openly he talked in this vein, the less likely he would be to remain in overall command. He was still a young man, in his mid-twenties, but with this pessimism, he had begun to think like an old man. It just didn't play to the young men who served beneath him and thought they were born to glory and immortality.

As Quantrill drifted off, I saw that the brief chat had yielded its intended results. Captain Bill put his head down in what looked to me like shame, but when he raised it again, it was the old eyeball-burning rebel stare I remembered. He only gave me a nod and walked to rejoin Bush and the other ladies who were now encircled by suitors.

Bill and Bush did make a dashing-looking couple that all present envied, despite her recent profession. We were a rough lot but forgiving in that regard. There were a few sanctimonious shits who worried about those things, but hell, I was the preacher after all and it was fine by me.

Over the next few weeks even the captains weren't getting along with Quantrill or anyone else. The best of friends were irritable with each other over the most insignificant slight. Every one of us was thinking about returning to Missouri and making the Yankees pay with blood. Spring was about to break up north. It wouldn't be long before the leaves sprouted on the trees and gave us the cover we needed to continue our fight.

There were rumors Price was going to mount an attack on Jefferson City. Once the Confederacy was back in power there, he would lead an assault on the Union in St. Louis. I'd join that fight on my own hook if I had to, but I was fairly certain the others would do the same. Looking back on it now, I'm not so sure why we had so much faith in Price. He'd disappeared down South for so long he'd almost become mythical, but then he had the political clout and the will to draw the Secesh, though in the field he wasn't much of a general. We would fight our guts out for him if he would only just return, if it wasn't another rumor, to liberate Missouri from those damn yankees.

While we waited to return, Quantrill and some of the men grew bored and were going on raiding parties in the outlying areas of Texas. They were abusing her innocent citizens as bad as Kansas Jayhawkers. I couldn't believe it when I first heard about it; even Captain Bill refused to put any stock into the news until Bill Gregg told us he'd seen it with his own eyes. He'd been on one of these so-called patrols. Quantrill had forced a loyal Confederate family to feed the men before robbing them of their horses and cattle. Gregg said he didn't want to be part of it, but Quantrill and some of the others might have killed him on the spot, so he had gone along with it. The next day some of the men under Quantrill's orders killed a Confederate officer for referring to his bunch in a derogatory manner. I believe the term used was "that brush crowd." It was a favorite phrase used to describe us Missourians straight from the mouth of General McCulloch. Gregg told us he was considering trying to join the regular Confederacy and perhaps fighting back East with General Jo Shelby. Captain Bill told him he had too much respect for him to tell him what he should or shouldn't do.

The sun was molten as it came over the ledge of the earth that morning. Captain Bill decided to take matters into his own hands. He knew it would look like all of the men were involved in terrorizing the good people of North Texas, so we settled up and paid General Ben McCulloch a visit. On March 30, 1864 we arrived at the City Hotel in Bonham, where McCulloch had his base of operations. There was a slight chill in the crisp morning air. The smells of breakfast fires and horse and mule dung and the sounds of the military and the citizens of the town going about their morning routine seemed especially loud after our relatively peaceful ride here.

In Bonham, the people scarcely looked our way. Though we weren't outfitted like regular Confederates, they could tell we were fighting men and paid us no mind, but we did receive serious appraisals from the soldiers, which made my hand trail down to the Lefaucheux.

Captain Bill gave me a grave look and shook his head. He was possessed of such a cool head off the battlefield—I felt proud to serve under him.

There were only a dozen or so of Captain Bill's closest men, so our approach wouldn't look like some kind of assault. After getting the lay of the town, we went back to the stables and paid to leave our horses there. McCulloch's men detained us at the door and ordered us to relinquish our firearms, though Bill refused to do this until a boy was sent with a note upstairs to the general and then he in turn sent a message back down agreeing to meet with us. But only two or three of us, said a sergeant with woolly sideburns sprouting from both sides of his face. *The rest must stay downstairs.*

Bill asked his brother Jim, and surprisingly he tapped me to accompany them. I thanked him as we climbed the stairs. He explained we needed cool heads for this situation as he placed a brotherly arm about my shoulder.

Much to our astonishment, General McCulloch greeted us cordially, though he failed to step around the battered oak desk to greet us and remained seated. It was clear he did not want unnecessary interruptions. He had a commanding, self-important air, but at the same time something about his demeanor struck me as confused. He allowed a book with a leather cover to shut and tossed it on his desk with a thud.

His room was likely the biggest suite in the hotel. The particular room we were in looked to be a kind of dining room, with a great table strewn with official documents and maps. A large, well-traveled steamer trunk stood partially open and revealed neatly hung formal clothing, uniforms, and other personal items. McCulloch offered us drinks all around as the country's most uncomfortable chairs were brought in from an adjoining room for us to sit upon. We took off our jackets and hung them on the chairbacks before taking our seats, owing to the heat of the day.

"So!" The general clapped his hands together suddenly. "What brings you here today, Captain Anderson—is it?" He knew as well as we did that the rank of captain was more of an honorary title, he seemed amused at even using the title himself. "I hear you have news of what is happening with Quantrill and the brush crowd around Sherman?"

Captain Bill nodded. He didn't allow the insult of "brush crowd" to deter him from his purpose here. He stood and gravely explained the situation to the general. "It's not all of the men who are behaving this way, but the men directly under Quantrill have been given free rein. It's a regrettable situation, but even he cannot control his own men. Something may have to be done."

"Please be at ease." General McCulloch motioned with his hand that Captain Bill should sit. "By *something*, I assume you mean that something must be done by me?"

"I can't say what you should or should not do," Captain Bill said and then slowly sat down. "But I wanted to tell you personally that it's not me or my men involved in this gross misconduct, sir. I'm most decidedly not telling you what should be done, but

I'm saying that this is the problem before us. Most of his men are just boys who have never been taught real discipline. If things continue as they have been until now, he might just ravage all of North Texas. Perhaps he could be sent away? Ordered to fight back East?"

"Or arrested!" General McCulloch's calm was suddenly broken. "You should know I'm well ahead of you on the subject of *Colonel* William C. Quantrill." He sneered when he said "Colonel."

"I've already written to General Bee down in South Texas about taking charge of Quantrill, and would you like to know what his response was? Well, he would have taken them over. Out west of Corpus Christi was where I suggested—for your ears only. When I gave Quantrill a direct order to report there, he flatly refused the command. He stated that his commission as a Partisan Ranger came directly from Jefferson Davis himself and that he took orders from no other man! A ridiculous statement! I should have had him shot for insubordination on the very ground he stood upon!" General McCulloch pounded his fist impotently on the table. It was clear the general was accustomed to his orders being taken as the edicts of God.

"What do you plan to do, sir?" Captain Bill asked. "If I may ask? My men and I will support you."

"Well, what do you think I'm going to do?" Spittle flew from McCulloch's lips. "I'm going to have that man arrested and court-martialed for disobeying orders! I've already ordered him to present himself posthaste to me right here! But I fear he'll never come or follow any direct order that's given him. Even if that order came down from the Lord above! This is the disadvantage of using mercenaries in this war. He behaves more as a chieftain of a barbaric tribe than an officer in the CSA."

"I've heard they sleep with their clothes on in Kansas in fear of Colonel Quantrill's return," Jim Anderson said. Bill put his hand flat out as a warning to his brother not to continue in that vein.

If McCulloch registered the non sequitur you couldn't tell it by the way he stared distractedly out the window of his hotel room.

"Yes, well," Captain Bill said. "If you don't mind me saying, you will have to arrest him forcibly. I've fought with him for some time now and he'll not come easily. He's a crafty one. I'd be surprised if he comes at all. Even in response to a direct order."

"We'll see," McCulloch said. He indicated that we should take up a strategic position outside and warned us not to approach Quantrill if he did decide to show up. He needn't have given us this advice, since we all knew how it would look to Quantrill if he got wind of our talk with the general. Show up to be arrested? It didn't seem likely, but Quantrill always did have a penchant for the unexpected maneuver. If he could find an advantage in it, he just might show. We collected our weapons and waited.

Much to our surprise, just before lunchtime, Quantrill and two hundred men rode into town. It was easy to spot Quantrill up front on his big black horse. He managed to look regal, lonesome, and estranged from his own men all at once. The riders kicked up a great cloud of dust in their wake, trailing packhorses and mules loaded down with supplies. It was rather an impressive sight, until they actually made it into town and I saw for the first time maybe what others saw. Some of the men looked all right, but the majority looked like a gang of cutthroat street urchins, or as if some prisoner-of-war camp had just opened its gates. The level of humanity Quantrill was attracting these days was troubling. Most of them were vicious boys, treasure hunting under the toughest pirate they could find.

We were holed up in a burlesque house kitty-cornered, about a block away, where we could see the front door of the hotel from an alley window. Our horses were tethered just outside to a post and ready to go. Captain Bill was anxious to see what would become of Quantrill. He had to witness the demise of the man himself. It was a sad end to the colonel's leadership, but he wasn't fit to lead anymore and anyone could see that. He didn't seem to have it in him to give actual orders, for fear of losing what passed for loyalty these days.

"As sure as he goes into that hotel," Captain Bill said, "he's done for. They'll arrest him, and McCulloch will probably have him hanged."

"Or shot in the ass!" Jim Anderson laughed but then immediately looked contrite.

"Damn." I shook my head. I couldn't help laughing at Jim's face.

Bill glared at me, "I wouldn't want to see that happen."

"I just didn't think it would come to this," I muttered. I'd never figured Quantrill would just ride into town and hand himself over to a man like McCulloch. He was the sort of military-correct bastard that stood for everything Quantrill despised.

Quantrill and his boys rode up to the front door of the hotel. Quantrill dismounted and stood there talking to his boys for some time. A boy held his black horse for him and every man looked nervous as hell with hands touching their pistols for comfort. They scanned the doorways, windows, and roofs for signs of ambush:

Daren Dean

any place where there could be an advantage. To all appearances, McCulloch hadn't taken any precautions. Where were his men? We had seen a few go into the hotel, but not enough to take the old man.

Quantrill and two lieutenants went in and didn't come out. The hands of time seemed to move entirely too slow. He had been in there for too long. My hands were sweating.

"I think maybe McCulloch got him," I said to Bill.

"Maybe," he allowed. "Let's wait a bit longer, Preacher."

Just about that time, the hotel door came flying open. Quantrill had guns in his hands and he had lost his hat.

"Boys!" Quantrill announced as cool as you please. "McCulloch says we're under arrest! I said the hell with that! Let's skin out of here!"

The boy holding Quantrill's beast handed the reins up to him. The colonel was on the hellbitch's back and thundering out of town before any of McCulloch's men could even react. Two hundred men thundering into the flatland under the midday sun. Now, McCulloch would have a mess on his hands. How to arrest such a charismatic man who was considered a hero for his daring raid on Lawrence? How to catch such a man? What to do with him if you ever did capture him again?

We just looked at each other with dumb grins on our faces.

"Colonel Quantrill." Jim shook his head in admiration. "That sumbitch!"

"Can't they arrest one man?" Captain Bill said in frustration. "Send Jake to get the rest of our boys immediately!"

Bill looked at me. "We better get out there and offer our services. McCulloch's men won't be able to find their own asses with both hands out there."

In short order, McCulloch ordered a Colonel Martin to pursue Quantrill and take him dead or alive. Captain Bill attempted to advise the man, but he was given a contemptuous look for his troubles. There had been no time for proper introductions.

We knew Quantrill would head straight for the Red River and Martin was sufficiently competent to figure it out too, eventually. After hours in the saddle, we managed to come close enough to them to see their false battle line on a ridge. It was none other than George Todd and his men bringing up the rear so the rest could escape. It was a maneuver we were well acquainted with, of course. Todd and Quantrill hated each other, but there they were supporting each other again.

I saw Ed Speight and a tough cuss called Barker at the front of Todd's line, just daring us to come at them. Martin was hot to engage their line, but it was the old trick of leading the pursuing force into an even stronger second line to be shot to ribbons. It was difficult but Bill eventually made Martin understand. So Martin's men took up positions and traded shots with them, but here we had the advantage. Not many guerrillas carried rifles anymore because of the shoot-them-in-the-face style of fighting most oft engaged in.

We advised Colonel Martin to send a second force to outflank them, but he said he would not divide his force. It was clear, Bill said, that Martin was not ruthless enough to catch Quantrill. He was more concerned with obeying orders and suffering no casualties. He made the same mistake so many of the Confederate officers made in dealing with Quantrill. They thought him a gentleman and they treated him as such, but this was why they always came up on the short end of the stick against him. He'd cut Martin's heart out and roast it over a spit in the Sni if he ever had the chance.

"If you're not going to listen to reason," Captain Bill said. "You no longer need our services. We're going to leave you to it!"

There were about twenty of us who had broken off. We sat our horses in the heavy timber, when lo and behold we saw horsemen on the opposite side of the road. We couldn't have planned it much better, except now we were outnumbered. Todd hadn't had the chance to rendezvous with Quantrill yet, and we were probably the only ones who could stop him.

Captain Bill started firing first. He directed us to spread out in the woods so it might look like there were more of us. That wouldn't fool Todd for long, but it was worth trying.

They fired back at us. The smell of gun smoke in the air. I thought I spotted Ed Speight and aimed carefully to hit him true, but I wasn't sure any of us were doing any good. They wounded one of us and we wounded one of theirs was the upshot.

"Come out onto the road and fight us like men unless you're a pack of cowards!" Captain Bill called out to Todd.

"You have the most men," Todd rejoined. "Come in the woods and get us, unless you're a pack of cunts!"

Bullets began to fly in earnest again. They whizzed back and forth like greedy hummingbirds. The tree I was hiding behind was chewed up by gunfire. The green bark beneath the old bark was clearly visible, even to me, where it was stripped and falling away like a taffy pull. At the same time, there were gunshots north of us, which we assumed to be Martin's men engaging Quantrill's gang. I couldn't help feeling like a penned heifer knowing the problem but not able to do anything about it.

The boys across the way were firing less and less. It was

clear to Captain Bill that they were slipping away one-by-one. Normally, Bill would have given the order to chase them down and start picking them off one by one as they retreated, but we all believed we would end up fighting together against our true enemy in Missouri in a few weeks. Back in Missouri, I would not have thought it possible that we would all be openly fighting against each other or that Quantrill and Todd would be in a pitched battle with Confederate soldiers. It showed me clear that we were on our own. Our homeland was in Missouri. We were strangers, and the logic of the world was upside down here in Texas.

"There go the sons of thunder, Preacher," Captain Bill said as he clapped me on the shoulder.

"There they go," I said.

"Todd gets away again," Arch said. "That cocksucker has cat lives!"

Captain Bill gave me a nod and turned his horse back toward the camp.

We heard later that Colonel Martin met George Todd and Todd gave him a good tongue-lashing that sent him packing back to McCulloch. Quantrill had managed to escape from another impossible situation.

I began to pray for an early spring. I was growing more disillusioned with our cause. It had turned into murder and piracy on the plains, as I featured the things we had done since Lawrence. Each day I saddled up and rode further from Mineral Springs, as if I could influence everyone else to do the same. It was like a magical compass pulling me ever further north. I'd even told Cole about my frustrations, but he agreed it wasn't a good time to head back, since there would be nowhere to hide. As painful as it was to wait, we had no choice.

Returning on one of my rides I came upon a rider sitting his horse overlooking the banks of the Red. It caused me to remember a time when a big unorganized group of us boys were riding near the Missouri River and out of sheer boredom we took potshots at the highborn on a steamboat on a pleasure ride. The paddle wheels churned like mad, the water boiled with the movement. They passed so close I could smell food being cooked on board. A couple of passengers on deck returned our fire. We didn't actually hit anyone, but you should have seen the exodus off the deck! How we laughed our asses off.

Since I had the advantage on the mysterious rider today, I slipped down off the horse and pulled him by the reins very quietly. Finally I saw that it was none other than Bill Gregg. He had been one of Quantrill's lieutenants since the early days. I wondered what he was doing out here.

So as not to get myself shot, I called out to him, and he spun around with a pistol in his hand so fast he had me foul.

"Oh," Gregg said, "it's you. I thought you might be Todd returning to bushwhack me. What are you doing out here?"

"Just riding," I said. "I'm anxious to get back to Missouri. I wish we could leave today."

"You're riding with William T., eh?"

I wasn't sure about how to talk to Gregg, so I decided to add a little pepper to my speech. "Why? Who should I be riding with in your expert, fucken opinion?"

"Ain't nothing wrong with William T., but he's a mite rash."

"Some might call that bravery," I said.

"He no longer cares if he lives anymore, since his sister was killed in that damn prison. That affects a man's judgment. He'll ride right into the middle of anything that a sane man might not. You see what I mean?"

"I find your meaning strange," I said, cautiously. "What do you mean to imply by this talk?" I wasn't about to tell him that my own wife had been murdered in that prison but he probably knew as much.

"We can both agree," Gregg said, "he's a sight better than Quantrill or Todd. George and Bill are going to lock horns one day, and it won't be pretty."

"Who you going to back if that happens?" I demanded to know.

"You probably already know the answer." Gregg rode his horse nearer to me. "I hate Todd, but I don't trust Quantrill either. They are both a sight too greedy. The men don't really trust Quantrill anymore. The boys under him now are too green for my liking. He's made it clear he's about to give it all up to Todd anyway, when I'm the one who has been with him all this time. I could lead the men, but he's going to let Todd take his men one by one."

"Why?" I asked.

"Because he's afraid of Todd," Gregg said.

"Are you afraid of him?"

"I'm afraid of both of them," Gregg pulled out a weathered cigarette case, put two in his mouth, lit them with a Lucifer match off his belt buckle and handed me one.

I took the procured cigarette from him, nicely packed and rolled tight, and smoked it gratefully, "Thanks pard."

Gregg squinted his eyes from the smoke as he inhaled and exhaled the green smelling tobacco, "I guess you know, they would shoot you in the back if it suited their purposes? I've been studying on joining up with the legitimate Confederacy. I've been thinking maybe Jo Shelby's outfit. Has something of that nature ever crossed your mind? You seem to be a steady lad with a good head."

"That's not for me," I said. "I saw a man at Wilson's Creek blown into vapor. He followed his orders to the letter and what did he get for it? The only thing left were his blood and brains on my face. The common man don't rate too highly in the ledgers of those West Point officers. Me and my brother Gid figured that's what comes from following orders. They use you up like pawns. Ain't you read up about Gettysburg and Vicksburg?"

"Don't you have faith in the Confederacy?" Gregg squinted at me.

"I have faith in me living another day," I said, taking another deep draw on my cigarette.

"That's why you're with this outfit, Preacher. Because you have the market cornered on faith." Gregg spit on the ground. "If you don't see me around again, you will know where I have gone. I do not desire to kill old folks and boys in short pants to line the pockets of men with the temperament of Quantrill and George. I've lost all faith in those two. And speaking of lost faith, Bill and George both talked of giving the money we collected at Lawrence to the farmers who helped us back in Missouri, but that was all talk. Make no mistake, Quantrill and the others don't care about Missouri. They're fighting for themselves."

"Who ain't!"

"I'm afraid you don't apprehend the full import of what I'm saying to you." He turned to his horse, bounced on the stirrup, and leapt into the saddle. "Why don't you query your Captain William T. and ask him whatever happened to ole Charley Hart? I am sure it will be a most enlightening tête-à-tête. And ask him whatever he did with all those Missouri ponies. He'll know what I'm referring to." He flicked the nub of his cigarette onto the ground.

"I don't know what you're trying to tell me, but I don't like your tone." I let my hand down slowly and meaningfully to my holstered pistol. The cigarette still burned in my lips and now I was squinting up at him.

"Once a bushman . . ." Gregg shook his head. "This ain't got nothing to do with loyalty or honor." His horse spun in a circle as he mounted. Over his shoulder he called out, "You're a damn fool, Ashby Marchbank."

I would never have seen hide nor hair of him again, but I asked if I could accompany him back to Sherman, where he wanted-ed to gather some provisions and maybe have a stiff drink before he left Texas. Later I would learn that he distinguished himself under Shelby's Missouri Brigade and even achieved the rank of captain. A real captain.

I made a note in the pages of my Bible to look into this mys-tery Gregg had left at my feet. Who was Charley Hart? What did he have to do with anything? Maybe he was an old enemy we'd have to put in the ground. At the same time, I was hesitant to ask Captain Bill this question directly. It struck me as imprudent with the current state of affairs, though once we were back in Rocheport I might pursue it. Of course, I had heard the rumors that before the war the Andersons were horse thieves. I had also heard about bad blood between Gregg and Todd, but Todd didn't like anyone save his own bloodthirsty sycophants.

The beginning of the end for Colonel Quantrill's leadership came to a head not long after. We were in camp, many were getting rip-roaring drunk. There might not have been a stone-cold sober man in the entire camp. Todd was standing in front of a fire and swaying back and forth slightly like he was on the deck of a ship. He was boasting as usual, the "flag of distress" protruding from the crotch of his trousers.

"I fight for the Confederacy! The real Confederacy! The one that's going to win this thing!"

Todd was walking around those gathered before the bonfire with a wild glimmer in his eyes and his brogue as thick as ever I'd heard it. It wasn't clear if he was giving a rousing speech or deciding on someone to pick a fight with. "If you boys want to back someone who's going to give it to Billy Yank or them Kansas cunts, you just stay with ole George Todd! I ain't like some who can't be relied upon. Those sumbitches are only out for themselves and don't have the sand to win. Why, I ain't afraid of no man in this outfit or any other!"

"What about me?" Colonel Quantrill asked with a sneer. He looked plumb sober compared to the rest. "Aren't you afraid of me a'tall, George?"

Todd gave a wink and then stumbled around quickly backtracking his cakewalk around the fire, even stepping onto orange glowing hot coals, until he came to stand directly in front of Quantrill. The two eyeballed each other before Todd finally said, "You're the only goddamn bastard I've ever been afraid of! Who ain't been afraid of the great bushwhacker *Captain* William Clarke Quantrill at one time or another! But the only trouble is—that time is nearly over."

He took out his pistol and fired it into the blue. Some of the boys jumped up and fired their shooters too. A great roar of approval went up from the boys, as it seemed to be all in good fun.

Until Quantrill whipped out his gun and fired at Todd over the campfire and, miraculously, the bullet missed its intended target. Ed Speight took Todd by the arm and pulled him away from the light and off behind the men. Todd took a drunken shot at Quantrill in kind and it whined and thudded harmlessly into a deadwood log used for a sitting bench by a young recruit near the fire.

"Kill him!" Quantrill ordered imperiously to the men in general, but no one moved. Eyes and glances cheated toward Todd as the men considered what to do exactly. No one wanted to shoot Todd, but Quantrill had given the orders so many times in the past it was difficult not to obey him.

The majority of those present began to back away toward Todd, but strangely John Barker, one of Todd's cronies, locked eyes with Quantrill and nodded his support. They were almost side by side when like one man they fired at Todd and again both missed. Then it was a morass of running, yelling, tackling hands and feet, as those present rushed to tackle both Todd and Quantrill to keep them from killing each other. No one relished the idea of losing either one or both of their most capable leaders. The men would not allow them off the ground until they gave their strongest oaths not to resume killing one another.

"I wasn't trying to kill him," Quantrill said. "You men did right not to kill George but damn it all! He should not fucken taunt me. I'm not amused by his antics or his drunken speeches directing thinly veiled threats against my person."

George Todd's eyes rolled in his head like a lunatic's. It could have been attributed to all the popskull he had imbibed. Ed Speight exhorted Quantrill to promise not to kill Todd that night.

Quantrill slammed his pistols into their holsters, "I promise not to kill him in the next five minutes, but I cannot promise him the sanctuary of tomorrow!" It was an oath that would have to do.

CHAPTER 18
Return from Exile
April 1864

George Todd rode out of the Mineral Springs camp with his men. They were heading back to Missouri. It was high time we all returned to the real country we were fighting over. Quantrill followed shortly thereafter with about seventy men and crossed the Red River at Colbert's Ferry. The captains all took their men north separately by different routes, so they wouldn't be so easily discovered as a single unit, an apocalyptic wave moving across the country. I even entertained a dream, a vision that Sterling Price might meet up with Quantrill and Todd and unite them in Arkansas with thousands and perhaps then they would take back Missouri. That's what the rumors were beginning to jabber about anyway: the notion that Price was fixing to mount a final assault on the Federals in Missouri and retake the state; thereby, providing new momentum for the Confederacy to win the war.

But until then we waited.

It might have been a day later when Captain Bill gathered us around his little cabin with his wife at his side and told us to get our possibles. It was time to go back and kick the Yankees out! *Hurrah!* We jabbed our guns into the pale-blue sky. The time of our emancipation was drawing nigh.

We all scattered and came together a couple of hours later. It felt good to be leaving the strong smells of horse offal and human waste in the camp. The men were always cooking something which seemed tempting when one was hungry but sometimes made the stomach sicken otherwise. Along with ole Maddox, I finished off a bowl of turtle soup and drank my fill of my last cup of coffee in the Lone Star State and slung the grounds over the fire in front of the tiny cabin we'd called home these past few months. I was ready to return north and renew our claim on our true homeland. We raced out of the camp in high spirits, some sixty-five strong of the most gritty fighters you can imagine churning up clods of red dirt.

I hadn't received many letters from home and wondered how mother had fared of late. I had never worried about her health. I cannot recall ever seeing her in a sickbed or seeing her feel poorly. But once I had arrived back on the farm I was surprised to find that my sister, Sarah, with her husband, John Lawrence, and the baby were there too.

I shouldn't have been surprised. Sarah was dressed in mourning black. The dress caught my attention because it was made from such expensive material, bought from a clothier in St. Louis. Our mama had died from common pneumonia and had been buried a week before I arrived with gifts for everyone. My joy turned to sorrowful torment. Sarah embraced me as soon as I stepped foot in the door and I traced the scar Jennison had given her and a tear leaked from her eye. We laughed, too, with bliss at being together again. She kissed my cheek and ruffled my hair with a teary laugh like I when I was a boy.

"You're so big now," Sarah said. "You look older. The war has made a man of you."

I didn't know what to say. Speechless, I embraced her again.

Melancholy made her beautiful. She had been transformed into a fine lady by Lawrence's money and her own God-given grace. I was filled with emotions and found I could not speak at the very sight of her. Perhaps the clothes and her new lifestyle attributed to her refinement. She had become an important lady in Howard County besides. The only thing I could think to say was, "Remember when you took a potshot at that Jayhawker Jennison?" But that just reminded us both of all the terrible things that had followed. A profound silence filled the cabin.

Sarah had placed new candlesticks upon the tables. They danced in a slight breeze that made its way through the house from the window. She made a wonderful meal for us out of fatback, beans, and giant biscuits that tasted like heavenly air. There was apple pie for dessert and we savored our food in silence. There was a tension in the air between Sarah and John but I assumed it was a private matter and didn't dream it had anything to do with my affairs, though it did in a roundabout way.

Lawrence smoked a cigar and didn't appear particularly grief-stricken. To be true, he had buried two wives already and had a grown son older than my sister who lived in Kansas City. Mr. Lawrence, as I called him, shook my hand gravely and called me "son." I had heard him say because he was a farmer and a businessman that he must remain neutral in the hostilities in Missouri. I demanded to know how he would accomplish that when one or the other rode up to his grand house and affixed a pistol to the end of his nose and demanded to know if he was sound on the goose. He smirked at me because he was the kind of man who felt loved more by God than other men. There were certain friends in high places, who I took to be Union men, who were already backing his plans to expand his holdings. I called him a Black Republican just to get his goat! When he heard during dinner that Quantrill's boys called me Preacher, he smiled and laughed in mocking delight. Even so, I labored to maintain my composure, since he was my brother-in-law. But then he made up an accent of someone from the deep South claiming to be a good Southern man and then just as easily his voice and demeanor changed so that he sounded like a Yankee and begged for his life as a good Union supporter. He next blew a trail of cobalt cigar smoke in my face with that smug look of his.

In an instant I was on him. In our skirmish we knocked over his chair and I succeeded in dragging him from the table by his shirt collar, though he was much larger, and out the front door and laid him out in the yard and slapped him pertly across the face with the flat of my hand. I spat at him like a wildcat. "How do you like that, ole son? Huh? Are you happy you got what you've been begging for, son?"

Sarah followed behind and begged me, "Don't! Please Ashby! Don't kill him! Don't kill my husband!"

But I unsheathed my Arkansas toothpick, grabbed him by his thinning hair, and threatened to scalp him if he didn't behave in the future. Just so he knew I was serious, I gathered up the billy-goat beard beneath his chin and cut it off roughly with the knife just so he wouldn't be so eager to trifle with me in the future.

Sarah gripped me by the wrist and again pleaded for me not to make her a widow. She reminded me of those brave women in Lawrence, and shame overcame me, so I allowed him to live, although I knew he would be plotting for my death now. He had political connections with the politicians in Jefferson City. It might be a cold day in hell before I could come back home.

He saddled up early the next morning to retire to his Fayette

The Black Harvest   291

farm. I assured him I could accompany Sarah home when our affairs were set in order.

"One more thing," he said. He sat his horse like a farmer and not at all like the gentlemen he took himself for.

"What is it?" I asked between gritted teeth.

"I mean to have this house and the land that comes with it," Lawrence said.

"You'll never get it," I said. "Son."

"Oh, I'll get it." Lawrence consulted his pocket watch before slipping it back into his vest pocket. "In fact, I'd say I have it all sewn up already."

"Over my bloody corpse you will!" I said.

"Have it your way, then." He tipped his hat with something like grudging respect and wasted no time heading to his homestead.

"There should not be a gossamer of doubt in your mind that you will die first!" I shouted to his retreating back, but the threat sounded hollow even in my own ears. He should have known that the men I knew would be only too happy to visit Fayette and set things to rights.

When I visited our family cemetery, not more than a half-mile away, it was to find the earth itself had been scorched under the burr oak at its center. Lightning had struck the tree. Our family grave markers stood abused and listing in the aftermath of the recent storm. It was just like the Burnt District itself and I felt there was some sort of metaphor in it, but I could not bring myself to contemplate it for long. I wanted to be at liberty to come speak to my parents anytime I wanted, but if John Lawrence sold the place, the family plot would fall into disrepair or be blotted out permanently. I rolled up my sleeves and worked to clean up our family plot. I wanted to put a black iron fence around it all one day.

Sarah said she had only just arrived to find the doctor had given our mother laudanum for her pain and assured her that everything had been done to reverse the course of the disease, but in the end she had succumbed. The dark little medicine bottle sat like a monument on top of the bureau, testifying to my mother's death.

The only blessing I could ascertain that had come from it was that it brought Gideon, also recently returned home, he from his sojourns in the Nevada territory. I was relieved to see him since hearing from John Thraikill that he might be dead. I was on my way back to the house from my prayers at our parents' graves. They were buried side by side as they had always wanted. Gid tipped the brim of his bowler and grinned lopsided at me as we walked the field toward one another. He looked like a banker from where I stood. The bushwhacker Gid had all but disappeared. Finally, I broke and ran to him. It was like we were boys again. His hands were pounding me on the back as we embraced. We laughed to think we had both thought the other dead at times over the intervening months of his disappearance. For a moment, I would be lying if I didn't say I entertained the idea that we could partner up under Captain Bill. I featured us riding through the towns and counties of Missouri and cleaning it up for the decent folk who were left there. Not to mention the friends and family we hoped might return.

"There he is!" Gid said. "I would call you Dingis, but I reckon you would shoot me dead. A dangerous Missouri bushwhacker you've become!"

"Gideon! Gid! What a moustache!" I cried. It was greased and curled up rakishly at each end.

"Oh ho, Ashby!" He twirled one end of his greased moustache. "I'm a businessman and must look the part! On the other hand, your face looks like the tail end of a dog!"

"I never thought such a terrible *whacker* like you, one of Quantrill's own men, would turn tail and run."

"Terrible was right!" Gid frowned. "Oh, I could pull my weight in a fight, but making money is more my speed. There's an endless line of Yankee cunts just begging to have their throats cut, brains blown out, and to be hanged from pin oaks minus their ears and scalps! I promise you, your arms will get tired before Lincoln stops sending them. But I'm tired of all that carnage. I chafed even under Quantrill. I'm my own man now. Once you get tired of killing Federals, you should come out West into business with me."

"Doing what, pray tell?"

We walked arm in arm as we had as boys, through a grassy field of white clover, goldenrod, bull thistle, and bloodroot. It was as if a wild garden had been prepared for our reunion.

We were trying not to think too strongly of our recently departed mother. We both had practice at quickly forgetting the dead. We would speak of her at length at the right moment, with Sarah present, but not for now. We kept our thoughts to ourselves. Instead, we reveled in each other's presence. He wore nice city clothes, a fine brown suit befitting a banker. His hair was longer, his face had taken the quality of an alabaster statue. Prosperous was how he looked. I felt a pauper in his presence. I noticed a swing in his step that couldn't be missed. An aristocratic calm. A kind of hopefulness I couldn't remember seeing in him before he left. It was strange to see him without his Colts. Maybe leaving the war behind was the right thing for him, but I couldn't feature it myself. I was not yet glutted on killing all the cocksuckers I could.

"When did you arrive?" I said.

"Only this *morn* on a boat in Glasgow," he said. "I must soon return."

"I would have met you there."

"Don't worry yourself over it."

"I only meant . . ."

"I have news!" He clapped me on the shoulder. "I own a bar!"

"The hell you say!" I said. "What would Pa have said about that?"

"Ah, yes, the respected Reverend Marchbank!" He did an imitation of our father wagging a disapproving finger in my face. We both laughed at the accuracy of it. Everything he didn't like he'd proclaimed a sin, right down to eating too much gooseberry pie at a dance. There was no winning in his judgment, though we had respected him more than any other man alive or dead.

Gid waved his hand to change the subject. "Anyway," he explained, "I should say I have a partner. We own a bar in a mining camp near Fort Churchill. After I labored as a miner for far too long, a friend suggested I get smart and provide the necessities of life for these men if I expected to really get ahead. Whiskey being one of the more popular necessities."

"How do you like living among the Yankees? Don't that grate on you at all?"

"You would be surprised at just how many Southern men are there," Gid said. My partner even flew the Stars and Bars over our establishment for several weeks! What a glorious sight! It did make those Federal troops from Fort Churchill cuss, but they liked whiskey as much as they liked bitching into their cups. It was quite a conversation starter. I had to pull out my Colts when quarrels became too vigorous! Finally, I convinced my partner—

Arthur McCarthy, you would like him—to fly the United States flag so we could avoid having our lives threatened every day by soldiers, though it could be amusing at times."

"You did? You convinced him to fly their flag?"

"Don't look at me like that!" Gid said. "Sure, it was fun for a while getting their Irish up, but like I told Arthur, we're there to make as much profit as we can—not get killed! The whole territory is under martial law anyway. I ran into a few Missourians, but most of them were either Feds or Dutch!"

"I was hoping you might have come home for good," I said. "Get back in the fight."

The hesitancy was clear in his eyes. His gaze focused off toward the horizon as we walked. It had not occurred to me that my brother would never return home permanently. After everything we had been through, it was unconscionable that he would choose to raise up the proverbial white flag after bearing the black flag for so many years.

I pictured us fixing up the house together. It could use a little paint. Maybe add on an extra bedroom or parlor for formal entertaining when peace finally came again. He could live there with a wife and start a new family. I might be allowed to visit and stay on occasion. I featured building a house on the property so we could still be together as brothers, despite it all.

"Gid?" I bent at the waist to look up into his eyes. "Gid?"

"I won't likely be coming back here." Gid spoke against bitter tears. "There's too much pain here. I have a successful business out West. Art may only be able to hold it together for so long. Anything can change at a moment's notice. I will stay for a few weeks at most, but then I must return. It pains me, but it would pain me more to stay. Don't ask me to fight with you. The Feds have the Confederacy outmatched. It's a losing battle and I don't want to die for something as insubstantial as honor."

His words cut through me to the bone. There was nothing I could think to say.

"Come back to Nevada with me!" Gid grabbed my shoulder in earnest. "You could work for me! We could sell this place and expand the business! It would be so grand—"

"No," I took him by the wrist and slid his hand from my arm. "I'll never sell. I'll never sell and I'll never give up this place. I've fought too long for Missouri. They'll have to kill me this time because they'll never put me out again."

He looked hurt, but he didn't attempt to convince me otherwise.

"You'd better see to the deed," Gid said. "From what I understand, John Lawrence may have sold it out from under us!"

"If he does, it will go badly for him."

"He's a powerful man in Howard County," Gid said. "Are you sure that's wise?"

"I mean," I said, "I will just move in with them. We are family after all!"

Gid clapped me on the back and produced a great belly laugh. "I hope you will give some serious thought to my proposal. It would do your soul some good to get away from all of this death. This is the day the Lord hath made! Rejoice and be glad in it, like the psalmist said!"

"I don't think I could live in peace," I said.

"The grass is green and beginning to grow," Gid said. "The dogwoods are beginning to flower."

"You noticed that, did you?"

Gid grabbed for an invisible pistol on his belt and drew it.

"You'll soon have the cover you need. It gives me the itch just thinking about it."

"Why don't you carry a gun?" I asked.

"Because traveling the highway, that's the quickest way to get shot by a constable or the state guard. They're packed away for travel."

"You sure you don't want to throw in one last time with Captain Bill?"

"Bloody Bill?" he asked. "I read the papers. Bill Anderson is a good man considering he started off as a horse thief, but he doesn't know the meaning of the word retreat. I fear that despite his bravery, he will get you killed. I beg you not to crash the gates of hell with him leading the way, brother."

"I'll take care," I said. "But I have one question for you? Who in the hell is Charley Hart?"

Gid looked like I had just slapped him across the face. "Who told you that name? Where did you hear it?"

"Why?" I asked. "Who is he?"

"Charley Hart was a Kansas schoolteacher who fell in with the wrong gang," Gid said. He hated Kansans and Missourians alike.

"Is he still alive?"

"Oh, he's alive all right," Gid mused. "That's the name Quantrill went by before the war. He'll get you killed quick as Captain Bill. Don't doubt that. If it suited him, he'd be the one to pull the trigger on you."

"Is that why you're not riding with Quantrill anymore?"

"And some of the boys told me to go and never come back or they'd make me disappear in the Sni Woods."

"George Todd and Ed Speight?"

Gid's face went hard. There was something he didn't want to tell me about the situation, so he remained silent on the matter. It was a mystery without end, I thought. He shook his head and closed his eyes as he fought off a memory.

"Just don't die for them," Gid said. "They ain't worth it. Make sure you keep your head. Don't sacrifice yourself needlessly for their cause."

It was my turn to pull away from him. I wanted to accuse him of disloyalty or the inability to care, but he was my brother and I couldn't hold his happiness against him.

As we approached the house, a spring storm was beginning to kick up its heels. The clouds were low upon our heads, like the bad mood of God's mad glory, as they often seemed in that part of the country as if you could reach up and touch them with your hands. A tendril of black cloud came down like a finger and pointed at the old place for me like a message from the archangel to protect it. I knew the celestial digit demanded vengeance for all of this death.

The rains began to splatter our hat brims as we quickened our pace toward the back door.

CHAPTER 19
Attack on Fayette

Now began the wild, wanton, stupid assault . . .
Not one of the enemy could be seen, but the
muzzles of muskets protruded from every porthole,
belching fire and lead at the charging guerrillas.
—Hamp Watts, one of
Bloody Bill Anderson's men

So there he was. A young man in the early prime of his life that history wouldn't ignore, though he just seemed another one of the type of boys we needed. The lad was wearing his own frilled guerrilla shirt with cartridges stuffed to overflowing in his big pockets. He was all of 17 and freshly recovered from being "fatally" shot for the second time, but he looked no worse for it. Jesse had taken a bullet at Simpson's Ford on Wakenda Creek. I'd been hit in the back of my left hand. The skin was puckered and black. Even Bill had been shot in the leg.

I recollect it was queer watching the kid do everything up close, including shoot, because he was left-handed like me so it was like looking into a mirror. Little Archie had taken Jesse under his wing, though you would have thought it would be Frank's lookout. Arch and Jesse became fast friends. Even though Arch was a little fella, no one questioned his willingness to kill, his handiness with a knife, or his ferocity. Without a single order being made from Captain Bill to Arch, we knew Arch would show

Jesse everything he needed to know to keep his head on his shoulders. Jesse was intelligent, possessed of a great many queer superstitions, but capable.

An old farmer with hair as white as cotton named Jed Adams plucked out a version of "Old Joe Clark" on his banjo and a few of the boys joined in drunken hilarity with the chorus. The twang of the instrument filled our hearts. They filled their little tin cups full of popskull whiskey time and again. I was the only one present enamored of a large pitcher of buttermilk. I poured myself a large glass of the sweet buttermilk and ate several hoe cakes with molasses to boot. I was waiting for the cook to finish up the eggs and bacon frying in an iron skillet.

"Good to have you back, Jess." I clapped him on the back just as he had taken a sip of coffee. He tried unsuccessfully not to spit it out. Captain Bill thought that was hilarious.

"Thanks, Preacher," Jesse said, but his eyes narrowed and his body language warned me not to try that again. "Good to see you're still walking the land of the living."

"This is where I aim to stay. No streets of gold for me anytime soon, if I can help it." I could see that his experiences had made him a boy not to trifle with so I decided to steer clear of that quick left hand of his. We were right close in age anyway. His eyes continued to burn me so I cozied back up to him and said, "I was just funning you, Jesse. I'm glad to see you back from Company Q."

Then much to my relief, he smiled heartily and clapped a hand on my shoulder. He showed me a right, good-sized knife and said, "Good to hear you say that, Preacher. I thought we were going to have pull out these pig-stickers and come to an agreement."

"Lord-Gawd," I laughed as stupidly and enthusiastically as I could manage. I was becoming a regular thespian in the war. The truth is, he made me nervous, though I thought I could handle him if I had to. "I hope it don't come to that."

"Time to move," Captain Bill said. "We've got a meeting to get to."

"Who with?" Frank asked. "General Price?"

Old Pap was about to make his gambit to take St. Louis according to the tongue waggers, but he would have to sweep out of Arkansas to do it. He'd sent couriers all over Central Missouri to find all of Quantrill's men to ask them to raise hell and make a commotion to distract the Federals from his target. We were only too willing to do our bloody part. Captain Todd, Captain Pool, Captain Yeager, and Captain Holtzclaw and others had turned the summer months into a terror of retribution for Missourians with sympathies for the Federals. But the truth to be told, some didn't care who was in the way. If they saw something they wanted, they took it. It no longer seemed to matter what a person's affiliation was, unless they could be useful. Frank told me about running across other bands of guerrillas who had gotten the short end of the stick and they found them hanging high in the trees. A troubling sight for our cause.

It became clear the Confederacy might fall back East, but we clung to the dream that we could play a part in taking back Missouri with Price. Of course, Pap didn't realize that Quantrill was doing well to command his bowels these days. I mean, no one wanted to listen to him anymore. What we didn't know then was that the General was esteemed by the average citizenry but the people in high command did not give much regard to his skill. He was known to be tentative in battle. We'd heard he had over twelve thousand men, but what I learned later was that many of those men weren't even armed. A ragtag rabble of deadheads at best, when we needed a horde of well-armed, bloodthirsty demons.

"Nope, not Price," Captain Bill told Frank. "We're meeting Todd and Quantrill up in Preacher's stomping grounds."

"Howard County!" I said.

"I can't hardly believe that shit," Little Archie said. "Them boys are like an old married couple, aye god! One minute they're fussing and then the next they're fighting half the Union Army together!"

"Believe it," Captain Bill said. "I already sent that boy . . . what's his name?"

"Hamp Watts," Arch supplied.

"Yeah, him," Captain Bill spat. "I sent that Watts to be sure if I showed my face at this meeting that those boys wouldn't start shooting. Once the boy returns, we'll see what Todd has in mind. I think he wants to attack Fayette."

"Attack the Fayette garrison! Does that seem smart to you, Bill?"

"Nope," Bill said, "but I reckon that rascal Todd has a plan."

"I'm all for that," I said. "In fact, there's someone there I'd like to pay a special visit to. My brother-in-law, John Lawrence."

Captain Bill gave me a nod. "Now, I have heard of him. He's got money too, doesn't he? I hear he's a Republican son-of-a-bitch and someone who is about to be robbed and beaten under unusual circumstances by the Kansas First Guerillas!"

I nodded eagerly. I couldn't think of many men I hated more. I'd been entertaining myself on long rides by imagining different ways to beat him, as if I could let him have it dozens of times, and he could come back to life only for me to put him down again. I imagined his ears on a necklace in one of my revelatory visions. *Damn you,* I said out loud to his specter. The images my mind could conjure had plagued and troubled me ever since I'd seen him last. I'd fallen away from the Lord and given in to all variety of sinful ways. "So long as my sister don't know I had anything to do with it."

The sound of cicadas in the trees filled the air. The alien bodies with their opaque wings and bulbous red eyes littered the ground. The wind itself was still. The sun was so hot it was easy to tell it was going to be Hell's parlor by noon. My body was already slick with sweat under the blue uniforms we wore over our regular clothes. Anderson, Pool, and Todd were still arguing with Quantrill about the best way to attack Fayette. We hadn't seen hide nor hair of Quantrill for weeks, but there he was today, as big as life, with a story about being on honeymoon and a toothache. It sounded like a stretcher, but then everything he said was something to take with a pound of salt.

"I will participate in this battle," Quantrill said, "but only as a private, since I deem it foolish to attack the courthouse and that blockhouse. It's too heavily defended here. Besides, I've already made a similar attack and it just got my boys killed. We can't afford these kinds of losses now, but I defer to your hardheaded natures one and all."

"We're going to take that town," Anderson said to Quantrill. "No matter what."

"Fine, *Colonel* Quantrill." Todd's Scottish brogue sounded more pronounced than ever. "If you're too much of a coward, I hope you will send your boys in when we need them."

"Most of their force has left, Colonel," Hamp said. "They sent out a heavily armed patrol after us from the blockhouse before you arrived."

"Ha!" Quantrill said. "That's good reconnaissance, but I do wonder how you're going to get at the militia holed up in there. It's impenetrable as a keep. I don't imagine they're going to throw open the doors and invite us in for a bow and curtsy."

Bill answered, "Very good, then, If you want to come along, that's fine but otherwise you can go back into the woods and hide with the cowards."

"I will fight, but I do so as a private." Quantrill gave Todd and Anderson a sneer, a hand to his hat in a mock salute.

"You said that already," Bill said.

I could see Quantrill's point, but we were all thinking ahead trying to imagine Ole Pap taking back Secessia and the land coming under Confederate deed. It amused me to think of Quantrill and Anderson, two Kansas men, fighting so hard over Missouri."

"Look pretty, boys!" Captain Bill called.

"It's easy to look pretty on a horse like this gentleman here," Frank said.

"What's his name?" I asked.

"I call him Little George," Frank said. "I got him off a farmer in Jackson County called Big George." The big palomino's tail swished when he heard his name called. Frank leaned forward and patted his chest.

Captain Bill led us nice and sedate down the main road into Fayette, all nice and comely-like wearing our blue-belly uniforms. We were, in fact, planning on riding right down the lion's throat, and they just might open the doors and come out. They had a man high up in the courthouse cupola eyeballing us pretty well. Jesse said he wished he had a buffalo gun or some other sharpshooter's piece so he could pluck him right out of the bird's nest. We laughed nervously at that, since we were all thinking the same thing.

The closer we came to the courthouse, the more we saw just how easy it was going to be. No one was particularly alarmed. An old farming couple was setting up vegetables for sale on a wagon. The hands on the courthouse clock read twenty minutes past ten in the morning. Dozens of people were teeming about in the business district, buying and selling their wares. A few men were obviously on their way to becoming drunk as Cooter Brown. Presumably those were the men who had left their better halves at home. All around, the competing smells of a late breakfast, piss, and offal steaming on the brick streets. I gave a nod to a well-dressed man on his way into the bank but then it all went to hell.

A black man on the sidewalk was wearing a new Federal jacket and stood aside to watch us pass. He loosely held the reins of a sway-backed nag that was cropping the grass close to the ground. I am not now sure who it was, but a man up front drew his pistol and shot the man dead. He had taken some effrontery at a slave or former slave proudly wearing a Federal jacket and decided to kill him immediately. The shot sounded like it had emanated from a cannon.

Most of our boys weren't the sort to wait for orders, but the truth was, our fine blue uniforms weren't fooling anyone now. Hamp Watts leapt off his horse and fired two pistols at once into the thick wood of the courthouse doors, but they were as impenetrable as a bank safe or the entrance to a mausoleum. In no time, muskets stuck out of the upper windows of the courthouse and rained down bullets over our heads in angry orange explosions from soldier and civilian alike. The blue smoke already made it impossible to see

Daren Dean

clearly. The courthouse was made of stone, so it was useless to continue to attack it. Thus, we regrouped and set our sights on the log cabins on a ridge inhabited by soldiers.

Not quite one hundred of us formed a battle line and we charged up hill at the soldiers in the cabins. They were already firing at us as soon as we started riding toward them, but most of the bullets in that first volley whined harmlessly over our heads. Still, they fired and unseated a few of our boys. This was enough to give pause to those in the front of the line. We peeked over the rise until someone decided what we should do next. It was soon clear we were going to take another run at the soldiers.

"That was like charging a stone wall that fires back." Frank drank deeply from a canteen of water. He handed it over to Jesse.

"I can't say I enjoyed that!" Jesse snatched at the canteen. "You couldn't see them. Just their damned rifles poked out." He took a long pull from the canteen before thrusting it upon me.

There were two dozen or so men left out in the field. They had been blasted off their mounts and were either dead or wounded. A pale horse lay gutshot where it had fallen atop its rider. It screamed like a woman being murdered. The man, one of Todd's, was likely dead. The horse screamed like a tortured woman and kicked its hind legs feebly.

"Someone with a rifle, put that animal out of its misery," Pool's rough voice called out. A minute or two later a shot cracked and the horse kicked its hind legs and then was still.

"See, Captain Bill's coming." Richard Kinney, a good friend of Frank's since Texas, nodded in his direction. "He's damned if he does and damned if he don't after cussing Quantrill."

"We're all damned if we do," Frank said. "Any order Captain Bill gives is an order I'm going to follow."

Jesse nodded.

"All right," I said.

A young boy was passing out torches. I took one and so did Jesse. He nodded at me.

"Mount up!" Captain Bill called. "Where the hell is fucken Quantrill?"

We could hear Pool and Todd charging their men to get ready to attack again. When we had formed up, we charged the log houses, and our boys were screaming "Scalp them!" We could hear the terrified men behind their portholes calling to each other to wait until we were upon them. I saw two men just ahead of me shot off their horses in quick succession. Jesse and I made it to one with our torches. We set the house ablaze and made a retreat from the side of the house so none of the soldiers within could draw a bead on us. I clapped the kid on the back in relief. He turned and gave me a grim smile.

All of a sudden Ed Speight's cadaverous face loomed in front of me on a horse he made appear small. His horse rammed Infernal and knocked me to the ground. Todd's henchman was on me and he held me down with one hand and raised a wicked-looking knife over his head. I knew in my heart that this was how I was going to die. I blocked his downward death strike and took the brunt of it on my forearms.

I clawed at his face, trying to gouge at his eyes, but I couldn't reach him. My desperation seemed to amuse him. He spat in my face. He laughed down at me as I continued to struggle for ten more seconds of life.

"After I kill you," Speight said, "I'm going to take one of your ears for my necklace, Preacher." His hand trailed down to his chest along a strand of gory ears like strange, rancid fruit.

Daren Dean

"Go to hell, Speight." I growled at him. I managed to lean forward and punch him as hard as I could manage in his nose with a stiff left, but he seemed not to notice at all. It hurt my hand like hell.

His eyes narrowed. He began to plunge the knife down to my chest again but suddenly the back of his head exploded as if a cannon ball had smashed into it. Blood and brains covered me. His eyes widened in shock and disbelief. His body turned as if he meant to confront his attacker, but he never saw who ended his life. It was none other than Jesse James, standing there still in a crouched position and pointing the pistol in his Devil's hand.

Jesse reached out his other hand, jerked me up, and boosted me back upon Infernal.

"Couldn't let him kill a fellow Missourian," Jesse said.

"Thanks, Jesse." I had narrowly escaped the boneyard. My hands began to shake, but no one would notice in the heat of the fight. They were stained with my own blood and stung from the black powder caked there. I felt cold, sick of the fighting. The closeness of death could not be denied. My memory made a photograph of Speight's death mask in my mind, which became intertwined with my own near death. I could not shake that somehow our souls had intermingled in that instant, when Providence had intervened and taken my enemy as a sacrificial lamb.

We rode back hard to the little ravine. Frank appeared concerned. He gave me a taste of what he called "ruckus juice" in his traveling flask.

He wanted to say something, but he didn't seem to know what. Kinney slapped me heartily on the shoulder and bade me buck up, not in an unkindly way. Everyone save Todd, had disliked the man, but there weren't many who could honestly say they didn't fear his talent for violence. If it hadn't been for Jesse, I wouldn't be spinning this yarn today. I guess the experience made me see Jesse the man, instead of the legend. And it was no big thing to him what he had done. When there was no other way around it, he didn't shy away from killing during the war or ever after. I guess he'd figured himself for dead once or twice, it had changed his outlook.

The house smoked and fired up, but the soldiers refused to leave it. One soldier came out coughing. His body was smoking like he had just stepped out of hell. Flames leapt from the arm of his jacket. He waved it around as if the air might put out the flame, until he was shot in the forehead and went down bloody and hard.

The death of Speight had not gone unobserved. Some of Todd's men came toward us. They meant to pay us back for killing the big man. Captain Anderson and Captain Todd had dirty, furious words over it. Given our current situation, they agreed to settle it at a later time. Todd indicated to his men to get back to the line.

I saw Quantrill for the last time riding his screaming mount into the worst fighting, to scoop up Jimmy Little, who had been shot through the hips and a shoulder and lost his little finger I heard tell about it later.

"He's been shot to hell, boys! I'll be back directly!" Quantrill hollered. He soon disappeared through the smoke and the terror into the woods. I watched the hole where he had entered into the woods, but he never returned.

A new volley belched hot fire and brimstone from the houses almost in unison. The air was heavy with blue smoke, it settled about our heads, creating an evil halo effect over the saints of the Lost Cause. Lost already but we did not want to believe it.

We had no choice but to give up Fayette. It was a turkey shoot. We were the ignorant turkeys. Our cold, dead bodies would be the prize, every one of them, if we didn't walk away from this fight. I would never have said it aloud, but Quantrill had been right. Our pistols were no match for the block house forts, even if the men picking us off from the portholes were Yankee cowards. They would not have survived five minutes out in the open against us.

"After him!" Todd commanded to no one in particular. His face was red and blackened by smoke. "Bring Quantrill back here. I will hang him from an oak tree!"

Not a man moved to obey. Todd stalked over to his horse, jumped on its back and without issuing an order to retreat, rode to the Glasgow road. We all began to follow suit. A few of our boys stayed behind long enough to recover our dead and wounded from the field. Eighteen of our men were killed, and over forty wounded. It was our first real defeat in weeks, and it came at a terrible time, at what might have been the penultimate moment for Missouri's independence. It was one of the few times we had actually outnumbered the men garrisoned inside and lost. There was no time to lick our wounds. We had been whipped.

CHAPTER 20
The Centralia Massacre

It was a quiet whistle stop called Centralia that will live in my memory until I'm moldering in a pine box, both for the terrible things we did there and for the lives we took. I thought I had become immune to all manner of evil that could be done to us. But it was the evil we did in return that was impossible to forget. It's like Frank told me years later, "They called it a *massacre*, but what did they think those Union boys would have done to us if they had the chance?" Still, it wasn't the sort of Christian morality Father had taught me.

I guess I wasn't completely lost, since the event still pricks my conscience to this day. There wasn't much more there than a brand new depot, two hotels, and a store to that place out on the prairie. The North Missouri Railroad ran from St. Louis to St. Joe. And there we were, the Kansas First Guerrillas, ready to do our terrible business under Captain Bill.

We rode into the town dressed in Federal blue. A couple of elder gents with fine suits and stovepipe hats stood on the gallery of the Eldorado Hotel looking down upon us importantly as they leaned on the balustrade. The taller of the two shook his newspaper, folding it under his arm, and removed his pince-nez in a gesture of disgust. It didn't take long before the men realized we weren't Yankees and quickly retreated inside.

It was quite a sight to see a town in our state looking like it had never even known about the war until we arrived. The necks of men, women, and children about popped off as they turned to gawk at us amid the shouts of the boys for them to stay off the street if they didn't want to end up in the cemetery. We were on edge, wondering what kind of progress Ole Pap was making and if we were about to be overrun by a superior force. If the Feds got word what the old man was up to, it would likely be put down before he even got started, but they were of the habit to make decisions slowly. Bloody Bill, just for the record, didn't really give a damn what happened anymore, but he had decided to fight until the Cause was done with him.

The tranquility of the little town had an unsettling effect on us, especially those of us who had family forced to leave the state under Order No. 11. Why should these people have the right to be so calm and unafraid? Something didn't smell right in this town, it was like the literal odor of the tannery wafting toward us with the breeze.

We decided we would give them a reminder that there was a war going on and war was ugly. The surprised, fat faces of the men and their wives and children made us long for that innocence we had lost. Is it so hard to understand that we wanted them to feel our loss? The truth is, we envied them. This place reminded us of our lives before the war had yet begun. The light reflected a blinding opaque white off the windows of the general store, and Arch shot out a pane for his aching eyes.

We were sitting our horses, contemplating just what level of hell to unleash upon the place, when Hi Guess rode up and his pony slid to a halt in front of Captain Bill with a familiar looking redheaded cuss. It turned out it was Mulvaney, my friend the Irishman, who pulled up just behind Guess on an especially no-

ble-looking appaloosa mule. It was a happy surprise since I believed him to be dead. Bill's moody warhorse hardly registered
Hi's inferior beast. I had already tied Infernal to a hitching post in
front of the Eldorado Hotel. My legs and back were stiff from all
the riding of late, just like everyone else. I hobbled over to hear
what was being said.

"Ho there, Fader!" Mulvaney slipped off the mule, tied the
beast to a post, and kissed my knuckles like I was the Pope himself.

I pounded him on the back as we embraced, "Good to see
you, my friend!" And it did my soul good to see the Irishman at
that moment. "I was beginning to think something terrible might
have befallen you."

"Not me, oh no!" He said. "Only the good die young!"

"Found this one dead drunk on the road," Hi Guess snorted at
the memory. The Irishman smiled his fey smile.

"What is it, Hi?" Arch asked. He nodded hello to Mulvaney.

Bill only glowered at what he expected to be bad news.

The rider's face was scratched and smudged in red clay. He
had a pipe clenched in his teeth and produced little joyful puffs
of smoke from it. His clothes were streaked in mud, though the
ground beneath our boots was relatively dry. The sun was already
baking the mud back to clay, and I could feel the sweat running
down my back.

"I'll kiss your ass if we ain't being followed," Hi Guess finally said. "We were camped along Young's Creek when we spied
some Yankees following us."

"That's a queer turn of phrase, Hi." Arch crossed his arms
impatiently.

"Who is it?" Bill leaned forward.

"We think it's an old boy name of Ave Johnston, a major in the Thirty-ninth Missouri Infantry," Hi said.

Mulvaney interjected, "They're Union, they've been following at a distance."

Bill nodded to encourage them both to give more information.

"I'm not sure I'd be too worried." Hi gave a few more puffs. "I rode back and surveyed them. It looks like a bunch of farmers riding nags and plow horses. A few are carrying regular-issue Enfield rifles. They couldn't catch up to us unless we let them. I ain't too worried. The major might be figuring on making trouble directly. He's carrying a black flag."

"A black flag," Bill mused. He shook his head, "Ain't he the Devil's own seed, then? I mean, at least we don't carry a black flag. I agree with you, but if they're waiting for someone else to meet up with like that Colorado outfit I've been hearing about, well, it could be a little more of a challenge. Those Colorado boys are gritty, and some of them have good horses, but they use old-fashioned French dragoons."

"We could send that Johnston a little welcoming party," Jim Anderson suggested.

"Great minds think alike." Bill winked.

"Yes, sir," Hi Guess said with a little salute. He made a show of backing up his horse and then did an about-face to gallop away. Jim shook his head in wonderment at Hi's horsemanship.

Hi waved at a man in fine duds watching over the proceedings from his second-floor window. An old man on the street uttered an oath as he yanked a child of six out of the street so he wasn't run down by Hi's mount.

I went with Jim, Mulvaney, and Little Archie into a fine-looking house, Arch sat back in a chair and propped his boots upon the kitchen table and told the woman there to make him some breakfast. She started to squawk about it until he pulled out his bowie knife and from a seated position, threw it so hard it stuck and shivered in the wood above the French doors leading to the parlor.

The woman wore an all-black dress with her hair tucked modestly under a black lace headdress. She had piled straw-hued locks. Her eyes were a lively blue like a marble, and her face was pale, unmarked like freshly strained milk. I picked up a locket, which bore the image of a colorful yellow beehive on a mauve table with bees hovering around the hive on a bluish-green background. I thought to *blag* it but instead set it back down out of respect. My father had been a fierce Anti-Mormon and told me about their beliefs and symbols, though I didn't understand the full meaning at the time. I knew they were convinced that Missouri was the Promised Land, and their kind in Independence called her "Zion" even though they had more or less been rooted out of the state officially many years gone by though they hadn't all left.

"Where's your husband?" Arch asked the woman. She recoiled from him, mute.

"I say, where's your husband?"

The woman pointedly did not answer.

"Don't you know some Dutch, Preacher?"

"I don't think she's German, Arch," I said.

"Ascertain her fucken lingua franca if you can." Arch motioned with his hand.

"Bist du Deutsche?" I asked her just to humor him.

She just looked over her shoulder at me with her wide-set blue eyes. The stove had already been lit before we came in, and she turned to busy herself with a cast iron skillet and frying eggs.

"Wo ist dein Mann?" I tried, but this time she pretended not to hear me. "She's not German. I'd say she's Mormon."

"You don't say?" Arch said. "They speak English. Why won't she answer me?"

"Maybe she don't like the way you smell," Mulvaney smirked. He sidled up to the woman and smiled while he poured himself a cup of coffee from the pot and sat down at the table. "PARDON ME, MA'AM!" Jim spoke to her as though she were deaf.

"Don't they live and travel in packs?" Arch asked. "Shouldn't there be a passel of little ones and other wives too boot? The men like to have harems, don't they?"

"Maybe I'll give it a whirl." Jim sized up the woman. "She appears to be a fine example of their stock."

"We thought you had already converted," I said. Jim was almost as handsome as Captain Bill. Women threw themselves at him and his fine duds.

"Pour me a cup too, Jim," Mulvaney said.

Jim took down another tin cup out of the cabinet and filled it up. "Damn these little teacups."

"Maybe she's got something to hide," I said. "But she ain't German."

"Where did you learn such good Dutch?" Arch asked suspiciously.

"Well, I don't know how good it is, but we had a neighbor named Meyer and his family who helped us out during hog-killing season when I was a boy. I picked up a little from him. I used to know more years ago."

Arch's eye traveled up and down the woman's frame. The fact that there was no man about made him think she was fair game.

I knew how he thought. It made me fearful for the woman.

There was a noise in the closet. Arch's eyebrows went up, and he slipped out of the chair with his pistol in hand. All of us were well armed. The woman was watching us all with a look of terror on her face. Her mouth fell open and she began to pant, but we were more worried about what might be in that closet.

Arch grabbed the doorknob firmly in his hand. The woman let loose a panther scream. He yanked the door open and a half-grown boy fell out in a heap on the floor with one hand raised in submission.

"Don't—" the young man said. "Please!"

Arch grabbed the towheaded boy by his hair and hauled him out of the closet and into the middle of the room. The boy was bigger than Arch, but he still had his baby fat on him. A spring colt of a boy he was. The look in his eyes was pure terror as he stared at Arch, who kicked him in the backside just to see him wince. The woman, as meek as could be a moment before, swung a pot from the stove and slopped the boiling water on the arm of my shirt. I screamed out in pain. Then Jim grabbed her by her forearms in an effort to steer her pot away from himself. Mulvaney uttered some colorful oaths and backed out of the room. The water burned something fierce, and I jumped up and down holding my arm. She managed to connect with the pot just above Arch's ear. It didn't hurt him much though he'd end up with a goose egg later, but he reached out and grabbed her wrist and shook the handle from her hand. I grabbed his left arm before he tried to hit her.

"It's all right, Arch," I said. "She's just trying to protect her cub."

Arch looked at me with death in his eyes. He was a little guy, but most everyone who had dealings was plumb terrified of him. There was no backing down in him. I wondered if he might pull out his pistol and shoot me right there or cut my throat with his Bowie knife in my sleep.

"You are right, Ashby." Arch's eyes relaxed. The firmness about his mouth melted. He gave me a nod. "Get this puke boy out of here, woman! I don't want to look at him."

"You leave my baby alone!"

"Some baby!" Arch said. He held up his hand like he might smack her down and she cringed as she skirted past him.

"What's your name?" I asked, stepping between her and the boy.

She stared at me for a moment, and I thought she wouldn't answer until she raised her chin at me and said, "Bullock, Rebecca Bullock."

I must have looked like an idiot to her then because I found myself staring into her blue eyes. My lips soundlessly repeated her name, and then she stepped around me.

"Well," Jim said, "she ain't Dutch."

Mulvaney inserted himself back into the room and laughed. His moods changed quicker than the weather in Missouri.

The woman leaned down and pulled the young man up off the floor like a sack of flour. He clung to her. The boy whimpered, tears streamed down his face. His hair was yellow like wheat just like his mother's.

"Bad men!" The boy said with a pout of a young child.

It was now plain to see that the boy was a simpleton. Intellectually, mentally, he was barely more than an infant. Arch ascertained this about the boy at the same time I did and the anger went out of him.

The woman took her boy up the stairs. Jim still stood where he was, holding a tiny cup of coffee in each hand by the tiny half-moon handles with pinkies extended, though I'm sure he wasn't aware of it.

"Maybe she's going to give him some titty," Jim said.

"I can take care of breakfast." I took off my Yankee jacket and rolled my sleeves up to my elbows as I moved to the stove and looked to see what sort of victuals I had to work with. There was bacon, eggs, and some leftover mush I thought I could heat up in the pot. We were all hungry for cooked food.

"Maybe we can tuck the lady of the house into bed next," Arch snickered. "Don't scowl at me, Preacher."

Mulvaney produced a deck of cards. They argued about playing Boo-Ray or poker. I told them I would play Faro. I loved that game, even if I still found it to be a sinful practice, but the Irishman only had one deck of cards on him so I quickly lost interest. Even Jim didn't seem to be interested though he loved gambling so I knew he would play. Somehow his money belt was always flush. Arch pulled up a chair. I could still hear the young man upstairs, braying like his dog had been eaten by a dirt-worshipper. The murmur of the woman's voice was comforting to my ear.

After I'd eaten my fill, I watched the boys play cards for a while and then decided to smoke a cigarillo and sip a little whiskey on the sly that I'd found in the cabinets.

The streets were bustling with our boys. I heard them talking about a train of the North Missouri Railroad that was on its way. It might have tens of thousands of dollars in Yankee payroll on it, they said. There would be passengers to rob to boot. The worrisome part was that we knew there could be soldiers aboard from back East and they might be inclined to put up a fight.

Before the train could arrive, a band of men were whooping and hollering that the Columbia stage was on its way. It was going to be a race to see who could rob it first. It made me laugh to see them in such high spirits. They had already had their fill of ruckus juice, by the looks of it. I saw others running down the street unraveling bolts of cloths and ransacking the stores. Arch and Jim would be sorely irritated that they had missed the chance to raise hell.

A boy I recognized by his blond peach-fuzz moustache was smashing a stack of dinner plates while an elderly woman stood calmly by with hands crossed over her breast, cursing him methodically. I couldn't help shaking my head when I saw another of ours unwinding a long bolt of yarn down the street purely to hear the distressed calls of the shopkeeper. I could see Captain Bill at the end of the street watching the chaos unfold with a grim smile. He never raised a hand to rein them in.

It was clear all hell would break lose when a couple of men rolled out a barrel of whiskey to the front of the mercantile and broke it open for all to partake. A great cheer went up. There were a cache of brand new boots being used as demijohns to fill up with whiskey and walk the streets by twos and threes. Two boys were seated on a yellow parlor sofa near the edge of the street and drinking from their makeshift demijohns with satisfied grins. I wanted to join in, but frankly I was much more worried about how what we were doing would benefit Ole Pap's efforts to take back the state. This was our last chance and here these boys were getting good and ripped instead.

"Yonder comes the train!" I could hear the strident call of an adolescent's cracking voice.

Not too far distant the locomotive hove into view from the

town of Mexico under a blinding sun lluminating the golden wheat, bull thistle, and the horsegrass riffling on the plain. A bent plume of black smoke belched into the sky and the iron horse gasped its black breath into the cyanic heavens. She was coming in fast around the bend over the flat prairie land. It was clear the throttle was wide open. It started screaming at us and I knew the engineer had been alerted to our presence.

I hollered at Arch and the Irish to come running and I went down to the tracks in time to see our boys picking up rails and ties to heave across the track amidst drunken curses and guffaws. Surprisingly, the grinding sound of the brakes on the cars screeching and spinning, an ear-splitting clank of iron over the hiss of steam, as the train appeared to slow against its better judgment.

The other boys who had robbed the coach were just riding up to meet the train now. It was coming in hot and fast and chuffing hard. We figured it was going to attempt to smash through the blockade, but as it came up from Young's Creek it began to slow and finally stopped next to the depot as usual. The men held their pistols up over their heads, firing celebratory shots into the air. Some of their agitated horses leap-frogged at the reports.

I was just walking up when the boys began to fire into the windows of the train cars. Glass exploded inward and bullets dug themselves into the outsides of the cars. Some of the women and children began to scream as they threw themselves down on the floor of the car. It was such a surprising sight that I pulled out my pistols and ran to join the fray, thinking that our drunken boys were taking fire. The closer I got, though, the more it became clear that the passengers weren't firing on them at all. I wasn't certain if any of the passengers were armed. Was this an order given by Captain Bill or just something they did to terrify the passengers so that none would defy them when they were robbed? You understand, there was no pay for risking our lives. The Confederate government certainly wasn't paying, so we had to take what we could to continue to fight.

The boys were piling rails and ties and anything they could onto to the tracks to keep the conductor from speeding through the whistle stop if he was of a mind to do so. Just as the train came to a dead halt, a pack of guerrillas jumped up and pointed their pistols in the faces of the engineer and his fireman.

The conductor was named Clark, his hands were in the air, a faraway look in his eye. His soul appeared to have left its perch.

"Don't kill us!" the fireman shouted in extreme fear. He was visibly shaking, walleyed with fear.

"Give me your watch and your cash, you son-bitch," a blond-whiskered bushwhacker growled. He was with a gang of our new recruits, still wet behind the ears.

"And then you won't kill us?" the conductor's forehead had traces of soot in the lines of his face.

"Aye."

The little, broad-shouldered man surrendered his timepiece and a drawstring purse with reluctance and was promptly shot in the chest for his trouble. The boy who shot him laughed cruelly and the others joined in. The bullet tore a huge gash in his chest. He fell to the ground but promptly picked himself back up like a soldier replacing another on the line. This prompted another bout of nervous and somewhat amazed laughter that a man who had received such a vicious wound was able out of fear or some kind of supernatural power to gain his feet so quickly.

"Should I blow his damn head off?" The newly whiskered young man asked rhetorically.

"No," I said. "Don't shoot him again, or I'll teach you what real unkindness is all about, brother." The hat on his head was tilted back at a jaunty angle. I snatched it off his head and tossed it to the ground with force and stomped on it with my boot. The look on the young man's face was utter astonishment. I nearly laughed in his face.

Why should I have cared? Why show mercy when the Federals would not? I don't know what it was about the railroad man that moved my pity, but I could not countenance such acts. The wounded man staggered forward and after looking around with a bewildered, almost beatific expression. His eyes fluttered heavenward.

"This is the end." His face went slack-jawed before he fell down to his knees dead. I wondered if he were coming to some understanding of his own death or a comment upon us all.

"Alpha and Omega!" One of the boys hissed like a curse.

The young man spun around in anger, his jaw jutted out. He stepped toward me quickly. He was taller, younger, and probably stronger but I stared him down with my will. I had reached the point where it all seemed preordained. This young man or some other might bring me low any moment, or I might introduce him to his new home in paradise.

"Don't!" one of his companions said curtly. "That's the one they call Preacher."

"The Preacher?" he asked, turning his head over his shoulder. "Him?"

"Come here!" Another man pulled him aside and spoke fiercely into his ear counseling him to restrain himself. "They call him Preacher . . ."

The worst of the anger ran out of the young man's face, I

Daren Dean

walked on, but then I stopped and turned and thought about killing the boy just for daring to offend me. There is a natural urge toward anger when your life is threatened. People always talk about fear, but there can also be rage. Before the worst of these thoughts could overwhelm, I saw that women and children were on one side of the train being herded away, and well over a hundred unarmed Union men were on the town side in various states of undress.

There was some wild buzzing talk in a harsh, guttural language—some of them were Dutchies. They were new to Missouri and couldn't have cared less about Union or Confederate, just so long as they came out on the winning side. I'd known a few good ones myself, as I said earlier, but this was not the general feeling toward them. They were the ones Captain Bill wanted to put down first. He had no respect for them. His eyes were nigh hemorrhaging fury.

Some of the children and babies were crying. I could see, just between the cars, the boys demanding the women's purses and jewelry. The men had already been picked clean of anything of value, from watches to cigars to mementos and fairly large sums of cash. The Federals had just been paid before being sent home and on board we found bags containing their pay— thousands of dollars in greenbacks. The war was just about over for them until they ran into us. They had almost made it too—poor bastards. Where would we put them all, if we took them prisoner? The local calaboose was so tiny it might hold two people in its cell. The only thing to do was to parole them.

"Skin off those uniforms!" Arch bawled.

Some of our boys came forward to really rob the Federals good, now that their clothes were on the ground. They rifled through the clothes, holding up greenbacks and expensive watches.

I must admit there were plenty of times I'd robbed too, but this day was particularly murderous. I could see Captain Bill and Arch were in a mood and there was no stopping them. Another captain might have talked Captain Bill down, but having so many Federals in his hands made him greedy about dispensing death. His fingers were tracing that hideous necklace at his neck representing all the men he had laid low in his life as repayment for his sisters. He was practically frothing from the mouth now.

The men stood there in their underclothes looking ridiculous.

"What are we going to do with them, William T.?" Arch asked.

"Why, parole them of course!"

"Yes!" Arch agreed. "Parole!"

There was no escaping his meaning; they were to be summarily executed.

"Many of you have killed good Southern men!" Captain Bill hollered down at them from where he sat his horse with the righteous indignation of a judge. "You Federals say that there's to be no quarter for us. Well, I say now that I ask for none and I offer none in return. From this day forward, every Union man who falls into my hands will be killed without mercy, just as you executed and scalped them less than a week ago and left their bodies to bloat on the prairie."

"That wasn't any of us!" A boy shouted an entreaty. "Surely you don't mean to kill us for something someone else done?"

Captain Bill answered, "But you are wearing the same uniform, and thus I hold every damn one of you personally responsible. I treat you all as one!"

"Oh, God!" A man wailed as he fell to his knees. "Please don't kill us! Please see reason, sir! We're just returning from Sherman's army in Georgia. We had nothing to do with the death of your men!"

"Shut him up," Arch said to one of the boys, who went over and walloped him on the side of the head with his pistol.

"Have you a sergeant in your ranks?" Captain Bill asked. "Have you?"

No man would answer, but it was far from silent. The women were screaming for their men, and children were bawling. Someone had set one of the sheds behind the depot on fire; whatever had been stored there was producing a foul smelling-black smoke. The train hissed like a dragon brought low. Many of the younger men were jabbering in disbelief now at the thought of their impending deaths.

"There's one there!" Jim pointed. "Get him. Bring him forward."

Two men grabbed the sergeant and escorted him to stand in front of Captain Bill's horse.

"What's your name, Sergeant?"

"Tom Goodman," the man said with his head bowed.

"He'll do." Captain Bill waved him aside with his captors.

Goodman almost collapsed. He had steeled himself to be shot in the head and when it didn't happen at that moment his feet went out from under him. They dragged him aside so he could watch the proceedings.

Captain Bill raised one hand in the air and the boys with their pistols and a few with rifles raised their arms. When he dropped his arm, that was a signal to fire! The Federals were in disbelief. Some of them held their hands in the air. Some were crying openly. Others stood stoically accepting their fate. About a dozen were dropped with the first volley. Some lay wounded in the dirt and our boys stepped forward and delivered killing shots to the head or the heart as necessary. The air was full of swirling eddies of gun smoke on the air currents.

I had fired my pistol into the Federals. I was not innocent. I admit that I wanted every last one of them to die so the war could end, but I felt then I was perhaps destined to die in the same way. If I were lucky I would die fighting instead of stripped naked and shot or hanged by the neck high up in the bows of a sycamore out in the wilderness for the buzzards.

Some of my brethren hooted and screamed excitedly. But I couldn't keep my black thoughts from pointing their damning fingers of blame at me now. I was glad to be alive. Glad to be the one doing the killing instead of being the one killed, but the land was full of Federals; it was even money if any of us was going to survive the next few weeks.

"Preacher," Mulvaney said as he appeared at my side, "don't let it eat you alive! They would have loved to do the same to you. That Major Johnson who's on our ass now bragged that he would have the heads of Bill and George on a post in no time! So you see, we aren't the only killers here. We're just the ones doing the killing today."

There was a commotion down the line. A mountain of a man who had been shot several times didn't know he was dead and fought like a demon. The voice of a Yankee hollered, "Get them bushwhackers, Val!" The way he ran right at the line of armed men made me recall a time as a boy when we had killed a wild, charging boar. The boar hadn't been afraid, neither was this man now intimidated by the guns in his face. I had to admire him because despite carrying so much lead in his body, he wanted to live! He cracked Ed Brown in the jaw with a hamhock fist and Brown went down like wheat before the scythe. The giant scooted his big, mostly naked body underneath the train and disappeared under the platform. A bit later he appeared on our side again with a thick chunk of wood in his hands. A couple of the boys ran up to grab him and were knocked flat on their ass. He turned to pick up a railroad tie and heaved it up over his head as if to squash us all with one mighty blow, but then we let him have it with our pistols. He must have been shot twenty times before he dropped to his knees and the railroad tie fell away harmlessly, "My Lord—" he cried, and then he lay still in an eddy of dust.

"Damn!" Captain Bill said. "What I wouldn't give to have twenty men like him fighting under me."

"I didn't think nothing was going to stop him," I said, incredulous. We stood there looking at his great body, streaming blood from his many wounds. The men passed by for a look at one of the wonders they would not soon forget. Even Ed, still rubbing his bruised face, stood by, shaking his head in utter amazement at this force of nature.

Arch and Ed and half-dozen others walked among the executed men. They would give a man a proper kick in the ribs and if he groaned, a quick shot to the head was meted out. There was one man who had multiple wounds but one of his legs continued to kick at the ground like a metronome.

"Lookee here," Ed said, "he's marking time!"

I hated like hell to do it, but I walked among them and if a man was still alive and in pain, I used the butt of a rifle I'd acquired for the purpose or stabbed him in the neck with the bayonet to send the sad puppet to oblivion. Every so often a pistol shot rang out.

Bloody Bill climbed down from his horse and personally scalped a dead sergeant with his buck knife and attached the bloody trophy to his horse's bridle to go with the others. The turkey vultures, ravens, and other scavengers were already becoming attracted to the macabre tableau we had laid out for them like a great feast for all the feral creatures in the country. The birds fiendishly circled the killing field. There were twenty-two dead Union men on the ground.

"Don't forget Goodman," Arch growled at me. "He's coming with us. We're going to trade him for Cave Wyatt."

"He's an evil dwarf, isn't he?" Goodman asked.

"Be still. He has ears like a fox."

I picked Goodman up off the ground where he had collapsed. I didn't want to look into his sad face or be responsible for his grief or his person. It was like trying to move a sack of feed. As soon as I got him up on his feet once, he seemed to throw himself down again in despair. This angered me, so I grabbed him up by his elbow out of the dirt and let him know that if he tried that again, I'd put him out of his misery for good. It was all I could do to keep the others from killing him, despite Captain Bill's orders he be kept alive. One after another of my bloodthirsty brethren ran up to spit curses within an inch of his face. He knew his time above earth was limited to the whims of madmen.

No one ever saw a face as miserable as the one he wore. It seemed like a fool's errand, Bill's plan for him. The Feds might have traded for Cave last year or before, but it wasn't likely they would exchange anyone this deep into the war. Not even this sergeant, who didn't look like a bad sort, but still he was the enemy. It was hard telling how many deaths of the boys in gray this one was responsible for. They had probably strung Cave up as soon as he had fallen into their hands. They were all merciless hypocrites who insisted we treat them as prisoners of war while at the same time hanging or shooting us if given the chance.

A couple of hours later, after we'd left the little prairie hamlet in chaos, we were hiding deep among the wildwood canopy near a creek. Todd was dressing Bill down for the unnecessary slaughter of the Federal soldiers back in Centralia. For his part, Bill sneered openly and suggested that Todd didn't have the balls for this line of work.

Captain Thrailkill mostly listened, but he added a word or two in an attempt to cool the argument. Clearly, subtlety was not really a specialty of either man. Dave Poole was operating as scout for Captain Todd. He broke up the argument for that day when he informed the bickering leaders that Johnston was about a mile away and leading a 120-man column.

The sun had spent the day playing peekaboo with dark rumbling clouds. It reminded me of a day a week or so earlier when the rain had come down in sheets with booming lightning strikes like cannon fire. Later we rode in our own column under a brief rain while the sun was still shining, dew-gold on the hayfield we were about to cross.

"We need to ride out and meet them," Dave said, "because they'll be on us directly!"

The captains put their heads together and came up with a simple plan. That braggart, Johnston, undoubtedly did not know he wasn't chasing just one of the captains but had in fact come upon a veritable hornets' nest. Anderson would take his men on horseback and ram it down their throat. While he kept them busy, Todd would make his move from the left with about sixty-five mounted men and Thrailkill would distract from the right with about the same number. They put a couple of green recruits on the prisoners, including Goodman, riding around with us.

I rode with Anderson and he had us spread out as much as we

could at the top of the rise where we could look down at Johnston and his force. I watched the captain closely as he spoke with Arch. He was worried, since he didn't know just how capable this Johnston was. Was the plan too simple? Was there another move here that didn't present itself in some obvious fashion? Did he have more men awaiting over the next hill to flank us after the attack began? This officer was either very confident or foolhardy.

Captain Bill's demeanor began to change. His worry changed to blood rage. I'd seen this transformation before. He fingered the necklace around his neck as he let the black thoughts do their work on his countenance. In his mind, these men were each and every one responsible for the deaths and injuries inflicted on his sisters. These were not honorable men in his mind; they were Federals. These were the men who had had a building demolished to inflict harm on women. These were men who wouldn't honor a parole and make a trade of men. They'd rather hang every one of us they caught, even if it meant their own would suffer the same fate.

It didn't take Johnston and his men long to register us and they began to make preparations. Captain Bill ordered us all to dismount and tighten our cinches on the horses so we didn't lose anyone on the charge down the hill. I had to punch Infernal in the gut so he'd suck in and I could tighten the cinch. He raised his back leg up like he might give me a kick.

"Save it for those boys down there, old man," I said.

Frank James, Frank Shepherd, and Richard Kinney were sharing a cigar while the last-minute preparations were being made. No doubt it was an expensive smoke from one of our recent campaigns, saved for a special occasion like this one.

"Ho Preacher!" Henry Williams sidled over to me, pulling his horse behind by the reins. "Don't the Good Book say something about he who lives by the sword dies by the sword?"

"Don't call me that no more, Henry," I said. "It seems worse than sacrilege now."

"Ain't you been called?"

I thought about that one for a time. It was a question I'd struggled with in my heart since Jennison showed up on the family property. "If I was called, it was for an apostate generation by the spirit of antichrist in the world."

"I don't reckon I understand you." Henry shook his head.

"I will say it plainly," I said. "We're living in the times John the Revelator spoke of as the Tribulation."

"Isn't there any hope of salvation then?" Henry leaned against his horse with his arm around its neck.

"Just don't call me Preacher."

"All right," he said, "Fair enough. But just what the hell is your given name?"

I looked up at him, a little surprised, and smiled. "Ashby. Just call me Ashby."

"Well, Ashby, do you think it applies to pistols too?"

"I expect it does," I shrugged uncertainly.

"He who lives by the Colt," he opined, "dies by the Colt."

I couldn't help wondering what Johnston thought when he rode into Centralia and saw all the mischief we had created. All those dead men of Sherman's littering the whistlestop must have given him pause. What made him think he could defeat us? He didn't have the experience or the men capable of doing it. The Colorado unit were the only ones in the area Quantrill or Todd had ever expressed any respect for—Anderson was no respecter of persons.

They tracked us down with the intent of sticking our heads on poles. Johnston was motivated for the same reasons many officers did what they did for as long as there had been armies. He wanted his name to be written gloriously in the history books. He knew he was the man to stop the infamous bushwhackers, Anderson and Todd. I wasn't sure about Todd but Anderson intended to keep killing Federals just as long as they kept showing up in front of him. In fact, we all knew this wasn't a war we were going to win. At best we might be able to fight them to a draw. Winning wasn't even the point anymore. War had become a way of life for us Sni-a-bar boys.

Before we could remount our horses, John Koger suddenly laughed and said, "Why look at those fools! They're going to fight us on foot! Sumbitch Johnston must think he's Napoleon." And sure enough, Johnston had ordered the "fourth men" to gather up their horses and lead them away. They appeared to be forming up a battle line and fixing bayonets.

We knew we were going to cut every last one of them down to a man. They didn't have a hope in hell now. Major Johnston was just another *gloryhound* fool. We climbed back in our saddles and sat our horses, waiting for the inevitable order.

Butch Berry let out a quivering rebel yell.

There they were, waiting for us below. It wouldn't have made sense for them to charge up the hill and fight through the little forest line of sycamore, white oak, and poplar. We had to sit back high in our saddles as our horses navigated trees, mossgrown stones, and scuppernong vines along the hillock as we made our way slowly toward them.

After we cleared the trees, Captain Bill shouted his command to charge. We dug in our heels and laid down our heads close to the necks of our horses. Mulvaney was between myself and

Frank James one moment and shot off his noble mule the next but there were only a few of us wounded in that first volley as these boys were inexperienced and didn't allow for the convexity and movement of the earth, nor the breath of the gods shooting down our necks. They managed a couple of volleys that were also mostly too high to do any damage. Jesse James made an incredible left-handed pistol shot straight into the eye of Major Johnston, killing him dead. It was a miraculous shot, his horse at full gallop.

My eyes fixed on a noble-looking man in blue with his trembling rifle and I shot him dead in the forehead as he was attempting to reload his single shot. I shot a boy in the neck as he was biting into a cartridge. My horse tried unsuccessfully to avoid a squat fellow but ran him over. Farther back the boys in blue were beginning to retreat in chaos so we shot the cowards in their backs. We rode hard for the fourth men. Some of them had the presence of mind to leap onto their mounts and ride off but inadvisably toward Centralia. Others sat their plow horses in round-eyed terror and more were running across the field on foot, having left their useless one-shot rifles on the ground unfired. Captain Anderson couldn't give a care. He told us to kill them all. Track them down and make them all pay with their lives. Our boys were riding the best horses Missouri had to offer; nary a farmer would escape us.

The pasture was covered in a hazy rifle smoke. I gave up the chase and circled back around to the field of battle. It was truly a bloodbath there, like some medieval painting of the underworld. Their black flag turned out to be an apron hoisted on a pole. I suppose it was meant to mock us. All the men had been relieved of their arms. Oh, a few swung their rifles at us and continued to put up a semblance of a fight but they were laughed at and executed. I saw one veteran who shall go nameless here but you would know him because he went on to become famous in the Wild West shows years later, use Johnston's decorative sword to hack two men's heads off and exchange their heads for different bodies—a brutal joke. There hadn't been a big victory like this since Baxter Springs, when we had disgraced General Blunt.

Bloody Bill himself took up an Enfield rifle and smashed it into Johnston's lifeless face. After this, he instructed Arch to scalp the officer; then Arch, with Jesse James, went about and made sure all the officers had been scalped. Arch and Jesse were only too happy to do it. The young man was at least a head taller than Arch, but anyone could see he admired the little man's brutality.

If we thought dealing all of this terrifyingly violent death would worry the Federals, we were sorely wrong in that. If nothing it seemed to make the state home guard and the Federals even more determined than ever. New commanders were being sent out to Missouri from back East to try their hand at capturing the worst we had to offer. Some of these officers also used useless tactics but they were battle tested and they had iron wills compared to the farmers riding mules and plow horses after us. Not to mention the continued brutality of General Ewing's military rule.

"What happened, Frank?"

"They killed ol' Dick Kinney," Frank said. "He was my best friend I've known in this war."

"I saw him go down," I sighed, "and they got the Irishman too. He was riding right next to me one minute on that odd appaloosa mule of his—and then he wasn't."

"That's his blood on my pants."

Frank rode off into the few remaining men with their hands in the air, trying to surrender, laying them all low with his Colts. He shot one man after another right center in their forehead as if they were nothing but vermin. Frank was a one-man exterminator on his own but then Jesse appeared at his side seemingly out of the curling gun smoke and they grinned like demons as they moved through the dead and dying men. I recalled the story Jesse had told me about getting shot while trying to steal a fancy saddle from a Dutchie only a few weeks earlier. By accounts it was a shot that should have killed him but here he was again just as right as rain. I wondered if he'd made a deal with the Devil himself.

Dave Poole was leaping from one dead body to another like a grim brand of Scotch-hoppers. Blue-tailed flies descended on the bodies like hell's blanket. I had never seen so many of the enemy die so quickly in a battle before as if it were preordained. Captain Todd rode up with a look of consternation on his face.

"What on God's green earth are you doing there, Dave?"

Poole stopped with one foot on the chest of one dead Yankee and the other foot on the back of another. "I'm counting them."

"You needn't walk on 'em to count 'em, boy," Todd said.

"They're dead anyway," Poole laughed. "I can't count 'em good unless I step on them. They won't feel it in this life nor the next."

"That's inhuman, Poole!" I shouted. I was overcome by the barbarity of his actions. Poole simply proceeded as if he hadn't heard me.

Captain Todd waved his hand at Poole's foolishness. Then he glowered at me and I felt the blood drain from my face. He had not forgotten nor forgiven how his man Speight had died. He hated me and I knew he would get me if he could. I reached for my pistol but he shook his head as if to say, *Not now, not today.* I gave him a mock salute in return so that even if he thought I was nothing but a chigger, I wasn't too afraid to fight the prick. After all, half my family were Scots too. He threw down his half-smoked cigar in disgust and slowly rode away.

Another man called McCracken had busied himself cutting off deceased Yankee heads with an ancient sword and placing them atop another dead man's body. It was a gruesome pastime. I didn't have the stomach for it. He smiled to himself while he worked and danced a jig to music only he could hear. I saw him muttering secrets into the ear of a surprised looking Yankee head as if the dead man were outraged by the partisan's words. The man had had fiery red hair and the detail alone made me want to retch.

I took my own flask of whiskey out and drained a quarter of it. I knew we would all be getting drunk that night. It was too much carnage not to be affected. I tried, unsuccessfully, to close my mind to the grisly scene.

I ordered a couple of new recruits and a slave to help me recover the body of Mulvaney from where he had fallen. I tried not to look at his face. He had a pained expression and was still gripping his pistol, like he might sit up and ask after his noble mule in his musical accent. His features were not those of a dead man. His body hadn't hardened his death mask yet. He had just been playing cards at the Mormon table and I did not want to feature his death nor believe the reality of it. The older and taller slave found a rough wool blanket for me and I wrapped Mulvaney in it as best as I could to cover and protect his face out of respect.

There was a farmer named Rayburn, a southern sympathizer, who let us use a gleaming black cabriolet that was a bit fancy for our purposes but somehow fitting. He said I could bury him out on his land in gratitude for fighting the Federals. We took the body to a clearing where I'd remembered passing by a pin oak near a creek. It looked like a right pretty place to spend eternity and I hoped Mulvaney appreciated it.

But my conscripts were anxious to get back to base camp and get drunk with the rest of the boys so I let them go. The slave sat with me and we shared a cigar I had brought from Texas. He said his given name was Sam but his real name was Yearie. Yearie wore a beard and something about his demeanor was more reflective than morose. He asked me a few questions about my friend and when I said he was a good man though a little mad he laughed in a rich baritone voice. He knew about madness and pain. We handed my whiskey back and forth until we had drained it.

"What will you do after the war is over?" I asked Yearie.

"Depends," he said. "Depends on which side wins."

"Of course," I said.

"God or the Devil." Yearie grinned. He had sized me up before he spoke his mind. "If the Devil win, I guess I have to keep on doing what I got to do. But if God wins this war . . . well that would change everything. I'd like to travel up North and see the world for one. Maybe get my own land. All my family scattered like the children of Israel to who knows where. I'd like to make my own new family on a piece of land I could work for my own self. Truth be known."

"That sounds nice," I said.

"I do hope God win this war, sir," Yearie stared ahead like he was seeing his future in the air before us. He turned to me with teary eyes, "Forgive me when I say, I hope your side lose."

I found a large creek stone to sit at the head of the Irishman's grave with Yearie's help and scratched out *MULVANEY* with the point of my Bowie knife. The sun was partially obscured by a flimsy veil of white clouds with gray underbellies and the thin light that shone down over the verdant field made the regret of a friend's death all the more poignant. The sky wept a few stingy tears for the Irishman. Yearie took the cabriolet back to Rayburn and left me there alone.

Small flocks of starlings began to appear over the marshy land above the hidden valley. As I sat and smoked and watched the sun begin to set, there appeared even more starlings in a sometimes thunderous murmuration overhead. The birds turned and flew through the air as one organism, creating shapes in the sky that I perceived as a black swan, a crouching lion, pyramids, twisters, a whale, Lincoln's stovepipe hat, the black Christ from Revelation, and suddenly a darkness so complete as to nearly blot out the setting sun. Then groups of a half dozen birds seem to be separating themselves and dipping to the earth like black hailstones. Many of the birds flocked to roost in the tree next to the Irishman's grave as I led my horse away from what could only be a holy place. I felt as though I'd been called to witness something ethereal and rare, but mostly it seemed to me to be a prophecy of the war's terrible end itself, if only I could understand nature's sermon. What I thought I saw was something I never wanted to see but that's how it often is with unwilling prophets.

Daren Dean

Chapter 21
The Day of the Lord

As Anderson is taking the place of Quantrel [sic] in the management of cutthroats in Missouri, the question is often asked, "Who is this Anderson, who is more blood thirsty than Quantrell!"
—**Leavenworth Daily Bulletin**

If I had fifty thousand such men,
I could hold Missouri forever.
—**General Sterling Price at Boonville upon meeting Captain Anderson and his men**

I'd thrown the remains of the rabbit I'd eaten for dinner down an embankment and sat before the little fire I could ill afford to enjoy. It wasn't a smart thing to do, but I didn't give a tinker's curse. The flames were low and hypnotic. I couldn't help seeing the faces of my family, friends, my brothers-in-arms, who had all passed into glory. So it was rather startling when suddenly two Yankees on horseback appeared just over my shoulder. My horse hadn't even made a sound at their approach. It was rather fortunate that we roamed the country in our stolen blue coats. Mine was fresh from a boy I had killed at Centralia. The boy's old dragoon misfired and the look of fear before I sent him on to glory lingered in my thoughts.

A black ball of terror landed in the pit of my stomach. My

hand instinctively went for the Colt. I figured I could either lie to them or I might have to shoot them point blank.

"What have we here?" a man with an old country lilt to his voice asked—causing me to do a double take. I could tell he was an officer by the chicken guts on his shoulder.

I turned and jumped to my feet, feigning relief and joy to be found by these two Union men. I saluted like hell. I couldn't see them too well in the hazy night. There was no moon. The trees just a few feet away were ink-blot shapes. The night clouds were bloated with rain. You could smell the rain in the air as it began to sprinkle. The little fire I'd made flickered. I let my hand fall from my pistol.

"Sergeant Thomas Goodman." I pretended to be the man we'd saved from Centralia. "I was on my way back home on the train from General Sherman in Georgia when we were attacked by bushwhackers! It was the worst I ever saw! Just terrible."

"Damn." the older Yankee shook his head sadly. "You were in a tight scratch then. I'm Cahalin, this is Pope." He gestured casually with his hand.

I shook my head and let my chin bob down on my chest. The advantage was mine since they couldn't see my face any better than I could see theirs. Their hats seem to roost on their heads in the darkness. The white hairs of the major's Vandyke glowed incandescently in the dark.

"How did you escape?" Pope asked.

"Their leader called for a sergeant," I said. "A vicious fellow he was. He had dead eyes. He wore a hat with a star on it. Dirty hair down to his shoulders. I figured I was dead then. They said they was going to parole us. Instead they took me captive, ordered the others to strip, and killed them all. It was worse than an execution. I waited until they all got drunk and made my escape. It was—" I surprised myself by actually weeping quite sincerely.

"That's all right." Major Cahalin held up his hand and seemed to listen to the night before continuing. "We've been scouting for the bushwhackers all night. Have you had any close calls?"

"I did have to hide in a ditch earlier this afternoon," I lied. "There was a rebel outfit moving southwest, but some of them were dressed in blue. I wasn't fooled."

Cahalin didn't answer right away. He appeared to fidget with the reins. "I don't know how all this violence will ever be quelled."

"Don't worry, Major," Pope said. "They're all but whipped now."

The blood rose to my face, only they couldn't see it. It felt like I was standing before a blazing furnace. It was all I could do to keep from killing them right then. The threat of the men behind them restrained my hand. If I did this thing, I might manage to escape but probably not. The odds were not in my favor. I had to play it smart like a game of euchre if I wanted to sweep this particular sweep. Arch would have followed them from a safe distance and snuck into their camp under the cover of night and slit one of their throats and retreated without making a sound to terrify them in the morning but I didn't have time or inclination for that.

It seemed like their palaver would go on all night. They offered to take me with them. I told them I was looking for a friend who I'd served with who had also been able to escape or so I thought. The younger Yankee gave me a queer look like he either didn't believe me or thought I was bit out of my gourd. He whispered into the officer's ear. I thought I might have only a moment to start shooting and avoid some grisly death by hanging or firing squad. The images of boys I'd known hanging high in the trees came to mind then. I would not allow that to happen without taking a couple of them to hell first.

The officer ordered a young private brought me a bedroll and a few supplies. It was quite a relief, I cannot tell you. I almost laughed.

So instead of being hanged, I had to continue to play my part as Sergeant Goodman. None seemed to notice that my uniform had no stripes. They weren't interested in one man alone. The night appeared to swallow them whole as they moved into the fog but I listened for a quarter of an hour in wonder just to see if they might send their rear guard after me.

It took a couple of days to locate Captain Bill and the boys. I'd arrived in Boonville a day late to miss the meeting between Old Pap himself and Bill. An elderly woman on the main road through town told me the story. She described Price's disgust at seeing the scalps hanging from the bridles, but I couldn't help thinking he might not have been so surprised had he seen firsthand the depredations Missourians had to endure and if he had been fighting for all of this time instead of biding his time in Arkansas for most of the war. The woman told me that Captain Anderson had presented the general with fancy dueling pistols he had been visibly delighted to receive but he had sent Anderson and his men across the Missouri River to destroy the North Missouri Railroad. It wasn't lost on the old woman (nor on Captain Bill I am sure), that the general direction the bushwhackers had been sent in was away from where Price intended to go out and fight. I tipped my hat to her and she gave me some venison to take with me on my journey. I didn't realize how hungry I'd become until I was wolfing down her generosity.

I sought to pick up their trail. My horse was tired and daw-
dling. I was surprised to find them camped outside of Albany. I
should have wondered why they were so far from any important
fighting or goal, though they were under orders from Old Pap himself. Looking back on it, it sure didn't make any sense except that
as I said he was intimidated or disgusted by our ways.

I was ushered back into the fold by none other than Clell
Miller. He was just a young boy, really, who Frank James had
introduced me to before. He was a Kearney boy too. He kept grinning and shaking his head. Everyone thought I'd been killed after
the defeat of Johnston's foolhardy troops.

A boy led Infernal away to put with the others.

"Preacher, we thought you—"

"Don't say it, Clell!" I said. "It's good to see you. Ain't you
too young for fighting?"

"I'm fifteen years old now! Almost as old as you!" Clell stuck
out his lower jaw. I could tell he was hurt, so I chucked him under
the chin to show him no hard feelings. He would later run with the
James-Younger gang and be killed in their botched bank robbery
in Northfield, Minnesota.

"What are we up to now, then?"

"You want a tug?" Clell held out a bottle of bark juice to me.

I didn't really want any, but I didn't want to offend him so
I took a polite sip. He was a good boy but it didn't take much
for him to start looking for a disagreement. He was a young and
moody boy eager to prove himself.

Clell then dipped two fingers into his pocket and pulled out a
newspaper clipping to show me a week-old copy of the *Lexington
Democrat*. My name was listed in the paper with other known
bushwhackers. We were all, if the article was to be believed, ter-

rible marauders bound for hell in a handcart under William T. Anderson.

I glanced up at Clell as I was reading, and he must have realized about how far down the page I'd read because when I looked up he pretended to get all weepy-eyed and rubbed at one of his eyes like a baby. He grinned real big at my laughter, and I went back to finishing the editorial. I guessed we'd next have to ride to Lexington and kill the journalist who wrote it.

Truth be told, I hadn't seen my name in the paper since I'd decided to go to the seminary but this time it felt momentous. It might be the last time I saw my own name in the paper. I couldn't shake the feeling that the death cloud was hanging over me. For better or worse now, everyone I knew, the quick and the dead, would know that I was fighting for a just cause though I can't say I felt particularly noble about it. The story painted us black and dirty as they could but I could recall the bard once said, "Conscience is but a word that cowards use, devised at first to keep the strong in awe."

I still wanted the war to be over and to go back to the way things were, but we all knew that was impossible. I'd never be that naïve boy I was before it began. We once thought if we showed enough pluck, they'd get sick of fighting against us but they would never let us be now. Most of us who were still around were going to keep going until they shot us out of the saddle. It wouldn't have made much sense to stop now. Thoughts of the resurrection came to me now. In particular, every man I'd ever killed passed in my memory.

Then I received a word of knowledge from my Lord before the campfire. The first such communication in a long drought. He bade me feature the dead lying in their plain or ornate coffins, in ditches, and in mass graves. He asked me to meditate upon their deaths and their everlasting life. I saw them all rise again on Jacob's ladder to meet their Maker in glory. He caused me to see that I was no different from them. I was no more or less noble. We all die. We all may apply through the gift of salvation to eternity with our Lord.

I rode high on this vision for an hour or two but then I saw those who were still fighting with a missing arm, digit, or eye. A long sleeve pinned just so. Don't misunderstand me when I say I did not feel sorry for them but I did feel empathy. We were one and the same and united under the same cause.

It was at this moment that I gathered the boys who would come to stand near the fire with me. I prayed out loud one last time to the Lord. I beseeched our God Almighty to protect these boys as they rode into the next battle. I prayed in the name of Jesus our Lord, the Anointed One, to intercede on our behalf to the Father. I howled and cried for Christ late into the night. I was drunk in the spirit. I prayed for their salvation. I read the familiar salvation scriptures to them from the Gospels and in Romans and Galatians. I wanted them to know what it would take to gain entry into paradise. Some of them cried as we sang the old hymns. By the end of the night, they each clasped my hand and called me "Preacher" without the customary irony. We went to sleep with the dream of peace on our minds and the Lord's grace, but on the morrow He would help those who helped themselves on the battlefield. We would kill, kill, kill . . .

It had rained lightly in the night. Frogs sang us to a peaceful sleep. When we awoke it was to the certain knowledge that we and the other partisans were being hunted all over the state. I'd been dreaming that I was asleep in a bed next to a beautiful woman with long dark hair. Or I assumed she was beautiful. She had beautiful features, such as lovely hair, fetching skin, and comely shape in her bedclothes. We were surrounded on all sides by beveled mirrors, an oriental rug on the floor and the room boasted gaudy tapestries and drapes. It wasn't clear to me if this was a room I had once been in or created from my own imagination. The more the fog dissipated from my mind, with each drink of Essence of Coffee I took, I was quite certain it was no room I'd been in yet.

I still wore my dirty boots in bed, but upon closer examination I could see it was chunks of bloody human flesh stuck to them, as though I'd been working in a human wine press. The woman let out a filthy moan. I touched her shoulder to pull her toward me, but it seemed just as I began to pull her closer, she would shudder back to the same position. Over and over again it happened. It was frustrating that I could not ascertain her features or know her countenance. The sound of a door slamming firmly shut awoke me abruptly. My body started toward the door but when I awoke I found myself wrapped in an oilskin under a white tent beneath a canopy of oak trees.

Captain Bill was eager to meet all comers as he took good care of his smoke-colored horse. I saw him whispering into the beast's ear and it rubbed its head against him just like a great cat. I noticed he was decked out more than usual. He wore a white wool hat with a long, fine black plume in it. He had a shirt of black cloth, elegantly embroidered, a fancy blue cloth vest, and a frock coat and matching pants of expensive cashmere. I wondered if he was going to a wedding or riding into battle today.

A blue jay was cantankerous on a low-lying sycamore branch, delivering a warning to us. We all checked and rechecked our pistols. I now carried ten pistols into battle. There were four on short hemp ropes attached to my saddle so I could empty the chambers and let them fall. Two were in my hip holsters. Two larger pistols were in saddlebags I'd fashioned. Still two more were plunged for the moment into my waistband. I'd learned a thing or two over the last couple of years.

Captain Bill was making some sort of prayer or exhortation to a picture in a locket. Arch had told me the picture was not of his wife, Bush, but of his sister Josephine.

A Confederate captain I'd never seen before stood conferring with Captain Bill. I asked Jesse who he was and he said it was Captain Rains, the son of a certain General Rains. How he'd come to be with us I wasn't sure, but perhaps he had been at the Boonville meeting with Old Pap.

Frank took Clell aside and was giving him a talking-to. He was so keyed-up that I thought he'd be the first one killed if we saw any fighting, which we were bound to do. I was smiling at myself at the sight of Clell looking so cowed, but then I heard gunshots and horses approaching across the field. The outriders, about fifty in number, looked to be lost from some Eastern outfit or other and it was our duty to show them the error of their ways. It would be easy *pickins*.

We mounted up and gave chase. Captain Bill led the way and I let out a bloodcurdling rebel yell as I had never done before. Arch rode past me with a pistol already in hand. We were riding in a fallow cornfield that rose up to a great hillock before us where our quarry had disappeared.

Our captain never hesitated as he led us first over the rise. At the top of the mound, there was a little vista that would have made a great lookout. What we saw below us made it unnecessary to spy out the land since the outfit we were after was galloping away from us down a lane closed on both sides by cedars and scrub oaks. Before we could even catch our breath, Captain Bill hupped his horse, and we had no choice but to spur our own horses to keep up with him or he'd be fighting the enemy virtually alone. The battle line opened for the unit we were hot after and then it closed behind them like a gate.

Now we were all on short notice with reins and guns out. I had no fear at that moment, since we'd won almost every fight we'd been in with Bill leading us, if you didn't count Fayette.

Arch was hollering at Bill, but he either could not or did not want to hear him. Bill and Captain Rains were pulling away from us hard on their fine horses, lathered to the withers, when the trees on our right erupted with hellfire, nearly bringing our charge to a sputtering halt. I had taken a grazing shot to the ribs but managed to stay on my rearing horse. The pistol fell out of my grasp but remained on its tether.

The air was filled with smoke like a dense blue fog. The same tactics we had long mastered had been used against us and now we had been lured by Cob Cox's men in the same way. I was able to control my horse and spurred it on to catch up with a few other riders but still behind the captains. They were heading for a wall of artillery firing enemy rifles. The branches and leaves above us were pruned by the minié balls.

Captain Bill drove his horse straight into the mouth of the blue-bellied beast. His horse leapt over the first men in the artillery line, unscathed, with Captain Rains two lengths behind. His Colts were dealing death to those boys and it seemed he and Captain Rains might whip them all by themselves before we could catch up. There was a big Federal officer on an iron-gray horse carrying a flag in his hand bellowing orders and I knew Bill would try to kill that officer first.

The battle noise seemed to disappear as I saw a few in the artillery turn to shoot and Bill went down off his horse. Had he slipped from his horse? It seemed inconceivable that he could have been shot. That was when Arch pulled up short and I followed suit. That naïve pie eater, Clell Miller, had tried to follow the captains into the line and was likely unhorsed and worm food already.

Now we looked to Arch for what to do next. He was twirling his pistol around over his head and we circled back around to take another run at them. We couldn't leave Captain Bill with that lot if there was any chance he was still alive, but we had been outmaneuvered and now it was plain we were outgunned. We charged them again, but they were ready for us and a few of us went down before their superior numbers. There was nothing we could do except escape for the time being. We rode off knowing they'd be hunting us down like rabbits now. Luckily my horse hadn't been shot, even though I had. When it was safe, I took a bit of remaining rope and tied myself into the saddle like we did when some of us were drunk and riding across the Indian territories.

Poor Bill. I hoped he was still alive, but I had a word of knowledge straight from the Lord told me he was dead. What I did not know was if I was going to make it without being shot in the back by our pursuers or hanged by the neck if and when I was caught. No word from the Holy Ghost. He had gone plumb silent on me. My mind wasn't right to receive.

Was he dead? Arch insisted we had to be sure. We would circle back and reconnoiter. If he were wounded and imprisoned, I knew Arch would want to bust him out. But his brutality and fame had been such that I knew they would never allow Bloody Bill Anderson to live.

He had terrified me more than all the other chieftains we'd followed; I respected him the most, though he had been the youngest of them. I felt I understood his reasons for fighting better than the rest since mine were of the same fabric. His story made sense to me because most of the particulars were true. If anyone had bothered to ask me, as much as I had loved the man, I would have said his soul would not rise again on the Day of The Lord. That didn't mean he wasn't a good man. The Almighty had always set his standards for men far too high.

About a week later, I read the following in the *St. Joseph Morning Herald*: "An avenging God has permitted bullets fired from federal muskets to pierce his head and the inhuman butcher of Centralia sleeps his last sleep."

Chapter 22
We Follow Clement

After the death of Captain Bill in the Guerrilla Confederate States Army, things began to change in a blazing rush. The Army of Missouri, under Ole Pap, was routed at virtually the same moment Captain Bill fell dead from his great black warhorse. Our dreams for Missouri were over, though none of us wanted to accept it, and many of us refused to believe it for at least another calendar year.

Captain Todd had been killed by a Yankee sniper on a scouting mission for Price outside of Independence. I was relieved, to say the least, though it was a blow to our cause. I wasn't exactly sorry the Scottish prick was dead, but I kept my tongue on the subject. Dave Poole took over Todd's men by unanimous vote until Old Pap and his army were driven back in defeat down into the wild Ozark forests of Arkansas for the second time. What was left of Price, including General Jo Shelby and his followers, retreated all the way back to Texas. Old Pap had turned out to be not much of a savior for the beleaguered state of Missouri.

Colonel Quantrill was shot on May 10, 1865, down in Kentucky by a Union bushwhacker named Terrell hired to find and kill him; he died from his wounds after a shootout about a month later. Quantrill, as slippery as ever, claimed to be a certain Captain Clarke, in the hope that would thus avoid saving his neck from stretching. Some of the boys were traveling with him, including Frank James, but I had kept myself busy doing what we had always done but this time with Jim and Arch leading us. It seemed natural enough, but the only thing missing was someone strong enough to veto some of Arch's wilder notions about what we could and could not accomplish.

Even though they said it was over, it didn't feel any different to us. Those of us who had been fighting for the duration weren't fit to return to peaceful living, having seen or committed too many grievous acts and remained above ground.

We had been tried in the "furnace of the affliction" as I heard one good Southern lady exclaim once she returned to what had been called the Burnt District after Order No. 11. The fire had not died out in what many a good person long referred to as "Quantrill's Missouri," though I'd never say it, knowing all I know about the man now. I had been too young to know that the man was a scoundrel. What Todd and others had accused him of had been true all along. He wasn't from Maryland but Ohio. There was no dead brother killed by Yankees, either. He had made it all up. Not that any man needed some moral reason to justify fighting, but to claim one went hard against even my own jaded principles. He had lived a charmed life for most of the war and had died in excruciating pain from his wounds. If his death was justly deserved, then I can only say, may not all of us suffer the death we merit. Some funerals would be attended by devils if this were the case.

In May of 1865 my blood didn't burn as bright for revenge as it had before. I knew I could not remain human if I did not give up this indiscriminate killing. There was no longer any hope for it. Arch was firmly in charge now, and he was as devilish and hungry for Yankee scalps as ever. The only problem was that we had to go to great and foolish lengths to engage the enemy, since we had all ostensibly given up—as the newspapers would have it. I knew I'd been sent on a fool's errand when Arch asked me to deliver a note demanding the surrender of the 180-man garrison in the town of Lexington, Missouri:

May 11, 1865
Major David, Lexington, MO
SIR: This is to notify you that I will give you until Friday morning, May 12, 1865, to surrender the town of Lexington. If you surrender we will treat you and all taken as prisoners of war. If we have to take it by storm we will burn the town and kill the soldiers. We have the force, and are determined to have it.
I am, sir, your obedient servant,
A. CLEMENTS

I delivered this message to Major Davis, who would have laughed in my face if he hadn't been so mad. He was still working on chewing up the better part of his sowbelly and johnnycakes. I could smell it on him. My own stomach growled so loudly in protest that he ordered a negro private to bring me a plate of the same.

Looking into the major's furious gray eyes, I thought I might be hanged immediately, but instead he gained control of his response, even if he was still red-assed about Arch's letter. For no more noble a cause than self-preservation, I made my face the residence of no particular emotion. I was simply a messenger carrying out his orders and the major would have to respect that.

He looked me up and down for an excuse to unleash his rage, but finding no ironic smile upon my lips, he apprised me of the current situation and to entreat Captain Clement to turn in himself and his men so all could go back to a relatively peaceful antebellum variety of life.

"There's something different in your demeanor," Major Davis said. "You don't seem like some of the Missouri bushmen I've interviewed. What is it? What makes you so different?"

I finished up my glorious breakfast in perfect ease, though they could have thrown a rope over a tree and squeezed the life out of me. But I knew the suspense was saving my life now. That is to say, they wanted to see what happened next, so they'd let me ride today to see if they had the chance to kill me tomorrow.

"I don't know," I said as I stuck a foot in the stirrup and mounted up pulling myself into the seat with the saddle horn.

"There's something—" He pointed at me with a thick, accusing finger. "You're no murderer, though I'm sure you have killed. How did you fall in with this bunch?"

"Jennison pulled me into it himself," I said. "If you must know. It was a violent baptism into the war I can guarantee you."

"Yes," the major said, "this makes some sense to me now. Too bad. Too bad." He shook his head as if he were sorely vexed by my plight in life. It made me want to draw my pistol, but I spat on the ground near his boot instead. I nodded and reined the horse away from the post. Major Davis waited there outside of the little building that functioned as his office as if I might tell him more about myself, or the war, or put the war in its proper perspective.

"What was your name again?" He asked.

Before riding off I looked over my shoulder at him, "They call me Preacher." I heeled the horse in his ribs.

"I suppose Clement will come wipe us now?" The mocking sound of laughter followed me out.

I allowed the reins to go slack and the horse pulled up short.

I sat the horse and then turned so my hand rested on her backside just behind the cantle. "Well, maybe not, but there's many a slip between the cup and the lip. Captain Clement would savor the opportunity to remove your scalp or put your ears on a necklace and wear it around his neck."

He was no longer angry now, but he rocked back on his heels and laughed while preening his moustache with his finger and thumb. I'd succeeded in amusing him. He waved me on.

I gave him the one finger salute and "yessir" treatment before riding back into the wildwoods where I related the major's response to Arch's epistle, which cause him no end of mirth. He laughed like a blackhearted lunatic.

We, of course, not only failed to capture both town and garrison, but we skirted around them. The war was over. We had nothing to gain by attacking a garrison. It seemed to me that we were now as relevant to the cause as gnats on a dog's ass. It upset me to think this way after so much death and sacrifice, but Clement would only get himself and the rest of us killed alongside him. And he did manage to get himself killed in the following year, in Lexington of all places! He had stopped behaving like someone who gave a damn. He was still as brave and willing to fight as ever but there was no great purpose behind it. I don't know if he found peace, but they slaughtered him in the street like a rabid dog that you kill from a great distance away. He had been a very small man in stature, but still the entire command in Lexington had feared him.

Not long after that I lost my horse on a final tour of the Sni hills. He had scars all over his body from the battles we had been in together. I wasn't sure how old he was since I inherited after the death of Roberts when we were being chased by Chief Mayes back in Kansas. He misstepped walking down a ravine and threw me on my back in a little creek. I heard his whinnying scream as we both went down together. I got up cursing only to realize his leg was broke—he was done for. He rumble low in his chest on his side in that ditch. I took off my gloves and rubbed his body down one last time taking care to stay clear of his foreleg. I stared into his great dark brown eye and saw myself in its reflection. I unsheathed a rifle I had recently purloined and did what was necessary.

Instead of these deaths making me thirst for revenge again, it made me want to disappear, so I did my best magician's act in various places around the state. I began to pose as a "Dutch" farmer, poor as Job's turkey, near Hermann in the Missouri Rhineland, but I didn't know much about wine except to drink it. My poor German didn't pass muster with those people, but they seemed to accept me for a time until the local constable found me one too many times drunk, face down in the street.

Nightmares stalked me. Lizzie's mangled body, her sweet face, called for help. I could not sleep unless under the influence of powerful spirits. If it wasn't her, Ephron was calling me in from the fields for dinner one moment and then I was looking at her in a pine box at her funeral again. The worst was when Jennison himself was shooting me in the chest and killing me for good. Perhaps that was what had happened. I was dead and my whole life had been the life of a shade going through the motions in a nightmarish war.

Edwards, the bullheaded journalist, was no longer listening or writing anything down. The wall lamp burned low, but brighter than it had before. His eyes had closed for a long moment before he pinched them open again.

Early evening had begun to fall, drawing the curtain of night around upon us. The parquet floor looked colder and dingier than it had when I'd first entered the office. He didn't want my story, only another record that corroborated his Confederate sensibility concerning the War.

I loved those boys but didn't see things so pure as I had when I was riding around God's country raising hell. I stopped talking then and sat back in my chair. The shouts of the stevedores working down by the river sounded sharp to my ear and the echoing bumps and crashes of the boats I'd come to associate with their work.

Edwards' appearance was more than merely scrofulous under the lamplight. His eyes were set deep in the black eye sockets of his face like one who had been recently disinterred from his final resting place. It turns out he'd die within the year and never write another word published about us. He had been one of us too, though I disagreed with his politics. The world had changed, but he would never admit it. His tongue would forever be a sword looking to thrust, cut, and sever. Oh, he had served honorably under Shelby in his "Iron Brigade." He had been brave; I would never deny it.

General Shelby for his part was spoken of in Missouri like some people spoke of General J. E. B. Stuart. Shelby's boys had even defiantly tried to join up with Emperor Maximilian down in Mexico, who refused to allow them to join his army but gave them land to settle down in Veracruz. Two years later, Maximilian was executed by Juarez and Shelby's men returned to the United States. It was over. They were Americans after all.

I ran into Frank James and Cole Younger one last time many years later in Boonville. I was trying to farm, but Mother Nature wasn't cooperating. I couldn't help thinking of that fine looking white mule Mulvaney rode into his last battle and thought about getting into the mule trade, which was strong across central Missouri. I'd recovered from my physical ailments, though I still carried remnants of iron from the nine times I'd been shot. Jesse had already been killed by that Ford boy a few years hence. Frank had been pardoned and he didn't have to hide now. He'd spent many a year moving from state to state under different aliases. Frank was a cagey one. He and Cole had started The Cole Younger and Frank James Wild West Company. They asked me to work for them and they took me to lunch in a little restaurant on Main Street. They looked like the sober fathers of the young men I had known.

"Come along with us to the bank." Cole gave me a serious nod.

"Now, what?" I stopped in the street. I wasn't about to go anywhere near a bank with Cole Younger and Frank James.

"That's right, Preacher," Frank said. "You don't think you just ran into us by accident, now, do you? We need one more man for a little job here."

"What the hell?" I spat. They both grabbed at my arms, even as I was trying to wriggle free from between them.

They were both grinning like groomsmen at a dance as they sidled up on either side of me and took me by the elbows so they could steer me toward the town's bank. It was a long straight avenue leading to the Missouri River at the other end.

They told me I looked peevish. Yes, I was angry because I thought they had matured with age and put away their outlaw ways.

"Aren't you men of commerce now? Because I'd come to the conclusion that you were—"

"Oh, how highfaluting he talks to us now in his middle years," Cole said.

"Indeed, Mr. Younger. Indeed so!"

"We don't even have guns, you fools! I can't help you rob a bank!" I protested. "Let me go, Frank! You and Cole have to understand, you're too old for all this nonsense!"

"Notice how he doesn't say he is too old," Cole said. "Just you and I."

"I had noticed," Frank made a tut-tut of disapproval. His balding pate shone under the sun.

I balled up my fist and took a wild swing at Cole, but he ducked me easily, though his bowler fell off his head and into the street. They both about fell out laughing on the street then. I looked about, more than a little confused. They had tears in their eyes from laughing at me. These were not men of commerce. They were Frank and Cole. Who else, what less, could they be?

"Can't you just see it now, Frank?" Cole held his swollen, fat belly through his fine suit of clothes.

"Ha!" Frank laughed. "Just what would happen if Frank James and Cole Younger walked into a bank together?"

"We better send in this old man here." Cole shook me by one of my shoulders.

I was still confused.

"We really do need to go to the bank for the show," Frank said, suddenly serious. He pulled out a little white snottinger and wiped the sweat off the inner band of his bowler. "We need cash for payroll. Besides, no offense, but nobody knows who the hell you are."

"I will not be talked to—"

"Except by us!" Cole slapped me on the back with the hilarity of their joke at my expense.

"Don't get so red-assed," Frank said. "I'll have the bearded lady show you some magic lantern slides to make it up to you. Besides, we know who you are and what you are capable of. "We're the ones that count!" Cole turned me by one shoulder and stared into my eyes for a moment. "You're the Preacher, by God."

The things we had done during the war, the men we had slaughtered, the friends and loved ones we had lost, danced across the vaudevillian stage of my mind as though accompanied by a Greek chorus and there did not seem to be enough goodness in these latter days to justify the death and meanness of those terrible times. The Day of the Lord is hard upon us, but His Judgment is delayed and measured out like flour through a sieve. Edwards, the irascible propagandist, is scribbling furiously like an archangel scribe something revelatory and probably profane. No doubt he's writing my epitaph and turning my person, my character, into the political rebel he's decided I will be. He wants to right the wrongs for the Outlaw State and ultimately make history run in reverse like memory.

As for me, in my way I have decided to continue to speak to the Lord and listen for His voice in the winds rushing through the pines and in the sounds of the bees and in the song of the red summer tanager.

Daren Dean

Acknowledgments

My deepest appreciation to everyone who read early versions of this manuscript over the years. My thanks to Jack Smith who edited and published an excerpt from the manuscript titled "Bad Company" in the *Green Hills Literary Lantern;* much admiration for the generosity of Evelyn Somers who helped immeasurably with this novel; I appreciate the wise words of Greg Michalson. Also, thanks to my colleague Nick Straatman for his insightful comments. Thanks to my parents, Larry Dean and Barbara Adams. Cassandra, Claira, and Finn—you sustain me in all things. For all your many kindnesses I tip my hat to: Billy Adams, Bryan Salmons, the Salmons family, Malcolm Todd, and in memory of Lisa Lester. Much love and respect to my friends: David Baker, David Collins, Anthony Connolly, George Foster, Eli Hastings, Michael Garriga, Steph Post, Randolph Thomas, Adam Van Winkle, and in memory of Margaux Fragoso. I can't say enough about my colleagues and students at Louisiana State University and Lincoln University of Missouri. Finally, my sincere thanks to Joe Taylor and University of West Alabama's Livingston Press for giving this book a home.

Author's Note

The following historical works were invaluable to me in writing this novel: Quantrill's War: The Life and Times of William Clarke Quantrill by Duane Schultz; The Guerrilla War, 1861-1865 by Albert Castel; Black Flag: Guerrilla Warfare on the Western Border, 1861-1865, Bloody Bill Anderson: The Short, Savage Life of a Civil War Guerrilla, and Bloody Dawn: The Story of the Lawrence Massacre by Thomas Goodrich; Three Years with Quantrill by John McCorkle; Noted Guerrillas by John N. Edwards; The Devil Knows How to Ride by Edward E. Leslie; Jesse James: The Last Rebel of the Civil War by T. J. Stiles.

Daren Dean is the author of the novel *Far Beyond the Pale* (Fiction Southeast Press) and the short story collection *I'll Still Be Here Long After You're Gone* (CJ Press). His latest novel, *This Vale of Tears*, was published in Fall 2021. His work has been featured in *The Huffington Post*, *Ploughshares online*, and *Bloom*. He holds an MFA in Creative Writing from the University of North Carolina at Wilmington. His work has appeared in numerous magazines such as Bull, The Green Hills Literary Lantern, Louisiana Literature, Maryland Literary Review, Midwestern Gothic, The Oklahoma Review, and StorySouth. In addition, he was recently nominated for two Pushcart Prizes in short fiction. Currently, he is an Assistant Professor of English at Lincoln University of Missouri.